Fairytales FROM VERANIA

TJ Klune

NEW YORK TIMES BESTSELLING AUTHOR

Fairytales From Verania
Copyright © 2021 by TJ Klune

Published by BOATK Books
http://tjklunebooks.com
tjklunebooks@yahoo.com

Cover Art by Reese Dante   https://reesedante.com

Published 2021.
Printed in the United States of America

ISBN: 978-1-7367186-0-5 (paperback)
eBook edition available

For Lynn, Mia and Amy.
Thank you for helping my words make sense.

THE UNICORN
IN THE
Tower

ONCE UPON A TIME, in a lost and lonely woods, a tower grew from the ground, stretching toward the sky. Made of black stone, the tower loomed over the trees for as long as anyone could remember. Vines had grown up the sides, leafy green plants mixed with sharp thorns that could slice even the most calloused of hands. This tower had no stairs, nor a door to allow entrance or exit, and honestly, it begged a profoundly serious question: what the fuck was the builder thinking? Who the hell built a tower this big without a godsdamn door? Talk about an extreme fire danger.

Thankfully, the builder—a spindly man named Norman Nelson—decided that he'd rather dance than build and left the world of blue-collar work behind to join an aerial dance troupe called the Flying Magnificents. He became the talk of the land until his untimely death involving an emu, an irate pirate, and the way his body exploded when he fell forty-two feet to the ground. It was pretty gross, and those in attendance who witnessed Norman's demise were never the same again, especially the child who caught the builder's eye after it popped out of his head. That child would grow up to be a serial killer.

But this is not a story about the builder or the future murderer. It's about the most beautiful creature in the entire world, one with a fiery disposition, the voice of an angel, and an ass that did *not* know how to quit.

Atop the tower sat a single window that looked out onto the forest. On a good, clear day, a voice could be heard from the tower, singing for all the world to hear. The people who lived in a village near the tower would often go about their day, listening to the singing and commenting to each other how pitch perfect the voice was, and that they were all extraordinarily blessed to have such a boon in their lives.

"Tra la la," the voice sang. "Tra la—ahem. Gods, my allergies are wreaking havoc on my throat. Let's try this again. Tra. Tra la la. There. That's better. Tra la la!"

I'm the prettiest who ever was, and no one can dispute!

Doesn't matter what I'm wearing: nothing or a suit!

And the people who hear me, they all say the same!

Dearest beautiful prisoner, won't you tell us your name?

"My name is—*godsdamn fucking balls of cock-sucking shit*. Who put this stupid fucking table here for me to walk into? I'll kill them! I'll kill them all!" The beautiful creature trapped in the tower blinked. "Oh. Right. I did. Because I'm the only one up here. And because it also really helps with the flow of the room. Never mind! Sorry, sorry, everyone! It was me. My bad!"

This wondrous vision's name?

"Gary the Supremely Attractive," Gary said, hooves clomping on the stone floor. "And don't you fucking forget it."

Yes, Gary the…Supremely Attractive. I guess we're just going with it now.

"Is that a problem, omniscient narrator?" Gary asked dangerously. The tip of his horn began to glow with an ethereal light. "Because if it is, I can think of at least six ways to kill you right this second, two of which involve me fucking you to death."

His name was Gary the Supremely Attractive, and he was the most generous and wonderful unicorn that had ever existed and did *not* need to follow through on his very pointed threats. But how did this unicorn end up here, trapped in an impenetrable tower?

"Ha," Gary said. "I'll show *you* impenetrable." He frowned. "Wait, that didn't make any sense. Hold on, let me try again. I'll show *you*—"

When Gary was born, he—

"Did you interrupt me? Huh. How about that. How. About. *That*. Oh, what do I have here? Is this a one-way ticket to Gore City? Why, I think it is!"

When Gary was born, he came into the world with the longest mane anyone had ever seen. In fact, the birthing process took much longer because of it. Gary's mother screamed as the foal finally fell to the ground but continued to push until a pile of wet hair spilled out of her, surrounding the baby as it tried to stand on its knobby legs.

Gary's father grimaced. "That was certainly something I didn't want to see. Yuck."

"He's perfect," Gary's mother said fondly as she nuzzled her young.

And he was! Aside from his ridiculously long mane, the hair along his body was as white as freshly fallen snow. His horn was thick and sturdy and his eyelashes glittered as if lined with stars. There had never been one such as he, and though his birth brought happiness to many, there was one who seethed in anger at the very sight of him.

A sorceress of unspeakable evil, one whose very name caused ice-cold shivers and a feeling akin to a horrendous bout of Irritable Bowel Syndrome.

"Hey," Lady Tina DeSilva said. "Can I babysit Gary?"

"Sure," Gary's mother said. "We were fretting about leaving him behind when we go on our swinger's tour, so this actually works out perfectly. No child should ever witness their father being railed by a centaur, at least not until they turn eighteen."

"Oh man," Gary's father said. "My thighs are already quivering. Derek promised me I'd get his whole arm this time instead of just his hand."

Gary's mother smiled. "Just so long as we stretch you out beforehand, I bet he gets all the way to his shoulder. It'll give you an idea of how it feels to give birth. I can't wait to see the look on your face."

"How…fun," Lady Tina said, although she looked like she was trying her level best not to gag. "I like you all so much, and I'm *not* planning on kidnapping your son and putting him at the top of a tower with no means for escape."

"Oh, good," Gary's father said. "I was worried about that specific thing so I'm glad we got that out of the way." He glanced at his wife before looking back at Lady Tina. "You do know that swinger's tours tend to last at least two decades, right?"

"You really have to dedicate the time to make sure you've gotten to everyone," Gary's mother said. "We don't like any swinger feeling left out. It can lead to jealousy, which is a very serious risk when it comes to partner-swapping. Open and honest dialogue is important."

Lady Tina waved them off. "I've got nothing better going on since I'm a lonely hag who'll never find a man unless I put a spell on him to love me forever."

[Editor's note: FUCK LADY TINA!!!]

"You'll get yours," Gary's mother promised her. "There has to be someone out there for you who doesn't mind your…you know. Entire existence."

They left the next day, promising to write as soon as they could, but told Gary not to expect much because they'd be very busy with Derek. And Vanessa. And Large Bill and Michael and Laura and Two-Dicked Darnell, so-called because he had two dicks for reasons that are better left unsaid. And that didn't even begin to describe Milo, the tentacle monster. Milo was their favorite. Because of the tentacles.

As soon as they disappeared over the hill that led from the village, Lady Tina whirled on Gary. "And now you're mine," she whispered as Gary bleated in terror.

She placed him at the top of the tower. How did she do that, you might be asking, especially when said tower didn't have a door? And the even bigger question was *why* would she do such a thing?

Because fuck you, that's why. It's just a story. No need to get caught up in logistics. Just go with it. Gods.

And there Gary remained for the next eighteen years, growing from a foal to a unicorn of unparalleled grace and beauty. But fear not! He wasn't alone. He had two of the best friends an imprisoned unicorn could ask for to keep him company.

The first was a bird named Tiggy, a great robin with an orange chest and black wings. "Bird," Tiggy said, hopping on the windowsill. "Bird, bird, bird. Tiggy a bird! Got wings. I'm awesome."

"Yes, kitten," Gary said, nudging at Tiggy's beak. "You are very awesome. I'm so lucky to have you at my side."

The second friend Gary had was a sickly weasel with mange named Sam. "I hate this," Sam muttered as his whiskers twitched from his place on Gary's bed. "I can't believe you made me a weasel."

"A *sickly* weasel," Gary said. "With mange that does not spread to the rest of us because it's very specific to weasels. Just go with it, for fuck's sakes. Gods, why can't you be happy for me? It's not always about *you*." His face twisted. "Oh look, I'm Sam! I'm so important because everyone loves me and inflates my already oversized ego!"

"You know what?" Sam said. "That's fair. My ego *is* oversized. Thank you for reminding me of my place."

Tiggy twittered. "Gonna eat worms. No one can say, no, Tiggy, no worms because Tiggy a bird. Birds eat worms. Yay, Tiggy!"

So, no, Gary wasn't alone. And while he dreamed of landing a man for his very own one day, he was an independent unicorn who did *not* need a man to define him, though he wished for one to curb the burning in his loins. And since everyone knows a unicorn reaches sexual maturity at the age of eighteen (a maturity that lasted until their death), no one should've been surprised that he was a horny motherfucker who'd like to sit on someone's face.

Out of *love*.

"I'm so lonely," Gary moaned, throwing himself onto his bed next to Sam, who squeaked angrily. "Though I know I don't need no mens in order to be my own unicorn, these constant erections are pointless when I have no one to stick it into."

"Gross," Sam muttered as he struggled to shove Gary's back legs off him. "And what happened to that pillow I gave you?"

A tear trickled down Gary's cheek, glittering in the low light. "I fucked it until the stuffing came out."

"Oh my gods," Sam mumbled. "Why did I even ask?"

Tiggy raised his wings before flying over and landing on the headboard above Gary's horn. "Need a mens?"

Gary sighed. "I think so, kitten. I love you both very much, but my penis would destroy the both of you, and then where would we be?"

Tiggy nodded. "Find you a mens?"

Gary tilted his head back to look at his friend. "You'd do that for me?"

Tiggy pecked Gary's horn. "Yep. Go find mens and bring them back. Eat Gary's flower."

Gary gasped. "My flower? Oh, dearest Tiggy, if only Sam could be like you instead of being a stupid weasel."

"Hate you too, bitch," Sam mumbled.

Tiggy grinned which, for a bird, was weird. Then he took to his wings, flying out the window in search of Gary's one true love, or at least a willing hole for him to pound into and rid himself of his sexual urges that would make even the most hardened of sex workers ask for double the rate.

"I wonder who he'll bring back?" Gary mused. "Perhaps a rough-and-tumble mercenary with a gaze of steel and death on his mind but a heart of gold, who is too afraid to open himself up again after he'd been hurt in the past by a man who didn't appreciate his finer qualities. He'll be reticent at first, but given time, I'll break through his armor and one day, he'll look upon me with an unexpected smile, and he'll find himself feeling things he didn't think he could feel anymore."

"Aw," Sam chittered. "That sounds nice."

Gary sighed dreamily. "It does, doesn't it? And then I'll fuck him until he screams for me to get him pregnant, even though it's biologically impossible given that we're both men."

Sam groaned. "And that's the opposite of nice. I don't know why I expected anything else."

Gary ignored him. "Oh me, oh my!" he cried. "I can't meet my future fuck boy looking like this! My mane and tail need to be combed, and my eyebrows need to be threaded—"

"You don't have eyebrows," Sam said.

"—and I haven't even douched in six weeks! Sam, I need your help."

"With the brushing," Sam said quickly. "And the threading. Sure, sure, I can do just those two things and nothing else without complaint."

Gary turned his head slowly to look at Sam. "And the douching."

Sam made himself as small as possible. "Oh, come on, man. Please don't make me do that again. The last time, I couldn't get the smell of chocolate chip cookies out of my fur for a week. Can you even begin to understand how you've ruined baked goods for me? Because you *have*."

"It's not *my* fault my digestive tract makes my shit smell like delightful confectionaries! I'm a godsdamn unicorn. That's *biology*. Don't be a bitter bitch because *your* poops are smelly little pellets that you leave on the floor for me to step in."

"I can't believe we're having this conversation," Sam moaned. "Who the hell is even gonna *read* this crap?"

"Lovely, odd people who have no problem exchanging their hard-earned money for the tales of my sexual prowess."

"Oh," Sam said. "Right. *Those* people. You'd think they'd realize that therapy is a much better outlet than gaping in horror at your shit-cookies."

"We don't judge them," Gary reminded him. "Also, the point of me doing all of this is so I can *be* gaping by the time my new man is done with me."

Sam hid his face in his little paws, whiskers twitching. "I have no one to blame but myself."

"Exactly," Gary agreed. "So pleased you realize that everything bad is your fault and that I'm the only light in your life. Now, if you'll get the douche kit out of the bathroom, we can start. Fair warning: I've been baking, and it's *not* going to be—"

Then, another voice filtered in through the window, sharp and clear:

Gary!

Gary!

Let down your mane

that I may climb and feed you grain!

Sam snarled as Gary rolled his eyes. "Gods," he growled. "This asshole again. I swear, she's so fucking needy." He rose from the bed as Sam jumped on his back and crawled up his neck, holding onto Gary's horn so he didn't fall to the floor. Gary went to the window and looked down.

Lady Tina stood at the base of the tower, a bucket of grain at her feet. She glared up at him when he bared his teeth at her. "I don't have all day," she called. "Hurry the hell up or I'll give your breakfast to orphans." She smiled to herself. "They're always so hungry, they'll eat anything."

"Are you going to let me out?" Gary demanded.

"Oh," Lady Tina said brightly. "Sure! I'll get right on that. I don't know what I was thinking. My apologies!"

"You're not going to let me out."

"No," she said. "I'm not. That'd defeat the purpose of me imprisoning you to begin with. You can't seriously be that stupid."

"Then *no*!" Gary bellowed. "I won't let you up, you damn wench! You haven't even told me *why* you're keeping me here!"

She frowned. "I haven't? Oh. Sorry, I thought I had." She grinned as she brushed a lock of her unfairly lovely hair from her forehead. "I'm going to sacrifice you by cutting your throat and bathing in your virgin blood on the first full moon after your eighteenth birthday. When that happens, I'll be the most powerful sorceress the world has ever known!" She cackled maniacally.

Gary gasped. "But my eighteenth birthday is *tomorrow*. And the next full moon is three days after that!"

"I know," Lady Tina said darkly as she tapped her foot against the bucket of feed. "I've had it marked on my calendar for nearly two decades. I'm positively aquiver with antici…pation."

"Ha," Sam said. "References. I like it when we do that."

"I'll never let you kill me!" Gary yelled. "You try it, and I'll fuck you up!"

"You don't want to mess with me," Lady Tina warned him. "I've waited too long for this moment, and I won't let you ruin my plans. Either you let me up, or you'll go hungry until it's time for me to rub your dismembered horn against my nude body."

Sam made a face. "Ew. There is something really wrong with her."

"No, thank you!" Gary said loudly. "I'm not hungry. Go away."

Lady Tina raised her arm, pointing a perfectly manicured finger up at him. "Mark my words, Gary the Supremely Attractive. In four days, I will straight up murder you and take your magic for my own. But! That doesn't mean we can't be friends before then. Come on. Let me up. I've got *all* the hot gossip from the village."

Oh no. His weakness. His nostrils flared as his eyes widened. "You *do*? Like what kind of hot gossip?"

"Seriously?" Sam said. "Dude, she's playing you!"

Lady Tina nodded. "Oh yes. Like how the man from the smithery has the hots for the werewolf who runs the taco cart."

"Oh please," Gary said. "Jason always gets nervous when Yousef comes in to have more forks made for his cart. That's not gossip, that's *fact*."

"Yes," Lady Tina said. "But did you know that Yousef already has enough forks to last him a lifetime?"

"Shut your whore mouth," Gary breathed. "So he's going *just* to see Jason? Oh my gods, that's amazing. Okay, you can come up. We need to make bets as to which one will break first and tell the other he can't live without him before…wait. Question. Is it bestiality if you fuck your werewolf boyfriend when he's shifted?"

"Yes," Sam said. "That's literally the definition of bestiality. If *you* were to have sex with a human, that's also bestiality."

"Well, then," Gary said. "Bestiality is fine. I'm glad we came to that conclusion. Lady Tina. Yoo hoo, Lady Tina! I've changed my mind. I don't have the time to talk to you. I'm busy living my best life."

Lady Tina's face turned red as she sputtered and snarled. "You listen to me, you ungrateful crap stain. Let me up, or I'll make sure your death is as slow and painful as possible."

Sam squeaked as Gary shoved his head out the window, looking down. Sam hung onto Gary's horn, trying to pull himself up. "Sam, if you please."

"Again?" Sam cried. "Dude, I just *went*!"

"*Sam.*"

Sam sighed. "Fine. But you owe me for this."

And then he pissed on Lady Tina.

She shrieked as she stumbled backward, droplets of urine dripping off her face. "It's in my *eyes*!" she screamed. "What the fuck is wrong with you!"

"Good aim," Gary said. "Better than last time, at least."

"Thanks," Sam said as Gary pulled his head back inside the tower. "I've been working on my aim."

"Now," Gary said as Sam jumped down to the floor. Lady Tina continued to make noises from somewhere below them, but out of sight, out of mind. "Tiggy will be returning with my new fuck boy, so we'll need to prepare. I'm thinking some eyeliner, some light mascara. Don't want to go *too* heavy, just enough to accentuate my mysteriousness. Ooh! And flowers. Yes, *flowers* for my mane and tail." He went to the mirror that hung on the wall, studying his reflection. He sucked in his stomach and posed, his front right leg raised. "Yes," he said, lowering his leg back to the ground. "I'm going to land myself a man, and he won't know what hit him."

"Just the makeup and the flowers, right?" Sam asked nervously.

Gary smiled at his reflection. "And the douching."

Sam cowered as Gary turned slowly toward him, an obscenely wicked smile stretching across his face.

Two HOURS LATER, Gary was ready.

"My word," he breathed as he swished his tail back and forth. "Do I feel pretty and absolutely clean from the inside out." He looked at the bed, where Sam lay on his back, paws in the air, frozen stiff. "You all right?"

Sam's eyes were glazed over. "The things…I've seen… no words. There are no words…to describe…the horrors I've witnessed. Should have sent…an emo…poet."

"You silly bitch," Gary said, as the flowers ruffled in his hair and mane. "I told you to hold the nozzle tighter. It's not my fault you weren't listening."

Sam stretched a trembling paw toward the ceiling. "Please," he whispered. "Gods, if you're listening, kill me. Kill me now."

Before Gary could tell Sam to stop acting like a drama queen (it hadn't been *that* bad), Tiggy returned, flying in through the window. He held a writhing worm in his mouth. Gary grimaced as Tiggy raised his head, slurping up the worm as his head bobbed up and down. "Taste like chicken," Tiggy said. He cocked his head. "What wrong with Sam and why it smell like bakery?"

"The douchening," Sam whispered. "The *douchening*."

"Tiggy!" Gary cried. "You have returned. What tidings do you bring? Have you found my one true love? Or, at least my one true cock? Tell me! Leave nothing out!"

Tiggy ruffled his feathers as he preened. "Found one." He flew from the windowsill and landed on the bed next to Sam, poking at his stomach until Sam curled up and tried to hide his head, rocking back and forth, muttering something about oatmeal raisin. Tiggy turned to look at Gary. "Good one, I think."

"Is he big?" Gary demanded. "And strong and handsome?"

"Yep," Tiggy said. "Big and strong and handsome. *And* alive."

"My favorite qualities! I must know more."

"Bouncy hair," Tiggy said. "And nice butt."

Gary threw himself on the bed next to his friends. "Oh, I have dreamed of such a day. A man to come and rescue me from my prison and fill me with his juices like he's preparing to roast me over an open spit."

"*That's* what you dream about?" Sam asked. "Gods, that explains so much."

Normally, Gary wouldn't allow such insolence, but today was a new day! A man was coming, a man who'd worship the ground Gary walked on. A man to take him from this tower to a life of luxury, where he'd want for nothing. A house to call his own. A full staff to take care of his wants and needs. And a husband with an overly-healthy libido who wanted nothing more than to rearrange Gary's guts. Just like every other almost-eighteen-year-old unicorn dreamed about.

"Where is he?" Gary asked. "Did you tell him where to find me?"

Tiggy pulled at a loose strand of the comforter before looking up at Gary. "He coming. Said he wanted to get sword first."

"His sword?" Gary asked. "What does he do? Oh, let me guess. Is he a lord? With his own manor and a lonely heart who is searching for a connection in the vastness of time and space? And a sword, which he uses to defend the meek and righteous all while shirtless, his back muscles shifting and covered in sweat from a... oh. Shit. Now I have an erection. Don't look at it. I'm shy!"

"It's right *there*!" Sam screamed, trying to roll away. "Pull it back! Oh my gods, why does it look like that!"

"Prude," Gary said. "It's a natural part of life. The sooner you get used to it, the better off you'll be."

"Can I go do weasel things?" Sam asked miserably. "Like, as far away from here as I can get?"

"Don't be ridiculous," Gary said. "My fuck boy is on his way, and I need you to talk me up before he rescues me. You better say nice things about me, or I'll make you watch when we consummate our love." He paused, considering. "You know when you say something out loud in jest but end up realizing it might be a kink you never knew you had?"

"No," Sam said. "I've *never* done that. Ever."

"Oh," Gary said. "Well, I guess there's a first time for everything." He shook his head. "Stop distracting me. This is important. Honestly, Sam. It's like you don't even know how to be happy for me."

"He made me pee on Lady Tina after she told him she was going to sacrifice him in a few days," Sam told Tiggy. "Please don't leave me alone with him again."

"Poor Sam," Tiggy said, pecking his head. "I love you, Sam."

Sam sighed. "Yeah, yeah, I love you too, you lug."

Then, the most erotic voice Gary had ever heard called up through the window, causing his butthole to clench.

Gary!

Gary!

Let down your hair

that I may climb and see my husband fair.

"He's *here*!" Gary hissed. "I'm not ready! Stall him so I can work through this panic attack!"

Tiggy flew toward the window as Gary put his head between his knees, breathing in and out, trying to calm his racing heart.

"Hi!" Tiggy called down. "You came! Good. So. How you?"

"Uh," the voice said, and Gary had visions of a burly man with large, hairy hands and an ass made for eating. "I'm…fine? Well, as fine as one can be who listened to a talking bird that demanded I follow it to find my one true love. This is a really weird Tuesday if I'm being honest."

"Aw," Tiggy said. "You're dumb. Pretty, but dumb."

"That's…not the first time I've heard that," the sexy voice said. "I said the poem you told me to say. Where is this Gary?"

"He already can't live without me," Gary whispered to Sam, who sighed heavily. "This is going so well. What do I do?"

Sam shrugged. "Tell him how you feel. Invite him up for a cup of tea."

"What if he wants to put himself inside me?"

Sam grimaced. "Then give me a head start so I can jump out the window and die."

"You're right," Gary said. "I *am* perfect. I have nothing to worry about."

"I never said—"

"I'll just mosey on over to the window, and once he sees me, his breath will be knocked from his chest as he gazes upon my everything. And then he'll remove all his clothing and we'll live happily ever after." With that decided, Gary approached the window, his heart thundering in his chest. He'd never been more excited in his life. Finally, *finally*, he was going to see the man who would take him away from all of this and give him the life he'd always dreamed about.

"Okay," he whispered to himself as he reached the window. "You can do this. Smile. Be polite, but *sexy* polite. Don't say something that might scare him off because of how intense it will be. Sultry yet practical. Think, Gary. Think. Ah! Got it." He fluttered his eyelashes as he poked his head out the window. "Why, hello there," he purred, voice dropping an octave, so much so it sounded like he was gargling gravel. "Why don't you come up and slip into something a little more comfortable. Fun fact. My asshole is named *a little more comfortable*."

"What," the man said. And it *was* a man. Yes, the *paragon* of man. He had muscles and wavy blond hair and a jawline that could slice concrete. His eyes were bright, and though he was frowning deeply, Gary could see he was packing in his trousers. He looked more than a little stupid, but Gary could deal with such things in the name of deflowering. He even had a sword, though it dangled toward the ground, the man's grip limp on the hilt.

"It is I," the unicorn declared triumphantly. "Gary the Supremely Attractive. Yes, you may continue to stare at me with that dumbfounded look. I will allow it." He lifted his head, posing so that the man might gaze upon his beauty.

"You're Gary," the man said dubiously.

"I am," Gary said, flicking his head so that part of his mane lay on the windowsill, ready to fall to the ground to have the man climb up and ravish him. "And you are my one true love who will save me from the tower and then let me mount you in a variety of ways until I am utterly satisfied. You are welcome."

"Whaaaat is happening," the man said, looking dazed.

Oh, the poor, pretty thing. He didn't seem to have a lick of sense in his abnormally-sized head. "Your name, my beloved?" Gary asked.

"Ryan," the man said. "Ryan Foxheart. Uh, look. I think there might have been a mistake."

"A mistake? Why, whatever do you mean? The only mistake I can see is that you're still wearing clothes. Do you have a six pack? You look like you should have a six pack."

Ryan blushed. "I mean, yeah, sure. I work out. Try to keep in shape, you know?" He flourished his sword unnecessarily. Gary was entranced. He couldn't believe how well this was going. "Gotta make sure I look good." The man flexed his arms, staring off into nothing as if pondering how attractive he was. Gary would have to curb that ego with his tongue.

"Well, it's working," Gary breathed. "Tell me, Ryan. Have you ever tasted the rainbow?"

[*Editor's note: It should be noted that Ryan Foxheart didn't want to be included in this story, saying that he, in no uncertain terms, does* not *"want to taste the rainbow, Sam, why would you let him say that?" Ryan's request for his removal from this story has been denied.*]

"Wow," Ryan said. "Those were certainly words you just said to me."

"Do I make your loins ache?" Gary asked, batting his eyelashes.

"Something aches, that's for sure," Ryan said with a wince. "It goes to show that I should probably stop following talking birds. This is the fourth time I've done that, and it never ends well for me."

"I want to see!" a whiny voice complained. Gary snorted sparks of green and pink when Sam crawled up his legs and stepped onto the window ledge. He looked down, and gasped. "Sweet molasses. Who is *that*?"

"Ryan Foxheart," Gary said. "Weren't you listening with your tiny ears? Wait. Hold up. Do weasels have ears? I'm just now realizing I don't know a damn thing about weasels. What the hell even are you? A weird rat thing or…?"

"Tiggy has wings," Tiggy said. "Bird Tiggy is the best Tiggy."

"Hello!" Sam called down obnoxiously. "I'm Sam! I like your sword and the fact that you exist."

Ryan scratched the back of his neck as he scuffed his boot in the dirt. "Aw, shucks. That's so nice of you to say. Thanks, Sam. I like your fur and the way your tiny eyes look like they're completely black."

That certainly wouldn't do. "Sam," Gary said through gritted teeth. "Would you *please* stop flirting with my fuck boy? Gods, it's like you don't even know your place!"

"But look at him!" Sam said. "He's perfect. Why can't I have him?"

Gary smiled. "Because, my love. You're a godsdamn weasel and you need to shut. The fuck. *Up*." He looked back out the window. "Sorry about that, Ryan! You know how it is with weasels. Give them an inch, and they're begging for the rest of the ten inches."

"Whoa," Ryan said. "I wish you hadn't told me that. You have sex with the weasel?"

Gary laughed daintily. It sounded as if someone was banging against a large bell with a sledgehammer. "Nah. He'd explode. And besides! I'm not interested in him like that. However, if you insist, he can watch our coupling. In fact, let's do just that. I believe the masses call it cuckolding, but I can't be sure. The books I've read were very unclear as to the practice."

"I think I'd like to not do that," Ryan said. "Oh no, would you look at the time. I just remembered I have a meeting six thousand miles away from here that I'm going to be late for if I don't leave right this second. Of all the damn luck."

"Hey!" Sam barked. "No cursing! What if there are children present?"

Ryan looked around, confused. "Why would there be children out here? This doesn't seem like the best place for them. No offense."

"There could be!"

Ryan sighed. "Fine, I'll think of the children. Darn. Shoot. Fudge."

"There," Sam said dreamily. "That's better. Will you do me a favor? Can you raise the sword above your head, bare your teeth and snarl something heroic?"

Ryan chuckled. "Gosh, I don't know if I could. I've never done something like that before. I don't even know how to—" The sword shot up into the air, the blade glinting in the sun. "I will protect the kingdom with my life, and not stop until the blood of my enemies covers the ground!"

"Oh my gods," Sam whispered aggressively. "Weasels have penises. Guess how I know that?"

Gary grimaced. "Nobody answer that. I'm already scarred enough as it is."

"Sam!" Ryan called up. "That's your name, right? Sam?"

"It is!" Sam said. "Thank you for remembering. You're so smart."

"I like the colors of your fur," Ryan said. He arched a devastating eyebrow. "They're very…colorful."

"Yeah, they are," Sam said. "You should see the colors on my underbelly."

"What the fuck," Gary said faintly. Then, louder, "Are you *for real* right now? You're supposed to be coming to rescue me and then we'll do things better left to the imagination! And since I'm *very* imaginative, you won't walk right for the rest of your pointless life!"

"The heart wants what the heart wants," Ryan said seriously. "I apologize, Gary the Supremely Attractive. Though your name fits you well, my heart belongs to another."

"Who?" Gary snarled.

"Sam," Ryan said.

Gary blinked, sure he'd misheard. "Sam. As in my best friend Sam? Sam the weasel who is sitting right next to me. The weasel who is the size of a small cat. That's who your heart belongs to? You want to be a weasel fucker?"

"No," Ryan said. "I want to be a weasel *lover*."

[*Editor's note: Ryan Foxheart said that if this last line was not removed, he'd sue the author for slander. Since Ryan does not know any attorneys and is also a kill joy, the line will stay as is. Free speech is paramount!*]

"Holy shit," Sam said. "*I'm* a weasel."

"I know," Ryan said. "The weasel of my heart."

"Yeah," Gary said. "I've decided that people named Ryan

Foxheart are the absolute worst."

"I have talons," Tiggy said, raising one foot, opening and closing his toes. "Talon Tiggy. Capitalized."

"Catch me!" Sam cried before flinging himself out the window. Gary's heart leapt to his throat as his friend fell toward the ground. Ryan dropped his sword and caught Sam deftly, cradling the weasel in his arms. Sam raised his head, nose twitching as he sniffed Ryan's face. "I love you," Sam whispered.

"And I you," Ryan said, petting Sam's back. "We'll never be apart for the rest of our days. Come, Sam. Let me take you from this place and give you the life you deserve. I have a large house with many rooms that need to be filled with the sounds of your cries of ecstasy as I give you my *real* sword."

"Yeah," Gary said. "This is pretty fucked up, even for us. Just when you think there's a line between decency and screwing a pseudo-rat, we just jump across it without a care in the world. I blame Ryan for all of this."

"Goodbye!" Sam called up as Ryan carried him away. "I'll come back and visit after I get that good, good Ryan Foxheart dick while you wither away into nothing!"

"Fuck you very much!" Gary shouted after him. "I won't forget this vile betrayal, you stupid bastard! And Ryan, you're a weasel fucker!"

The last Gary saw of Sam and Ryan was when they crested the hill that led away from the tower, Ryan kissing the top of Sam's head.

"That weird," Tiggy said. "Sam and Ryan gonna do stuff?"

"Yes," Gary said, collapsing dramatically on his bed. "And it's going to break so many laws, I can't even begin to fathom. But enough about them. Tiggy, what about me? I only have three days left until I get sacrificed!"

Tiggy puffed out his chest. "Find another mens. Save Gary. Promise."

He flew out the window, leaving Gary staring forlornly after him. "Where is my true love?" he lamented. "Isn't there someone out there for me who wants to get all up in my bidness even though I'm not a weasel? There must be *someone*." He looked down at his mane, which cascaded off the bed and lay in luminous piles on the floor. "Someone who'll climb my mane, and then pull it until

I scream. Is that too much to ask for? Oh, woe is me! I'll be alone forever! And by forever, I mean until Friday when I get sacrificed. Oh, woe! So much woe!"

Gary turned his face into the pillow and cried glittering tears.

OVER THE NEXT THREE DAYS, Tiggy brought back a multitude of men, though none were up to the challenge.

The first of whom was an older man with a nose that looked like it could have been a penis at one point. "Why the hell am I even here?" the man muttered, glaring up at the tower. "I'm far too busy for this nonsense."

"Name is Randall," Tiggy said, hopping on the ledge. "Old, but kinky. Likes group sex."

"Interesting," Gary said. "But nah."

Randall flipped them off before hurrying away, mumbling under his breath that he'd once had a group of assassins come after him, but ended up with all of them on their knees, worshipping his balls. What a nutter.

Next was a willowy boy man with large ears and a propensity for all things blueberry. Todd—a ridiculous name if there ever was one—looked frightened but determined. "Dad said I could take over his restaurants if I find a spouse. He didn't say what species they needed to be, but that's on him."

"How fascinating," Gary said, though he meant exactly the opposite. "Tell me, if it came down between me and the restaurants, who would you choose?"

Todd puffed out his thin chest. "You, of course."

Gary glared at him. "You would choose me over the business your father built from the ground up? How delightfully ungrateful. Next."

The third man Tiggy returned with was far better, a kingly sort with a barrel chest and a devious twinkle in his eye. Daddy as fuck, as Gary liked to say. His name was Anthony, and he bowed low, arm across his chest, the other folded behind him. "I have heard tales of your beauty. They didn't do justice to the vision before me."

"Ooh," Gary said. "Now that's what I like to hear. Tell me more about myself."

It turned out that Anthony was very descriptive, and though it filled Gary with happiness, there was still something missing. Regretfully, he sent Anthony away, but only after having him do a slow turn so he could get a full view of that Dad bod. He had a great ass.

The next visitor was different. He was younger, for one. He looked like he'd once been a twink but was on his way to being a twunk, the more muscular version of a twink. It was very rare for twinks to turn into twunks. Usually, they just turned sad. This man had somehow managed to avoid that pitfall.

"His name Dustin," Tiggy said. "He a prince."

"Now that's what I'm talking about," Gary said, staring down at Dustin.

[*Editor's Note: "Dustin" is Justin, who doesn't know about his inclusion in this story, and it should be kept that way. He's already threatening execution for that thing last week that was totally done by accident.*]

"I want to fuck you," Dustin said. "I want nothing more. I've heard about you for years, and when you were sleeping, I've sat underneath your tower, listening to the dulcet tones of your snores, like music for the weary soul."

"Huh," Gary said. "How…expectant to hear that the Grand Prince *Dustin* is through fighting his feelings for me and is making his intentions known."

"Exactly that," Dustin said. "I have suffered in silence for so long, but I'm through with remaining quiet. I must have you. I dream of you, Gary. Of your supple body, and your quivering muscles. I want you to hold me down and choke me. I want you to fuck me with your horn. If you'll let me, I'll sit on your face until my legs give out."

"Wow," Gary said. "Just going right for the butt play. I approve."

Dustin nodded. "My loins burn for you. The heat is overwhelming. I can't live without you one moment more."

"Yikes," Gary said. "You're starting to come across a little clingy. Dial it back, just a little. And burning loins? That sounds like a serious medical issue, my guy."

Dustin took a step toward the tower. "You've lit a fire in me, and I never want it to go out." He rubbed a hand down his chest before cupping his junk obscenely. "Oh, the things I'll do to you."

"Gross," Tiggy said, cocking his head from side to side.

Dustin leered up at the window. "Gonna fill you with my baby juice."

Gary blinked. "Did we know that Prince Justin—oh, *excuse me*, Prince *Dustin*—has a breeding kink? I feel like we should know that he has a breeding kink."

[*Editor's Note: Justin does not have a breeding kink, as far as we know. We asked Ryan, but he turned around and walked away without answering.*]

"Yeah," Dustin said, his lips curling into a devastating sneer. "I'm freaky like that."

"That's pretty obvious," Gary said. "And while I'm normally one to celebrate kinks, I will *not* become a husband who lives only to pop out babies. I respect myself too much for that."

"But," Dustin said, "I love you."

Gary scoffed. "Of course you do. I'm the best thing in your entire life. But I'm afraid that love is not reciprocated." He looked off into the distance, as if pondering roads not taken. "Please, go, and know that I would've been the best you'd ever had."

"I'll never take another lover," Dustin vowed as tears streamed down his cheeks. "As the gods as my witnesses, I will never love one as much as I love you." He choked on the last word, his body wracked with sobs.

"Gods," Gary muttered. "This fucking guy. Tiggy, I'm really starting to doubt your tastes in mens."

"Dustin has penis," Tiggy said. "Gary wants penis. No problem."

Dustin fell to his knees, pounding the ground with his fists as he wailed Gary's name over and over.

"Okay," Tiggy said. "Few problems."

"My word," Gary said. "He's really going for it, isn't he? Maybe I should fuck him. Just a little bit. You know, as a treat."

But before Gary could put this offer out, Dustin rose to his feet, wiping the tears and snot from his face. "Before I leave, might I see your asshole? It will help me get through the cold, lonely nights ahead."

Gary rolled his eyes. "Then you'll go?"

Dustin nodded. "I swear on my love for you."

"Fine." Gary turned and lifted his tail, sticking his rear out the window.

"Oh," Dustin breathed. "I understand art now. I understand the beauty in what the gods have created. It's an entire universe I'll never explore. Curse you, gods! You show me this and then snatch it away? How dare you!"

"Yes, well," Gary said as he pulled his rear back inside. "That sounds like a you problem. Later, gator."

Dustin eventually left, vowing that he'd live a life of celibacy from this day forth, seeing as how no other asshole would ever be good enough. The last they heard of him was a final scream: "Gary! *Gaaaarrrrry*!"

As the final night fell, Gary lay on his bed, face in his pillow. He'd never felt more alone in his entire life. Not that he had much life left. Tomorrow would come, and Gary would be sacrificed by Lady Tina. He'd remain a virgin for all eternity.

"Tiggy fix," Tiggy said, alighting on Gary's horn. "Tiggy fix, okay?"

Gary sniffled. "No, friend. This is the end of the road for me. I've accepted that." He closed his eyes. "I just wish…"

"What?" Tiggy asked.

"I just wish I could have felt a hard cock in my person before I died. Is that too much to ask for?"

"Does Tiggy have penis?"

Gary opened his eyes. "I…don't know? Frankly, I have no idea about bird anatomy."

Tiggy bent over, ruffling his feathers. "Can't find it."

"It's okay," Gary said with a watery smile. "I appreciate the effort, kitten. I don't know that I would have felt it if you had."

"Rude," Tiggy said.

"Maybe when I cross beyond the veil, there will be mens

waiting for me," Gary whispered. "Tall, brutish mens who want nothing more than to ravage me for hours on end. They won't even bother taking turns, descending upon me all at once, and all my holes will be plugged, including my ears. Doesn't that sound wonderful, Tiggy?"

"Uh," Tiggy said. "Sure."

"But alas," Gary said mournfully, "I won't know until Lady Tina takes her blade and slices my throat. Oh, Tiggy. Maybe this much beauty isn't meant to exist in the world. I'm too pure and lovely to stay here. Yes, yes, I can feel the call of the veil. Come, it says, come. And then you won't stop coming."

"I like blasphemy," Tiggy said. "Gods boner!"

"I agree," Gary said. "The gods will also probably want to take me over and over again. I guess death won't be so bad, so long as the orgy doesn't let up when I cross to the great beyond."

"Sleep," Tiggy said, pecking Gary's horn. "Tomorrow be better."

And so Gary slept, and when he dreamed, he didn't dream of the stars. No, he dreamt of bukkake, of mens with rough hands holding him down and jerking off onto his face.

As the moon began to lower, he smiled in his sleep.

HE AWOKE WHEN HE HEARD the chirping of a bird. He opened his eyes, blinking slowly. "What is it?" he mused out loud. "What has awakened me from my slumber on this, my final morning?"

"Gary!" Tiggy called from outside the window. "Quick!"

Gary rose from his bed and clomped toward the window, his mane trailing after him. He looked down at the ground beneath the tower, but the road was empty. He turned his face to the sky and found his friend circling above him. "What is it, kitten? What tidings have you brought me on this, the day of my death?"

"Found a mens!" Tiggy cried.

Gary's eyes widened. "You have?" But then he shook his head.

"It doesn't matter, kitten. It's already too late. The sun is rising, and with it, my ending!"

Tiggy landed on the window ledge, hopping excitedly. "Big mens," he said. "*Biggest* mens."

Though his heart thundered in his chest, Gary tried to tamp it down as best he could. He was used to disappointment, and wouldn't let himself get his hopes up again.

Oh, who was he kidding. "The biggest mens? What on earth are you talking about?"

"Found him," Tiggy said proudly. "Found a good mens. Come and eat your flower."

"But where is he?" Gary asked. "There's no one on the road! Unless…Tiggy. Dearest, *Tiggy*. Is he invisible? I've never considered such a thing. That'd be crazy fucked up, having an invisible man do my butt. Isn't that fucked up? But now that I've said it out loud, I might be completely on board with that. Hold on, let me check." He lowered his head to peer between his legs. "Yep, getting chubbed up here. Invisible mens, whoever you are, I see— okay, I don't *see* you, but you get what I mean."

"Not invisible," Tiggy said. "He *flying*."

A shadow crossed over the tower as if a great creature blotted out the sun. Gary turned his face toward the sky in wonder.

A flash of black and red, the pumping of incredible wings.

"Who," Gary breathed, "the fuck. Is *that*."

"It is I," the beast growled, sending a delicious shiver down Gary's spine. "The bringer of lust. The purveyor of sexy shenanigans. I have prowled the world in search of one who makes my many hearts roar with the fires of indecency. And I have found him. I *smell* your ripeness, a fruit waiting to be plucked. And, as I always say, once you go plucking, it's time for fucking."

Gary blinked prettily. "That…doesn't make any sense."

"I know!" the beast bellowed. "It doesn't *have* to!" Gary gasped as the beast's wings spread wide as he lowered himself to the ground, the earth rolling beneath his talons, causing the tower to tremble. He raised his head until he was just underneath the window, forked tongue snaking out and flipping back and forth rapidly. His dark eyes narrowed, scales glittering in the sun. "Hello, my pretty," the dragon—for yes, it *was* a dragon—purred. "There

I was, minding my own business, chasing floofy little rats who think they're better than me. Fuck those sheep! Fuck them right in their stupid faces!" A lick of fire bloomed from his mouth, causing Gary's erection to become more pronounced. "As I was listening to their screams, a bird fluttered overhead, telling me of the most gorgeous creature trapped in a tower. A creature unlike any other that has ever existed. I had to see for myself." The dragon leered at him. "And I find myself without disappointment."

Gary laughed, high-pitched and obnoxious. "Are you talking about little ol' me?"

"I am," the dragon said. "Tell me, oh great beauty. What is your name? I'd like to know what I'm going to be screaming later."

"Gary," he whispered daintily.

"Gary," the dragon rumbled. "Gar. Ry. My gods, has a name ever rolled off my tongue so easily? I think not." He reared back, standing on his back legs, wings spread wide. The muscles in his chest and arms were enormous, and Gary wondered what it would feel like to be crushed in them. "Gary. I am the Beast from the East. Those that hear my name cower in fear. I am…Kevin."

In his eighteen years, Gary had never heard a more erotic name. "Kevin," he said, the word foreign on his lips. "*Kevin*."

"Oh yes," Kevin said. "Say it again."

"Kevin!"

"Again!"

"*Kevin*!"

"Again!"

"*KEV*—"

"Tiggy gonna go do bird things," Tiggy said, backing away slowly. "Tiggy no taste the rainbow."

"Yes, yes," Gary said, distracted. "Fine. You go do that. Whatever. Bye."

Tiggy rolled his eyes and took to the sky.

"Well," Kevin said. "It looks as if we're alone. I wonder what we should do now?" He brightened. "Ah! I know. Let's fuck."

Gary looked away. "But how do I know if you're my one true love? That's the only way to break the curse."

"Curse?" Kevin asked. "What curse?"

[Editor's Note: There's no curse. Gary, this isn't a story with a curse. You can't just add things because—]

"The curse of how tight I can clench my asshole," Gary said.

[Editor's Note: Godsdammit.]

"Oh," Kevin said. "Is that all? Because I know how to test that curse out."

"You do?" Gary asked, fighting against the hope welling in his chest.

Kevin grinned at him, all fangs. "You bet your sweet ass I do. I'm hella cool."

Gary shook his head. "This is all so sudden. I barely know you, and yet... you don't feel like a stranger."

"I can be a stranger," Kevin said. "If that's how you want to play it. I got your stranger danger right here, baby."

Gary shuddered in pleasure. "You'd do that for me?"

"Yes," Kevin growled. "I do anything to—I mean, I'd do anything *for* you." And then he began to sing.

Gary!

Gary!

Let down your mane

That I may pull so you shriek my name!

"That almost didn't rhyme," Gary said. "But I'll allow it." And with that, he jerked his head, his mane spilling out the window and down the length of the tower. The white hair glittered in the sunlight as it fell toward the ground, the ends of which scraped the bottom of the tower.

"Tell me," Kevin said, brushing his nose against Gary's mane. "Does the carpet match the drapes?"

"Maybe you should come up here and find out," Gary whispered.

"I'm coming," Kevin rumbled. "And pretty soon, you'll be able to say the same." His talons pierced the tower as he began to climb.

"Okay," Gary said. "Ow. You're climbing on my—*ow*. Ow! Move your stupid feet, you overgrown sex lizard!"

The dragon's head appeared in the window. He grinned razor sharp when he saw Gary waiting for him. He tried to push his head through the window. He didn't fit. He frowned and tried again. Still didn't fit. "Okay," he said. "We didn't really plan this out very well."

"You're still stepping on my mane!" Gary cried, head jerking as Kevin slid on the tower.

Kevin winced. "Sorry, sorry. Just trying to…oh, for fuck's sakes. Who the hell built this window so small? My penis won't even fit in here!"

"Wow," Gary said. "That was information I didn't know I desperately needed."

Kevin's large tongue fell from his mouth, wrapping around Gary's ankle and rubbing up and down slowly. The tongue pulled back, brushing against Kevin's lips. "Now I've had a taste of you," the dragon growled. "And I want to go back for *seconds*. You wanna be my love buffet? Get you a sneeze guard and everything while I scoop you out from your warming tray."

Gary had never heard such sexy words hurled toward him that way. "Yeah," he panted, flexing his glutes as he spun in a slow circle. "You want to pay a flat rate for all you can eat macaroni and cheese while you sit in a sad, cracked booth with others who're regretting all their life's choices that led them to even enter a buffet?"

"Hell yes," Kevin said. "And then after I eat all that gooey overbaked macaroni and cheese, I'll go to the soft serve machine and pour that white cream in a bowl. And then you know what I'm going to do? I'm gonna cover it with hot fudge."

"Oh my gods," Gary said, half out of his mind with lust. "You gonna put sprinkles on it? You gonna put sprinkles *all over it*?"

"So many godsdamn sprinkles," Kevin promised darkly. "I'm gonna *cover it with sprinkles*."

[*Editor's Note: WHAT IN THE ACTUAL FUCK, GARY!*]

Gary moaned. "And then, later, you'll be sitting on your couch and your stomach will hurt and you'll regret ever going to the buffet in the first place."

"I will," Kevin agreed. "I'll regret so hard, especially when I get the shits later. All that dairy, just wreaking havoc on my digestive tract."

"Yes!" Gary cried. "Yes!"

"I'm gonna huff," Kevin said, "I'm gonna puff, and I'm gonna fuck you so godsdamn hard!"

Gary blinked. "Wait, what? That's not the right story. We're doing Rapunzel."

"I'm ad-libbing. Just go with it."

"Oh. Right. Carry on."

"By the hair on your chinny-chin chin," Kevin snarled. "let me right the fuck in!"

"Oh, is this too sudden?" Gary lamented. "I know what my heart and dick are telling me, but this sounds too good to be true!"

"I've got you, baby," Kevin said, tongue falling once again from his mouth and circling Gary's horn, the grip tight as it rose up and down. "Now that I'm here, you'll never be alone again." His tongue moved faster until Gary couldn't hold back. A rainbow shot from his horn, splattering the walls and ceiling. His knees grew weak as he tried to stay upright. "That's it," Kevin said. "Let it all out. Get that shit all over my face."

"What the hell is going on here?" a voice shrieked.

Kevin pulled back, tongue dragging through the mess of rainbow on the ground. Gary rushed to the window. Looking down beyond Kevin, he saw Lady Tina standing on the road holding a dangerously sharp dagger, her face twisted furiously.

"Who's that?" Kevin asked. "I already don't like her. She sucks ass."

Gary sighed. "She's coming here to sacrifice me so she can bathe in my virgin blood and gain all my powers. She's the one who put me in the tower in the first place."

"She *what*?" Kevin growled, snapping his fangs angrily.

Lady Tina didn't even flinch. "Get your disgusting talons off my unicorn! I have plans for him, and I won't be denied!"

"Your unicorn?" Kevin asked. "*Your* unicorn? Listen here, you gangrenous gash, Gary is *mine*."

Gary's heart fluttered in his chest at the possessiveness in the dragon's voice. Although he was a strong, independent unicorn who didn't need no mens, he'd be lying if he said that it didn't please him to hear Kevin speaking in such a way.

"You can't have him!" Lady Tina cried. "I've waited for this day for nearly two decades, and not even one such as *you* can stop me."

Kevin turned his head back toward Gary. "My love," he said. "Give me just a moment. I'll be right back. I expect you to be ready for me to enter you upon my return."

"How big is it?" Gary called after him as Kevin flared his wings and leapt from the tower.

"Your insides will never be the same," Kevin said as he lowered to the ground. "If you weren't a magical creature, it'd probably end up in a serious medical emergency."

"So, big, then. You could have just said that."

"I don't like to brag," Kevin said. "Okay, that was a lie. I love to brag because I have a lot to brag about. I literally have the biggest dick in the world. It's the size of a thirty-seven-year-old man."

"Dreams do come true," Gary said with a sigh.

Lady Tina, for her part, didn't look scared as the dragon loomed over her. She narrowed her eyes into slits, her mouth a thin, bloodless line. Then, with a screech, she darted forward, the dagger raised above her head. "Taste my wrath!"

"Yawn," Kevin said before raising his front leg, curling his digits, and flicking against Lady Tina's chest. Gary expected her to fly back and hit the ground hard, but apparently the dragon was stronger than even he knew. Instead of being knocked off her feet, Lady Tina exploded, blood and gristle flying around in ropey arcs. What remained of her face landed in a tree. The dagger—still held in her dismembered hand—hit the road and skittered in the dust.

"Hurray!" Gary cried. "Exactly what Lady Tina DeSilva deserves!"

"Ew," Kevin said, shaking his hand. A string of intestine hung from the tip of his talon. "There's a reason I'm mainly a vegetarian. Look at all that disgusting meat. Blech." He rubbed his talon on the ground, the intestine dragging in the dirt. "Why won't it get *off?*" He shook his entire leg. The intestine finally fell to the ground in a wet heap. "There. Done and done!"

"I'm free," Gary whispered, barely believing in his own words. "Oh my gods, I'm *free.*"

"Yeah, you are," Kevin said, turning around and climbing back up the tower. "Free to get railed. Which is what's going to happen next. I can't wait to hear it described in excruciating detail, so much so that even the most hardened of people would fall to their knees and beg to the gods to kill them so they don't have to hear anymore."

And they lived happily ever after.

THE END

"Wait, *what*?" Gary growled. "This isn't the end! I'm about to get *laid*. We're not going to—"

THE. END.

"Nope," Kevin said. "Fuck that and fuck you. We're doing this. We're doing it so damn *hard*." He whipped his tail against the tower, causing it to shudder and shake, stone crumbling. He did it again and again until the tower began to lean precariously. He rose on his hind legs, pushing against it, his head just underneath the window. "Jump on me," he said. "And let us desecrate this place in the name of queer loving."

"My bakery is open for a private event," Gary purred as he crawled out the window, his mane trailing after him. He landed on Kevin's head, careful so he didn't hurt the love of his life. "And there's only one person who's invited. Guess who that is?"

"It'd better be me," Kevin said as he pushed the tower with all his might. It tipped and tipped and *tipped* until it fell with a jarring crash, a cloud of dust and rock billowing up in the air. "And you should know, I have a mighty need for your confectionaries."

He lowered his head toward the ground. Gary leapt off him, landing perfectly as a breeze washed over his mane. He looked over his shoulder at Kevin as he raised his tail. "I hope you like banana nut bread. Because that's what I've got cooking."

"I'm gonna banana nut all over you," Kevin swore as he descended.

THE END. THE END. THE END. THE END. OH MY GODS, THE *END*.

"Wait," Gary cried as the dragon's tongue slithered out, nostrils flaring. "One more thing!"

Fine. *What?*

Gary grinned as the sounds of moist slurping filled the air.

"Ryan Foxheart is a weasel fucker. There, all done! You can go now. You should probably run unless you want to watch what's about to happen. He's…oh. *Oh.* Ooh, yes, oh my gods, you get that bread, you disgusting fuck lizard! You *get it.*"

And then these two assholes lived happily ever after.

The end.

Also, Ryan is *not* a weasel fucker.

SAM
AND THE
Beanstalk

ONCE UPON A TIME in the Kingdom of Verania, a kickass boy was born on a farm outside of the City of Lockes. His parents were hardworking, and at times, life could be difficult, but they were alive and had all their teeth. Which was very important.

The family—mother Rosemary, father Joshua—was poor, but they did their best to provide for their son, Sam. They lived far enough away from everyone that it was usually just the three of them. Sam grew up safe and loved, though he often turned his face toward the sky, wondering what else was out there. He was happy with his life on the farm, knowing that it was the Haversford legacy, and would one day be his. Over the course of his first eighteen years, Sam sprouted like an unruly weed, growing up and up and up, his limbs long and gangly, his mouth always moving.

When he worked the farm, he often stared at the City of Lockes rising in the distance with a sense of unease. He wasn't *scared* of the tall buildings with their colorful flags, nor the crowds of people hurrying to and fro. He was seven the first time his father took him to the city on one of his monthly visits to sell the fruits and vegetables and flowers grown on the farm. By the time the day ended Sam was exhausted, never having spoken to so many different people in his life.

While he could appreciate the noise and bustle of the city, he preferred the solemn quiet of the farm, the sounds of chickens and cows music to his ears. And yes, perhaps he was a bit lonely. The nearest farm was half-a-day's walk, and the owners were an older couple without any children. Sam grew up without anyone close to his age. There were nights when he longed for more, but it was a negligible thing. He knew his place in the world.

But times grew tough as the years went on. Someone had apparently decided that fast food was much better, and therefore, sales of Haversford produce fell off dramatically. Sam and his father often returned with half their goods still unsold, Joshua smiling tightly and saying that the tides would change, and that they'd be all right in the end.

But Sam could see how much it weighed on his parents, how hard they worked for so little return. It seemed pointless, and although Sam doubled his efforts, they were more in the red than not. Every now and then, as Sam lay in his bed, sleep only a fanciful wish that wasn't coming true, he'd overhear his parents talking in the kitchen in low voices.

During one such conversation, near Sam's eighteenth birthday, his mother was tearful, his father consoling her as best he could. "We'll figure it out," Dad said quietly. "I don't know how, but we will. We're due for a bit of good luck. So long as we remain firm in our convictions, I know we'll see this through as we always do."

Sam closed his eyes against the ache in his chest. He hated how defeated his parents sounded, though they always put on a brave face where he was concerned. They wouldn't let their worries become his own, telling him that he needed to focus on becoming the best man he could.

On the morning of his eighteenth birthday, Sam was in the fields, pulling weeds from the flowerbeds, the sun beating down on his back. Sweat dripped from his brow, but he barely noticed it, hands digging into the soil, dirt underneath his fingernails.

"It'll be all right, Morgan," he said, glancing over at his prize Mashallaha rooster, a proud bird with rainbow feathers and a bright green wattle. Morgan had been a gift for his sixteenth year, and he was Sam's best—and only—friend. Not the best conversationalist, but Sam didn't mind. There was another boy with big ears and a nervous disposition who lived on a farm miles away, but for the most part, Sam only had Morgan. He grinned as Morgan pecked the ground, eyes black as he pulled a writhing worm from the soil. He tilted his head back as he swallowed the worm. "You'll see. We'll be okay. I promise."

Morgan ruffled his feathers in response.

"Exactly," Sam said. "You always know how to make me feel better."

When Sam returned to the house for lunch, he found his mother and father sitting in the kitchen, their heads in their hands. He paused in the doorway, worried that something had happened while he'd been out in the fields.

Dad lifted his head, smile strained. "Sam, I was just about to come looking for you."

"What's wrong?" Sam asked, slumping down in the empty chair across from his parents. His mother patted his hand and poured him water from a wooden jug. He drank deeply, throat working before setting down his cup. "You look like someone died. Oh my gods, did someone die? Who? Did their nipples explode?"

Dad snorted. "You and exploding nipples, I don't know where you got that from."

Sam shrugged. "It happens. I think."

Dad and Mom exchanged a glance that lasted only a few seconds but said much. Whatever was going on, it wasn't good. "We got another notice from the bank," Mom said quietly. "We're behind on the mortgage. If we don't come up with a way to pay what we owe, we might lose the farm."

Sam hung his head. "How bad is it?"

"Bad enough that we need to make some tough choices," Dad said. "But not so bad that we'll forget we have each other. We're Haversfords, we always come out all right in the end. This is just a bump in the road." He sighed, shaking his head. "Another bump."

"What can we do?" Sam asked, thinking hard. "There has to be a way to fix this. I could…" His eyes widened. "I know! I could go to Meridian City and work for Mama. She always has a need for sex workers. I saw the flyers for it the last time we were in the City of Lockes. Just think! I could get paid while also getting rid of my virginity. Win win!"

Mom and Dad stared at him.

Sam slumped in his chair as he folded his arms. "What? I'm just spit balling."

"While I appreciate you wanting to help," Mom said slowly, "perhaps we should consider other options before deciding on sex work."

"My body, my choice," Sam muttered.

"Oh boy," Dad said. "There isn't enough wine in Verania where this conversation would be palatable. Let's try a few other things first."

"I'd be a good sex worker," Sam argued. "Maybe even the best."

"Yeah," Mom said. "If those drawings you hide under your mattress are any indication, you certainly have an active imagination."

Sam groaned, face hot. "Those aren't mine! I'm keeping them for…a friend. Yes, a *friend* who…you don't know because… they're…not…real? Godsdammit!"

"What are these drawings now?" Dad asked, brow furrowed.

"Nothing!" Sam said hastily. "Nothing at all. Just art! You know how I have an extreme appreciation for art." Sam did not, in fact, have an extreme appreciation for art. The drawings were very erotic, and showed men in various impossible poses, all of whom seemed to like having things shoved up their butts if the expressions on their faces were any indication. Sam wouldn't know; he'd never had a boyfriend—or anyone, for that matter—who wanted to put things inside of him.

"Is that what we're calling it now?" Mom asked, sounding amused. "Because your definition of art seems to involve quite a bit of chest hair."

"I have an idea!" Sam said brightly. "Let's talk about something else and never circle back to this particular topic."

"It's probably for the best," Mom said. "Especially since the pages were a little…stiff."

Sam glared at her. "You're enjoying this way too much."

She shrugged. "I live on a farm with two men and a bunch of animals. Have to get my kicks somewhere."

"We need you to sell Randall," Dad said. "He's a good bull, but he's past his breeding prime." Dad shuddered. "Though that doesn't stop him from trying to mount anything and everything he can climb up on."

"No," Sam said. "Oh noooo. Anything but selling Randall. That makes me so sad. Oh, my heart. How it hurts."

"You're smiling," Mom said dryly.

He was, but only because Randall was a fucking asshole who had apparently decided that Sam was the most annoying thing on the planet. Anytime Sam got near him, the bull's nostrils would flare as his eyes narrowed, hoof pawing the ground in warning. His horns were really sharp, and Sam knew Randall would buy him a one-way ticket to Gore City if he wasn't careful.

"You think we could get something for him?" Sam asked.

"At least enough to carry us through the next month," Dad said. Sam studied his father, noting the slump of his shoulders, the dark circles under his eyes. "And that's all we can ask for. We just need a break." He shook his head. "Sam, take Randall to the market in the city, and see what you can get for him." He looked sternly at his son. "And don't take the first offer you get. Make them work for it."

"I know how to haggle with the best of them," Sam said, puffing out his chest. "Don't worry about a thing. I'll take care of it."

Mom smiled. "We know you will. And when you return, we'll celebrate your birthday. I can't believe you're already eighteen." She sniffled as she wiped her eyes. "My little boy, all grown up."

Sam stood from his chair, walking around the table until he stood behind his mother. He wrapped his arms around her, his face in her hair. He turned his head to see Dad smiling at the both of them.

"Happy birthday, kiddo," Dad said. "We may not have much, but we are thankful for what we *do* have. And that includes you."

"Fucking Randall," Sam mumbled as the bull once again stopped on the road, refusing to move another inch. The city was still a couple of hours away, and the sun was high in the sky, beating down on them both. "Come on, you stupid cow. Walk!"

Randall snorted, shaking his head, the length of rope cinched tightly around his neck. Sam pulled as hard as he could. His feet slipped on the dirt, and he fell on his ass with a grunt. "Oh, fuck you, dude. Seriously. You suck ass. I hope whoever I sell you to likes stringy meat, because that's all you're going to be."

Randall lowed in response before lowering his head toward the ground, grazing on the grass at the side of the road.

Sam was about to push himself up when a husky voice spoke from behind him, the accent melodious. "What is it we have here?"

Sam turned to find an old woman standing in the road, wearing a heavy blue cloak, the hood of which rose over her head. Wisps of white hair hung down around her ancient, craggy face, her skin dark, her gaze sharp. She leaned on a wooden staff with ornate carvings that looked like a snake dragon monster thing. She tapped the staff against the road twice. "A boy," she said. "Yes, a boy."

"Who are you?" Sam asked, rising slowly, taking a step away from the stranger.

"I am called Vadoma," the woman said, eyeing him up and down. "And who be you?"

"I be Sam," he said. "I've never heard the name Vadoma before."

The woman chuckled, the sound like a dry desert wind over golden sand. "No, I don't expect you would have. As far as I know, there is only one with the name."

"Neat," Sam said. "I'm having such a wonderful time. Now, if you'll excuse me, I have to get this motherfucker to the market so he can be butchered." He pulled on the rope again, but Randall jerked his head, causing the rope to slide against Sam's palms. He hissed as he dropped it, shaking his arms against the burn.

"He doesn't appear to want to go," Vadoma said.

"Fun," Sam said. "I really appreciate how observant you are. Just an idea, but maybe you could go do that somewhere else. Like, really far away from me."

"I have a proposal for you."

Sam balked. "Uh. Okay? No offense, but you're old, dude. Not sure I want to get married to you."

Vadoma snorted. "Not that kind of proposal, you idiot. An exchange of goods. You give me the bull, and I'll give you magic."

That caught Sam's attention. "Magic? What the hell are you talking about? You can't just *give* someone magic. That's not how it works. Magic is only for wizards."

"Bah," Vadoma said derisively. "Wizards. They think they're all high and mighty, but they're not. They're no better than anyone else. And I wouldn't be giving *you* the ability to perform magic."

Sam eyed her warily. "Your sales pitch might need some work, if I'm being honest."

Vadoma reached into her cloak then pulled out her hand and held it towards him. "This is what I offer." She opened her hand, and there, laying on her palm, were three black beans.

Sam waited for the punch line.

There was none.

She bounced her hand, the beans rattling together as if they were made of stone.

He squinted at her. "You want me to give you my bull in exchange for beans? Do…do you not know how commerce or the fair exchange of goods works?"

"These aren't normal beans," Vadoma said. "They are imbued with magic. Plant them in the light of a full moon, and they will grow until they reach the sky."

"Are you on meth?" Sam demanded. "Because you literally sound like you're on meth."

Vadoma frowned. "That's not how to use the word *literally*."

Sam threw up his hands. "I feel like you're missing the point entirely. Do you know what my parents will do to me if I return with *beans*? Holy shit, they'd be so pissed off. And there's not even enough there for a full meal. I'd rather eat Randall."

Randall bellowed behind him. Without looking back, Sam flipped him off.

"You shouldn't eat these," Vadoma said. "If you do, your innards will explode."

"Okay, crazy lady," Sam said. "I'm gonna be on my way if it's all the same to you. A piece of advice? Maybe don't accost people in the road and try to give them beans in exchange for a horny old bull. That's just stupid."

He turned, meaning to grab the rope and get Randall moving. But before he could, the woman spoke again. "Oh, my. I forgot to tell you the most important part."

"Oh my gods," Sam muttered. "You're *still* on this? What the fuck."

"Beyond the clouds," the woman said. "A treasure beyond your wildest dreams lies hidden. The beans are the key to this treasure."

Sam turned slowly, heart rabbiting in his chest. "And why

would you give them to me? Why not go for the treasure yourself?"

"Because I'm old," Vadoma said. "My body is weary, and I no longer have it in me to reach for the sky. And I like you."

Sam chuckled weakly. "Still not my type, dude. I prefer someone who's a little less…you."

"This treasure," Vadoma said, taking a shuffling step toward him, "is more than enough to save your farm. In fact, you and your parents will never want for anything again."

A chill ran down Sam's spine. "I never told you the farm was in trouble."

She grinned, her teeth yellowed and crooked. "Think, Sam. You take these beans from me, and all your fears and worries will melt away. The sky treasure will be yours."

If it was normal treasure, Sam might have stood strong. But *sky* treasure? Sweet molasses, how fucking rad did that sound? Sky. *Treasure.* Why, the very words were enough to get him to chub up, something he wasn't exactly proud of, given the present company. "What's the catch?"

She blinked. "The catch?"

"The *catch*," Sam insisted. "There has to be a catch. No one gives away something like that for nothing."

"I told you," she said flatly. "The beans for the bull. That's all I require."

Sam gnawed on the inside of this cheek. Visions of gold and jewels danced before his eyes, his mother wearing a crown of rubies, his father holding a golden scepter. All in all, they looked awesome, and he felt his resolve crumbling. "Okay. Say I entertain this. What kind of return program do you have in case it doesn't work? Do I get Randall back or store credit or…?"

Vadoma closed her hand. "Perhaps I was wrong about you. I thought you were ready for the beans, but it appears I was mistaken."

"No, no," Sam said quickly. "I'm ready for the beans. Like, so ready. I just…" He shook his head. "Fine. If you *promise* there's sky treasure."

"I promise," Vadoma said. "That, and so much more. Do we have a deal?"

He glanced back at Randall, who looked up at him, jaw moving side to side as he chewed. He lifted his tail, letting out a long, sonorous fart, all while never breaking his gaze.

"Deal," Sam said. "Seriously, Randall, you're the worst."

Vadoma smiled widely. It wasn't a very pleasant sight. She rushed forward, thrusting the beans into Sam's hands before hurrying around him to pick up Randall's rope. "No take backs," she said. "The deal is done. Remember, boy, plant them under the light of the full moon. Tonight. If you don't, the magic won't work."

Sam stared down at the beans in his hand. They were such tiny things. He barely felt the weight of them on his palm. "Do I have to water them or something? Give them fertilizer?" When Vadoma didn't reply, he turned.

The road was empty. Vadoma and Randall were gone.

Sam chuckled uneasily as he looked around. "Uh, crazy lady? Where'd you go?"

The only response came from the birds flying high above.

"Uh oh," Sam whispered. "Buyer's remorse is setting in. I'm so fucking screwed." And with that, he began to trudge home.

"YOU DID WHAT?" Dad bellowed.

Sam winced in the kitchen as his parents glared at him. "Yeah, see, I *knew* that was going to be your response, but no worries! If you give me, say, seven more hours, I'm sure I'll be able to come up with an appropriate response that'll make everything better. Let's reconvene first thing in the morning and pick it up then. Great! Glad we had this talk. I'm just gonna mosey on out of here and leave you two lovebirds to it."

He turned to flee to his room.

"*Sam.*"

His shoulders slumped as he turned back around, his father's anger a palpable thing. He could deal with that. He was a loudmouthed teenager; his father had been pissed at him more times than he could count.

But it was his mother that gave him pause. She didn't look angry. No, she looked *sad*, and even worse, disappointed, as if she couldn't believe her only son could do something so stupid. Heavy guilt bled through his ribcage, lodging firmly underneath his heart. He couldn't meet her gaze, finding something interesting to stare at on the floor.

"How could you do this?" Dad asked, scrubbing a hand over his face. "I asked you for *one thing*, and you just…" He shook his head. "You gave the bull away. For *beans*."

"Magic beans," Sam muttered. Then, "Okay. I know how it looks, and you have every right to be pissed off at me—"

"Oh gee," Dad said, and Sam took a moment to appreciate how snark was apparently genetic. "Since we have every right and all."

"—but what if it works?" Sam said, pushing through the ache in his chest. "What if they *are* magic? It could solve all our problems!"

"Or," Dad spat, "you could have done exactly what I asked, and we wouldn't be having this conversation."

"Joshua," Mom said quietly. "Don't go so hard on him. He's… trying."

Not exactly the ringing endorsement Sam had been hoping for.

"I need him to try *harder*," Dad snapped as Mom rubbed his arm. "Always with his head stuck in the clouds, these flights of fancy that have no place in the real world." He glared at Sam, his mouth twisting. "What were you thinking?"

"I don't know," Sam admitted. "It just…it all happened so fast, and then when I turned back around, the woman and Randall were gone. Disappeared into thin air!"

"I don't believe you," Dad said. "There's no such thing as magic beans."

"It's not so bad," Mom tried again. She peered down at the beans on the table. "Perhaps I can mash them up. Put them in some hot broth. Would you like that, Sam? Would you like hot smashed bean broth?"

Sam groaned. "Well, if you're wondering if I could feel worse, have I got news for you."

Dad gaped at him for a long moment before his resolve steeled. "I'm going out to the barn. Sam's chores still need doing."

Sam startled. "No, Dad, you relax. I can take care of them."

But Dad was already heading toward the door. "Don't bother. Wouldn't want to find out you traded the rest of our animals for a magic cucumber." And with that, he banged the door open, the hinges protesting in a metallic shriek. Sam heard his father muttering to himself as he stalked across the yard toward the barn.

Mom sighed. "Give him time, kiddo. He'll come around."

"I'm sorry," Sam whispered. "I thought…"

"I know," Mom said, going for a smile but failing spectacularly. "But your father is right about one thing. Your head *is* always in the clouds, Sam. And while that was all well and good for a time, you're eighteen now. You're becoming a man, and you need to realize that actions have consequences. You need to start thinking about your future. The farm will one day be yours, and you'll need to step up to the challenge." She looked down at the beans with a frown. "Such a fuss over something so tiny."

"I'll fix this," Sam said. "I don't know how, but I'll make it right. I promise."

"We love you," she said. "More than anything in the world." She hesitated. "This woman…did she have a name?"

"Yeah," Sam said. "Weird, too. Never heard anything like it before. She called herself Vadoma."

Mom's eyes widened briefly before her face smoothed out. "Vadoma. How…curious."

The tone in her voice threw him off-kilter. "Do you know her?"

"No," she said. "I don't know her at all. It doesn't matter. We'll make the most of what we have, as we always do." She brightened. "Oh, and a boy stopped by earlier. Nervous little thing." She nodded toward a vase of flowers sitting near the sink. "Brought you those. What was his name? Todd. Yes, Todd. Seemed as if he wanted to wish you a happy birthday."

"He has pretty rad ears," Sam said.

"But?"

He shrugged. "Doesn't really do much for me. He's nice, and sweet, but I don't feel the same way."

Mom chuckled. "A heartbreaker, just like your father. Todd would make a good husband, but I don't think he could handle all your…Sam-ness. You need someone who appreciates you for all that you are. He's out there, somewhere. And I can't wait for the day you meet him."

He watched as she turned away from him, humming under her breath, a lonely little song that caused Sam's eyes to sting. He scooped up the beans from the table and left her standing in the kitchen, sashaying back and forth.

NEAR MIDNIGHT, Sam stepped quietly through the house, wincing as the floorboards squeaked underneath his boots. "*Quiet,*" he hissed at Morgan, the rooster clucking as he followed Sam down the hall.

Morgan cocked his head up at Sam, beady black eyes darting around.

Sam made it to the door, pushing it open while holding his breath, listening for his father's snores to stop. They didn't, and he sighed in relief as he stepped out into the cool night air, the light from the full moon above bathing the farm in an ethereal light.

"Stupid beans," he muttered as he crossed the yard toward the fields behind the barn. "Stupid Randall. Stupid Vadoma. Stupid *Dad.*"

Morgan trilled in response as he hurried after Sam.

"I know," Sam replied. "But I'm mad as hell, and I'll bitch about whoever and whatever I want."

Morgan clucked.

Sam rolled his eyes. "Oh, like *you* could have done any better. You weren't even there. I dare you to try and say no to a crazy lady who wants to give you magic beans. And now that I've said that out loud, I might see the problem. But! *Sky* treasure. Everyone knows that sky treasure is the best kind of treasure."

Morgan, in fact, did *not* know that. He made a low, guttural grunt.

Sam threw up his hands. "*Yes,* I know how that sounds. But your entire existence is eating and pooping, so you don't get to say a damn thing about this."

He crossed the field until he stood in the middle. He looked up at the vast array of stars shining down around him. Maybe his parents were right. Maybe his head *was* stuck in the clouds, but how could they blame him? He didn't want this life. If he were honest with himself, deep down in his secret heart, he'd wished upon these very stars time and time again for all manner of things, both big and small. The gods never listened, but that didn't stop him.

He fell to his knees in the dirt, pulling the beans from his pocket. He scowled down at them. "You better be worth it," he warned them. He dug a small hole in the ground before dropping the beans into it. He turned his face toward the night sky and whispered, "Please, oh please, let this work."

He covered the beans with rich soil. He chuckled bitterly when nothing happened. Not that he expected it to, at least not right away, but still. Nothing.

He lay down on the ground next to them, Morgan pecking at the ground near him. He folded his arms behind his head and looked at the thin clouds passing in front of the moon. "If you're up there, sky treasure," he murmured, "I'm coming for you."

And then his eyes grew heavy, and he drifted on a sea of stars. His mouth parted as his eyes closed, and the boy named Sam Haversford slept as a cool breeze ruffled his hair.

HE WOKE WHEN Morgan squawked angrily. Sam blinked as he sat up, the sky beginning to lighten in the east, the black of night fading into a cold indigo. He yawned, stretching his neck side to side, trying to work out the kink. Smacking his lips, he wriggled his nose as something tickled it. A leaf. It felt like a leaf. Which was odd, seeing as how this field was mostly empty, already having been harvested.

His vision sharpened as he focused on…the leaf. A fat green leaf, bigger than any he'd ever seen before. His gaze rose from the leaf to see *another* leaf. And then another. And then another, all thick and fibrous, with vines that curled and beckoned.

Sam raised his head as he stood slowly, heart stuttering, a vise closing around his lungs, making it almost impossible to breathe.

There, in the middle of the field, was a great tower of green, a stalk bigger than even the widest of tree trunks. He tilted his head back in wonder, looking up at the stalk that stretched toward the sky, disappearing into the clouds.

"Um," Sam said. "What in the actual fuck."

Morgan squawked again, and Sam tilted his head back as far as it could go. Morgan stood on a limb of the stalk, about twenty feet off the ground, feathers ruffled. He called down to Sam again.

"I'm dreaming," Sam decided. "That's all this is. This is a dream, and I need to wake up." He pinched himself viciously. "*Ow.* Okay. That didn't work. I probably shouldn't try it again." He did it anyway. "*Ow.* Godsdammit! Wake up!"

Morgan crowed, and Sam looked back up in time to see Morgan hopping higher and higher, moving from one limb to the next. "Morgan!" he shouted as quietly as he could. "Get down here!"

But Morgan didn't listen, continuing to go up and up and up.

"Oh, just you wait," Sam snarled. "When I get my hands on you, I'm going to stuff you with so many herbs and spices. You'll be *delicious*. Get your ass back down here!"

Morgan ignored him, growing smaller the higher he climbed.

Sam didn't hesitate. He gripped the vines of the stalk. They seemed strong and firmly fixed to the massive tower growing in the field. He began to climb after his only friend.

Ten minutes later, Sam Haversford came to a startling realization: he was deathly afraid of heights, and it was *extremely* easy to vomit off the side of a beanstalk. Thankfully, Sam hadn't eaten before going to bed, so it was mostly yellow acidic bile that hung from his bottom lip in a disgusting string. He wiped his mouth, carefully, before hugging the stalk as best he could. Sweat dripped down the back of his neck as a bird flew near him. "Okay," Sam said, voice trembling. "Just climbing a beanstalk toward sky treasure. You know, like normal people do."

He looked up, leaning back as far as he dared. He couldn't see Morgan anymore, nor could he hear him. He thought Morgan would probably scream if he'd fallen, so he must have reached the top. With a fatalistic resolve, Sam pushed himself on, climbing higher and higher, ignoring the burn in the muscles of his arms and legs.

He stopped and rested every now and then, and by the time the sun crested the horizon, he could no longer see the ground, having passed through the clouds, mist falling over his hands and face. At one point, in the middle of a particularly grumpy gray cloud, his hand slipped, and he almost fell, managing to grab onto a heavy leaf at the last moment. Wheezing, he tried to calm his racing heart.

"Onward," he whispered tiredly. "Ever onward."

Time passed, and the clouds grew thicker, heavier, as if they had weight to them. He pressed his hand against a bit of fluff near his face, amazed when he pulled his arm back and could see the imprint of his fingers in the cloud. He laughed, his fear momentarily abandoning him, replaced by wonder and delight. He broke off a piece of cloud and shoved it in his mouth, where it dissolved into smokey water on his tongue.

"Such a weird Thursday," he muttered as he continued on.

The clouds above him began to brighten as if backlit by a great fire. He squinted against it, pulling himself up and up and—

He broke through the top of the clouds. The sun shone down on him, the light warming his face. The top of the stalk thinned into a small vine, curled at the edges. He looked around, seeing blue sky above, and white clouds below. He almost fell from the stalk when he saw Morgan, standing near the vine.

On top of a cloud.

"Okay," Sam said. "That's not something I expected to see today, if I'm being honest." Carefully, he stretched out his leg, pressing his toe against the cloud Morgan stood on. It gave a little before firming. Taking a deep breath, Sam bellowed as he leapt from the stalk, eyes closed.

He fell briefly, heart in his throat until—

Until his feet met something solid, the impact jarring his legs.

He opened his eyes.

He stood on a cloud, Morgan only a few feet away. Sam froze, sure that he was about to fall through the clouds to his death. He waited a beat or six before pumping his fists in the air. "Yes! *Yes*. I did it!"

Morgan was not impressed.

But it mattered not to Sam. The beans had done exactly what Vadoma had said they would: they'd led him to the sky, and here there would be treasure, his for the taking. He couldn't wait to see the look on Dad's face when he came back down, heavy with gold and sapphires and rubies. He wasn't so magnanimous that he wouldn't rub it in his father's face, at least for a little while.

He took a step forward, the clouds holding his weight. Laughing, he crouched down next to Morgan, running a hand down the rooster's back. "Don't scare me like that," he scolded. "You've got wings, but you can't fly."

Morgan pecked at his hand.

"I know," Sam said, kissing the top of his best friend's head. "We'll be careful. Come on. Let's find that treasure. I wonder where we should...look...."

He gasped when he saw a broad, winding road made of red brick leading further into the clouds that rose like mountains on either side. "There," he breathed. "I bet that's what we have to follow." He picked up Morgan, setting the rooster on his shoulder. "All right. Let's do this."

He put his feet to the road, marveling at the red ornate bricks, each carved with swirling lines of green and gold that glittered in the sunlight. Morgan clucked in his ear as they passed between two great clouds, the peaks of which looked like snow-capped mountains. A bird burst through the cloud mountain on the right, leaving wispy swirls in its wake as it flared its wings, rising high on a current of air. Sam watched it as it passed in front of the sun, black wings spread wide. It circled above him before flying off further down the road, which curved around a cloud and disappeared.

Sam hurried down the road, trying to follow the bird. He rounded the corner and skittered to a stop, eyes bulging from his head.

There, in the distance, at the end of the red brick road, stood a castle.

It wasn't like the castle in the City of Lockes with its many towers and turrets. This castle was a large cube, made up of the same red brick that Sam stood upon. And it was *massive*, bigger than Castle Lockes. Sam thought that Castle Lockes could fit inside of it with room to spare. A flag rose from the top of the square building, fluttering in the breeze, white with the symbol of a giant eye at its center.

"I wonder who lives there?" Sam asked Morgan. "I bet it's

someone cool, because you'd have to be to live in a castle in the sky."

Morgan pulled on the lobe of his ear.

Sam rolled his eyes. "Uh, *yeah*. Of course I'm going inside, we didn't come all this way to turn back now. And need I remind you that *you* were the one who came up here first. If we die, it's all your fault."

He approached the castle, listening intently to hear if anyone would come out and welcome him. Or murder him. It could really go either way. As he got closer, he could see large doors at the front of the castle, made of steel and wood. The castle loomed above him, and he'd never felt so small in his life.

They stopped at the front of the castle, looking around to see if there was perhaps another entrance. There didn't seem to be, so with a trembling hand, he reached out and knocked firmly on the door.

The banging of his fist echoed like a heavy drum.

Boom.

Boom.

Boom.

He stepped back and waited.

Nothing.

He frowned. "Maybe no one's home? I suppose we could walk around the castle and see if there's any other way in—"

He jumped when a latch slid open on the door in front of him, and a glittering eye stared out. Morgan tittered a warning in his ear.

"Who the fuck are you?" the eye demanded. "If you're selling magazines for your marching band, we don't want any! Who the hell reads *magazines* anymore? Go blow your tuba somewhere else, you twink!"

Sam frowned. "Magazines? I'm not selling magazines."

The eye blinked. "Oh. Then what *are* you selling? Avon?" The voice laughed. "Nah, just kidding. You don't look like you've moisturized ever, and those eyebrows are a *travesty*."

"Hey!"

The eye narrowed. "Leave!" The latch slid shut with an audible *snap*.

Sam banged on the door again. "Come back! I just climbed a beanstalk for, like, three whole godsdamn hours, and I'm not leaving until I get what I came for!"

The latch slid open again, the same eye peering through. "Bossy twink," the voice said. "I approve. Maybe there's hope for you yet. I'll allow you entrance, but only if you answer my riddle."

"A…riddle?"

"Yes! Everyone knows that you must answer a riddle before going into a sky castle. Fucking amateurs, I swear to the gods. You only get one guess, and if you fail, then you die. Are you ready?"

Sam swallowed thickly. "Can I have some time to think about it?"

"Sure!" the voice said. "Take all the time you need."

"Really? Oh man, that's rad of you. Thanks. I'm—"

"I *lied*," the voice snapped. "You don't get any time at all! Ready yourself, twink. Some like to be on top. Some like to be on the bottom. Either way, it involves a bed. What is it?"

Sam thought hard. "A…bunk bed?"

"What? No! I mean, yeah, okay, that kind of makes sense, but I was talking about two mens fucking!"

Sam blushed. "Oh. Right. Uh, yeah, that works too."

"Well, let's call that a practice one. Since I'm feeling generous today, I'll allow you one more chance. It will be your *last*, so you better not screw this up! Here it is: When I go in, I can cause some pain. I'll fill your holes when you ask me to. I also ask that you spit, and not swallow. What am I?"

Sam remained silent for a moment, thinking as hard as he ever had in his life. And then it hit him. It was so obvious! "A dentist," he said with conviction.

"Wrong!" the voice cried. "It's that one goblin I had a brief sexual interlude with fifteen years ago named Johnny! Everyone knows you have to spit with goblins, because their jizz has magical properties that change your lower intestines to mush! Gods, you're really terrible at riddles."

"How the hell am I supposed to know about a goblin named Johnny?" Sam demanded, Morgan clucking in agreement.

"That sounds like a *you* problem," the voice said. "Okay, since I'm feeling *really* generous, I'll give you *one more chance*. Ready?

Here it is: I—oh shit."

Through the door, Sam heard another voice, masculine and strong. "Gary, what are you doing? You know you're not supposed to be guarding the door. That's *my* job."

The eye disappeared. Sam stood on his tiptoes, trying to peer through the latch. He could see what looked like wisps of hair lifted over a strange, crinkly opening. It took him a moment to realize he was inches away from a butthole, and he reared back, gagging as his mouth filled with saliva.

"Maybe if you were *doing* your job," the first voice—Gary?— retorted, "I wouldn't have to step up! You know I shouldn't be working in my condition. I'm very delicate!"

"I was in the bathroom," the other voice responded. "I was gone for five minutes." Then, "Who are you talking to?"

Another eye appeared, this one smaller and green. It widened in alarm as it looked out at Sam before the latch slammed closed. Sam pressed his ear to the door, trying to hear what was happening on the other side.

"It's a *twink*," Gary snarled. "A twink who…why are you breathing like that, Foxheart? Also, follow up question: why is your face all red and why are you sweating?"

"It's a *man*," Foxheart said, voice high-pitched and breaking. "He's…he's *beautiful*."

A pause. Then: "I have some serious concerns about your taste in mens. But I suppose that's neither here nor there. Don't just stand there with your mouth agape like *I* was gaping after Johnny. Fucking open the door, you dumbass. Fair warning: he's an idiot who couldn't answer my riddles, even though they were obvious."

"But, my *hair*. I haven't brushed it today!"

"Oh, good gods," Gary muttered. "You're the worst. All of you. Good help is so hard to find. Move, you useless lump of male virility who *still* won't have a three-way with me and my husband for reasons I'm not quite clear on."

"Really," Foxheart said. "You're not clear. Like, at all."

"Shut your whore mouth," Gary snarled. "I'm in no mood for your sound reasoning. It's your loss, anyway. You'll never get the joy of knowing how Kevin's tongue feels when it's brushing against your liver."

Sam made a face as Ryan said, "Yeah, see, I think I'm good with missing out on that. And, I don't think I understand how anatomy works. Where is your liver, exactly?"

But Gary didn't reply. Or, if he did, it was lost under the sound of the great doors opening with a mighty groan. Sam stumbled back, Morgan's feathers bristling against his face. It took a moment for Sam's eyes to get used to the semi-darkness through the doors, but when it did, his jaw dropped.

Before him, stood a magnificent unicorn, his body white, his mane and tail streaked with violet. His horn jutted proudly from his head; his front leg raised as if he were posing.

"Yes," the unicorn said. "It is I, Gary. Gaze upon my wondrous and nubile body and—mother*fucker!*" He grimaced as his head lowered, eyes narrowing as his lips pulled back over his large, square teeth. "I *knew* this one was going to give me trouble."

It was about this time that Sam noticed the unicorn was very, very pregnant. His belly bulged on either side of his body and hung low to the ground.

Sam had never seen a unicorn before, much less a pregnant one. He didn't even know that male unicorns could get pregnant. He was about to ask about it, but the words died in his throat when another figure stepped forward.

He was the dreamiest dream to have ever been dreamed. His wavy blond hair sat perfectly coiffed on his head above a nervous smile. His eyes were the brightest green, and he wore a sleeveless tunic, the muscles in his arms ropey and magnificent. He appeared to be around Sam's age, perhaps a year or two older. He took a step forward, and Sam forgot how to breathe.

"Hi," the man whispered, gaze roving over Sam's face.

"Hi," Sam whispered back, body vibrating as if lightning-struck. His palms were sweaty, and he cleared his throat, trying to maintain some semblance of decency that didn't involve him climbing the man like a godsdamn tree.

"I'm Ryan," the man said. "Ryan Foxheart."

The most perfect name for the most perfect man. Sam swallowed thickly. "I'm Sam."

"Sam," Ryan said. "I like your name."

"Thank you," Sam said, scratching the back of his neck. "I like your everything."

Ryan beamed at him and said, "Wow. Wow, wow, wow. You're so…I want to…can you…*will* you—"

"*Boring*," Gary said, shoving Ryan to the side. "Pay attention to me now. I'm more important than Ryan. As you can see, I'm the most beautiful creature in existence, and I demand that you tell me so. I'm very delicate and I need positive reinforcement by way of compliments about—*oooh*. Ow, ow, fucking *ow*."

And then a wet splat appeared on the floor behind the unicorn.

"Well, crap," Gary said. "I think my water just broke. Ryan, get my husband. Sam, boil water and bring me— aaaaaaaaaaah*hhhhhhhhhh*! It's coming! Oh my gods, it's *coming*!"

Gary shuddered and shook, the muscles in his body tensing as he ground his teeth together. Sam would have nightmares for the rest of his life at the sounds happening at the rear of the unicorn's body. It sounded as if a crowd of a hundred drunk selkies were all stepping on overripe grapes at the same time. Gary's eyes bulged from his skull as he screamed.

A sharp *clunk* sounded from behind him as a golden egg the size of Morgan fell from his rear, covered in rainbow slime that sloughed off the egg onto the ground.

"There," Gary said, breathing hard. "That's better." He shook his head, mane flopping back and forth. "Gods, you'd think with how many things I've had shoved up there, it'd get easier for stuff to come *out*. My body is a wonderland."

"Whaaaaaat is happening," Sam said.

Ryan sighed. "Yeah, I said the same thing the first time it happened. And the second. And the third. Don't worry, you'll get used to it eventually." He grimaced down at the egg. "Or that's what I keep telling myself, anyway."

Gary snorted sparks of blue and yellow. "You try having a dragon for a husband. It's not *my* fault his semen makes gold in my stomach. But he doesn't like condoms because, *babe, they just don't feel as good*. Fucking sex lizard. Gods, I love him so much." His eyes narrowed as he swung his head toward Ryan. "Speaking of," he said, voice low and dangerous, "I thought I told you to go find him? What the fuck are you waiting for? Sam can pick up my ass egg."

"Yeah," Sam said. "I'd really rather not, if it's all the same to you."

Gary turned back toward him slowly. "What was that?" he asked sweetly.

"Nothing!" Sam said quickly. "I'll get right on that." That egg would be enough to take care of his family for the rest of his life. Maybe if Ryan and Gary were distracted, he could—

A great voice bellowed, "My love! I heard your asshole expanding and I've come to partake in the revelry!"

A black dragon with a red underbelly landed behind Ryan and Gary. Sam slapped his hands over his mouth, trying to cover up the scream that tore from his throat. The dragon was huge, his dark eyes glittering as his nostrils flared. He lowered his head, tongue slithering out and brushing against the egg. "Ah," he said, snapping his lips. "That's some good eats right there. I thought there to be buggery afoot, but it seems as if I was mistaken."

"*Hup*," Sam gagged. "*Hup. Hup. Hup.*"

The dragon ignored him, rubbing his snout against the unicorn. "Look at you," the dragon purred. "My light, my darling. You did so well."

"Of course I did," Gary said, kissing the dragon on the cheek. "But if you think you're going anywhere near my ass for the foreseeable future, you're probably right. Kudos."

It turned out that Sam had a bit more to vomit, which, you know. Neat.

He raised his head to find the others staring at him, Ryan with a goofy expression on his face, Gary grimacing as if he hadn't just *shat out an egg*, and the dragon—Kevin?—eyeing Sam as if he were a four-course meal.

"Ah," Kevin rumbled. "And who do we have here?" He grinned, many fangs on display. "It's been a bit since we've had a twink. Tell me, little twink, do you like what you see?"

Sam wiped the bitter spit from his mouth. "I honestly have no idea how to answer that."

"Great," Gary muttered. "He's an idiot. Just what we needed."

"He's *not* an idiot," Ryan growled, causing Sam to blush furiously. "He's awesome and cool and his name is Sam."

"Oh, well fuck me upside the head," Kevin said. "We've never had a *Sam* before. Can I have the first go at him?" He swiveled his head. "Is there a signup sheet, or…?"

"We don't even know why he's come," Gary said. "He could be here to try and steal from us. You can't just let in every poor waif with buggy eyes and semi-good hair."

"Thank you," Sam said, because his mother and father had raised him to be polite. "And, if I'm being honest, the thought of stealing the golden egg literally crossed my mind, like, three minutes ago. But that was before I saw the dragon so now I'm reconsidering many, many things." He grimaced as he glanced at the egg. "Is there…is there a half dragon, half unicorn in that? Is it going to hatch and crawl out and beg for us to kill it because its lungs are on its back and it's leaking fluids out of every orifice like some terrible monstrosity that has only existed in my nightmares?"

They all stared at him.

Sam shrugged. "Dudes. Someone had to ask. Might as well be me. I have no idea what's going on."

"As if *I* would ever want to be a parent," Gary said with a sniff. "I'm far too selfish to care about anyone but myself." He nudged his horn against Kevin's leg. "Did you hear that? He thinks there's going to be a *baby*."

"The only babies are the ones I eat when you shoot down my throat," Kevin said, and *that* wasn't something Sam ever wanted to hear.

"Delightful!" Gary said happily. "I'm having so much fun. No, Sam, there is no baby. It's solid gold." His eyes narrowed. "And if you try and steal from me, I will stomp on your pancreas."

"Noted," Sam said. "Though, to be fair, I don't know what my pancreas does."

"He's so stupid," Gary said, sounding oddly fond. "Look at his stupid face spouting ridiculous words."

"How did you get here?" Ryan asked, taking a step toward Sam.

Sam sighed. "It was this whole thing involving a bull, this weird old lady with magic beans, and my inability to understand the complexities of capitalism."

"Yeah," Kevin said. "I hear that. We've all been there before."

"Really?" Sam asked. It would make sense. How else would all of them have gotten up here? For all he knew, Vadoma had a billion magic beans and suckered a shit ton of people like she'd done Sam.

"No," Kevin said. "Because that's dumb." He laughed. "Magic beans. That's ridiculous."

"You live in a castle in the sky," Sam said. "And I just watched Gary lay an egg. I don't know if you get what *ridiculous* means." He blanched. "No offense or whatever."

"I like him," Kevin said as Ryan grinned. "He can stay, so long as the big guy is okay with it."

Sam's heart tripped all over itself when Ryan grabbed him by the hand, tugging him into the castle. He nearly faceplanted on the ground when he slipped in the rainbow wetness around the egg, but instead of falling to the floor, he was held up against a strong chest. He raised his head to find Ryan's face inches from his own, lips parted over a hint of teeth. Sam curled his fingers into Ryan's tunic and blinked slowly.

"I got you," Ryan said, eyes soft and warm.

"Ew," Gary said from somewhere next to them. "It's like watching weasels in heat."

Sam cleared his throat and took a step away from Ryan. Ryan didn't seem to like this very much, given that he reached out and took Sam's hand in his own once more. "And who's this?" he asked, nodding at the rooster on Sam's shoulder.

"Morgan," Sam said. "He's my best friend."

"Your best friend is a rooster?" Kevin asked. "That's weird."

"You fuck gold into unicorns," Sam said without looking away from Ryan. "Shut up."

"Okay, now *I* like him," Gary said. "It's gotta be the birthing hormones still coursing through my body, but I'll allow it. Where *is* the big guy, anyway?"

Big guy? Sam mouthed to no one in particular. Kevin was already the biggest thing Sam had ever seen. He didn't know if he was ready for the *big guy*.

But that mattered not. Because before he could take another step, Ryan's hand still gripping his own, the entire *castle* seemed to shake as if an earthquake (cloudquake?) had begun to shake the entire sky.

And then a deep voice spoke from the shadows, causing Sam to squeak and tremble in fear.

Fee Fi Fo Fum

I smell the blood of a Veranian

Be he alive or be he dead

I'll hug him close and call him friend.

Stunned, Sam barely felt Ryan drop his hand. He looked over to see Kevin sit back on his haunches, raising his front legs and… snapping? Repeatedly?

Ryan was doing the same. Even Gary was sitting on his butt, bashing his front hooves together.

"Uh," Sam said. "What are you doing?"

Gary rolled his eyes. "Have you never heard poetry before? If you have fingers, you're supposed to snap to show your appreciation. Oh, who am I kidding. You're a poor, uncultured twink. You've probably never been to a poetry slam before."

"We do it every time he has a new one," Ryan said. "It makes the big guy happy when we do."

Sam immediately began to snap as hard as he could. It took him a moment to realize everyone else had stopped. Face growing hot, he lowered his hands slowly, Morgan tugging on his hair.

"He's gonna like you," Gary said ominously. "But whatever you do, don't piss him off. He can be a bit temperamental when he wakes from a nap."

The floor shook again as the shadows far above Sam shifted. He yelped when a massive bare foot stepped out from the darkness, covered in russet hair that curled near the toes. The foot was attached to a gigantic leg almost as big around as the beanstalk. Sam tilted his head as far back as it would go, gaze rising up the leg to a torso with heavily muscled arms hanging on either side of it. The torso led to a neck, then to a *face staring down at him.*

"Oh my gods," Sam whispered fervently, his bowels loosening.

A giant towered above him, his wonderful face adorned with a wide smile, each of his teeth the size of Randall. He crouched down, knees popping so loud, Sam had to cover his ears. Morgan screeched, wings bashing against the side of Sam's face before he jumped down, running in a dizzying circle, squawking in terror.

The giant bent his face toward Sam, nostrils flaring as he sniffed the air. His face screwed up, and before Sam could react, he sneezed.

It was as if Sam stood at the edge of a hurricane, his clothes whipping around him as he took a stumbling step back.

"Sorry," the giant rumbled as he wiped his nose. "Allergies. Cloud pollen bad this time of year."

"Tiggy!" Gary cried, prancing around the giant's feet. "So many things have happened since you settled down for your after-breakfast nap. I laid another egg! Kevin learned how to make smores with his fire, and I'm sure Ryan did…. something. I have no idea what, but he thinks he's useful, so let's not try and take that from him. Also, this is Sam. He came up here by planting his bull next to beans or whatever. He came here to steal from us! Isn't that fucking *crazy*?"

"Steal?" the giant said with a frown.

"No!" Sam yelled. "I'm not going to steal!" He paused, considering. "Well, not anymore. Funny thing, that. It turns out I like being alive and not squashed, so I changed my mind to allow that to be my immediate future." He smiled as much as his fear would allow, hoping it would appease the giant.

"No steal," the giant said. "Not nice. Steal and I smash. I smash you *gooood*."

Now *that* Sam believed. The giant's fist seemed as big as Sam's entire house. If the giant decided to smash, there'd be nothing left of Sam but a puddle that looked like it'd been expelled from a unicorn's butthole. "I agree," Sam said, nothing if not diplomatic. "In fact, I can go. Yes, that sounds like the best idea. I'll just head on out, back to where I came from and you'll never have to see my face again. So, bye! Goodbye, everyone! Bye, Gary! Bye, Kevin! Bye, Ryan!"

But before he could turn and run as fast as his legs could carry him, a gigantic hand closed around him, lifting him from the ground. He struggled to no avail as the hand brought him close to the giant's face, who's brow furrowed at the loud, insignificant speck he held.

"Stealing wrong," the giant said firmly, his cinnamon-tinged breath wafting over Sam's face. "No steal. Be nice."

Sam nodded so hard his neck cracked. "Yup! I completely agree. Stealing is wrong, and I will be the nicest person who's ever existed. Watch!" Sam grinned at the giant. "I like your face. And you've got a good grip! I can barely feel my bones crushing together."

The giant sat down on his bum, the castle groaning around them as his fist tightened around Sam. It didn't hurt, but just a bit more pressure and Sam's intestines would probably burst through his stomach.

He startled when the giant brought him to his great chest, rocking back and forth. Sam opened his mouth to give thanks for still being alive, but instead of speaking, he got a mouthful of the giant's coarse shirt. "Mine," the giant said. "Pretty Sam. I love him. I keep him? I keep him."

"A stray?" Gary said, aghast. "We don't even know if he's gotten his shots. He looks like he's covered in fleas. Tiggy, you can't just keep every pretty that wanders in here."

"My pretty," the giant—Tiggy?—insisted. "I keep him." He pulled his hand away from his chest. Sam felt his gorge rise as the giant flipped him upside down, shaking his fist. "Bad fleas. Go away, fleas."

The blood rushed to Sam's head, dangling high above the ground. "I don't have fleas!" he bellowed.

The giant turned him back over, opening his hand. Sam hugged Tiggy's thumb as hard as he could, not wanting to slip and fall. He closed his eyes, breathing heavily through his nose, waiting for the giant to straight up murder him, compliments be damned.

"No fleas," Tiggy said. "Friend. My friend Sam. No one else."

"I found him first," Gary said, sounding annoyed. "He's my friend too!"

"I found him *second*," Ryan snapped. "Which means he's also my friend." Sam blushed when Ryan winked up at him. If he survived this day, he was going to have to motorboat the shit out of dat ass. Granted, he'd never done that before, but if the drawings under his mattress were any indication, you just had to go for it without worrying about technique. Let your tongue do the talking, as Sam always said.

(He'd never said that before in his life. He was, as it turned out, a virgin prude who grew immediately sweaty at the thought of faceplanting into Ryan's butt.)

"I found him third," Kevin said. They all looked to him. He shrugged. "What? Everyone else was saying it. I didn't want to be left out. Sam is my friend too. My *sexy* friend who looks as if he could use a good dicking or six. Hey, Sam. Hey. Hey, there. You want some dragon dick? Yeah, you want some dragon dick, don't you? Good thing that I'm the only dragon, then." He looked off into nothing, thoughtful and regal. "I always knew I'd be called upon to destroy a human twink named Sam with my sexual prowess. I never thought the day would come. Fortunately, it has, and there is going to be *so much coming*."

Sam had never been offered a dicking from a dragon before. "That's quite a proposal. Can I think about it and get back to you?" Then, another thought struck him. "If I said yes, am I going to have to poop out a golden egg? Because that sounds gross." His eyes widened. "What the hell am I talking about? I'm not going to have sex with a dragon!"

"Boo," Kevin said. "And also rude. I'm pretty much the best at sex. Ask Gary."

"Eh," Gary said. "You're all right."

"Oh no," Kevin whispered. "My ego."

"I volunteer as tribute!" Ryan yelled.

When Sam woke up next to the beanstalk that very morning, he'd had no idea anyone would be fighting over him. He found he was pretty good with this turn of events. He looked up at Tiggy, the giant's head cocked. "I don't have fleas," he said. "And I won't steal from you, I promise. I'm not a jerk like that, even if I thought about it." He sighed and leaned his head against Tiggy's thumb. "What a strange day this has been."

Tiggy crooked his thumb, rubbing the top of Sam's head. "You be our friend?"

Sam didn't even have to think. "Hell yeah, dude. I'll totally be your friend. I've never had a giant as a friend before. This is wicked awesome. Tiggy, right? That's a good name."

Tiggy puffed out his chest. "Tiggy best name."

"It is," Sam agreed. "I like your house! Er...castle. Or whatever this place is. How did you all get up here?"

"Ooh," Gary said. "Story-time! I'll go first. One day, I was running along a rainbow because that's what unicorns do, as everyone knows. And then I found this castle in the clouds. The big guy here lived all by himself. He was sad and lonely. I couldn't have that, so I decided to stay."

"I was flying," Kevin said. "I caught the scent of my beloved's ripe body odor and followed my nose as the heavens parted and revealed the source of the smell. At first, Gary wanted nothing to do with me, but that only lasted two minutes until I showed him just how long my tongue was."

"It's very long," Gary purred, rubbing up against Kevin's leg obscenely.

"It is," Kevin growled. "And I couldn't allow anyone else to claim this immense beauty. Well, at least without me watching. So, I stayed and never looked back."

"Ryan," Gary said gleefully. "It's your turn. After I ran on rainbows, after Kevin found his one true love, remind us how you came to be here?"

Ryan glared at Gary before turning his face up to Sam, who peered down at him from Tiggy's hand. He raised his sword, flourishing it spectacularly and completely unnecessarily. "There I was!" Ryan said, voice booming. "In the middle of a ferocious sky battle. I stood on the deck of a blimp, my sword speaking the language of war. Blood spilled, and yet it wasn't enough. My thirst couldn't be quenched!" He leapt forward, stabbing his sword into nothing. "I was outnumbered ten to one! Things were exploding left and right. Ka-*boom*! I thrust my sword. Ka-*pow*! Take *that*, villains! I am Ryan Foxheart, the best swordsman in all the world! Hi*yah*!" He parried and thrust, his feet light and quick. "But I was too cocky. I didn't hear the captain of the enemy vessel behind me." He whirled around, sword swinging out in a flat arc. He took a step forward, folding in on himself, clutching his stomach. He gasped, raising his face toward the ceiling. "I was stabbed," he groaned. "Right in the gut." He stumbled backward, looking betrayed and in immense pain. "My back hit the railing of the blimp, and as the villain advanced on me, I raised my sword one last time."

"Oh my goodness," Sam whispered. "I want to put my face on your face."

"Just when I was about to meet the gods," Ryan continued, "the railing gave way with a loud *crack*!" He flailed his arms as he tilted backward. "And then I fell through the sky, hurtling toward the ground far below. Oh, did I mention this was also in the middle of a storm? Because it *was*. Thunder rumbled. Lightning flashed! Rain slapped against my skin, and I *knew* it was my end."

"What happened next?" Sam demanded, practically breathless

in excitement.

Ryan grinned. "I landed on a cloud near the castle. Tiggy and Gary and Kevin found me no worse for wear."

Gary snorted. "What an interesting retelling of events that absolutely did not happen." He flipped his mane. "Ryan slipped on a sponge on the deck of his ship and fell overboard. He was a trader, not a heroic captain of a blimp. He didn't even *have* a blimp. It was this rickety old thing that broke apart as soon as it hit the clouds. And he had a cut on his finger that he was convinced was going to cause him to lose his entire hand."

"It was a big cut! A gaping wound! The blood was *gushing*, and I—"

"It healed in two days," Gary said flatly. "It didn't even leave a scar."

"You suck," Ryan muttered, scratching the back of his neck. "Just because I refused to have relations with you and Kevin doesn't mean you get to embarrass me in front of guests."

"No one likes a liar, Foxheart," Gary said. "The twink already has a boner for you. No need to embellish."

Ryan's head jerked up. "He does? You *do*?"

"Well, not now since everyone is looking at me," Sam mumbled. Desperate to point the conversation elsewhere, he glanced at Tiggy. "And you? How did you come to be here?" He knew it was going to be the best story out of all of them, filled with magic and danger and romance, just like in the books Sam absolutely did not read.

"Sky giant," Tiggy said. "Where I live. My house."

Sam waited for more.

Tiggy just stared at him.

"Oh," Sam said. "That...huh. That makes sense. I've never heard of sky giants before."

"Last one," Tiggy said. "No other sky giants. Only Tiggy."

"You're alone?" Sam asked, feeling strangely sad. "But you're so cool!"

Tiggy grinned, pleased. "Pretty Sam," he cooed. "Best Sam."

"He's not alone," Gary said. "He has us, obviously. He's our precious kitten, and no one gets to give him crap about anything, not while we're around."

"He looks like he can take care of himself," Sam said, appraising the giant before him. "All those muscles. I bet no one messes with him."

Tiggy laughed, a deep, rumbling sound.

"You'd think," Gary said. "But he's a soft marshmallow who needs to be protected at all costs. We're his best friends, so that means the job is up to us. All bark, no bite, that one." Gary grinned at him, and Sam didn't like the looks of it. "You should've seen what happened the last time someone tried to steal from him. Quite a rude fellow who thought Tiggy was dumb and therefore, could be taken advantage of quite easily."

"What happened to him?" Sam asked.

"Kevin ate him," Ryan said with a wince. "I don't know if you realize this, but when a dragon eats a person, it can get pretty… messy."

"All dem bones," Kevin said proudly. "Cronch, cronch, cronch."

Sam nodded. "Well, then it's a good thing I have decided not to steal anything. Because that's mean, and you're all pretty great."

"And what about you?" Gary asked. "Aside from being stupid and taking beans in exchange for a bull." He nudged Kevin. "This fuckin' guy, right?"

"Yes," Kevin said promptly. "I am trying to fuck this guy. Thank you for reinforcing my wants and needs."

Ryan groaned. "You guys are so embarrassing."

Sam shrugged as he struggled not to fidget. He thought maybe these weird beings could be his friends. Best talk himself up and make him seem like they couldn't live without him. "I'm nothing special. I live on a farm with my mom and dad. That's it. I don't really do much else aside from work." Welp. That didn't come out like he wanted it to.

"Wow," Gary said. "Riveting. I'm so glad I asked. You seem like a particularly important person." He lowered his voice as he looked at Kevin. "They just let anyone up here now, don't they? Pretty soon, we're going to be surrounded by twinks who dance to terrible music while they do ketamine in the bathroom because they're desperately sad and begging for acceptance."

"I see no problem with this," Kevin replied.

"Sam stay," Tiggy said. "Sam stay forever and ever. I love him. He's my squishy."

Sam had never been the squishy of a giant before. He found he didn't have a problem with that. He hugged Tiggy's thumb as the giant peered at him. "I can't stay forever," Sam said quietly. "My mom and dad are probably worried about me." They'd probably already awoken and found the beanstalk in the field. He shuddered to think what they made of it.

"Forever," Tiggy insisted. "No leave. Stay with Tiggy. We have cake."

"Cake?" Sam gasped. "It was my birthday yesterday, and I didn't get to have *any* cake because of the whole beans-for-a-bull thing."

"You've never had cake until you've had Tiggy cake," Ryan said. "It's the best I've ever tasted."

Tiggy lowered Sam to the ground. Sam hopped off, Morgan clucking at his feet, pecking the leg of his trousers. Ryan looked like he was going to take Sam's hand again, but he stopped, blushing as he scuffed his boot against the floor. "Happy birthday," he muttered. "How old are you?"

"Eighteen."

"Oh thank the gods he's legal," Gary said. "Don't want to make *that* mistake again." He circled around Sam, eyeing him up and down. "Farmer, eh? Don't really have many muscles. You look like you delegate more than anything."

"I have muscles," Sam said, flexing his arms. Not much happened there, though, and Gary laughed at him. "Hey!"

"It's okay," Kevin said. "Everyone is shaped exactly how they're supposed to be." He lowered his head toward Sam's rear. "Oh look! I already found the cake!"

Sam smacked Kevin across the snout. "Don't be crass. I'm a strong, independent man and I will *not take your shit*."

"We're keeping the sad boy-man," Gary announced. "Though, the name Sam isn't really doing anything for me. From this day henceforth, your name shall be Rex Steel."

"Rex Steel," Kevin said, practically chewing the words. "A CEO for a large company that deals in image rehabilitation for celebrities. He's harsh and mean but always gets what he wants because he's so attractive. And *we'll* be the interns at said company, working for free during our summer break from college with our big dreams and even bigger dicks. Uh oh! Mr. Steel just called for a meeting with all the interns and guess what? He's instigated a no-pants rule. It's a good thing I *never* wear pants."

"Or," Sam said, "you can just call me Sam and everyone is required to wear *two* pairs of pants."

"I quit!" Kevin cried. "Just because I'm an intern doesn't mean I'm not a person! You will respect my autonomy. I'm *leaving*, and I will never—oh no!" He fell onto his back, legs kicking in the air, wings spread out underneath him. "I've fallen and landed in a sexy position. I sure hope no one tries to take advantage of me and my innocent nature!"

"This is pretty much the norm around here," Ryan mumbled.

Gary's horn began to glow pure white. "Now *I'm* Rex Steel," he growled. "And I've just come from my office where I was conducting business because I'm a businessman. You there. Intern whose name I pretend not to know even though you've already wormed your way into my heart with your supple college body. Do you have the financial reports I asked for?"

Kevin moaned. "I do, Mr. Steel. There are bullet points. *And* a spreadsheet."

"I'm gonna spread *your* sheets," Gary snarled, as if he hadn't just birthed out an egg twenty minutes ago. "Wait, that's not erotic. What the hell am I talking about? Gotta get this right. Rex Steel. I'm Rex Steel. Red leather, yellow leather. Red leather, yellow—"

"You're *ruining* it," Kevin hissed out the side of his mouth. "Do it right." Then, louder, "Oh, I'm just a young man from a small town now living in the big city trying to take it one day at a time. How I wish I made a livable wage and had health insurance instead of being forced to live in capitalistic slavery!"

"You've been a bad intern," Gary said, advancing on Kevin. "Report to my office at once. I have your quarterly evaluation to go over. Suffice to say, I'm not impressed, though I have a few ideas on how you can earn my respect. Here's a hint: it involves you proving you don't have a gag reflex. For *business*."

"Run!" Ryan cried, grabbing Sam by the hand and pulling him between Tiggy's legs as the giant stood. Sam glanced back only once, and what he saw would be burned into his head for the rest of his days. As it turned out, Kevin wasn't the only one with a long tongue, and things were immediately wet in ways Sam would unfortunately remember forever.

Ryan led him further into the castle, Morgan and Tiggy trailing after them, the rooster landing on Tiggy's foot and digging his talons in to hold on. "Funny bird," Tiggy said happily as Morgan squawked up at him.

They passed by a set of stairs that led to another floor of the castle. "Our rooms are up there," he said, jerking his head toward the stairs. "There are empty ones, if you want to stay the night. Or whatever. There's an empty one right next to mine and everything."

"You all just…live here?" Sam asked as he looked around, head swiveling side to side, taking in the enormity of the castle. He couldn't believe something so wondrously large could exist without others knowing.

Ryan nodded. "Yeah, it's pretty great. We all work together to keep things going."

"What about your family? Don't they wonder where you are?"

"Nah, I didn't really have anyone waiting for me. And even if I did, I'm not much for the ground life. It gets too complicated. Up here, I can be whoever I want to be."

That sounded fine to Sam. "You don't miss it at all? Being on the ground?"

Ryan shrugged as they entered the biggest kitchen Sam had ever seen. It had to be, given that Tiggy could stand upright inside it. Massive cupboards lined the walls in front of a working stove that gave off sweltering heat. A table just the right size for a giant sat in the middle of the kitchen. "Not really," Ryan said. "Everyone always seems to want something down there, and they don't care who they hurt to get it. Up here, we take care of each other. The only time I go to the ground is when I trade some of our treasure for anything we need." He smiled up at Tiggy. "The big guy helped me fix my ship. He can pretty much do anything."

"Ryan good," Tiggy said. "Ryan friend. Tiggy likes friends." He picked Ryan and Sam up, setting them on top of the table. Sam laughed when he saw a much smaller table sitting on top of it, perfect for someone his size. "Sit," Tiggy said. "I make cake." He turned toward the cabinets and pulled out a large bowl, setting it on the counter as he hummed to himself. He bent over, scooping up

Morgan and setting him next to the bowl. The rooster immediately began investigating, claws clicking as he ran back and forth.

Sam did as requested, sitting in one of the empty chairs. Not to be outdone, Ryan dragged another chair over until it was next to Sam's, sitting so close their legs bumped together. Sam held his breath, waiting for Ryan to pull away. He didn't.

Sam watched as Tiggy began to work, crushing large eggs in the bowl, each as big as the cart Dad used to take goods into the city. He didn't know what kind of creature the eggs came from, but he didn't want to ask. Tiggy reached up and pulled a bag of flour from the cabinet, setting it down next to the bowl.

"He makes the best cakes," Ryan said, bumping his shoulder against Sam's. "Even better when it's someone's birthday."

"He doesn't need to go to all this trouble," Sam said, guilt gnawing at his ribcage. "I don't need—"

"He likes it," Ryan said quietly. "It makes him happy. He's..." Ryan sighed, shaking his head. "Before we got here, he was all by himself. He didn't have anyone and lived alone in this big castle with no one to talk to. I think he was lonely, so when we all came it gave him a sense of purpose. He takes care of us as much as we take care of him. I know he's big, but you don't need to fear him."

"I'm not scared," Sam said, watching as Tiggy moved expertly, a bit of flour already on his nose. "He's big, sure, but no matter how big or small you are, you deserve to be as happy as anyone else."

Ryan didn't reply, and Sam looked over at him. Ryan's mouth hung open before snapping shut, his teeth clacking together. "Uh," Ryan said. "So. Can I just." His cheeks puffed up as he blew out a stream of air. "Wow, I did *not* think I could be this nervous. Ugh."

A trickle of sweat dripped down the back of Sam's neck. "What're you nervous about?"

Ryan laughed too loudly before slapping a hand over his mouth. "Nothing!" he said, voice muffled, eyes panicked. "Nothing at all!"

"Oh my gods," Sam breathed. "Please tell me there's no Missus or Mister Ryan Foxheart, because my heart couldn't take it."

Ryan flushed so hard Sam thought his head was going to explode. He dropped his hand, picking at a crack in the table. "No. There's...there's no missus or mister." He glanced at Sam out of the corner of his eye. "Is there a Missus or Mister...Sam?"

"Nope!" Sam practically yelled. "And even if there *was*, I'd divorce them immediately which, now that I've said it out loud, kind of makes me a terrible person."

"Nah," Ryan said, hand inching toward Sam's as if he thought he was being smooth. He really wasn't. "I happen to think you're pretty cool."

"So cool," Sam agreed. "Like, everyone looks at me and says, 'Oh shit, here comes Mr. Cool." He winced. "Or something."

The sound Sam made when Ryan's pinkie touched his own is better left to the imagination. He wasn't proud of it, but he didn't try and pull his hand away. "Mr. Cool," Ryan whispered. "That's a good name. Sam Cool."

"Yikes," Sam said as Ryan's hand covered his. "I lied. My last name is Haversford, not Cool."

Ryan chuckled. "That's even better."

Sam wasn't sure how to proceed from here that didn't involve him demanding Ryan divest himself of all his clothing immediately. But since that wouldn't do, he tried to slow things down. The problem was his brain highjacked his mouth, and he blurted, "I want to sit on you forever."

Ryan's eyes bulged. "*What?*"

"Nothing!" Sam cried as Tiggy chuckled warmly. "Ignore me. The air up here is thinner than I'm used to and it's making me say my thoughts out loud. Which I normally do anyway, but not like this!"

Ryan hesitated. Then, "You can sit on me as long as you want."

Sam wheezed, sounding like the hinges on a door that hadn't been opened in a millennium. "Sweet molasses. I like the sky."

"Fee Fi Fo Fum," Tiggy said. "Ryan gonna get him some. Will be sweet and filled with power 'cause Ryan gonna eat that flower."

Sam immediately snapped his fingers before the words sunk in. "Whaaaaat."

"Tiggy!" Ryan yelped. "You can't just *say* stuff like that!"

Tiggy glanced back at them over his shoulder, dark eyes dancing in amusement. "I Tiggy. I say what I want."

Ryan groaned, hands over his face. "You're going to scare him away."

"Nah," Tiggy said. "Sam likes it here. He stay forever."

Sam swallowed thickly. He'd never been good at making friends, and now that he had the chance, he was unsure of how to proceed. Tiggy seemed much gentler than a giant should be, but then Sam had only heard stories of their rage. People whispered about the land of giants, far to the north beyond an empty castle made of ice in the snowy mountains. How angry they always were, destroying anyone who dared to cross them. And while Sam didn't know much about these people, he didn't think Tiggy was like that at all. Strange, he mused. It was so strange how all it took was opening his eyes. Perhaps there were giants who *were* awful, but then humans could be just as bad, couldn't they? Why should he judge a group of people based upon the actions of a few? Even if Tiggy was the exception to the rule, Sam pondered on how easy it was to spread rumor and innuendo.

And yet…

"I can't stay forever," he said quietly. "My mom and dad are probably worried out of their minds. I can't do that to them."

Tiggy stiffened, his hands freezing over the bowl. Then, "They come here. Live with Tiggy. Be Tiggy's Mom and Dad too." He reached up and pulled down a set of cake pans. Sam watched in amusement as Tiggy plucked a pair of the smallest pans out of the middle with the tips of his fingers. These tiny pans were like the ones Sam's mother had in her own kitchen. Tiggy poured the cake batter carefully into each pan. It took only a drip or two to fill the smaller ones.

"They would like you," Sam said as Tiggy carefully juggled all the pans as he carried them toward the oven. He used his foot to lower the oven door. A great wave of hot air washed over Sam, causing him to blink rapidly. "All of you, but I…" He shook his head. "I don't know. They were mad at me last night. They might not want to see me again."

Tiggy closed the oven door, bending over and peering in through the thick glass in the front of the oven. He nodded, before standing upright and turning toward the table. "Be mad," he said thoughtfully. "Allowed. But not mad forever. Mad because they love you. Mad because they want best for Sam." He scrunched up his face, tongue sticking out between his teeth. "Okay to be mad sometimes, but not for long time. Anger eats you. Makes you hollow."

Giants, Sam had also heard, were stupid and brash. They didn't have a single intelligent thought in their oversized heads. That, as Sam was learning, was bigoted bullshit. He didn't think he'd ever met someone more profound. Granted, it could all be a ruse. All of this could be. But to what end? Tiggy didn't seem like the type to grind Sam's bones to make his bread. Or cake, as it were.

The world was a much bigger—and ultimately, much stranger— place than Sam ever expected it to be.

"You're very smart," Sam said. "I like you, Tiggy."

Tiggy grinned. "I like you too. Good Sam. My Sam. Come. Cake baking. Tiggy show you things." He set his hand on the table. Sam didn't hesitate, rising from his chair. Ryan did the same, rushing forward to help Sam onto Tiggy's palm, taking Sam by the hand and gripping it tightly. Sam turned and pulled Ryan up next to him. Ryan stumbled a bit, his chest bumping against Sam's, their faces inches apart. He really was the most handsome man Sam had ever seen.

"Sorry," Ryan whispered, not moving away, his breath warm on Sam's face.

Sam stared into those bright eyes, his skin alight and vibrating. "I don't mind."

Tiggy lifted his hand carefully, holding it in front of him as he moved around the table and left the kitchen behind. They went through a large doorway off to the right, sunlight streaming through open windows, a cool breeze bringing in the scent of crisp rain. Tiggy chattered away, telling Sam how he'd built the castle with his own two hands, the materials brought from the ground by birds. As if they could hear him talking about them, a group of large birds—some almost as big as Kevin—landed on a windowsill, chirping brightly, their rainbow plumage on full display. Sam startled when Tiggy chirped *back*, the birds cocking their heads as if they understood.

"They love him," Ryan whispered as Tiggy stroked the biggest of the birds with a large finger. "He says they belonged to the sky first and allowed him to stay. They bring anything we need if I can't get down to the ground. He repaid them by building an aviary behind the castle for them to seek shelter when it storms."

"It storms?" Sam asked as Tiggy kissed the top of the bird's head.

"Worse up here than down on the ground," Ryan said. "They're rare, but when they hit, the wind and rain make it impossible to go outside. Sometimes, it lasts for days, but we're safe in here, and the birds know they have shelter in the aviary. They come and go as they please because Tiggy says that no one should be shackled to the ground, much less birds. They have wings for a reason."

"Is that how you felt?" Sam asked. "Shackled to the ground?"

Ryan shrugged. "Not always, but here I don't…" He paused, looking up at Tiggy. "Here, I don't have to worry about being something I'm not. I can be whoever I want to be. Tiggy showed me that. Same for Gary and Kevin. I know it sounds a little weird, but we're free in the sky. Like the birds."

"Free," Sam whispered. And though the guilt of leaving his home behind was ever present, it wasn't as harsh as it'd been even an hour before. Dangerous this, he knew, but yesterday he was a boy with his feet firmly planted on the ground. Now, he was in the sky and he didn't know if he would ever want to leave.

Tiggy left the birds to their chattering as he moved further into the castle. "Our rooms," he grunted, shoving open a door. Inside was the biggest bed Sam had ever seen. It had to be at least half-a-mile wide, the pillows looking like mountains at the head of the bed. Drawings covered the walls, some in chalk, others carved into the stone. Sam couldn't make sense of most of them, the lines and swirls seeming without rhyme or reason. But carved into the wall above Tiggy's bed were figures he recognized. A stick figure towered over a unicorn and a dragon and a man with a little sword. Though somewhat crude, Sam could see the love and care it'd taken to get the carvings exactly right.

Sam gasped in delight when Tiggy pointed out a set of smaller doors near the floor against the far wall. One—the larger of the doors—had dragon wings burned into the wood, along with a unicorn horn right through the middle. A second, smaller door, had the symbol of a sword on it.

"Those are our rooms," Ryan said. "Gary had his own before he and Kevin got married. Gary moved in with him. Tiggy helped us build each room when we got here. I've got my own bathroom and everything."

Tiggy lowered them to the ground, and Ryan helped Sam jump off the giant's palm. Ryan took his hand, leading him to the sword door. He grinned over his shoulder before pushing the door open.

The room was cozy. A set of mismatched armor hung on the wall, Ryan telling him that he'd once wanted to be a knight in Castle Lockes before he decided to take to the sky. A bed sat against the back wall, covered in thick blankets. "It gets cold at night," Ryan told him, patting the blankets. "The fires from the kitchen blow heated air through vents, but it can still get chilly."

Sam laughed as he went to a bookshelf, heavy with tomes, many with cracked bindings. The books were varied in topics: some about gardening, others about construction. Sam snorted when he saw a copy of *The Butler and the Manticore*, a book his mother had swooned over time and time again.

"Come," Tiggy rumbled through the door.

They left the room, Ryan leading the way to yet another door next to his. He pushed it open. It was sparse compared to the other rooms, devoid of personality. It had a bed and empty shelves, and a door that led to a small bathroom. "This was Gary's room before he and Kevin boned," Ryan said with a grimace. "It took four hours after they met the first time. At least, that's what Gary says."

"Two hours," Tiggy said from outside the room. "Saw things. Bad things. Squishy. Wet."

Sam shuddered. "They're certainly…together."

Ryan leaned against the doorway, watching Sam as he moved back and forth in the room. He went to the window next to the bed, pushing it open and peering out. All he could see for miles and miles was blue sky and white clouds, and the bright, bright sun shining down. "This could be your room," Ryan said nervously. "If you want."

Sam hesitated. He'd never wanted anything more, but he wasn't sure if he could accept. He had his place. His father was counting on him. The farm would be his one day. It was his legacy. "Maybe," Sam said, though he didn't know how he could make it work. He was old enough now to make his own decisions, but he couldn't leave his parents behind. He loved them too much to ever consider such a thing. But that didn't mean he couldn't visit, right?

Thoughts swirling in a storm, Sam turned and saw a great eye peering through the open doorway, blinking slowly. "I like it," he said. "You did good work, Tiggy."

The skin around the eye crinkled. "Thank you. I like making things. Makes me happy. Makes others happy. Need happiness to get through bad times."

Sam nodded. "We all do."

Ryan closed the door as Sam walked back out to Tiggy. "Show you one more thing," Tiggy said, hand on the floor. Sam jumped up, turning around to pull Ryan up with him. The giant lifted them up, leaving the bedroom behind and heading down the hallway.

At the end of the hall were a pair of doors, almost as tall as Tiggy. Off to the right, near the floor, a smaller door, too small for a giant, but just the right size for everyone else in the castle.

"Important room," Tiggy said.

Sam frowned. "Why?" The doors, though quite large, were unadorned, plain, made of wood and metal. A latch sat in the middle, and underneath, a keyhole.

Tiggy stared down at him, brow furrowed. "Trust you? Good person?"

"I want to be," Sam said honestly. "I make mistakes, but I always apologize and try to make things right."

Tiggy studied him for a long moment before nodding. Ryan exhaled explosively, looking relieved for reasons Sam didn't understand. Tiggy shifted, and Sam looked up in time to see him reach in the collar of his shirt and grab a gold chain around his neck. He pulled on the chain until a large, silver key rose from his shirt. Carefully, he put the key into the lock, twisting it to the right. The tumblers clicked as the door unlocked. Tiggy put the chain back over his head, the key resting against his chest. And then he pushed open the door.

Sam's jaw dropped when he saw what lay inside. Piles of glittering jewels, towers of coins of varying shapes and sizes. Gold bricks stacked in rows that almost reached the ceiling. And eggs! So many golden eggs, Sam's breath whooshed from his chest as if gut punched. Gary and Kevin had obviously been busy. Which, you know, gross.

"Holy fucking *sky treasure*," Sam breathed. His eyes bulged from his head as he took in the contents of the room. He'd never seen such riches in his entire life. He doubted anyone on the ground had. And with that, a chill: if anyone knew about the treasure, they'd stop at nothing to get it. And though a strange, deep hunger curled in his bones, he did his best to shove it away. It wasn't his. It never had been. And he couldn't steal from them, not after he'd gotten to know them. Even if only a handful would change the course of his and his parents' lives, it wasn't Sam's to touch.

And with that thought firmly lodged in his head, the treasure began to lose some of its luster. "It's weird," Sam said to no one in particular.

"What is?" Ryan asked as Tiggy stared down at them.

Sam shrugged. "Everyone wants what's in here. They go to war over it. They kill each other over it. And they think it brings them happiness, but in the end, it's just rocks and stones carved to make you think they're important."

Tiggy nodded sagely. "Just rocks and stones. Pretty, but so are clouds and lightning. Don't steal those, do you?"

Sam sighed. "I'm sure people would try if they only knew how. Don't you worry about someone trying to take your treasure?"

"No," Tiggy said. "Because I smash."

"Tiggy does the best smashes," Ryan said proudly, causing the giant to blush. "No one messes with us because he protects us."

"So much smashing," Tiggy muttered, pulling them out of the room and locking the door once more. "Cake time. Think lemon frosting and tea."

Sam looked at the treasure once more before pushing it out of his mind.

"CLOSE EYES," Tiggy ordered in the kitchen. He'd set Sam and Ryan back on the table. They were joined by Kevin and Gary, Kevin laying on his back on the table, rubbing his stomach and yawning widely. Gary had an *I-just-got-boned* expression on his face, and Sam wished he hadn't realized that. Morgan pecked at a bit of seed Tiggy had laid out for him, head rising up and down.

Sam looked up at Tiggy. "Me?"

Tiggy nodded. "Close eyes, pretty Sam."

Sam thought about asking why, but instead, did as he asked. He heard the others moving around him, whispering, but he couldn't make out the words. Gary laughed about something, but it sounded sweet and lazy, a low chuckle that warmed Sam's bones.

"Eyes closed?" Tiggy asked.

"Yep!"

"Okay. Still closed?"

Sam grinned. "Promise."

He heard the table rattle in front of him, and then Tiggy said, "Surprise!"

Sam opened his eyes.

There, in front of him, was a cake with yellow frosting. Atop the cake sat candles, their flames flickering. Sam counted, and his throat closed when he got to the last, the eighteenth.

A birthday cake; Tiggy had made him a birthday cake.

Ryan watched him, wringing his hands together. Gary lay against Kevin's side, head resting on the table, his horn sparkling.

Sam's eyes stung unexpectedly. He wiped his face with the back of his hand. "This is for me?"

Tiggy nodded. "Birthday. Celebrate because Sam friend. Sam important. Eat cake, be happy. Sam happy?"

Sam smiled up at the giant. "The happiest. This is the nicest thing anyone has ever done for me."

"Well, that's just sad," Gary said, though he sounded amused. "You should really get out more."

"Not yet," Tiggy said as Kevin reached for his own, much larger cake. "Sing first. Birthday song for Sam."

Kevin rolled his eyes but pulled his claws back. "You better do this for *my* birthday. Last year, you didn't make *me* a cake."

"Gave you sheep," Tiggy said.

Kevin sighed dreamily. "Ah, yes. You did, didn't you? Remember how they screamed when I chased them? That was the best day."

"You eat sheep?" Sam asked, stomach twisting.

"Nah," Kevin said. "I just like to hear them scream."

"Oh. That's…cool. I guess."

Tiggy cleared his throat as Ryan leaned over to Sam and

whispered, "You're gonna love this. He makes up his own songs for each of us."

Sam was about to ask what Ryan was talking about when Tiggy said, "And a-one. And a-two. Annnnnnd…"

And then he began to sing.

Fee Fi Fo Fly
Sam in castle in the sky
Climbed a tower to the top
With strong heart that doesn't stop

Fee Fi Fo Foo
Hello, Sam. How do you do?
I your Tiggy, your giant pal
Made you cake, watch me scowl!

Sam burst out laughing when Tiggy did just that.

Fee Fi Fo Flum
Ryan trying to get him some
Tries too hard, might overshoot
But that's okay, it's kind of cute.

"Tiggy!" Ryan shouted, burying his face in his hands as Kevin and Gary chuckled.

Fee Fi Fo Fig
Tiggy the biggest of the big
Though heart is soft and full of love
Lonely in the clouds, in the sky above

Everyone quieted, watching the giant. Tiggy sniffled, looking away.

Fee Fi Fo Fum
Sometimes Tiggy feels so glum
But then his house filled with laughter
And Tiggy lived happily ever after.

"The end," Tiggy said, and looked stunned when Sam rose from his chair, clapping as hard as he could. Kevin and Ryan and Gary joined in, and the kitchen filled with the sounds of their applause.

"That was the best song ever!" Sam crowed. "Holy shit, dude. You thought of that all on your own? That's fucking epic."

Tiggy grinned. "You like?"

"No," Sam said, but before Tiggy's face could fall, he added, "I *loved* it. That's much better than like. How the hell are you not famous? I'd listen to you sing every day if I could."

Pleased, Tiggy nodded at Sam's cake. "Blow out candles. Make wish. Keep it secret so it comes true."

Sam looked around at the others at the table, all watching him. He thought hard for a moment before thinking, *I wish they would be my friends for always.* And then he blew out the candles. The flames stuttered before going out, leaving little wisps of smoke.

"Now?" Kevin asked.

"Now," Tiggy agreed.

Kevin face-planted in his own cake, causing Gary to squawk as frosting and crumbs of cake flew up into the air.

Ryan sliced the cake as Sam poured the tea. Tiggy had his own plate and cup, and though he could have done exactly as Kevin did, he waited until each of them was served. Once they had their own slices, he nodded, and began to eat.

As they whiled away the rest of the day, Sam wondered if wishes could come true, if only one was brave enough to reach for them.

EXHAUSTED, SAM DIDN'T GIVE much thought to climbing back down the beanstalk. Though he worried about the panic his parents must be in, he didn't think he'd do himself any favors trying to go back to the ground. He could slip quite easily, especially given how full of cake he was. Though a little voice whispered in the back of his head that he was making a mistake, he readily accepted Tiggy's offer of staying the night.

Gary and Kevin had already gone into their room, closing the door behind them. It took only moments before unholy sounds began to filter through the door, and try as he might, Sam couldn't block them out, even though Ryan stood in front of him, looking shy and edible.

"So," Ryan said.

"So," Sam replied.

"Oh my *gods*!" Gary wailed from his room. "How are you—is that *peanut butter*? What the hell is wrong with—you know what? Never mind. I'm into it. You freaky fuck lizard, *yes*. Make me your PB&J!"

"Today's been a big day," Ryan said.

"You have no idea," Sam said, wondering if Ryan was thinking the same thing *he* was, and it mostly involved kissing until they were breathless.

"Yeah," Kevin growled. "I'm gonna give you *all* the P. All the B. And you're gonna be filled with so much J, you won't be able to walk without sloshing."

"I enjoyed it, though," Ryan said, glancing at Sam before his gaze darted away, cheeks pink.

"Me too," Sam said quietly. His hand twitched as if it had a mind of its own, wanting to reach out and cup Ryan's face.

"This is the grossest thing we've ever done," Gary moaned. "I'm your sack lunch, and you need to reach inside it until you find the bag of chips your mom put in it at the bottom, even though she knows the chips will be crushed."

"Hell *yeah*," Kevin snapped. "I told my mom to put the chips at the *top*, but she didn't listen. She tries so hard, but she works a lot, so she's sometimes distracted. But that's okay because I *found* the chips."

"I guess I should just...go to bed," Ryan said. "Since it's late, and all."

"You should," Sam said. "I know I'm tired."

"What's this?" Kevin growled. "Did I find the cookies she packed? I did! And wouldn't you know? They're *double stuffed*."

Gary gasped. "They are? All that extra filling. What are you gonna do with it? Are you gonna break it apart and lick the stuffing out before putting the cookies back together, held together because of your saliva which you'll then dunk in the thermos of milk she thoughtfully included?"

"So tired," Ryan agreed. "I can't imagine what it must be like for you, though. Don't worry. The bed is really soft and…big."

Sam nodded aggressively. "So big. Like, the biggest bed I've ever seen. Well, you know. Aside from Tiggy's." He glanced at the giant's bed, where Tiggy lay snoring loudly, his lips flapping.

"I'm opening the thermos!" Kevin bellowed. "Uh oh, it's spilling! Oh gods, I'm so clumsy. Look at this mess."

"Spill it!" Gary screamed. "Spill that entire thermos of milk all over and lick it up! Make such a mess that the lunch ladies glare at you because they know they'll have to clean it up when we're done!"

"Yep," Ryan said, nodding just as hard. "His bed sure is big."

"Where did he even find a mattress that large?" Sam mused out loud.

"With their hairnets and their bushy eyebrows raised in judgement," Kevin grunted. "But they *like* cleaning up the messes, even if they say they don't. Fuck off, Edna! We'll finish when we're good and ready!"

"Edna!" Gary groaned. "Edna, *look away*. Kevin is about to eat his entire lunch, and you are far too pure to witness such a feast."

Ryan cleared his throat. "Um. So. Good night."

"Good night," Sam said.

Ryan turned to head to his room. Before he could take another step, Sam reached out and grabbed his arm. He pulled Ryan to him and hugged him as tightly as he could. Ryan sighed, bringing his arms up around Sam, clutching at his back. They swayed back and forth as Gary and Kevin ascended to the end of their lunch period with words and animalistic snarls that shan't be uttered here. Suffice to say, it sounded as if Kevin ate everything his mother had packed. Or something.

Eventually, Sam stepped back, dropping his arms. Ryan looked like he was going to say something else. Instead, he shook his head, smiling ruefully. "See you in the morning?" he asked hopefully.

"In the morning," Sam said, trying to work up the courage to kiss Ryan. But before he could, Ryan stepped back, nodded his head, and left Sam listening as Edna (sounding suspiciously like Kevin with a higher voice) came and yelled at Gary and Kevin for making such a mess in her cafeteria.

SAM EXPECTED TO nod off immediately. The bed felt like clouds, his pillow the softest thing he'd ever laid his head upon. But instead of drifting off into dreams, he lay awake, staring up at the ceiling, listening to Morgan cluck in his sleep. He missed his mother and father, though he thought if he went back to the ground, he'd miss his new friends just as much. He'd only known them for a day, but he felt as if they'd been friends for ages. He wondered what it would have been like, had he met them in another life.

Late into the night, he heard movement outside his door. He sat up, listening to the sounds of heavy footsteps that caused his bed to rattle and shake. Rising carefully, Sam moved from the bed toward the door, cracking it open and peering out in time to see Tiggy leaving the room. He looked back at the bed. Morgan still slept, his breaths slow and deep.

Gnawing on the inside of his cheek, Sam decided to follow Tiggy to see what the big guy was up to so late at night.

Even moving at a jog, it took minutes to reach the doorway that led into the castle. By the time he walked through, Tiggy was gone from the hall, though Sam could still hear his footfalls. He followed the sound toward the front of the castle. Sweating heavily, a stitch in his side, Sam ran after Tiggy as he opened the front doors, leading out into the clouds.

He hesitated as he saw Tiggy sit down on the clouds in front of the castle, hands flat on the ground behind him as he tilted his head back toward the night sky.

The air was cool as Sam stepped from the castle. He looked up, and a lump formed in his throat as he saw the field of stars above him, so close and yet still so far. The moon—heavy, full—shone down onto the giant, casting a long shadow that stretched for what seemed like a mile. Sam had never felt so small in his entire life.

"Hullo, Sam," Tiggy said without looking at him.

"Hi," Sam said nervously. He stepped onto the cloud in front of the castle, approaching Tiggy. "Couldn't sleep?"

Tiggy shrugged. "Little bit. Wanted to see the sky."

"It's big," Sam said, stopping next to his new friend. "Bigger than even you."

Tiggy chuckled as he lowered his hand. Sam climbed on top of it, and Tiggy raised him until he was level with the giant's shoulder. He stepped off and found a good spot to sit, just above Tiggy's clavicle, feet dangling down. "Bigger than even me," Tiggy echoed. Then, "I like it."

"What?"

Tiggy waved his hand at the sky. "The bigness. I big. Bigger than anyone. But when I sit here, I small. Just like you."

"Yeah?" Sam said. "Do you like to feel small?"

"Sometimes. Reminder."

"Of what?" Sam asked, laying down on Tiggy's shoulder, hands folded under his head.

"No matter how big, something always bigger. Grander. Makes me remember that I big, but I can be small too."

"I wish I could be big like you," Sam said.

Tiggy laughed quietly. "Then you not be you and I like the Sam you are. You not giant. But your heart is."

Sam turned his head over to look at the side of Tiggy's face. "How do you know?"

"See it," Tiggy whispered. "In your eyes. They light up. At Ryan. And Gary. And Kevin. Cake. Tiggy home."

"And Tiggy too," Sam said. "They light up for you too."

Tiggy was quiet for a moment. Then, "By myself. For long time. Thought I didn't need friends. Quiet. Too quiet. Then find friends. Came here. Made me think."

"About what?"

"Better together than alone," Tiggy said. "Everyone needs someone. Some just need one. Others need many. I needed three. Got them. They stay. Make Tiggy proud and not lonely."

"I'm glad you're not alone," Sam said.

Tiggy shook his head, and Sam gripped his shirt to keep from sliding off. "Didn't know needed another. Had three. Now have four. Tiggy happiest when there are four."

"Kevin," Sam said. "And Ryan and Gary. That's only three."

"Sam is four," Tiggy said. "Pretty Sam. Funny Sam. Tiggy's Sam."

Sam blinked against the burn in his eyes. "You included me?"

"Yep," Tiggy said, smacking his lips. "Good boy. Good man. Head in the clouds, but now *in* the clouds. Go no higher because high as you can go."

Funny, that. Though his parents had tried, Sam didn't think they understood him, not completely. They loved him unconditionally, and Sam gave as much in return. But here, now, he marveled at the vastness of the world. People spent so much time looking down, digging into the soil, backs hunched and faces grim. If only they knew what lay hidden beyond the clouds. Sam didn't know how he could ever go back to life on the ground. The very thought caused his heart to ache.

Tiggy must have taken his silence wrong, as he said, "Like it here, right?"

"Yeah," Sam said with a sigh. "I like it here very much."

"Stay?"

Sam closed his eyes. "I don't know, Tiggy. People are counting on me. Dad and Mom already work themselves to the bone. They need me to help them survive. We take care of each other. We love each other. I can't abandon them. That wouldn't make me happy, even if you all do. It's…complicated."

"You are own person," Tiggy said. "Make own choices. Parents love you. Happy with whatever you decide."

"How do you know?" Sam whispered.

"They love you," Tiggy rumbled. "Love means raising up to sky. Letting go so wings work and you learn to fly."

"Really?"

Tiggy nodded. "Really. You go, I understand. I miss you, but birds not caged. Birds free to go wherever wind goes. So long as Sam remember to spread wings, Sam be okay."

"I'd miss you, too," Sam said softly. "All of you."

"No decision now," Tiggy said. "Watch sky. Look. See?" He raised his hand, pointing a finger toward a group of stars off to the east. A constellation, one Sam knew well. David's Dragon, an old god who watched over them all. "Big," Tiggy said. "Bigger than you. Bigger than me. We be small together."

They stayed there as the moon crossed the sky, as the stars twinkled. Eventually, Sam's eyes grew heavy, and he fell asleep, listening to Tiggy's breaths. When he dreamed, he dreamed of stars.

HE AWOKE TO the sound of alarms.

Confused, he looked around as bells rang from somewhere in the castle. Last he remembered, he was out with Tiggy in the clouds, but he now found himself in bed, Morgan blinking slowly as his feathers ruffled.

"What's that sound?" he asked aloud, a sense of dread worming its way into his chest.

He jerked his head when someone pounded on the door. Jumping from the bed, he rushed toward it, throwing it open to find Ryan dressed in his mismatched armor, sword drawn, his expression filled with worry. "What is it?" Sam asked. "What's wrong?"

"People," Ryan said. "They're coming up the beanstalk. One of the birds came to warn Tiggy."

Sam blinked. "What? Who? Is it my mom and dad?"

"I don't know," Ryan said, gripping his sword. "But it's quite a large group. Maybe your parents are with them." He hesitated. Then, "Did you tell anyone you were coming up here?"

Sam blanched. "No." He scrubbed a hand over his face. "But the beanstalk was right outside our house, and I told them about how the beans were supposed to be magic." Shit. If his parents thought he was in trouble, of *course* they'd send people after him. He needed to fix this while there was still time. He couldn't let anyone get hurt because of his mistakes.

Before he could tell Ryan they needed to hurry, Ryan brought two fingers to his lips and blew out a sharp, piercing whistle. A moment later, the flap of wings filled the air, and Kevin swooped into the room, landing near them, talons causing sparks as they scraped along the stone floor. "Get on," he growled as he lowered his head. "Gary's with Tiggy at the front of the castle."

Ryan hoisted Sam up onto Kevin's neck before climbing up himself. He sat behind Sam, wrapping his arms around his waist and holding on tightly. "Go," he snapped.

Sam's stomach sank to his feet as Kevin rose swiftly into the air. Wind buffeted his face as he reached forward, clinging to one of the spines on the back of Kevin's neck. The dragon flew from the room, heading toward the front of the castle. Ryan's arms tightened around Sam, his forehead pressed against Sam's neck. "We'll be all right," Ryan said. "You'll see. Tiggy can handle them."

Sam didn't *want* Tiggy to have to handle anything. He only wanted the giant to know peace and happiness. This was all his fault. He'd become distracted by all the wonders he'd found in the sky. He'd never forgive himself if something happened to any of his new friends. Thoughts racing, Sam held on for dear life as Kevin swooped through the front doors of the castle. Tiggy stood on the clouds, Gary at his feet, horn blazing as brightly as the sun, multi-colored sparks shooting from his nose.

Kevin landed near Gary, wings flaring before his feet touched the clouds. He lowered his head, allowing Sam and Ryan to slide off his neck. Sam almost fell to his knees, but Ryan was there, holding him up with one hand, the other holding his sword.

Tiggy crouched down above them, his large eyes troubled. "People," he rumbled. "Coming to the sky."

Sam reached up and touched Tiggy's chin, feeling the scrape of the giant's stubble against his palm. "I didn't mean for this to happen. If they're…if they're coming for me, I'll try and hold them off as best I can."

"Not your fault," Tiggy said kindly. "Sam friend. Tiggy love Sam. No matter what."

Sam swallowed past the lump forming in his throat. "Back at

you, big guy."

Gary bounced on his feet, shaking his head from side-to-side, mane flipping back and forth. Morgan, for some reason, stood on Gary's back, wings spread as he crowed. "These bitches," Gary muttered. "Gary gonna bring the *pain*, you just wait and see. Come to steal *our* treasure? Oh, have I got a ticket for *you*. Guess where it goes to?"

"Gore City," Kevin and Tiggy and Ryan all said at the same time, much to Sam's glee.

"Damn right," Gary snapped. "It's been far too long since I got to stab someone. Why, I can't even remember the last time—okay, that was a lie. It's been seven years, six months, twenty-seven days, eight hours and twenty-two minutes since I straight up murdered a man. To be fair, he didn't understand the meaning of the word *no*, so he had it coming." He paused, considering. "Also, he was a mass murderer I was hunting back when I was still a private investigator."

"Wait," Sam said. "What?"

"No time for backstory!" Gary cried. "Sure, it'd be colorful and would explain so much about how I am the individual who stands before you today. And *yes*, there is intrigue and suspense and explosions and so much sex that I'm surprised I'm not *riddled* with chlamydia, but that will have to wait for another day!"

"No, seriously," Sam said. "*What?*"

"I love you so godsdamn much," Kevin growled, nuzzling Gary's head.

"Of course you do," Gary said with a haughty sniff. "I'm the best thing that's ever happened to you." He glanced at Sam, expression softening. "We're not mad at you, Sam. Get that idea out of your fool head right now. You're one of us." Then his eyes narrowed as he raised his head, towering over Sam. "But if you betray us, there will be nowhere on the ground or the sky you can run that I won't find you. It may not be today, or tomorrow or even a year from now, but a unicorn *never* lets go of grudges. It's what makes my species so endearing."

He thought about arguing, but Gary had fire in his eyes, and Sam didn't want to get burned. Thinking fast, he said, "Let me try and talk to them first. If my parents are with them, I know I can fix things." He looked up at Tiggy. "I don't want any of you to get hurt."

"No hurt," Tiggy agreed. "We stand together. Friends."

"Friends," Sam whispered as Ryan squeezed his hand.

And so they stood there in the sky in front of an impossible castle, together. Tiggy cracked his knuckles, the sound so loud, it could have been thunder. Kevin belched a lick of fire, teeth bared. Gary shook his head from side-to-side, horn glowing brightly. Ryan flourished his sword like the hottest douchebag Sam had ever seen. He hoped they'd live through this day so he could tell him as much.

As for Sam? He squared his shoulders, stood tall and proud. He wondered if his clothes were billowing, a thought that he'd never had before, but now that he had, he knew it'd make him look extremely badass.

They didn't have to wait for long. Soon Sam heard many footsteps marching toward them up the red brick road that led from the beanstalk to the castle. A moment later, the first of the invaders rounded the large cloud mountain and came into view. Sam blinked when he saw the men and women carrying pitchforks, scythes and even a hammer or two. A few even had torches, the fire flickering in the wind.

The front of the group came to a stop at the sight of what lay before them. More and more people appeared, crashing into the backs of those in front. At least two dozen humans, all of varying shapes and sizes and ages. Sam startled when he saw most of them were farmers, just like his parents. Not a contingent of knights like he expected. He recognized almost everyone in the crowd.

Sam pulled out of Ryan's grip, stepping forward in front of his friends. "Halt!" he bellowed. "You are trespassing on private property!"

"That'll show them," Gary muttered. "Oh look, no it didn't."

Sam ignored him as Ryan came to his side, sword at the ready. "Cease and desist! Stop!"

"They already stopped," Ryan pointed out unnecessarily.

"Oh," Sam said. "Right. Uh. Okay. I can do this." He raised his hand, trying to quiet down the frightened whispers coming from the crowd. However, they weren't looking at him. All their faces were turned upward, staring at Tiggy, who wiggled his fingers in a wave.

Before Sam could demand to speak to whoever was in charge, his mother and father pushed through the crowd. Dad stumbled a bit as he took in what lay before him, but then he shook his head, determined as Sam's mother said, "Oh my gods. It was real. Joshua, it was all *real*."

"Sam!" Dad cried. "*Sam*." And apparently not giving two shits that a dragon, a unicorn and a very tall giant were all growling at him, he rushed forward, scooping up Sam in his arms, hugging him tightly, lifting him off his feet and spinning him around. "My boy," he whispered. "I was so scared for you."

"I'm fine," Sam said, slightly embarrassed at his father's display, but not enough to make him stop. Though he'd only been gone for a single day, he'd missed his parents. He laughed when Mom kissed his head frantically as Dad set him back on the ground. Both rubbed their hands up and down Sam, asking him where he'd been hurt. "Did they torture you?" Dad asked, brow furrowed. "I'll kill them. I'll kill them all."

Sam rolled his eyes. "Okay, first, almost everyone here is bigger than you, so you'd probably be the first one to die. And *second*, no one was tortured. We had cake."

"Cake," Dad repeated. "You weren't tortured and you had *cake*."

"Yep," Sam said. "Tiggy made it for my birthday. He sang me a song and everything. It was pretty rad, if I'm being honest." He glanced back over his shoulder, grinning up at the giant who blushed at the praise.

"But," Mom said, sounding breathless. "I…Todd volunteered to climb up here last night. He said he saw you and…and the giant. He said the giant was the most terrible thing he'd ever seen, and that you were his prisoner."

Sam perked up. "Todd's here? Did he bring his ears?"

Mom squinted at him. "Well, yes. They're attached to his head."

"*I* have ears!" Ryan cried. "*Two* of them."

They all turned to look at Ryan. He shrugged. "What? I do. See?" He turned his head side to side. While Todd's ears were the most perfect thing in all of creation, Ryan's ears were right up there too.

"Sam?" Dad asked. "Who is that man and why is he showing us his ears?"

Before Sam could reply, Ryan stepped forward, looking

nervous. "Hello," he said stiffly, bowing as low as his armor would allow. "I'm Ryan Foxheart. This is my sword. Which, I think you'll find is better than anything *Todd* could bring."

"He's right," Todd said mournfully from somewhere in the crowd. "I only brought this piece of wood I found on the road."

"Ha!" Ryan said. "Sucks to be you." He puffed out his chest, his wavy hair bouncing on his head. "Sure showed him, eh, Sam?"

"Oh my gods," Sam muttered. "I'm gonna do you so gross later, you don't even know."

"What," Dad said.

"What," Mom said.

"Whaaaaaat," Ryan said.

"No time!" Sam yelled. "No one is attacking anybody!" He glared past his parents at the crowd. "And how the hell do you have *torches*? Are you telling me you climbed all the way up here with them?"

"They weren't lit," Dad said. "We waited until we got up here to do that."

"Oh," Sam said. "That makes sense. Forward thinking. Good on you."

"Sam," Ryan said.

"Right, right. People of Verania! I know what this looks like. But I'm not a prisoner, and Tiggy and Gary and Kevin and Ryan didn't try and stop me from leaving. I stayed here by choice."

The crowd mumbled warily but didn't lower their weapons.

"That's it?" Gary snapped. "That's the best you got? Gods, twinks. They can't do anything aside from look pretty and flash their buttholes. Never send a twink to do a unicorn's job." He pranced forward, light spilling from his horn in a thick stream that was oddly sexual in ways Sam didn't want to think about. The crowd reared back as Gary approached them, sizing them up. He leaned forward towards one man—Harry? Something like that— with a tremendous mustache and a barrel chest. "You," Gary said. "You there. Hello. I saw you eying me. Do you see something you like?"

Harry—or was it Graham?—scuffed his feet. "A little bit," he admitted.

Gary craned his head forward, lips grazing over the man's

cheek. Sam grimaced when the man's eyes fluttered closed. "Tell me," Gary purred. "Have you ever tasted the rainbow?"

"Not yet," Harry or Graham or possibly Adam said. Sam really needed to pay more attention when being introduced.

"Gary!" Kevin yelled. "Ask him how he feels about tail-play!"

"Sam," Mom said. "Why is Morgan riding that unicorn?"

Sam shrugged. "It's a sky thing. It's best not to question it or pretty much anything else that's happening. Gary, stop flirting with that man. Harry or Graham or Adam, stop being interested while I'm trying to save the day!"

The man pouted as he folded his arms. "My name is Chuck."

"Yeah it is," Gary whispered. "And does Chuck like to fu—"

"*ENOUGH.*"

The crowd gasped and cowered as the sound of Tiggy's voice bowled over them. Gary winked at Chuck, turning around and flicking his tail in the man's face before rejoining his friends.

"Well?" Kevin whispered as Gary resumed his place at the dragon's side.

"Easy pickings," Gary murmured. "If we don't end up having to murder them all, we'll take Chuck for a test-drive."

"Hella cool," Kevin said. "Hella, hella cool."

"What is this place?" Dad asked, looking around. "Sam, what have you done?"

"I planted the magic beans," Sam told him. "And then a beanstalk grew and I climbed up here to find the sky treasure that Vadoma promised me. But guess what? The *real* treasure was the friends I made along the way. Oh, and there's real treasure, but *friends.*" He waved his hands at said friends.

Everyone stared at him.

Sam scowled. "What? It's true."

"Sir," Ryan said to Sam's father. "If I may."

Dad nodded slowly, eyes narrowed.

"Really?" Ryan said. "Oh man, I thought you were going to say no. Crap. Um. Hold on a second. Working…through…my thoughts. Annnnnd. Wait. Got it! No, that doesn't make sense. I mean, why would you have potatoes?"

Sam sighed. "That's Ryan. He's special."

"Really selling it here," Gary muttered.

"And that's Gary," Sam said, pointing at the unicorn. "And Kevin. Ignore all those fangs. He's a vegetarian."

"Yes, I am," Kevin said. "But not a vegan, because those people are insufferable."

"And that's Tiggy," Sam said, pointing up at the giant towering over them. "This is his castle, and he's probably the nicest giant I've ever met. Granted, he's the only giant I've met, but still. He's awesome."

"Tiggy awesome," Tiggy agreed. "Tiggy smash, but also Tiggy bake and sing and—"

Sam didn't see who threw the rock. It came from somewhere in the crowd, arcing high into the sky.

And then it bounced off Tiggy's shin and fell onto the cloud.

Tiggy frowned down at it. He lifted his head slowly, eyes narrowed.

And that certainly wouldn't do. Sam glared at the crowd, and said, "Fee Fi Fo *fuck whoever did that*. What the hell is *wrong* with all of you!"

"My bad!" a voice from the crowd said. "My hand slipped! Won't happen again. Please don't smash me."

Tiggy seemed to consider it, and then smiled. "Okay. Didn't hurt. Tiny, tiny humans."

"See?" Sam said. "Everything is fine. You didn't have to come up here. I would have come back down eventually."

Dad sighed. "Sam, you disappeared. We woke up yesterday and found you gone with a giant beanstalk growing out of our yard. Did you really think we wouldn't come up after you?"

Sam shrugged. "Well, I didn't think you'd bring an angry mob, so I guess we're even. Torches, Dad. You brought *torches*. It's freaking *daylight*."

"That's what I told him," Mom said. "But you know how your father gets. He does love his torches."

Dad sure did, and it was oddly charming. "Okay," Sam said. "I'll allow that. I'm fine, though. Better than fine. They've treated me like I belong."

"You do," Tiggy said. "My Sam. Pretty Sam."

"We like him," Ryan said. "Maybe even more than like."

"He's just talking about himself," Sam whispered to his parents. "We didn't have an orgy or anything. And I wish I really hadn't said that last part."

"So do we," Mom said.

"Mister and Missus Haversford," Ryan said, and Sam did his level best not to swoon. "I know I might not look like much, but I promise you that I think your son is the best thing in the world. And if you'll give me permission, I'd like to ask him on a date where I'll bring him flowers and tell him how handsome he is over plates of spaghetti. And you have my word that I won't attempt anything… untoward until at least the third date."

"Fuck that," Sam growled. "I'm gonna stick my hands down your pants before we even get to *dessert*."

"He learns so quickly," Gary said in a tearful voice. "He's growing up right before our eyes."

"That's my son!" Kevin cried. "You rail that wannabe knight, kiddo!"

"Oh boy," Mom said. "I'm not even going to touch that one."

"That's cool," Kevin said. "I'll do the touching for you. I have no boundaries."

Dad approached Ryan, who stood stock still. Dad circled him slowly, eyeing him up and down before stopping in front of him. "You care for my son?"

Ryan's head jerked up and down. "Yessir."

"And you want to take him on a date?"

"Yessir."

"Hmm," Dad said, stroking his chin thoughtfully. Sam knew it was all an act, but let his dad have his moment. He'd earned it for the worry he must have felt over the last day. "Hmm. *Hmmm*."

Ryan said, "I know I don't look like much, but—"

"So you said already," Dad grunted. "But if my boy thinks of you the same way, you look like enough to me." His glare melted as he smiled warmly. "Never doubt your self-worth, Ryan. It takes a man with a good heart to stand up to others *for* others." He reached up, settling his hands on Ryan's shoulders. "And you seem to be a good man." His grip tightened, fingers digging in. "That being said, if you hurt my son, I'll tear your spine out through your mouth. Do you believe that?"

Ryan nodded, eyes wide.

"Good," Dad said cheerfully. "Then you have my approval, not that you needed it. Sam can speak for himself. I trust his judgement."

Ryan looked confused. "Wait, really?"

"Really," Dad said. And then he hugged Ryan just as hard as he'd hugged Sam. "Put your back into it, Ryan. We Haversfords are huggers. It has to last at least a minute for it to count. Might as well get the practice in now."

It lasted almost *two* minutes, which was uncomfortable for most everyone, but Ryan didn't seem to want to let Dad go.

"This went better than I expected," Sam whispered to his mother.

"Because of the torches and the pitchforks?" she whispered back, a fond smile on her face as she watched Dad and Ryan.

"Because of the torches and the pitchforks," Sam agreed.

Dad and Ryan parted, but Dad didn't seem to want to let Ryan go, slinging an arm around his shoulders and pulling him close. Ryan looked dazed, but happy.

"So let me get this right," Gary said, causing everyone to look at him. "All this hubbub and there's going to be no murder?"

"Murder bad," Tiggy said. "Hurray for no murder!"

"I'll let you murder me," Kevin said. "Stab me in all my hearts and everything."

"Aw," Gary said as he melted against the dragon. "You say the sweetest things, but it's already too late. My bloodlust is waning and being replaced by a different kind of lust. Oh, Chuck! Yoo hoo, Chuck! It's your lucky day. We're not going to kill you. Instead, you're going to find out you have orifices you never thought you'd use before."

Chuck pumped his fist in the air. Sam wasn't sure if he was happy for his friends or disgusted beyond measure. It really could've gone either way.

Tiggy looked down at the crowd amassed before him. "Hungry?" he asked. "I make you food. Come. Come."

With that, he turned around, heading back toward the castle, whistling so loudly, people had to cover their ears.

"I need to see his kitchen," Dad said over his shoulder as he hurried after Tiggy, leaving Ryan looking slightly bereft. "How often do I get to say that about a giant? Never. That's how often."

The crowd seemed unsure at first. Unsure, that is, until Todd marched forward resolutely. He smiled at Sam as he passed them by. It was the catalyst the others needed, all of them laying down their farming tools and snuffing out their torches as they followed the giant into the castle. Chuck walked between Gary and Kevin, eyes glassy as Gary whispered into his ear, Kevin's tail flicking back and forth. Sam wondered if he'd ever walk again by the time they were done with him.

Mom said, "I better make sure your father doesn't talk Tiggy's ear off. You know how he gets." She kissed Sam on the cheek. He thought she'd leave, then, and she turned to, but stopped at the last moment in front of Ryan. She studied him before leaning forward and kissing his forehead. "Welcome to the family," she said, laughing when Sam and Ryan both sputtered nonsensically. "I look forward to getting to know you." She trailed after the others.

"So," Ryan said. "That just happened."

Sam shrugged. "I knew we'd take care of it. Mom and Dad can be a pain in my ass, but they're pretty cool overall." He bit his bottom lip. Then, "Did you mean what you said?"

"About what?"

Sam huffed. "About dating me and flowers and spaghetti."

Ryan's eyebrows nearly disappeared into his hairline. "Oh! Uh. Yes? *Yes*. If…if that's all right with you and you think I'm—*oof*!"

Sam tackled him which, in the end, wasn't exactly the smartest move seeing as how Ryan wore armor. They landed on the clouds, Sam on top of Ryan. This wasn't fate, Sam thought. This wasn't destiny. This could be his by choice, but only if he were brave enough to take the chance.

As it turned out, Sam Haversford was quite brave when it counted. He leaned his head down and right before he kissed Ryan for the first time, Ryan smiled.

It was then Sam learned that kissing while smiling was fucking *awesome*.

THINGS CHANGED, AFTER, now that the people of Verania knew there was a castle in the sky. Most were excited and spoke in wonder at what lay beyond the clouds, especially after Tiggy opened up their home for anyone who wanted to visit. He offered tours three times a week, ever the consummate host. Those who came for the tours were treated to sights unlike anything they'd ever seen before, complete with cake at the end of every trip while being serenaded by a Tiggy original.

Instead of making everyone climb the beanstalk, Ryan repaired his ship and brought groups of people up for the tours. They didn't charge for it because Tiggy said they didn't need the money, given that Gary could literally shit out golden eggs after getting fucked by Kevin. He didn't say it *quite* like that, but everyone knew what he meant.

It should be noted that Chuck never walked right again, but he never complained. He eventually settled down with a handsome centaur named Stephen. Sam's dad converted the barn on the farm into a bed and breakfast for those who traveled far to visit the castle in the sky. Chuck and Stephen ran the day-to-day operations of the B&B, allowing Dad to focus on the farm itself.

Sam decided to live in the castle. He saw his parents a few times per week, and he and Ryan always went down on Sundays for dinner, a little tradition they enjoyed, giving themselves time away from all their responsibilities.

No one was surprised when, a few months after Sam had arrived, he moved all his possessions into Ryan's room. They thought they were being subtle, but Gary immediately called them both out before dissolving into glittery tears, wailing his happiness directly into Sam's ear.

On a cool fall night, Sam awoke in their bed. He heard Tiggy moving just outside their room. He knew where the big guy was going. He leaned down and kissed Ryan's forehead as he snored. Tomorrow, Sam promised himself. Tomorrow he'd tell Ryan he loved him for the first time. He couldn't wait.

He rose from the bed, grabbing one of Ryan's coats and pulling it on before leaving the room. He made his way through the castle and out the open doors. Just as he expected, he found Tiggy sitting on a cloud, looking up at the stars.

Though he tried to be sneaky, Tiggy always seemed to know when he was coming. "Hullo, Sam," the giant said, face still turned toward the sky.

"I'll get you one of these days," Sam said as Tiggy lowered his hand for him to climb on. Once he took his familiar place on Tiggy's shoulder, he sighed happily. They did this, every now and then, just the two of them. He wouldn't change it for anything in the world.

"So pretty," Tiggy whispered to the stars. "So big."

"Feel small?" Sam asked, laying on his back on Tiggy's shoulder.

"Small," Tiggy agreed. "And big. All at same time."

"That's good, my large friend."

"Yep," Tiggy said. "The best."

Sam watched David's Dragon glittering in the heavens. "Tiggy?"

"Sam."

"You're not lonely anymore, are you." It wasn't a question.

Tiggy chuckled, the sound causing Sam to vibrate. "No, Sam. Not lonely. Not anymore. Tiggy never be lonely again."

"Good," Sam said, eyes growing heavy. "I love you, dude. You're the best giant anyone could ever ask for."

Right before he drifted off to sleep, he heard Tiggy whisper, "My pretty Sam. Fee. Fi. Fo. Fum. I smell the blood of a Veranian. Tiggy happy Sam found home, forever my friend, never, ever alone."

And you know what?

They lived happily ever after.

THE Good BOY

O NCE UPON A TIME, in the kingdom of Verania, there lived a man of great renown. His name was Jason, and he was the owner of a chain of popular restaurants that promised family-style dining with peculiar items on the menu, most of which involved blueberries for reasons people didn't quite understand. Though it sounded disgusting, most discovered that a blueberry glaze on top of fried onions was strangely palatable, and Jason found himself more successful than he'd ever dreamed, all at the tender age of twenty-six.

On a bright summer evening, on a girl's night out, a woman came into the main restaurant. She and her friends drank blueberry martinis and giggled sweetly, their faces flushed as they whispered to each other each time Jason asked if they needed anything else.

Jason didn't need to go to their table as he had a full wait staff. But he felt drawn to them. Well, to one in particular. She was pretty, her hair raven black, her eyes a lovely shade of brown that reminded Jason of chocolate shavings on top of blueberry clusters, a signature dessert. But, strangely, it was her ears that Jason noticed first. They were small, though they stuck out far from her head, poking through the strands of her hair. Jason had never considered himself an ear man before that moment; in fact, he questioned if that was even a thing. But for some reason, he found her ears endearing, and by the end of the night, he learned her name: Laura. And with this knowledge, he fumbled awkwardly as he asked if he could see her again.

She blushed and smiled. "Yes. I'd like that quite a bit."

A year later, Laura and Jason were married in a festive ceremony surrounded by their closest friends and family. Everyone commented that they'd never seen a couple so in love before and knew their love would be everlasting.

Ten months after their wedding day, the happy couple welcomed their first—and who would turn out to be their only—child, a boy they named Todd. And though Todd took after his father in appearance, his ears stuck out from the sides of his head just like his mother's. Jason was in love the moment his son was placed in his arms.

They lived happily, but not ever after. A few days after Todd turned ten, his mother fell ill and never recovered. No matter what the healers did, she began to waste away, and two months before Todd's eleventh birthday, Laura passed beyond the veil.

Jason was devastated, as was his son. They clung to each other in their grief, trying to make sense of the destruction left in the wake of Laura's untimely death. It hurt for a long time, but lessened as the years went by.

So much so that when Todd turned fifteen, his father came to him and said, "I've met someone."

Todd looked up from his homework on the kitchen table. He frowned, sure he'd misheard. "Met someone," he said, voice meek and mild. Todd was an anxious boy, perpetually wringing his hands and sweating. He hadn't quite grown into his lanky limbs yet, more often than not tripping over his own feet. The other kids at school mocked him for such things, and he took it in stride, knowing it showed their lack of character more than anything else. Once, they'd made fun of his ears until he'd socked one bully square in the mouth. After that, people didn't mention his ears again. After all, there was so much more to mock Todd about.

Dad nodded. "I have. It's only been a few months. I didn't want to say anything until I was sure it was going somewhere."

Todd frowned harder. "And it is?"

"It is," Dad said, sitting in the chair across from him. He folded his hands on the table, looking at his only child. Dad was big and strong, something Todd hoped he himself would be one day. "I'm thinking of asking him to marry me."

Todd knew his father was bisexual. He'd been very honest about that, especially when Todd himself had gone to him a couple of years before, telling his father he thought he was gay. Though his father had been immediately accepting of his son, Todd could have done without the conversation that followed, especially since it became very graphic as Dad fumbled through a sex talk that involved dental dams and kink, something a thirteen year old did *not* want to hear from his only parent. He'd practically run screaming from the room when Dad decided to bring up watersports, sure the therapy he'd require would need to be intense.

Dad had dated a few times that Todd was aware of, a woman here, a man there, but nothing he'd brought up to his son. If he was ready to discuss it now, he must be serious.

"Okay," Todd said, setting down his pencil and giving his father his undivided attention. "Do you love him?"

"I think I do," Dad said. "He's funny and smart, and though he has a bit of a sharp tongue, he makes me happy." Dad smiled. "He's a good guy, Todd. And better yet, he adopted twins when they were babies, and raised them on his own. They're your age. If this all goes as I hope it will, you'll have a stepbrother and stepsister."

Todd wasn't sure how he felt about that. For the longest time, he'd been the center of his father's world. He never wanted for anything, and the thought of sharing his father's attention with not one but *three* people caused his stomach to twist nauseously. Was his father trying to replace him? Replace his mother?

Dad reached across the table and took Todd's hands in his own, squeezing gently. "I know this is sudden, but he makes me happy, kiddo. I'd like you to meet him, if you think you'd be up for it. But remember, no matter what happens in the future, your mother was and is one of the most important people in my life. And you are too. If you don't like him, or his children, we'll work through it together. You can talk to me about anything. You know that, right?"

"Yeah, Dad. I know." He scrunched up his face. "Do they want to meet me?"

Dad beamed at him. "They do. I've told them all about you, and they're as excited as I am." Then, nervously, his smile fading, "What do you think?"

Todd shrugged. "If it's what you want." If his father was happy, then Todd would be happy for him. His dad had sacrificed so much in the name of his son, and it was the least Todd could do to support him. "When?"

A knock came at their door. "Right now," Dad said, standing up from the chair. "Surprise!"

Todd groaned, lowering his head to the table. "Seriously, Dad? You couldn't have warned me?"

Dad patted him on the shoulder as he rounded the table. "Best to jump in with both feet rather than inch toward the edge, don't you think? It'll be amazing. You'll see."

DAD'S NEW BOYFRIEND was a unicorn named Gary.

Todd didn't know what to do with this information that didn't involve banging his head against the nearest wall. He gaped when the unicorn clomped through the door, his mane—white with streaks of green and gold shot through it—wavy and soft when it smacked against Todd's face. "Jason," Gary said, his horn strong and large as he studied Todd. "Why didn't you tell me your son was so handsome?"

Todd blushed, looking down at the floor, trying his damndest not to grimace at the sound Gary's lips made when they smacked against his father's cheek. "Hello, sir. It's nice to meet you."

"*Sir*," Gary exclaimed. "Listen to this guy. *Sir*. So polite! I approve. Tell me, dear Todd, did your father raise you to be this way, or did you figure it out all on your own? Ha, just kidding. Your dad is a delight, and I'm so very pleased to meet you."

Todd lifted his head. "Really?"

"Really," Gary said. "I've heard so much about you, I feel like we're family already." He batted his long eyelashes, which glittered like they were filled with stars.

Dad grinned, gaze darting back and forth between them.

"That's…nice," Todd said, nothing if not diplomatic. He wasn't quite sure what to make of the fact that his father seemed to be in love with a unicorn. Though he'd never met a unicorn before, he'd heard stories of their…well. Let's just say that Todd was aware of a unicorn's penchant for promiscuity (not that there was anything wrong with that!) and couldn't believe Dad had landed one all for his own. Sure, it wasn't exactly…orthodox, but love was a powerful force. If Dad was sure about Gary, then Todd would do his best to feel the same way.

He cleared his throat and said, "I like your mane."

Gary laughed, a shrill sound that caused Todd's shoulders to stiffen. "Oh, you are *precious*. I could just eat you up. But I won't." He turned and began to nibble on Dad's cheek. "I have to save my appetite for your daddy."

Todd hid his grimace as best he could, especially when he saw Gary's tongue scrape against Dad's neck in an overly familiar way.

Gary pulled away from Dad and turned his head toward Todd once more. "You're fifteen, right? My son and daughter are the same age! I'd ask if you knew them, but I don't think you quite run in the same circles. The little darlings go to public school. You're in private school, aren't you?"

Todd nodded, unsure of what he was supposed to say.

Dad stepped in to save him. "Only the best for my boy. The gods have smiled upon us, and I've made my fortune in the name of my son. All I have will one day be his, and I know my business couldn't be left in better hands." He winked at Todd. "But not for a long time to come. He's still got a bit of growing up to do, and I plan on living for decades yet."

"Oh, Jason," Gary purred. "That's so…*wonderful*. And even though I don't give two shits about your money—fortune, did you say?—it's nice to know you have been able to provide so ably for Todd. And this *house*. Fuck me sideways. Could it be any bigger? Gods, our voices are *echoing*." He left them standing in the foyer as he pranced through the house, exclaiming over every little detail.

"What do you think?" Dad asked, wincing as a crash came from the kitchen, followed by an "Oops! I hope you didn't need that table!"

Todd said, "He seems…alive." Then, in a rush, "I mean, he's cool. A unicorn? That's different."

Dad laughed. "I know! Isn't it grand?" He stepped forward, settling his hands on his son's shoulders. "Nothing will ever replace your mother. She was the best thing that ever happened to me because she gave me you. I know this is sudden, but I know she'd want us to be happy."

Todd thought Mom might have a few words to say about Dad's choices, but he kept this to himself. Forcing a smile, he said, "Sure,

Dad. Gary's great." Another crash, this time sounding like plates being flung against a wall. "A little destructive, but great."

Before Dad could reply, Gary stuck his head back into the foyer, chewing something wet. "Hey, Todd! Have you ever been able to tell your teachers that a unicorn ate your homework? Because guess *what*. Chomp, chomp, chomp." He laughed. "I'm delightful. You're welcome."

Todd smiled weakly. "Ha, ha. You're so fun."

Gary grinned, razor sharp. "And don't you forget it. Jason. Yoo hoo, *Jason*. I do believe you promised me a tour of your bedroom. I'd like to take you up on that offer right the fuck now. I'm *moist*."

"Coming, my dear!" Dad said, leaving Todd to stand in the foyer, wondering what the hell had just happened.

A MONTH LATER, Todd met Gary's children for the first time. Over the past weeks, he'd gotten to know Gary, for better or worse, and he thought he knew what to expect when meeting his son and daughter.

He was so very, very wrong.

"What's wrong with your ears?" Tina asked, her blonde hair hanging in ringlets.

"They're awfully big," Justin said, his handsome smile cold and knowing.

Though twins, they didn't look anything alike. Justin was tall and muscular for a fifteen year old and carried himself as if he were royalty. His thick brown hair was luxurious, and though Gary wasn't wealthy—something the unicorn had stressed time and time again, claiming they were a salt of the earth sort of family—Justin still wore expensive trousers, and a tunic made of the finest silk. He sat in Todd's tearoom as if he'd always been there, legs dangling over the armrest, loose and relaxed.

Tina was smaller, though no less terrifying. Her fingernails looked like claws, sharpened to a point and painted blood-red. Her dress was blue, a sash cinched at the waist. But it was her knowing gaze that worried Todd the most. She barely seemed to blink, and this chilled Todd to the bone.

Gary and Dad were in the backyard, saying they wanted to give the children time to get to know each other without interruption. Todd wasn't quite sure how he felt about that, but he knew this was important to Dad, and he wanted to make him proud, even though he wanted to run and hide away in his room.

Todd slumped in his own chair, barely able to raise his head. "I don't…know? They're just my ears."

Tina laughed, and though it sounded pretty, it grated against Todd's skin. "Oh, are we going to have fun with *you*. Isn't that right, Justin?"

"Yes," Justin agreed. "So much fun. Say, Todd, how many bedrooms does this house have?"

"Um. Twelve? We don't really use them all, but Dad said that—"

"Twelve," Tina said. "Twelve whole bedrooms. For just the two of you? Oh my. Don't you get lonely?"

Todd shook his head. "Not really. Dad's busy a lot, but I am too. I have my schoolwork, and I help out at the restaurants almost every day. I don't have time to be lonely."

Justin scoffed, his tunic open at his throat, revealing miles of tan skin that Todd couldn't help but sneak a peek at. Though Justin disturbed him, Todd couldn't deny how attractive he was. Bad thoughts, these, especially if Dad and Gary married. Justin would be his stepbrother, and that wouldn't do. "Sounds like you're a busy bee," Justin said, tapping his fingers against his raised knee.

"I try," Todd said.

Lady Tina lifted her teacup to her lips, taking a dainty sip. She grimaced. "Oof. This needs sugar. Too strong for my taste."

Todd immediately stood, going to the tea cart and grabbing the bowl of sugar cubes and setting it in front of Tina. The twins exchanged a look that Todd couldn't parse through. Then they fixed their gazes on Todd, and he wondered if this was how prey felt when cornered by a predator.

"Todd," Justin said slowly. "I've always said tea is best with a pastry or two. I'd like a scone. Now."

Todd nodded, and hurried to the kitchen. By the time he returned with a plate of blueberry scones, Tina and Justin had their heads together, whispering furiously. They stopped when he coughed, not wanting to be rude. They gave him matching smiles as he set the plate on the table before them.

Justin picked up a scone, pulling at the flaky pastry but not eating. "Such a submissive little thing, aren't you?"

Todd blanched, feeling his face heat up. He tried to speak but croaked instead.

"He is, isn't he?" Tina said, leaning forward as she stared at Todd, her chin cupped in her hands. "Do you like to be told what to do, Todd? Does it make you feel good to serve?"

He spluttered. "That's not—I don't—I can't—"

Justin and Tina laughed, and a trickle of unease wormed its way into Todd's head. He'd never examined this part of himself too closely, fearful of what it could mean. He liked order, structure, and yes, part of that meant a strangely uplifting feeling he got when he was told what to do. It wasn't exactly…sexual, but Todd wasn't quite clear yet what *sexual* meant. He didn't know if there were others who felt the same way and didn't have it in him to ask. It felt like a secret, one he'd kept hidden away, locked in a box surrounded by chains.

But the fact that Justin and Tina had picked up on it so easily? That caused Todd's blood to turn to an icy sludge. He wasn't a doormat. He never had been. He knew how to say *no*. But for some reason, their knowing gazes caused his voice to dry up, and he fidgeted, hoping against hope that Dad would come in and save him.

He didn't.

"Yes," Justin said with a dangerous smirk. "I think we're going to get along smashingly. Father will be quite pleased to know that."

"Oh yes," Tina breathed. "He'll be so happy to know that we'll have a brother who only wants to see us happy. Isn't that right, Todd?"

Todd looked away.

"WELL?" DAD ASKED, later that afternoon after the others had left. "What do you think? Justin and Tina seemed to like you quite a bit. Said you were…how did they put it?" He brightened. "Ah, yes! That you didn't leave them wanting for anything. Such a good host."

Todd warmed briefly at the praise, though it did nothing to melt the ice in his chest. "They were all right, I guess."

Dad laughed. "A ringing endorsement if I ever heard one. I'm so happy you got to meet them, Todd. I worried, a little. I know they can be a handful, but Gary said their bark is worse than their bite. Don't be intimidated by them. You're my son, which means you're strong and brave." He wrapped his hand around Todd's neck, pressing their foreheads together. "I think we can make this work. But only if you want. I won't do anything without your permission."

Todd sighed, knowing he'd already lost. Dad was happy. Todd wanted to see him smile more than anything. Since Mom's death, Dad hadn't smiled as much as he used to, the tinge of grief settled on his shoulders like a shroud. But ever since he'd met Gary, that weight seemed to have been lifted off him, and who was Todd to stand in the way of that? If anything, he only had three more years until he became a man and could step out into the world on his own. His father was counting on him.

Todd said, "We can make it work. Just…"

Dad jostled him a little. "Just what, kiddo?"

He sniffled, eyes burning. "You promise you won't forget me?"

"Never," Dad whispered. "Never, ever, ever. You are my son, the reason my heart beats. Though things might change a little, you are and always will be my first priority."

Relieved, Todd said, "Thanks, Dad."

DAD AND GARY WERE MARRIED in a boisterous affair attended by many important people. Todd stood at his father's side as his best man, Justin and Tina next to Gary. The air was redolent with flowers of red and blue, yellow and white. Dad wore his finest suit, tailored for just this occasion. Gary was resplendent, his mane streaked with green and blue, a lace veil over his face.

Dad lifted the veil and kissed his new husband to the cheers of all.

GARY AND JUSTIN AND TINA moved in the next day. "Oh," Gary said as the movers brought in box after box. "It already feels like home! Well, sort of. We'll have to redecorate from top to bottom and replace much of the furniture. Paint on the walls, new flooring, and these window shades are hideous, so we'll need to have those replaced immediately. But still! Just like home."

"We're very lucky," Tina said, eyes wide as she looked up at Dad. "Thank you for welcoming us."

"Yes," Justin simpered. "We're so grateful that you rescued us from our hovel—I mean, that you married our father who has nothing but love in his heart and no desire to take anything for his own."

Gary snarled at his children before turning back to Todd and his dad. "Don't listen to them, dear. They're a little…exuberant. They obviously don't know how to keep their *godsdamn mouths shut*." He laughed, horn glittering. "But today isn't about them. It's about me and joining this wonderful family. Jason, love, let's leave them to it. I have an ache in my loins that only you can cure."

"Oh my," Dad said. "We should see to that immediately."

They disappeared up the stairs, leaving Todd with Justin and Tina.

"Todd," Tina said with a shark-like grin, all teeth. "Carry our things to our room, won't you? Justin and I would help, but we're exhausted from the last few days. You're a good boy, aren't you?"

"Such a good boy," Justin said.

Todd flushed, hating the surge of *something* in his body that wished for them to call him a good boy again. He did as he was asked.

DAD DIED THREE MONTHS LATER.

Gary's face streaked with tears, body wracking with sobs as he told Todd that Dad had fallen down the stairs quite by accident. "I told him not to try and clean the chandelier by hanging off the railing!" he cried, his mascara running down his face. "But he just wouldn't listen! He slipped, and fell back *over* the railing somehow, and then tumbled down the stairs! Oh woe. Woe is me! I am a widow. Whatever shall I do?"

Gary threw himself to the ground, wailing at the unfairness of it all. Tina and Justin hurried to comfort their father, whispering words of solace into his ears as they rubbed his snout.

"My gods, Todd," Justin hissed. "Can't you see he's suffering? Get him something to drink! And you better make it strong."

"He needs it," Tina cooed, pressing her face against Gary's neck. "Don't be so selfish."

Numb, Todd drifted toward the kitchen, hoping this was nothing but a dream. Once they couldn't see him, he sagged against the wall, his knees no longer supporting his weight. He cried as quietly as he could, face in his hands.

"AS PER HIS LAST WILL AND TESTAMENT," the solicitor said a week later, "Jason has left all assets, both monetary and tangible, to his son, Todd. The restaurants. The house. The fortune he'd amassed."

"What," Gary said.

"What," Justin said.

"What," Tina said.

They all turned slowly to look at him.

Todd wrung his hands, knuckles popping. Dad was only three days in the ground, and he hadn't yet found a way to get a handle on his grief. The only reason he wasn't in bed at this very moment was because Gary had forced him to get up and attend this meeting. He didn't care about the money or the restaurants. He wanted his father.

Gary laughed, but it didn't sound as if he were amused as he turned to glare daggers at the solicitor. "I'm sorry. I must have misheard you. As you are undoubtedly aware, I recently married Jason, may he rest in peace. I'm sure he must have made an addendum to the will as I clearly asked him to. He wouldn't have left a grieving spouse with nothing."

The solicitor shook his head. "There is no addendum. On Todd's twenty-first birthday, he will inherit everything. Jason made sure that his son would be well taken care of. The money will be placed in a trust, overseen by a team of financial advisors Jason hired, who will also see to the day-to-day operations of the restaurants until such time comes when Todd is ready and willing to take over."

Gary's eyes flashed darkly. "But he's only a *child*. A sweet, wonderful child who I love as if he were my own. That kind of responsibility isn't something he should have to carry on his shoulders. Look at him. He's so sad. A sad, sad little boy. Don't you think it'd be better if someone smart and wonderful and completely innocent of any nefarious actions—say, myself—ran things for him? These advisors sound sketchy. I loved Jason, but he didn't always have the best judge of character."

To that, Todd agreed, though he kept his mouth firmly closed.

"Yes," Gary continued. "I believe that it should be left for me to handle. After all, I know Jason meant to leave us *something*."

The solicitor smiled grimly. "I'm sorry for your loss, but these are my client's last wishes." He glanced at Todd. "However."

"Yes!" Justin whispered. "I *love* howevers."

"Me too," Tina whispered back. "It's one of my favorite words."

"Todd is still a minor," the solicitor said. "And from what I understand, he has no other family. Is that right, Todd?"

He nodded, head jerking up and down. "Mom's parents died when she was young. And Dad's parents were never in the picture."

"Remember when we were orphans?" Justin asked Tina. "That was a shitty time."

"Good thing we're not anymore," Tina replied. "I'd just hate to have *that* hanging over my head again."

"Children!" Gary trilled. "Daddy is trying to have a business meeting, and you're *interrupting.*"

Justin and Tina folded their arms and pouted.

"My apologies," Gary said to the solicitor. "My precious angels often forget they're better seen than heard. Now, to the matter at hand. As you know, I have so much love in my heart, and it guided me to adopt Justin and Tina. Though they aren't of my blood, they are my own. I would gladly adopt Todd as well. That way, we can all be a family in his—*our* home. Would you like that, Todd? Yes, you would, wouldn't you? You wouldn't dream of kicking us out onto the street, would you?" He looked at Todd, eyes wide and wet.

Todd shot up in his chair, his heart in his throat. "I…"

"That settles it," Gary said, eyes drying immediately. "I'll adopt Todd, and we will all live together as we work through the terrible loss of Jason. Oh, and a question, if I may, absolutely apropos of nothing that we're currently discussing." He leaned forward, smiling sweetly. "What would happen to the assets if, say, Todd died suddenly and completely by accident? After all, his mother passed unexpectedly, as did his father. Who's to say the same won't happen to our lovely Todd?" He chuckled. "Bit of bad luck, there."

The solicitor frowned. "Then by Veranian law, all assets would pass on to the next in line. Absent of any prenuptial agreement— which Jason did not include—that would mean his spouse."

"Huh," Gary said. "How. About. That."

THE FOLLOWING WEEKS went as best as could be expected given everything that had happened. Todd did his best to avoid Gary and Justin and Tina, hiding away in his room. It was summer, which meant no school, and Todd spent most days curled up in his bed, a small portrait of his parents clutched in his hands.

At night, he'd sneak down when everyone was sleeping, and eat by candlelight in the kitchen, listening just in case someone heard him. After he finished, he'd return to his room and try to sleep, though mostly, he laid awake, staring at the ceiling, wondering how things had gone so wrong, so quickly.

Three weeks after his father's death (which had been ruled an accident, Gary saying that Jason had always been such a klutz as he wailed at his loss, the constables looking like they'd rather be anywhere else), Gary came into his room without knocking and said something Todd did not expect.

"I need your room."

Todd blinked, pushing himself up on his bed, back against the headboard. "What?"

"Your room," Gary repeated. "I need it. It's far too big for someone such as yourself, and when I—*we* have guests, we want to make sure they're comfortable."

"There are eleven other bedrooms," Todd reminded him.

Gary whirled on him, eyes narrowing. "You can count. How fun. Yes, there *are* eleven other rooms. Tina has one, as does Justin and myself, which means there are only *eight* other rooms. But I need *nine.*"

Confused, Todd asked, "For what?"

Gary flicked his mane. "Since your father—a desperately complicated man—decided to not watch out for his family after he departed, I have to make money *somehow.* Which is why I decided to open the house up as the premier bed and breakfast in the City of

Lockes. Isn't that exciting?"

No, it really wasn't. "But…this is *my* house. And *my* room."

Gary blinked rapidly, eyes shining. "It is, isn't it?" He sniffled. "Which is why I know you won't let us become destitute or try to argue against my idea. I've always said that you were the most kind and giving boy I'd ever met." He leaned closer, dropping his voice. "Don't tell Justin I said this, but you're the son I've always wished for. Justin sucks. I'm Team Todd!"

Todd stared at him, unable to speak.

"Good," Gary said. "I'm so happy you see it my way. Pack up your things. You're moving to the attic. And when you're done with that, I have a list of chores for you to do. You better hurry. The list is long, and you have a lot of work ahead of you. How do you feel about robin egg blue for the walls? Ha, just kidding. I don't care what your opinion is, so long as you know how to hold a paint brush."

And with that, Gary left the room, tail swishing behind him.

Todd lay back down on his bed, pulling the comforter over his head.

THE ATTIC WAS DUSTY AND DARK, the only light coming in through the single grimy window at the opposite end. Todd lit a candle, swinging it back and forth, grimacing at the number of cobwebs that hung from the rafters. The air was thick and musty, and the floorboards creaked with every step he took.

At the back of the room lay a mattress on the floor. He set his pack upon it before sitting down. The lumpy mattress wheezed obnoxiously. Todd put his face in his hands, head pounding, nose leaking from all the dust.

But before he could start to feel even more sorry for himself, he startled when a tiny voice squeaked, "Who is he? Why is he up here? I swear to the gods, if he tries to steal my stuff, I'll give him the plague!"

"*Quiet*," another voice whispered harshly. "He'll hear you! And I *told* you about the plague thing. We'll never overcome the stigma if you keep feeding into stereotypes!"

"I'm a *rat*," the first voice replied. "You really think I give two shits about political correctness?"

"Who's there?" Todd asked, voice trembling as he wrung his hands. "Show yourselves!"

"Now you've gone and done it," someone muttered. It sounded as if it came from behind a large box in the corner of the attic. "We had it good here, and you went and ruined it. He's gonna lay down traps and I won't be able to resist them because I *need that cheese*."

"You do like cheese. Such a cliché. I love you so hard, even if you don't quite seem to understand that you're lactose intolerant."

"I love you too, and I am *not*."

"Yeah, keep telling yourself that, Ryan. But *I'm* the one who has to smell your cheese farts. And newsflash: they're *gross*."

Todd stood swiftly, moving toward the box. Without hesitation, he lifted it up…

….and screamed when two large rats stared up at him with beady black eyes, their whiskers twitching.

The rats also screamed. It was quite the new experience for Todd. For one, he'd never been a big fan of rats. Secondly, he was unaware that rats could make such a noise, much less talk. He stumbled back, dropping the box. Something inside it broke as it hit the floor, but Todd only had eyes for the two fat rodents, their tails tangled together, their tiny ears cocked in alarm.

Before Todd could scream again, one of the rats stepped forward. He was black in color, his tail a pale pink. "Whoa, dude," the rat said. "Just chill. It's cool. I promise. I was just kidding about the whole giving-you-the-plague thing. I was tested two weeks ago. I'm clean!"

The other rat—slightly larger and smokey gray—sighed. "Sam, you're scaring him. Let me try." His little legs scurried as he rushed forward, stepping in front of the black rat as if shielding him. He stood on his hind legs, nostrils flaring as he eyed Todd warily. "Hello. My name is Ryan. This is my boyfriend, Sam. We're not going to hurt you, so long as you don't try to hurt us." His eyes narrowed. "My teeth are very sharp. I once chewed through five feet of brick, so your skin would be no match for me."

The black rat peered over Ryan's shoulder. "He's very proud of that fact. And honestly, I wanted to give him shit over it, but it was pretty hot. The brick never stood a chance against my boo."

"Aw," Ryan said, puffing out his chest like a douchebag. "Thanks. I did my best, and that brick—"

"You're…you're *rats*," Todd spluttered.

The black rat—Sam?—snorted. "Nothing gets past this guy, huh? Hey, look, everyone! This cool dude knows what rats look like!"

Ryan rolled his eyes as he wrapped his tail around Sam's middle. "Be nice. It's probably a shock to hear us speak."

"You can *talk*," Todd said rather hysterically.

"Of course we can," Sam muttered. "What, you think you're the only one? Man, you really need to do something about that ego. Just because you're human doesn't mean you're better than us. *I* can squish my body down and fit through even the smallest of holes, so suck it."

"I don't think I'm better than you!"

"Good," Sam said, coming to stand at Ryan's side. "Because this is *our* attic, and if you're going to be staying up here, you'd better invest in some earplugs. Ryan's a screamer, and I won't have the dulcet tones of the pleasure I give him muffled because you're a prude."

"What," Todd said.

"Rat sex," Sam said as if Todd were the idiot. "Lots and lots of rat sex."

"You're gay *and* you can talk?" Todd asked faintly.

"Hell *yes*," Sam said as Ryan nibbled on his ear. "We're here, we're queer, so you better fucking get used to it. Gay rat rights!"

Todd's legs gave way, and he sat on the floor with a grunt. The rats—fat little things—cocked their heads as they watched him.

"Today has been a very weird day," Todd whispered, looking down at his hands.

He flinched when Ryan approached him cautiously, Sam whispering that if things went south, to go for the eyes first. Ryan, in fact, did *not* go for Todd's eyes, instead putting his tiny paw on one of Todd's boots. "It's okay," Ryan said. "You don't have to be sad. The attic isn't so bad. In fact, it's the nicest place we've ever lived."

"You should have seen our last place," Sam said, rolling over on his back, legs kicking up in the air as he started to clean himself. "It was a fucking hole, man. We had to move when this dumb kid found us in the kitchen trying to get the crackers."

"You hissed at him," Ryan said.

Sam chuckled. "Right? He shit himself and everything. It was hilarious." He looked at Todd. "They called an exterminator, but we were already thinking about moving, anyway, so no big deal."

"And you… moved here?"

"We did," Ryan said. "Just the attic, though. We don't go down into the house often, just to be safe. I don't want anything happening to Sam."

"He loves me," Sam said dreamily. "He's the hottest rat I've ever seen. Isn't he hot?"

"Uh," Todd said.

"Rude," Sam said with a sniff. "I'd rather have him than a pink monstrosity such as yourself."

"He didn't mean that," Ryan said hastily.

"Yes, I did. Why do they have so much skin? Where is the *hair*? Humans are weird looking. I mean, sure, *objectively*, some of them are attractive, even if they all look like they have mange. They don't even have tails. What the fuck is up with that?"

"How long have you been here?" Todd asked, wondering if he was feverishly sick and caught in a nightmare. That would make more sense than having a conversation with rat boyfriends.

Ryan scrunched up his face. "Six…no, wait. Seven months."

"We even built a nest and everything," Sam said. "Look!" He righted himself and scurried over to the wall underneath the window. There, at the base where the wall met the floor, was a hole that looked as if it'd been chewed through. Todd crawled after Ryan, lowering his head toward the ground so he could see inside.

The hole opened up into a small space in the wall. Inside was a pile of soft blankets covered in bits of hay and twigs. The center of the pile was depressed, as if that was where the rats slept.

"Pretty kickass, right?" Sam said as he jumped onto the blankets. "Tiggy got us the blankets as a housewarming present."

"Tiggy," Todd repeated. "As in…*Tiggy*. My dad's mule?" The

mule was stabled in the barn behind the house. He was a kindly thing, always happy to see Todd whenever he did his chores. But Todd had never heard him speak a word, which meant one of two things: either Tiggy hadn't felt comfortable talking to him, or Todd was high as balls and none of this was real. He couldn't decide which seemed more plausible.

"Yeah," Sam said. "He's our best friend. Good guy, that Tiggy. When we moved, we were in between places for a bit, but he let us stay in the barn with him until we moved in here."

"And he can talk too?"

Sam grinned, his large front teeth digging into his bottom lip. "Obviously. All animals can talk, but people choose not to hear them. You should really work on that as a species, especially since you all seem hell bent on destroying everything you can get your hands on. Humanity blows."

"I have no idea what's going on," Todd said helplessly.

"That sounds like a you problem," Sam said.

"Why are you up here?" Ryan asked. "Don't you have your own room?"

Todd shook his head as his chest hitched. "Um. My…dad. Died unexpectedly. My stepfather made me move up here because he's turning the house into a bed and breakfast."

"Oh," Sam said quietly. "I'm sorry to hear that. If it makes you feel better, we're orphans too."

"No," Todd said as he sat back on his legs. "That doesn't make me feel better."

"Well, then, fuck you very much. See if *I* ever say anything nice to you again. Here I am, showing you our home and opening up to you about how my parents got caught in a trap when I was a wee slip of a rat, and you—"

"*Sam,*" Ryan said in warning.

"Yeah, yeah," Sam muttered as he came back out into the attic. "I hear you. Sorry, dude. You're Todd, right? We've heard you in the house before. Your dad seemed nice. Better than that asshole he married." He grinned up at Todd. "Hey, I got something that'll cheer you up! Ryan and I shit in the pockets of one of Tina's coats. When it gets colder, she'll pull the jacket out of the closet and when she sticks her hand in the pocket, she'll get shit hands!"

Todd was startled into laughter. "You did *what*?"

"It was my idea," Ryan said smugly. "Sam wanted to poop on her pillow, but that was too on the nose. Secrets poops are the best kind of poops."

"I'll give him that," Sam said, looking fondly at Ryan. "He may not look like it, but Ryan can be devious when he really wants to be. Come here, boo. I'm about to give you some sugar."

When Todd woke up this morning, he hadn't expected to be forced into the attic only to watch two rats make out. It was quite illuminating. And also disgusting, especially when Ryan did something that made Sam squeak as they rolled on the floor.

"There," Sam said, lips smacking as he pulled away. "That's the ticket."

Ryan looked dazed, the hairs on his face ruffled and slightly wet. He shook his head. "This is going to be so great, you'll see. We'll be roommates and everything."

"Oh my gods," Sam whispered. "We're *roommates*."

"I suppose," Todd said slowly. "It'll be nice to have someone to talk to. Gary and Justin and Tina aren't exactly the best conversationalists."

"That's because they're stupid," Sam said. "Stick with us, kid. We'll watch your back. You know what? Since I'm feeling so generous today, I'll make you an honorary rat. Huzzah!"

Todd smiled for the first time in weeks.

"TODD!" GARY YELLED. "I better be able to see my godsdamn reflection in the floor, you hear me? I want it *spotless*."

"Todd!" Justin bellowed. "My bedsheets need changing! Also, empty my chamber pot, won't you? Dinner last night didn't agree with me, and the smell is making me gag!"

"Todd!" Tina shrieked. "I'm having the girls over later for our fan club, and there'd better not be a single lick of crust on the tiny watercress sandwiches I need you to make, or so help you gods, you'll live to regret it!"

Todd was not smiling. His back hurt, his hands were dry and cracking from all the cleaning chemicals he'd been forced to use. In the six months since his father's death, he hadn't had a moment of peace, forced to work from the moment he woke until he collapsed into his bed at night. He hadn't been allowed to return to school, Gary telling him that he didn't need to worry about such things, especially since he had so much to do at home. The bed and breakfast was set to open just after the new year, and Gary had ordered a complete renovation of the house. Todd hadn't even had time to go out to his father's restaurants, but so long as Gary couldn't get his hooves on them, he counted himself lucky.

The only light in Todd's miserable life were Sam and Ryan. They weren't so bad for rats, and though he wished he could forget how…exuberant their coitus was, it was a small price to pay in order to have someone to talk to.

They'd also introduced him to Tiggy, even though Todd had known the mule for years. It was different now, though, given that apparently Tiggy could talk just as well as Sam and Ryan.

Sort of.

"Todd!" Tiggy bleated when he went to the barn. "Hi, Todd!"

"Tiggy," Todd said in greeting as Ryan and Sam ran into the barn ahead of him and jumped into a pile of hay. "How are you today?"

"I'm a mule," Tiggy said proudly. And he was! His coat was brown and black with splotches of white on his chest and stomach. His large ears were pointed, the left one flopping over. His tail was thick and bushy, streaked in browns and whites. He was a jovial fellow, always happy no matter what happened.

"So you've told me repeatedly," Todd said as he poured grain into Tiggy's bucket. The mule pranced around him before burying his face in the bucket and eating noisily. Todd stroked the skin between his ears.

"Tiggy," Sam said. "Can we take a bit more of your hay? Ryan hasn't been sleeping very well, and I want to make our nest better."

Tiggy nodded through a mouthful of grain as he lifted his head. "Yep. My hay your hay. Todd want some hay?"

"Nah," Todd said. "I'm good. Thanks, though."

"Todd sad?" Tiggy asked, ears twitching against flies that circled his head.

Todd shrugged. "I don't know. I don't know how I feel."

"He's a teenager," Sam said as he gathered up hay in his tiny paws. "All those hormones. You should just jack off. It'll make you feel better."

Todd groaned. That wasn't something he liked to think about. Masturbation wasn't exactly at the front of his mind, especially when he lived with amorous rats. And even if he *didn't* live with rats, he was always too tired to do anything but sleep when he finished for the day. Gary never ran out of things for him to do, and he'd spent the day wiping down every baseboard in the house simply because Gary saw a smudge on one downstairs.

"I have hormones," Tiggy said. "Also have hooves. Fun!" He pressed his snout against Todd's chest. "Todd has no hooves, but that's okay. Todd is good person, and Tiggy likes him."

Todd brushed Tiggy's head, fighting a smile. Regardless of how else his life had unexpectedly turned out, he still had friends. Granted, they were rodents and a fake horse, but still. It was better than having nothing at all.

"Todd!" Gary screamed from the house. "I found a *hair on the floor*. I demand that you sweep the entire house again!" Then, "Oh, it's from my mane. Ha, ha, that's funny. And you will also *mop the floors too*. Todd? Todd!"

"I gotta go," Todd mumbled as he left the barn behind and headed for the house.

AND THAT'S HOW IT WENT, for the next couple of years. The bed and breakfast opened, and Todd had never been busier in his life. Days and weeks flew by, the seasons changing as they always did, but Todd kept his head down, working as hard as he could. He dreamed of the day when he turned twenty-one and could take control of his father's empire. He was always aware, never letting

Tina or Justin or Gary stand behind him when he walked down the stairs, and he counted the knives in the drawers every morning just to be safe. One couldn't be too careful, especially given how carefully Gary watched him.

Once, shortly after Todd's seventeenth birthday, he'd awoken to Sam and Ryan's shouts, the attic filling with smoke. He leapt from his bed, choking as he hurried toward the hatch that led down into the house. Smoke billowed through the cracks, and he flung the hatch open to find someone had put a bunch of candles on top of the ladder near the hatch. He'd managed to blow them all out before the wood of the house caught fire.

"Oh, silly me!" Gary said when Todd had asked after it. "I meant it to be a surprise for your birthday. I must have forgotten to put them on a cake or tell you that they were there. Oops!"

"Who the fuck does he think he is?" Sam ranted when Todd had returned to the attic, opening the window to try and clear the smoke out. "I'll fucking kill him! I don't give two shits that he's a unicorn. Fuck him in his stupid face!"

"You can't," Todd begged, scrubbing a hand over his face. "It'll only make things worse for me. I just have to last a few more years. Once I turn twenty-one, I'll be able to deal with it then."

Sam muttered under his breath as Ryan tangled their tails together. "Are you sure?" Ryan asked, sounding worried. "Gary is escalating. You might not make it until you're twenty-one."

"I can handle it," Todd said, sounding stronger than he felt. "Let them do their worst."

"Todd!" Justin shouted from somewhere in the house. "One of my boyfriends just left, and I need you to wipe down the windows in my room! He made a mess when I was fucking him against it."

Gary's laughter trickled up through the floorboards. "I've raised you well."

Todd's shoulders hunched as he made his way once more to the hatch.

THERE WERE GOOD DAYS, and bad days, though the bad days seemed to happen more and more frequently. Todd held on the best he could, swallowing down the retorts that bubbled in his throat any time Gary or Justin or Tina screamed his name. He didn't hate them; Todd had never hated anyone in his life. It seemed like such a waste. But that didn't mean he wasn't irritated beyond belief and kept reminding himself that his twenty-first birthday would come sooner rather than later.

"Catch!" Justin cried, and Todd managed to duck just in time as a sword hurtled over his head, quivering as it embedded itself in the wall behind him.

"Oh dear," Tina said as Todd managed to keep from slipping down the stairs after stepping in a puddle of syrup that had mysteriously appeared on the top stair. "Do be careful."

"Fuck," Gary growled when Todd was not choked to death after somehow getting wrapped up in the curtains he'd been cleaning. "I mean, oh, good. You're still alive."

"Are you a masochist?" Sam asked one night as Todd collapsed onto his bed. "No judgement, but that's the only thing I can think of to explain you. Do you like pain? That's gnarly, dude. I had Ryan chew on my leg once to see if I could get it up, but that shit hurt."

"No," Todd said dully. "I'm not a masochist."

"Oh," Sam said. "I'm out of ideas, then."

Todd turned over on his bed, facing away from the rats staring at him from the footboard. "I just…I don't know. I know it sucks, but I like being told what to do. It makes me feel safe to have order."

"Right," Sam said slowly. "So you like structure. Nothing wrong with that. We don't kink shame here, especially since I have a few of my own that are probably better left to the imagination."

"He's very imaginative," Ryan said.

"You have to see how terrible they are," Sam said. "You don't deserve to be treated like that. You need to find yourself a man who'll tell you what to do but will do it in a way that shows he loves you, if that's what you want."

Todd laughed bitterly. "Because *that's* going to happen. I'm not even allowed to leave the house unless they need something. I'll never meet anyone while I'm here." He turned onto his back, staring up at the ceiling. "Two more years."

"But what if you don't make it that long?" Ryan asked quietly.
To that, Todd had no answer.

SHORTLY AFTER TODD'S TWENTIETH BIRTHDAY—on a fall day, the air crisp, the leaves turning shades of red and gold—he heard Justin and Tina speaking excitedly in the kitchen. Todd tried to avoid them as much as possible, but something pulled him toward the kitchen, a strange curl in his chest that felt like fire.

"—and we'll look our best," Justin was saying, his lips curled back over his teeth in the approximation of a smile. "He won't know what hit him. He'll look at us and forget everyone else exists."

"Of course he will," Tina said, tapping her fingers against a piece of thick paper on the table in front of her. "Those other bitches don't even deserve to stand in his presence. I'll fucking cut them if they try."

"Dear sister," Justin said, "I do like it when you become stabby. What are we going to…Todd. What are you doing?"

They turned to look at him, gazes narrowed.

Todd shrugged. "Just making sure everything is clean and ready to go for breakfast for our guests." He set down the bag of pastries he'd purchased at the bakery on the counter, pulling a large plate from the cabinet. He knew they were still watching him as he arranged the pastries on the plate. He ignored them as best he could, hoping they'd continue talking about whatever they'd been discussing. It sounded exciting, something Todd longed for.

"Forget him," Tina snapped. "We have to think about what we're going to wear. I hear he likes leather."

"Of course he does," Justin said. "There's a reason everyone calls him Sir instead of his real name. He's very…dominant."

Todd paused. Sir? Who were they talking about?

"Ooh," Tina said with a shiver. "That gave me chills. When it comes down to just the two of us, who do you think he'll pick?"

"Me, of course," Justin said. "I'd make the best husband

someone like him could ask for."

Tina scoffed. "Bullshit. He needs a *wife*, someone soft and beautiful like me. A feminine touch."

"Who?" Todd blurted, growing cold when Tina and Justin fell silent. He didn't turn around, not wanting to see their expressions of derision pointed at him again. He didn't expect them to answer and was surprised when Justin did just that.

"A Lord of Verania," Justin said. "One of the king's closest advisors. He's decided to throw a ball for every eligible man and woman in Lockes. He's looking for a spouse."

"Which lord?" Todd asked, trying to keep his voice even.

"Lord Tremaine the Firm," Tina said. "Also known as Sir."

Todd swallowed thickly. He'd seen Lord Tremaine only once, from a distance when he was out on an errand for Gary. The man was slightly terrifying, large as he was wide with a head of wavy black hair and a permanent scowl on his face. He had a scar over his right eye that stretched down to his cheek from where—allegedly— he'd been attacked by an intoxicated centaur. The centaur had gotten a lucky swipe in, or so the story went, before Lord Tremaine had removed all his kneecaps in the space of thirty seconds. Lord Tremaine was not to be trifled with, and Todd stayed as far away from him as possible. If he'd found an empty alley and jerked off furiously, that was no one's business but his.

Todd cleared his throat. "He likes to be called Sir?"

Tina laughed obnoxiously. "Yes, he's quite kinky. I don't like it, but he's rich and when he chooses me, I'll change him until he's exactly as I want him. After all, that's the point of getting married."

Justin snorted. "Or he'll choose *me* and take me away from this hovel to live in his manor outside of the city." He reached over and patted Tina's hand. "You can visit when we're not busy with his dick in my ass."

"You slut," Tina growled. "He'll *never* choose you. You've slept with half of Lockes."

"And you've slept with the other half," Justin reminded her.

"I have *needs*. It is *not* polite to slut shame a woman. My body, my choice."

"You just did the same to me!"

"You're a man," Tina said flatly. "No one gives a crap about what men do."

"I guess that means I'll go too," Todd said, more to himself than anyone else.

Once again, Justin and Tina turned to stare at him. "What was that?" Justin asked.

"Yes, Todd," Tina said sweetly. "What was that?"

Blushing, Todd pushed himself through it. "You said every eligible man or woman was invited to attend. I'm eligible."

Tina's lips tugged down into a half-sneer. "You're just the help. You'll be too busy to attend a ball."

"Far too busy," Justin agreed. "In fact, I have a list of chores for you to do that'll last at least the next seven weeks."

"Children," Gary said, clomping into the room, his horn twinkling with an ethereal light. "You're being so mean. Stop it. Todd is right, of course. He *is* an eligible man and can attend if he so chooses."

Tina and Justin gaped at their father, and Todd tried his level best not to smile. He was surprised Gary had spoken up for him, but he wasn't going to try and fight it. Maybe Gary wasn't so bad, after all.

"But," Gary said, drawing out the word until it was at least twelve syllables long. "That doesn't mean he can shirk his responsibilities here at home. Todd, if you finish all your chores by the time the ball happens next week, you can attend."

"Thank you," Todd whispered.

Gary grinned at him. "I wouldn't thank me quite yet." He tapped his glowing horn against the table. A bright light flashed, and when it dimmed, a long list lay on the table, spilling out onto the floor and extending all the way to Todd's feet. "This is the list of chores I created, with help from Justin and Tina. We only want the best for our B&B, and our guests deserve our gratitude, don't you think?"

Todd's stomach sank as he looked at the list. "You want me to rebuild the *chimney*?" he asked incredulously.

"Not quite," Gary said. "I want you to rebuild the chimney *after* you've done the first two hundred and seventy-three items on the list. It's why their numbered, you simple boy. Rebuilding the chimney is number two hundred and seventy-four, right after creating a cream that will get rid of these damn crow's feet around my eyes, and right before finding a type of spoon I saw thirty years ago in a market in Meridian City that I absolutely must have right this second even though I haven't thought about it in decades. Do all of this, and yes, you may attend. In fact, I insist upon it."

Justin and Tina smiled.

OVER THE NEXT WEEK, Todd worked as hard as he ever had. He barely slept, working on the list Gary had given him with an intensity that should have scared him. He'd gotten Gary's word, and he wouldn't let the opportunity go to waste.

Gary pronounced his eye cream marginally acceptable, and seemed flustered when Todd presented him with the exact spoon he'd been looking for, having traded for it with an oily man who specialized in exotic spoons. On the morning of the ball, Todd marked off the last item on the list, face and hands caked with dust from having spent the night rebuilding the chimney to Gary's specifications.

"Yes," Gary said flatly, gaze running over the list. "I guess… you finished everything. Huh. I did not expect that." He glared at Todd as he raised his head. And then he smiled, and Todd's blood turned to ice. "Except…"

"Except," Todd said, hands curling into fists.

"What are you going to wear?" Gary said, smile widening. "You can't go looking like *that*. This is a ball, Todd, not a swap meet in an abandoned field. You're just going to embarrass me looking like you are." He paused, considering. "And yourself, of course."

Todd looked down. His trousers were covered in dust, his shirt torn at the hem. Gary was right. He couldn't go looking like this, but none of his finer clothes fit anymore. He'd shot up to almost six feet tall in the last couple of years, and his fanciest suits would be too short and tight.

He hung his head. "No, I suppose I can't go looking like this."

Gary smacked his lips. "Oh, poor Todd. Nothing ever seems to work out, does it? Ah, well. At least you tried. Take heart in knowing at least no one can take *that* from you."

He left Todd sitting by himself, the chore list forgotten.

TODD TRUDGED UP TO THE ATTIC, defeated and heartsore. He tried to convince himself that it didn't matter, that Sir wouldn't have noticed him even if he'd gone, not with people like Justin and Tina in attendance. They were beautiful in ways Todd wasn't. At the very least, their ears didn't stick out from the sides of their heads.

He entered the attic and closed the hatch. The afternoon sun cast shadows on the floor as light streamed through the window. He was about to lay face down on his bed when Ryan ran out from behind a row of boxes in the corner of the attic. "Todd!" he said, practically tripping over his own feet. "*Todd.* Hurry! Sam needs help!"

Todd jerked his head up as Ryan turned around and ran back toward the boxes. Todd hurried after him, hoping that Sam wasn't too hurt.

He skidded to a stop when he rounded the boxes, jaw dropping.

"Surprise!" Sam and Ryan shouted.

There, resting upon an old coat rack, was the finest suit Todd had ever seen. The trousers were green like summer grasses. A white button-down shirt sat underneath a vest of black leather, inlaid with golden thread that looked like shooting stars. Todd raised a shaking hand, touching the clothing he'd never seen before. The fabric of the shirt was soft, and the vest looked like it'd fit him perfectly.

"Where did this come from?" Todd whispered.

"We made it!" Sam said. "We measured you when you were sleeping—and nothing else!—and then Ryan and I gathered the materials and with Tiggy's help, made you this suit for the ball!"

"You made this," Todd repeated.

"Hell yeah we did," Sam said. "Rats are amazing. Not only can we go for weeks without drinking water and have excellent memories, we're also fantastic tailors. Weird, right? Rats are the best."

"You did this for me?" Todd asked, still disbelieving what he was seeing.

"Yep," Ryan said, leaning against Sam. "We saw how hard you were working, and we wanted to help you out so you can go to the ball and try to woo Sir."

Todd sniffled, eyes burning. "I don't know about all of that. He probably wouldn't even notice that I was there."

"Bullshit," Sam muttered. "Dude, you're hot in that sort of way people would say, 'Yeah, I guess I can see that. He's not for me, but someone might like it.'"

"Wow," Todd said. "That's…. something."

"I mean, you're not *bad* looking, especially for a human. Your ears are rad as balls. Ryan's are better, but yours are right up there."

"My ears are only second to Ryan's," Todd repeated dubiously. "Do…do you know what compliments are, or…?"

"Sir won't know what hit him," Ryan said, whiskers twitching. "You'll see. Come on, put it on so we can make sure it fits."

It did. It fit like a dream. The shirt was a little tight across the shoulders, and the trousers advertised his business downstairs more than he cared to admit, but other than that, Todd almost didn't recognize himself as he looked in the cracked and dusty mirror, Sam sitting on his shoulder, trying to fix the collar of his shirt. "Damn, boy," Sam said. "If I wasn't with the love of my life and was cracked out of my mind, I'd hit that."

"You stay away from Sam!" Ryan snapped as he tied Todd's boots. "You get your own man."

"That's what he's gonna do," Sam reminded him. "You know you're my one and only. No one does tail play like you."

"Darn right," Ryan muttered as he pulled the bootlaces tight. "There. All done. Well? What do you think?"

"I think this is one of the nicest things anyone has ever done for me," Todd murmured as he turned this way and that, studying his reflection. "Thank you. Both of you. I won't forget this."

"Aw," Sam said, rubbing his nose against Todd's cheeks. "You got this, dude. We believe in you. You'll see. Tonight is going to be the best night of your life. Make sure you douche before you go in case Sir wants to get all up in your butthole. A good bottom knows how to prepare for his top. Oh, that reminds me. I also made you a douche out of butter and lilacs! Is there *anything* I can't do?"

AS THE SKY BEGAN TO DARKEN, Todd—not freshly douched, no matter how much Sam said he needed to: "I was just kidding about the butter!"—descended from the attic, his fine clothes catching the candlelight and making him feel better than he had in a long time. He heard Gary and Tina and Justin gathering in the foyer. Steeling himself, he took a deep breath and approached the stairs.

The first step creaked, causing Gary's head to jerk toward him. "There you are, Todd. I need you to get the… earrings from… what are you *wearing*?" He sounded breathlessly irritated.

Tina and Justin also looked up at him, Justin frowning hard, Tina's face pinched.

Todd brushed his hands down his front as he walked down the stairs. He wanted to curl in on himself but wouldn't give them the satisfaction. He was his father's son, and he would hold his head high.

"Something I threw together," he said. "As you reminded me, I need to look my best for the ball."

"*Dad*," Tina snarled. "You said he'd never go!"

"You *promised*," Justin whined.

Gary snapped out of his daze, shaking his head. "Children, we discussed this." He smiled, though it didn't reach his eyes. "Todd completed his chores and found acceptable clothing. Of course he can attend."

Todd nodded but didn't speak.

A strange expression crossed Gary's face, too quick for Todd to parse through it. Then Gary said, "Well, let's go. We don't want to be late. The rain has finally let up, so we'll want to head out in case it returns. And careful, careful, children! The streets are muddy. Wouldn't want to get anything on your fine clothes."

Tina and Justin smiled at the same time. "Of course, Father," Justin said.

"Yes, Father," Tina agreed. "I would just *hate* to have something happen."

Tina went to the door first, followed by Justin. Gary trailed after them, leaving Todd to shut the door to the house. Taking a deep breath, he turned to follow the others…

…and gasped when mud was flung at him, streaking him from head to toe.

"Oh *no*!" Gary cried as he continued to kick up mud from the street in Todd's direction. "I can't get it off my *hooves*. It's *everywhere*! Oh my. Oh dear. Oh no. Get off, you bedeviled mud! You're so sticky and wet!"

Todd couldn't move as splat after splat of mud coated his face, his chest, his trousers. It stung his eyes, but his arms weren't working. He could only stand there as Gary stopped kicking, Tina and Justin bent over, hands wrapped around their waists, laughing as hard as he'd ever seen them. A strange buzzing noise filled Todd's head, followed by a wave of black shame that caused his vision to narrow into pinpoints.

It was about this time that Todd wished he'd grown up differently and had no qualms in committing a triple homicide. Unfortunately for Todd, his mother and father had done right by him, and though his fingers twitched dangerously, he managed to keep from lunging at Gary and strangling him until his eyes popped out of his head, his tongue lolling out of his mouth as a death rattle rumbled in his throat.

Mud sloughed off him, splatting onto the ground as the last drops of rain fell. Gary pranced on the cobblestone road, mane flipping over his head. "Oh dear," Gary said, voice filled with barely disguised glee. "I am so sorry, Todd! I don't know what I was thinking. What an absolute mess you are. You can't go to the ball looking like that! You should go get changed."

"I have no other clothes," Todd said through gritted teeth.

Gary snorted sparks of pink and yellow. "How disappointing! Well, I suppose you'll just have to stay here. Be a love, would you? Have tea ready for when we return. I expect it'll be late, so you'll have to stay up and watch for us. Come, children! Your future husband awaits."

Tina and Justin continued to laugh as they followed their father down the road, rounding a corner out of sight.

Todd couldn't help the tear that slid down his cheek as he turned back toward the house.

"WHAT THE FUCK?" Sam snarled when Todd climbed back into the attic. "What happened? You were gone for, like, five minutes!"

"Gary," Todd said dully. "He…" The words wouldn't come out no matter how hard Todd tried. Trembling, he began to remove the clothes, grimacing at the mud on his skin. The clothes fell to the ground with a wet *splat*. Wearing only his underwear, Todd stumbled toward his bed. He knew he needed to wash up, but he didn't have the strength. He collapsed on the bed, curling up with his knees to his chest, mud smearing against the comforter and pillow.

Sam and Ryan sniffed the clothes, muttering to themselves about the evils of unicorns, and how they'd have their revenge. Ryan said he'd leave droppings in the kitchen. Sam told him to think bigger, and that they'd have to shit in Justin's mouth when he was sleeping. Both agreed this might be a step too far, and that they'd table the discussion for now.

Todd didn't move as the rats climbed onto the bed, Sam laying a paw on his shin. "Are you all right, dude? I'm sorry this happened. You didn't deserve this."

"Sam's right," Ryan said quietly. "You're a good guy, Todd. Also, if it makes you feel better, that underwear does nothing to hide your penis. Congrats! It seems pretty big, but then I'm a rat, so most things are big to me."

Todd moaned, turning his face into the pillow to hide his tears. He couldn't understand how it'd gotten so bad. He'd done his best, but it apparently wasn't good enough. He wished his mother and father were here.

He flinched when Sam's whiskers brushed against his face. He opened his eyes, Sam inches away, nose twitching.

"Hey, champ," Sam said. "I know it seems bad right now, but you can't let this get you down. It's what they want, to see you so defeated. You can't let them win."

"They already did," Todd whispered. "I don't know what I was thinking to begin with. It was never going to work out. Even if I'd gone, Sir would've seen all the other pretty people and ignored me. I'm used to it by now."

"Stop it," Sam snapped. "You're the coolest human I know. If Sir didn't notice that, then he sucks too. You'll find someone, dude. I promise. A big, burly man with a stern disposition that hides how soft his heart is. You'll see. He'll spank you until you're screaming and then put soothing cream on your butt and bring you strawberries as he tells you all the things he loves about you."

"Oh, how I wish that were true," Todd said. "But it's not to be. I'm going to be alone, trapped in this house and forced to do whatever they tell me to. I'll never escape."

Sam sighed as Ryan joined him. "You gotta have hope," Sam said. "Without hope, you'll sink into despair."

"Sam's right," Ryan said, patting Todd on the cheek. "It'll turn out all right in the end. You have to believe."

Todd rolled onto his back, looking out the window. The sky was fading into darkness, and the stars were appearing, little twinkling lights that caused a lump in Todd's throat. "I wish I could. I wish I could with all my might. I wish, I wish, I wish—"

A loud crash from downstairs, followed by cursing.

Todd shot up in his bed, heart thundering. "What was that?"

Sam ran to the end of the bed, head cocked as he stared at the hatch that led down into the house. "Did they come back? Quick! Find a belt you can use as a garrote to slip around their necks until they vomit and die!"

"Why don't you have a sword?" Ryan muttered. "Swords are wicked awesome." His ears were stiff above his head as he listened. "It sounds like only one person."

"A robber," Sam breathed. "They're coming to steal our stuff! We have to stop them. I saw this play once about a kid left alone in his house and two men came to steal from him. He created a series of ever-increasing diabolical traps to thwart the robbers. It was played for laughs, but the kid was a fucking psychopath. We should do it. Get cans of paint and tie them to strings!"

Todd rose from the bed, creeping toward the hatch. He lifted it carefully, wincing at the creak of the hinges. He held his breath as he peered down into the house. It sounded as if someone was in the kitchen, but he couldn't tell what they were doing.

And though he was frightened, it was smothered in a heavy blanket of anger that fell onto his shoulders. Who the hell did they think they were? Todd was tired of this shit, and with a furious growl, he descended the ladder, Sam and Ryan jumping down after him.

They crept down the hall toward the stairs, listening at the movement coming from below. Todd thought he heard someone muttering, but he couldn't be sure. They reached the bottom step and tiptoed toward the kitchen, Sam and Ryan staying close to Todd's bare feet.

He pressed himself against the wall, sliding down inch by inch until he reached the entryway to the kitchen. Taking a deep breath, he tilted his head around the corner.

A strange figure sat at the table, drinking a cup of tea. Todd gasped at the sight. It appeared to be a…woman? Possibly. He couldn't be sure. She wore thigh-high red boots made of shiny leather, her legs long and lean, the muscles in her thighs strong. Her sharp fingernails were painted black, matching the barely decent strips of fabric that crisscrossed her body, hiding her business, but only just. Her skin was lovely and pale, her arms covered in bangles that knocked together when she lifted her teacup once more. The woman's hair was white, cascading down her shoulders, the ends curled up. She didn't look at them as she said, "Todd, won't you join me?" Her voice was husky and sweet, though tinged with something akin to danger.

"Who are you?" Todd croaked.

"Ah," the woman said. "I'm the answer to your wish."

"Holy shit," Sam said, scurrying into the kitchen and circling the woman's chair. "Lady dude, I don't know who the fuck you are, but I want to be you when I grow up."

The woman smiled down at Sam. "But then you wouldn't be

you, and the world would be much darker because of that. Also, I'm one of a kind, so fuck off."

"I love you," Sam breathed feverishly.

The woman chuckled. "Of course you do."

"Hello, ma'am," Ryan said nervously as he stepped into the kitchen. "You are the scariest thing I've ever seen, but in a good way. I think. Please don't rob us."

The woman snorted elegantly. "You have nothing here I want. Todd, if you please. Join me so we can begin."

Todd hesitated, but did as he was asked. He stayed as far away from the woman as possible, back pressed against the counter. The woman tracked every step he took, her smile widening as her gaze crawled along his body. Todd realized he was streaked with mud and only wearing underwear. He covered his junk as he blushed furiously.

"Hmm," the woman said. "I can work with this. Not quite a blank canvas, but still. There's something there." She tapped her fingernails against the table, never looking away from Todd.

"Who are you?" Todd asked again.

The woman rose from her chair. She was much taller than Todd expected. She seemed to dwarf the kitchen, her presence undeniable. "I have been called many names in my long life. But you may call me Mama. I'm your Fairy Drag Mother."

"My *what*?" Todd blurted.

"In your heart of hearts you wished upon the stars," Mama said. "And I heard you. I appear to those who are in need of me, those who are kind and good but who also need some help in getting a piece of ass."

"That settles it," Sam announced. "You're the best person I've ever met in my life. No offense, Todd. You're all right." Then, under his breath, "But not as cool as Mama."

Dazed, Todd could only nod.

Mama said, "We have a lot of work ahead of us. I'm asking you to trust me. I will help you get to the ball and make an entrance the likes of which Verania has never seen. What happens after is up to you, but I will give you the tools in order to land a man."

"I have no idea what's going on," Todd said faintly.

"She's a *fairy*," Ryan hissed at him. "Listen to her before she eats your pancreas!"

Mama waved her hand. "I already had pancreas for lunch, so I'm good. Now, Todd. From what I understand, you're hoping to meet Sir, is that correct?"

"Ye-es?" Todd said or asked, he wasn't sure.

Mama clapped her hands. "Perfect! Now, hold still. This might feel unpleasant."

Before Todd could react, Mama wriggled her nose, pursed her lips, and said, "Flora Bora Slam."

An unseen force struck Todd in the chest, knocking him back against the counter. He closed his eyes as his skin heated up, his teeth rattling in their sockets. A wind kicked up from somewhere, washing over him, causing his hair to flop on his head. By the time it died down, Todd was struggling to breathe, gripping the counter behind him.

"Whoa," Sam whispered. "Todd. *Todd.*"

"Look at him," Ryan whispered back.

Todd opened his eyes.

Mama said, "What do you think?"

Todd looked down, eyes bulging as he saw the clothes he wore. His feet were clad in black boots, the buckles a shiny silver. His legs were encased in tight black leather trousers lined with tiny crystals that glittered in the candlelight. His chest was covered in a heavy harness that wrapped around his middle and shoulders, heavy D-rings hanging down. He tugged at one of the rings, disbelieving it was real. He'd never worn anything so fine before, and it settled him in his skin in ways he didn't expect.

"Fuck me," Sam said. "Todd, you got it going *on*. Look at dat ass. Look at it!"

"It's a very nice ass," Ryan agreed.

"Boy's got cake," Mama said. "Best to show the assets."

"Ha," Sam said. "Word play. Nice."

"What the hell?" Todd said. "How did you do this?"

"I'm a fairy," Mama said. "I can do anything. Watch." She looked down at Sam and Ryan at her feet. "Bippity boppity fuck."

Sam and Ryan writhed on the ground before their rat-ness melted away with a loud *pop*! Smoke filled the room. Todd coughed roughly, waving his hand in front of his face. He yelped when the smoke dissipated, revealing two men standing next to Mama. One had a dark complexion, his eyes wide as he rubbed his hands up and down his body. The other was a handsome strong-looking man with wavy blond hair and bright eyes, his mouth hung open as he stared at the other man. "Sam?" he whispered.

The man jerked his head up. "Yeah? That's—*Ryan*? Ach! Gross! Why do we have so much hairless skin! I don't like this! Bad touch, bad touch! We need to…" He frowned, pulling at the waistline of his trousers and looking down. "Oh my gods, look at the size of my dick! It's *huge*. And jiggly. Huh."

"Me too!" Ryan cried, dropping his pants. "Look at it!"

Todd immediately averted his gaze.

"I'm gonna bone you until you're cross-eyed," Sam warned him. "You thought rat sex was hot, just you wait. It's cold outside, so I need to split you like firewood. Also, my fingers have never been this big before, so I need to stick those in you as well just to see what all the fuss is about."

"Aw," Ryan said. "You say the nicest things."

"You will be the coachmen," Mama said, sounding amused. "You'll take Todd to the ball."

"But we don't have a coach," Sam said as Ryan pulled up his pants. "How are we supposed to get him there?"

"We have two legs," Ryan reminded him. "We can always walk." He took an exaggerated step toward Sam and preened when Sam said he was the best walker he'd ever seen before.

Mama rolled her eyes. "Please. Walking is for suckers. Follow me, lovelies." She whirled on her heels, heading toward the back door that led to the barn.

Sam and Ryan grabbed Todd by the arms, dragging him out the door. Todd tried to dig his heels in, but his friends were much stronger as humans then they'd been as rats. They didn't seem to *quite* have the hang of walking on two legs, and they almost fell to the ground once or twice, Sam lamenting his lack of a tail, but he subsided when Ryan told him that his ass certainly didn't need a tail.

They found Mama in the barn, standing in front of Tiggy, who bleated happily as she scratched his ears. "Todd!" Tiggy cried, lips pulled back over his teeth. "Fairy lady says Tiggy gonna be a *stallion.*"

"Tiggy!" Sam said. "It's me, Sam!"

"And Ryan!" Ryan exclaimed, bending down and scooping up hay and shoving it in his pockets. "I need that for later."

Tiggy squinted at them. "Sam? Ryan? You human now?"

"Hell yes we are," Sam said smugly. "Pretty badass humans, if you ask me." Then he frowned. "But this is only temporary, right? I mean, no offense, humans are neat and all, but I like doing rat things. Ryan, stop chewing on the wall!"

Ryan grumbled as he pulled away from the wall, mouth full of wood shavings. He spat a wet wad of wood onto the floor. "Sorry. Force of habit."

"It is temporary," Mama said. "At the stroke of midnight, the magic will end, and you will all return to how you once were."

"Sounds fake, but okay," Tiggy said,

"Why midnight?" Sam asked. "Is that going to be enough time for Todd to woo Sir?" He glanced at Todd before looking back at Mama. "He's a little…shy."

"Fine," Mama said. "Twelve thirty."

"Breaking my balls here," Sam muttered. "And I can say that now because I have balls."

"Me too," Ryan said. "Three of them."

"Oops," Mama said. "My bad, sorry."

Ryan frowned. "What? Why is that bad?"

Mama ignored him, looking back at Tiggy. She sucked in a breath and blew it out directly in his face. Tiggy staggered back in his stall, collapsing onto the ground out of sight. Another poof of smoke rose in the stall, and when it cleared, a beautiful black stallion stood, his coat shiny, his mane a smokey gray. "Tiggy a *horse*!" Tiggy cried as he pranced around the stall. "Horse Tiggy is best Tiggy!"

"Now," Mama said. "I need a pumpkin."

"A pumpkin?" Todd asked. "For what?"

"For the carriage, of course."

Todd scratched the back of his neck. "Uh, I don't have a pumpkin. I don't even know where to get one at this time of night. I think I have a cucumber in the kitchen. Would that work? No, wait. We ate that last week."

"A cucumber," Mama repeated.

"I have no idea what's happening!" Todd snapped. "If you'd *warned* me about all of this, I would have stocked up on produce!"

"Gods," Mama muttered. "This job isn't as easy as it used to be." She shook her head. "No matter. A bucket. You have that at least, don't you?"

"He has so many buckets," Sam said. "Like, I've never seen someone own that many buckets before."

"We have four," Todd retorted.

"Right," Sam said slowly. "That's a shit ton of buckets, dude. What are you, a bucket factory? This fuckin guy."

"I found one," Ryan said, holding a metal pail out to Mama.

She nodded. "Set it on the floor and step back."

Ryan did as she asked before grabbing Sam and pulling him away. Sam laughed, and then they were eating each other's faces. They apparently weren't used to human teeth and tongues, and Todd gagged when Sam licked Ryan's face repeatedly while Ryan tried to bite Sam on the forehead.

Mama raised her hands and said, "Mothercracker."

The bucket rattled on the ground as it began to twist and grow, metal creaking loudly in the confines of the barn. Tiggy neighed as Sam said, "Don't put your tongue in my *eye*, you jerk!" An explosion of light and air filled the barn, Todd covering his face with his hands, breathing heavily. When the magical storm faded, he dropped his hands and gaped.

There, sitting before him, was a metal carriage, with four oversized wheels, the spokes lined with sharp spikes. At the front was an ornate steel bench covered in red fabric the color of blood. The doors to the passenger seats were black and carved with fire-breathing dragons.

Todd didn't move as Ryan hooked Tiggy up to the front of the carriage. Tiggy accepted the bit in his mouth easily, winking at Todd. "Look!" he said through a mouthful of metal. "Tiggy kinky! Pull on my reins!"

"Yes, this is going to go so well," Mama said. She looked at Todd. "Remember: twelve thirty, and the magic will end. You'll be as you once were."

Todd shook his head. "Shouldn't I be as I always am now? If I hope to woo Sir, don't I need to be myself?"

"You are," Mama said. "Just with a little extra. Oh! That reminds me. One last thing you need to complete the outfit." She snapped her fingers, Todd yelped when a mask appeared in his hands. It matched his outfit, black and lined with crystals with two holes for his eyes, and a raised ridge for his nose. The ends of the mask curled up wickedly, giving the appearance of horns.

"Why are you doing this?" Todd asked as he traced his finger over the mask.

"Because I love love," Mama said, not unkindly. "It is the greatest force on this planet, and one that pierces all the darkness."

"Wow," Todd breathed in awe.

"And you also need to get fucked within an inch of your life."

"There it is," Sam said as he climbed up onto the bench. "Todd, we're wasting time. Put on the mask and get in. Operation Land Todd a Dom is a go. Tiggy?"

"Ready!" Tiggy said.

"Ryan?"

"Having so little hair covering my entire body is weird," Ryan muttered as Sam helped him up onto the bench. "I'm cold."

"Todd, get your ass in gear!"

Todd startled, and moved toward the carriage. Before he stepped into the carriage, he looked at Mama. "Thank you. I think. I reserve the right to take that back if this all blows up in my face."

Mama shrugged. "Honestly, it could go either way. But remember, Todd: the clothes do not make the man. You have to dig deep within and find your fire. Burn brightly, and all will be in awe of you."

"Great," Todd mumbled. "Because *that's* something I'm capable of." He sat down on the carriage seat and Mama closed the door behind him with a terrible finality.

"Don't fuck this up," Mama said. "You only get this one chance. Make the most of it."

Todd slumped in the seat, mask resting in his lap. "How do I know if I'm doing it right?"

"Easy," she said. "If you find yourself bent over a table with an ass full of lube, then you're golden."

"*What?*" Todd wailed. "But I don't—"

"Tiggy!" Sam cried. "To Sir's manor!"

Tiggy reared back, front legs kicking in the air. When they fell back to the ground, Tiggy tore from the barn. Todd turned back to look at Mama, but she was gone, a cloud of glitter swirling in the air.

THE BALL WAS IN FULL SWING by the time they arrived. A boisterous crowd streamed into the stately manor, men and women dressed in leather and wearing masks as they chatted excitedly. Todd gulped when he saw some on all fours with leashes attached to collars around their necks being led by smiling owners who nodded in greeting at those around them. A few others were completely covered in latex from head to toe, taking awkward steps to get up the stairs.

"Okay," Sam said as Tiggy came to a halt. "Todd, you're up. Remember what we talked about. Be confident, but demure. Don't let people walk all over you. Know your boundaries. If you're uncomfortable, say so."

"I'm uncomfortable," Todd said.

Sam ignored him. "Don't be too eager. Make Sir come to you. Always stand in his line of sight, but don't look like you're fishing for his attention." He shook his head. "I really wish you'd douched, dude, but we can't do anything about that now. Now, how do you feel about nipple clamps?"

"Badly!"

"Oh. Well, then I guess it's a good thing I don't have any. Now that I think about it, I don't know why I asked. And if I'm being *really* honest, I've never been to a human party before, so I have no idea what's going to happen. If there's cake, bring some for us."

"Ooh," Ryan said. "Get me a corner piece. Those are the best ones."

"Okay!" Sam said happily. "That's it. We've taught you all we can. Go."

"*That's* your advice?" Todd demanded.

Sam shrugged. "I'm a rat. I don't know three quarters of what I'm talking about. Get out. Ryan and I are going to find a dark corner and do things to each other that's better left to your imagination. Here's a hint: it's gonna get weird."

"So weird," Ryan agreed. "I'm apparently a very bendy human. I'm pretty sure I can put my hands flat against the ground without bending my legs."

"Oh my gods," Sam whispered. "Todd, get. The fuck. *Out*."

Todd stepped out of the carriage, sweat trickling down his back. He raised the mask, setting it on his face. It fit perfectly, as if it were made for him and only him. It didn't have a strap to hold it in place, but it didn't seem to matter.

He took a deep breath, letting it out slowly. "Okay. I can do this. I can do this. Sam, would you—"

He turned in time to see the carriage driving away, Sam cackling as Ryan did something with his mouth that Todd wished he hadn't seen.

He approached the stairs, jumping when a man bumped into him. The man—a burly fellow with a handlebar mustache and a gap between his front teeth—grinned at him. "And who do we have here?" he purred, pulling himself to his full height. "Are you alone, boy? Where's your Daddy?"

"He died when he fell down the stairs," Todd said. "But I think my stepfather murdered him, even though it was ruled an accident."

The man blinked. "What."

"Yeah," Todd said. "It was this whole thing."

"What," the man said again.

"Gotta go," Todd muttered, hurrying up the stairs and getting in line. He popped his knuckles as he approached a heavyset woman standing near the door, a list in her hands. She marked off each name when she was told who was entering, jerking her head toward the entrance. Music poured out through the open doors, sounding like a cat being rubbed against violin strings. It wasn't to Todd's tastes, but then he'd never been to this kind of party before.

When it was his turn, the woman arched a thin eyebrow at him. "Um," he said. "My name is Todd."

"You married?" she grunted.

"No."

"You have a partner?"

"No. I'm single."

She eyed him up and down, a smile like a sneer tugging at her lips. "Surname?"

He panicked. If someone recognized his name—say, Gary—this would all be over before it began. He thought quickly before blurting, "Haversford."

She glanced down at her list. "Don't see a Todd Haversford on the list. You sure you're at the right place?"

Todd hung his head. "I don't know. I just…needed a night away from everything. Maybe I shouldn't be here. I'll go."

He turned to leave but stopped when the woman cleared her throat. "Oh look," she said. "Silly me. Your name is right here." He watched as she scrawled TODD HAVERSFORD at the bottom of the list before checking if off. "My mistake." Her smile warmed slightly. "Go ahead, kid. Have fun, but only go as far as you're comfortable with, all right? People here know to respect your boundaries, but if anyone gives you shit, you come find me, and I'll take care of it."

"Okay," Todd whispered. "Thank you."

She jerked her head toward the doors before barking, "Next!"

Todd moved into the house, immediately overwhelmed by the sights and sounds around him. The house was magnificent, far bigger than any he'd ever been in before. Lord Tremaine the Firm had obviously done well for himself. The foyer was spacious, opening up under vaulted ceilings. A grand staircase led up to the second floor, but it was roped off, with two men in suits standing in front of it.

Todd followed the crowd past the stairs, neck creaking as he looked around, taking in the manor. He'd never felt so small in his life, and desperately tried to ignore the people pressed against the walls around him in various stages of undress. He passed a room with an open door where a small group had gathered to watch a man being whipped, his ass red as he demanded more, more. The woman with the whip—her head shaved, her teeth bared—did as requested, and the man thanked her profusely.

Todd's blood heated at the sight. He didn't think it was for him, but then he'd never tried. He wasn't quite sure how he felt about pain. It scared him a bit, but then the woman caressed the man's face with such love in her eyes that Todd had to look away. If only someone could look at him that way.

The line of people moved toward two open double doors, and Todd gasped when he saw the ballroom. It seemed bigger than his entire house, a huge chandelier of crystal hanging from the ceiling at the center. The walls were white brick, the dark wood of the floor gleaming as if freshly polished. A group of musicians had set up in the corner—mostly nude, which was a new experience for Todd—plucking their strings sweetly. Tables had been set up at the edges of the room, people nibbling on diced fruits and slivers of meat, drinking from flutes of sparkling water. There didn't seem to be any alcohol, which Todd was comforted by. He'd like a little liquid courage, but the tradeoff meant that no one else would be too intoxicated, or so he hoped.

He couldn't believe the amount of people in the ballroom. There had to be hundreds. His heart sunk to his feet. If everyone was here for Sir, how would he even have a chance? Add to the fact that there appeared to be…demonstrations happening, men and women in various stages of undress, some attached to large wooden crosses and getting flogged, others laying out on tables while hot candle wax was poured on their bare chests and stomachs. There was even a man with a dark complexion laying on a table in the middle, his body covered with slices of oranges and kiwis, guests plucking pieces up and eating them. Todd was not going to eat food off a naked man. He had his limits, after all.

He was so distracted by the sights and sounds of the room that he didn't watch where he was going. He bumped into someone and was ready to apologize when he froze. A horn turned in his direction, and bile rose in his throat as Gary eyed him up and down. "Watch where you're going," Gary snapped.

"Sorry," Todd said, dropping his voice an octave. "My apologies."

"Yes, you should be sorry." Gary stared at him for a moment before turning back to the small crowd amassed around him.

Todd ducked behind a group of men and women who wore masks completely covering their heads, zippers across their mouths. That had been too close. Thank the gods for the mask. He needed to be more careful. Gary hadn't recognized him, but that didn't mean he wouldn't at some point. Tina and Justin, too, though Todd couldn't see them. He went to a darkened corner of the room, trying to make himself invisible. Maybe he shouldn't have come. It wasn't as if—

The musicians ended with a flourish, and everyone turned as one toward the back of the ballroom, looking at a large set of doors. No one spoke. The silence was unnerving. Even the people getting hot wax poured on them fell quiet, turning their heads, dreamy smiles on their faces.

Todd grabbed a flute of water from a passing waiter, sucking it down, coughing as it dribbled out onto his lips. His throat was parched, and a strange pressure pulsed behind his right eye. He wanted to leave, but he couldn't make his feet work. He wished he'd just stayed at home with Sam and Ryan and Tiggy.

But these thoughts faded when the doors opened, and *he* came into the ballroom.

Lord Tremaine the Firm—also known as Sir—walked confidently through the doors. Todd's knees grew weak at the sight of him. Sir looked as dangerously handsome as Todd remembered, the scar on his face white and puckered, stark against his dark complexion. His black, curly hair fell onto his shoulders, his mouth twisted in an approximation of a smile. He wore a sleeveless vest with no shirt underneath, his chest hair black and gray. A thick vein ran down his right arm, the muscles bunching as he walked with confidence. He was tall—he had at least six inches on Todd—and his presence couldn't be denied. He knew what he looked like and made sure everyone else did too without so much as a word. He frightened Todd, but it was a *good* fright, the same feeling Todd got when he walked down the stairs and missed the last step, momentarily falling until landing with a jarring crash.

Sir walked into the center of the room, next to the table with the man covered in food. He stroked the man's cheek before plucking an apple slice from his throat and eating it. His jaw ticked as he chewed. Todd sighed as Sir swallowed.

"He's so fucking hot," Todd heard a woman whisper, and he silently agreed. "Gods, I hope he picks me."

Her friend laughed. "You couldn't handle him, dearie. Sir likes things done his way, or no way at all. You wouldn't last a week with him."

Todd wasn't sure anyone could. He straightened when Sir cleared his throat. When he spoke, his voice was softer than Todd expected, though it still carried in the quiet of the ballroom.

"My friends," Sir said. "Thank you for coming tonight. I hope you find the satisfaction you seek, either by your own hand or the hand of another."

His captivated audience chuckled, whispers rolling through the crowd.

"I see many familiar faces," Sir continued. "Some that I've known intimately, others who have *wished* for the same. And while I ask that you partake in whatever your heart desires within the boundaries of consent, tonight is different for me. Two months ago, I turned forty years old. I thought it would be just another day, but I found myself with a feeling I'd never felt before. It wasn't quite loneliness, but something so close, I don't know that it matters. I've lived a fortunate life filled with the finer things and carnal pleasures of the flesh. But I find myself missing the comfort of having a partner, one who I can take care of above all others. While I have enjoyed a non-monogamous lifestyle, I have come to the realization that I need more than that now. I'm not as young as I used to be, and while I'm not concerned with progeny, I can't seem to shake the notion that I want someone to come home to, someone who I can hold in great regard. I have asked you all here tonight, friends and strangers alike, in hopes to find this person. This may be a fool's errand, but I won't know unless I try." He grinned, razor-sharp. "That doesn't mean I've grown soft. I'm still the same Sir you've known, and I will have your respect."

The audience applauded, Todd joining in though his hands shook.

"Let us celebrate!" Sir shouted above the din. "Tonight is a night for love and revelry. Thank you for coming, and I look forward to meeting the eligible citizens of the City of Lockes."

The crowd surged forward, descending upon Sir, blocking Todd's line of sight. He sighed, slumping back against the wall. He'd never felt more out of place in his life. He didn't know anyone here aside from Gary and Justin and Tina, though he did recognize a few of the upper crust, having seated them in Dad's restaurant. He couldn't let them know he was here, fearing Gary would make a scene.

And with that, Todd decided he'd stay in the corner. He'd give it an hour, and if nothing changed, he'd leave to find Ryan and Sam and head home. At the very least, he came. No one could take that away from him.

THE NIGHT WORE ON. Moans and wails filled the ballroom. Todd saw glimpses of Sir amongst the people, glaring at the men and women who threw themselves at him like they had a right to. Sir met each them with a dark smile, touching their faces as they quivered in front of him. Others began to dance in a waltz far more risqué than Todd had ever seen before, causing him to blush and look down at his feet. Still others disappeared in pairs or groups, their intent clear as they rubbed bare flesh with heavy hands.

He was mostly ignored, hidden in the shadows. Every now and then, someone would see him. Once, a man with large feathers hanging from his ears attempted to talk to him, but Todd mumbled nonsense until the man gave up and left him alone.

Eventually, Todd felt a pressure in his bladder, and he sighed, pushing himself off the wall. He needed to find a restroom. He would leave, after, he decided. He'd seen enough. There was no way he'd talk to Sir, not with how many people were here. He should've expected this, but he still felt a twinge of sorrow. He didn't know why he'd thought more would happen. But still, he'd managed to escape the attic for at least one night. That had to count for something. He'd return home, curl up in his bed and try to get some sleep before he was put to work in the morning.

He pushed his way through the crowd, fumbling over his words as he asked one of the wait staff where the restroom was. He was pointed to the doors Sir had just walked through. "It's the first door on the left," the waiter told him before dismissing him completely.

Todd went through the doors, stepping out into a long hallway lined with paintings of flowers and boats on an angry ocean, the sky dark, the large waves like mountains. He found the door to the bathroom, but when he tried to open it, something slammed against the other side, followed by a heated growl.

"Sorry," Todd said, backing up slowly. "I'll just…wait my turn."

He stumbled away from the door, not looking where he was going. His back hit another door, and he yelped when it opened, causing him to fall on his ass. He winced at the low flash of pain in his rear, bringing his knees up to his chest. "What are you *doing*?" he snapped at himself. "You don't belong here. Gods, I can't do anything right."

He rose to his feet, meaning to leave the room before he was caught somewhere he shouldn't be. He paused when he saw the room appeared to be an office of sorts: a large, oak desk sat near the far wall, covered in folders and loose sheets of paper, thick scrolls with scratchy writing.

And books! So many books, it took Todd's breath away. Shelves lined the walls from floor to ceiling, hundreds—no, *thousands*—of tomes on display. Todd went to the shelves, fingers trailing over the titles. He chuckled when he saw three copies of *The Butler and the Manticore*, a book his mother had sworn by when she was alive. He plucked one from the shelf, flipping through the pages. He'd read it himself a time or two, trying to see what his mother had. It wasn't exactly his favorite, but she had cherished it. He allowed the memories of her sitting in the bay window to fill his head, her forehead scrunched as her eyes darted along the words.

"I miss you," he whispered, putting the book back on the shelf. "I wish you were here." Then, "Well, not *here* here, because that would scar me more than I already am."

He was about to turn and leave the room—hopefully the bathroom would be vacant—when he heard voices from out in the hall. Panicking, Todd looked around, trying to find someplace he could hide. The only door was the one he'd come through. Behind the curtains? Out the window?

The voices grew louder, and Todd ran towards the desk, shoving the chair back and hiding underneath, his breath harsh in his ears. He covered his mouth, trying to calm his racing heart as a voice said, "I thought this door was closed."

Todd's eyes bulged.

That voice belonged to Sir.

"Oh no," Todd whispered into his hands.

"We could lock it, Lord Tremaine," another voice said. "Let me know when you've finished, and I'll make sure of it. Is there anything you require?"

"No," Sir said. "Thank you, Gabriel. I won't be long."

"You shouldn't be," Gabriel scolded, and Todd couldn't believe he was talking to Sir like that. "This ball is for you. It wouldn't do to have you hiding away in your office. You're supposed to be out there finding a spouse."

"I know," Sir muttered, the floor creaking as he stepped into the room. "But it's not working out as I'd hoped. Everyone out there is trying too hard."

"Or you're just not trying hard enough," Gabriel retorted. "Lord Tremaine, you wanted this, remember? I served your father, and I promised him before his passing that I would care for you. But you're making that difficult. You say you want to settle down, but then you dismiss everyone who tries to form any sort of connection."

"I can't force it," Sir said, sounding amused. "When I marry, I plan on it being the last relationship I ever have. I'm getting too old for these silly games."

Gabriel sniffed. "At least we're in agreement there. Collect your thoughts, my lord. But if you're not back out in the ballroom in fifteen minutes, I'm dragging you out by your hair."

"Promises, promises," Sir teased. "If only you were a bit more submissive, Gabriel. All our problems would be solved."

Gabriel snorted. "I'm sure my husband would have a thing or two to say about that. And the only reason I do what you tell me to is because I'm in your employ."

"And even then, it's like pulling teeth."

"Yes, yes, your life is so hard. I don't know what I was thinking. My apologies, Lord Tremaine."

"Get out of here," Sir said, sounding absurdly fond. "I promise not to stay in here long. Just a little while to clear my head. And when that's done, I'll return to the ballroom with a smile firmly fixed on my face."

"What about that boy…what was his name? Ah, yes. Justin. Or even his sister, Tina. They come from a good family."

Todd snarled into his hands, teeth scraping against his palms.

Silence.

Then, "Did you hear that?" Sir asked.

"Hear what?"

Todd silently begged the floor to open up and swallow him whole. It did not happen.

"Nothing," Sir said finally. "I thought…Justin, you say. Or Tina. Which ones were they?"

"The ones with the unicorn. Gary, his name is."

Sir groaned. "*Those* two. Right. Beautiful, both of them, but they aren't to be trusted. Gary was trying too hard to pawn them off on me. And Justin and Tina were…"

"Were?" Gabriel prompted.

"Not to my tastes," Sir said. Relief swept over Todd, vast and complicated. "They only seemed to think of themselves, and what *I* could do for *them*."

"Right," Gabriel said slowly. "And you got all of that from the two minutes you spoke with them."

"Gabriel," Sir said in warning, and Todd felt a shiver run down his spine, hot and cold all at the same time. Just one word, but in that tone of voice, Todd thought his heart would explode.

"Whatever," Gabriel muttered. "I'm done with you now. I have things to do. Fifteen minutes, my lord. Not a moment longer."

The door closed. Todd held his breath, hoping that Sir had followed Gabriel.

He hadn't. Todd heard him sigh and mumble something under his breath. The floor creaked once more as Sir moved through the room. Todd tried to make himself small as possible, curling in on himself under the desk. So long as Sir didn't try and sit down in his chair, Todd wouldn't be seen.

But the gods apparently had a devious sense of humor. Sir rounded the desk and sat heavily in his chair, pushing back away from the desk, his thick thighs flexing under his trousers as he rocked back, rubbing a hand over his face. Todd could see the long line of Sir's body, only a couple feet away. He looked massive, the biggest man Todd had ever seen.

And then Sir sat upright, feet firmly planted on the floor as he pulled on the desk, bringing the chair closer. Todd flinched when

Sir's knees nearly brushed his face. Mere inches separated them, and Todd didn't move a muscle as he listened to Sir breathe.

Careful, he thought. *Careful.*

Sir stayed at his desk for what felt like hours, papers shuffling, not speaking a word. And though the fear of discovery still coursed through Todd's veins, he began to relax slightly, Sir a calming presence. Todd wondered what it'd be like if this was real, if he belonged to Sir, sitting at his feet, awaiting his beck and call. Sir would reach down, every now and then, rubbing his hands through Todd's hair, and Todd would know he was a good boy, even without hearing the words. Sir would love him for it, and Todd would never have to be lonely again.

He was lost in this fantasy when Sir said, "How long do you plan on staying down there?" Sir's boot nudging against Todd's shin.

Todd yelped, head bashing the underside of the desk. "Mother*fucker*," he groaned.

Sir scooted his chair back, grinning as he leaned forward, looking underneath the desk. His eyes narrowed when he saw Todd. "And what do we have here?" His smile widened, all teeth. "Are you lost, boy?"

Todd lowered his gaze to the floor, adjusting his mask when it slipped a little on his face. "No," he whispered. "Not...not lost. Just..."

"Just," Sir repeated. "Just what? Hiding in a room where you shouldn't be?" He nudged Todd again, causing him to look up at Sir. The smile faded as Sir studied Todd. "Thought you'd try and get me alone, did you?"

"No!" Todd blurted, wringing his hands. "That's not—I didn't—I swear it's not like that."

"Uh huh," Sir said. "Then, may I ask what the hell you think you're doing?"

"I was trying to find the bathroom," Todd babbled, unable to stop the words pouring from his mouth. "But it was occupied with *sex*, and then I fell in here, and saw all the books and then *you* came in, so I hid."

Sir didn't speak.

"I'm sorry," Todd said, voice pitched high. "I didn't mean it. I shouldn't have come in here. I'll just go." With that, he crawled out from underneath the desk, careful to avoid touching Sir, though the man didn't make it easy as he didn't move an inch. He managed to make it to his feet, Sir's gaze boring into him. He rounded the desk and fled toward the door.

He only made it halfway when Sir growled, "*Stop.*"

Todd did, skin thrumming. The chair creaked behind him as Sir rose. Todd counted his every footstep, getting to six before Sir said, "Turn around."

Todd did, unable to stop himself. He raised his head briefly to find Sir leaning against the front of his desk, arms folded across his considerable chest. Todd averted his gaze to the floor, fingers twitching at his sides.

"Eyes on me, boy," Sir said, and Todd was helpless to do anything but. Sir looked him up and down, and Todd felt every second of it. He tried to keep his breaths even, but he was light-headed, and itching to run as fast as he could. Strange this, as it warred with wanting to obey every word out of Sir's mouth.

Sir didn't move from the desk. "I don't recognize you. Have we met before?"

"No," Todd said.

Sir arched an eyebrow, mouth in a thin line.

"No, *Sir*," Todd said hastily.

"Better," Sir said. "Is this your first time attending one of my celebrations?"

"Yes, Sir."

"How old are you?"

Todd swallowed thickly. "Twenty, Sir."

Sir nodded. "I see. Will you remove your mask?"

A question, not an order, but Todd didn't want to get this wrong. "I'd rather not, if it's all the same to you. Sir."

"Of course," Sir said. "We can keep the charade of anonymity for now if that makes you more comfortable. Your name?"

Another question, but Todd thought he was on shakier ground. He blushed furiously as he said, "I…I like…"

"You like," Sir said.

"Boy is fine," Todd said in a rush. "If it pleases my lord."

"Boy," Sir said, chewing on the word. "I see. Tell me, *boy*, why do you look so nervous? Do I frighten you?"

"Yes," Todd whispered. "Very much, Sir."

"Enough that you want to leave?"

Todd hesitated. Sir seemed to be giving him a way out, but now that it was on offer, Todd wasn't sure if he wanted to take it. "N-no. Sir."

Abruptly, Sir stood upright from the desk, taking two giant steps toward him. Todd closed his eyes and whimpered low in this throat. Sir didn't touch him, though Todd could feel the heat emanating from him. Sir circled him slowly, passing out of sight behind him before reappearing on Todd's other side. Never before had Todd felt so bare, so on display, and though part of him still wanted to run, it was dwarfed by a strange need to make Sir proud. So Todd didn't move, standing stock-still as Sir stood in front of him once more. He barely kept from flinching when Sir raised his hand, brushing his thumb against Todd's bottom lip, the scrape of his skin causing Todd's mind to blank out.

"Lovely," Sir murmured. "Have you ever been with a man before, boy?"

"No, Sir," Todd choked out, Sir's thumb still against his mouth.

"A woman?"

"No, Sir."

"Curious," Sir said, dropping his hand. "And now you find yourself in the den of the beast. Brave, that, for one so innocent. What should I do with you?"

Pull my hair. Smack my ass. Make me kneel. Help me not feel so alone. Todd said none of this, swallowing it down and locking it away.

Sir nodded as if Todd had spoken. He turned on his heels, going back around his desk and sitting in his chair. Todd stayed in the middle of the room, not sure if he'd blown his chances and was being dismissed. He was about to apologize again when Sir said, "I'm thirsty, boy. There's water in a jug near the door." He looked down at the papers on his desk, picked up a pen and began to write. When Todd still hadn't moved after a minute, Sir raised his head slowly, arching an eyebrow. "I said, I'm thirsty."

"Yes, Sir," Todd said hastily, turning around and practically running toward the small table next to the door. He fumbled with the jug, almost dropping it as he picked up a wooden cup. His hands shook as he poured the water, droplets splashing out onto his hand. He kept the cup as level as possible, gripping it with both hands as he brought it to Sir, who didn't look up at him as he set it down. Todd stood awkwardly next to him, unsure of what he was supposed to do next.

He was about to back away slowly when Sir said, "There are pillows in the drawer underneath the bookshelf. Bring me one."

"Yes, Sir," Todd squeaked, rushing toward the drawers he'd seen when he'd come into the office. He opened the top one, gasping when he saw what was inside. Dildos, each bigger than the last, some of rubber, others made of wood. He heard Sir snort behind him as he closed the drawer harshly, causing the bookshelf to shake. He moved to the next drawer. No better, as it held steel handcuffs, scarves of silk, and what looked to be a leather flogger. The last drawer held the pillows he needed. He grabbed the one off the top—white and soft, feeling as if it was filled with feathers— and brought it back to Sir.

"On the floor," Sir said without looking up. "Set it down next to me."

Todd did and stood upright once more, fidgeting, almost hoping Sir would give him another task. It felt good to be useful.

"Do you have any pain in your knees?" Sir asked, scrawling his signature on a scroll.

"My…my knees? Sir?" Todd asked.

"Your knees," Sir agreed. "Do they pain you in any way?"

"No? No, Sir."

"Good. Any other medical issues I need to be aware of?"

Todd's brain fritzed. "Like…"

Sir sighed as if annoyed. "Is there anything that would prohibit you from kneeling?"

"No!" Todd said, far too loudly. "No. I'm…good. Sir."

"Good," Sir repeated. "That remains to be seen. Knees on the pillow. Hands folded behind your back. If at any point you need to move, ask. I don't want you to be uncomfortable. You will not upset me if you need to move."

"Yes, Sir," Todd said, the relief in his voice palpable. "Thank you, Sir." He fell to his knees on the pillow, taking a deep breath and letting it out slowly.

"Back straight," Sir said, still not looking at him.

Todd straightened.

"Good boy," Sir said, and Todd warmed as if his insides burned.

He tried to clear his mind as best he could, casting away all his doubts and nervousness. It wasn't as easy as he'd hoped, but the pillow was soft, the scratch of Sir's pen comfortable. Sir continued to work as Todd knelt next to him. It felt like a dream. He couldn't believe he was here with Sir. If this was all he'd ever get, he'd take it, and gladly.

He was startled from his thoughts when someone knocked on the door. Todd bit his bottom lip hard enough to draw blood, nerves prickling once more.

"Enter," Sir said.

The door opened. Out of the corner of his eye, Todd saw an older man enter, with thin white hair and wearing robes of black and red. "Your fifteen minutes are up," the man said sternly, and Todd knew this to be Gabriel. "Ten minutes ago, in fact. You need to—am I interrupting something?"

"You are," Sir said, though he didn't sound irritated. "I'll be out shortly."

"O...kay," Gabriel said slowly. "People are asking after you, my lord."

"I'm sure they are," Sir muttered, looking up at Gabriel. "The night is still young, Gabriel."

"If you insist."

"I do."

Gabriel chuckled. "My apologies, Lord Tremaine. I'll make sure your guests are otherwise entertained in your absence. A troupe from Meridian City has arrived and will be performing. That should give you enough time to...do what you need to."

That caught Todd's attention. What, exactly, did Sir need to do?

"Noted," Sir said. "I don't want any further interruptions. I'll be out when I'm ready."

"Yes, my lord," Gabriel said, though his gaze was fixed on Todd. He didn't seem upset, merely intrigued. When Todd glanced at him out of the corner of his eye, Gabriel smiled quietly and winked before leaving, closing the door behind him.

"He means well," Sir said lightly. "He helped to raise me along with my father after my mother passed. He thinks that makes him my parent and gives him the right to fuss over me."

"He loves you," Todd croaked out. "Sir."

Sir's pen paused mid-scratch. "He does. And I him. I wouldn't be here today without him." The pen resumed. "Tell me, boy, do you have someone to love you?"

"No," Todd whispered. "Well, maybe a little. I have…friends."

Sir paused again. Then he lay the pen down on his desk and sat back in his chair. He turned his head to look at Todd with an inscrutable expression. "Are your friends here?"

"No, Sir." They were, but not like Sir meant. Also, they were rats in human shape, but that didn't seem to be something to say out loud in case Sir decided he was off his rocker and threw him out on his ass.

"And what of your parents?"

"They…died. My mother when I was young, and my father a few years ago, Sir." Todd sniffled, trying to blink away the burn.

Sir's expression softened. "I see. Thank you for your honesty. It's something I require. I don't like being lied to. Do you understand?"

"Yes, Sir."

"Will you lie to me, even if you think it'd make me happy?"

"Sir?"

Sir frowned. "It was a simple question, boy. Will you lie to me if you think it's what I want to hear?"

Todd started to nod but stopped himself. His parents had always instilled the need for truth in him, no matter what. Though he wasn't sure of his place currently, he had never liked to lie, even though he felt like a fraud. "No, Sir. I wouldn't lie to you, especially when you're wrong."

"Wrong," Sir said, lips quirking. "Do you think I'm wrong often?"

Uh oh. "I have absolutely no idea. Sir."

Sir laughed, a deep sound that warmed Todd's bones. "I am. All the time. But most pretend I'm not, always trying to end up in my good graces, even when I'm clearly in the wrong. Only Gabriel calls me out for my mistakes. That's not how it should be." He rubbed his jaw. "A person who kneels for me must have their own mind. And while I am in control in all ways, I would hope that a person I let close to me understands that I would value their counsel. But that requires trust, and not just from myself. One such as you would need to learn to trust me."

"One such as me, Sir?" Todd asked.

"Yes," Sir said, as if that answered everything. "I'm going to touch you, now." Todd closed his eyes when Sir's hand wrapped around his neck, tugging him forward. Todd allowed it, knees still on the pillow. His forehead pressed against Sir's thigh, his mask making it awkward, but Todd didn't mind. He groaned quietly when Sir's hand moved up to his hair, fingers digging into his scalp. He was aroused, but it felt like a minor thing compared to the sense of peace that bowled through him. He breathed Sir in, leather and clean soap. Sir's grip tightened on his head, holding him in place.

"There," Sir said. "That's a good boy."

Todd trembled but didn't speak, hands still clasped behind his back. He felt detached from his body, as if he were floating like a balloon on a string. His shoulders relaxed, and Sir scratched his nails against his scalp.

"Boys need a firm hand," Sir said as Todd closed his eyes. "Someone to guide them, to help them grow. Direction, but not so much that they can't forge their own path. I want to control you, boy, but only because I see the potential in you. You aren't like the others who've knelt for me before."

"You don't know me," Todd whispered, refusing to open his eyes. He didn't want to see if Sir was upset at his words. He didn't know if his heart could take it.

Sir's hand paused in his hair before the fingers dug in once more. It didn't hurt. It was firm, grounding. "No," Sir said quietly. "I don't. But I will if you allow me the honor. This isn't about just me and what I want. Some might think because I'm dominant, any relationship I'm in would be lopsided. But what they don't realize is that you have just as much power as I do. Perhaps even more so. If anything, for this to work, we'd need to be equals, even if others can't quite see it that way. Is that something you think you can do?"

Todd turned his face into Sir's thigh. "I don't know," he said honestly, voice muffled. "What if I mess up?"

"Then you do," Sir said. "Though it might not be without repercussions, it's my hope that you learn from your mistakes, and avoid making the same one again. But that can be easier said than done. Believe me when I say I know that better than most. I'm not infallible. I have made mistakes, most I regret. I won't demand perfection because that's impossible. All I ask of someone who kneels for me is that they honor the position and understand this isn't one way. I need a partner in all things." He sighed as he brushed Todd's hair off his forehead. "I'm getting older, boy. The things I once wanted aren't what I'm looking for now."

"Is that why you had the ball?"

"It is," Sir said. "Rather, it's why Gabriel demanded we have it. He saw that I was floundering, withdrawing in on myself. It was his hope that I'd meet someone to chase away the loneliness. I thought it a fool's errand, but I find myself not displeased with the results."

Todd flushed, his mouth dry. All of this felt like a dream, as if he'd wake up in his own bed in the attic, Gary and Justin and Tina screaming at him to get out of bed and get to work. He didn't know what he'd do if that happened. "I don't know what I'm doing," Todd whispered. "I'm scared."

"Of me?" Sir asked, no censure in his voice.

Todd shook his head against Sir's thigh. "Not…exactly, Sir."

"Then what are you scared of?"

"Myself." He swallowed past the lump in his throat. "And of how much I want this."

Todd yelped when Sir's hands hooked under his arms, pulling him up as if Todd weighed nothing. It was dizzying, this feeling of floating, and Todd shivered when Sir turned him around, his back against Sir's chest. Strong arms wrapped around him, holding him close, anchoring him in place. Todd couldn't hold his head up, instead letting it fall back against Sir's shoulder, their cheeks scraping together. Sir was bigger than him by quite a bit, but Todd relished in it.

"You're shaking," Sir said, his mouth near Todd's ear.

"I'm sorry. I'm—"

"I didn't ask for an apology," Sir said. "An apology is an implication that you've done something wrong. You haven't. It was merely an observation, boy. Are you cold?"

"No." He tried not to squirm, but Sir wasn't making that easy.

"Ah," Sir said, sounding amused. "Are you warm?"

"Yes," Todd gasped.

"I see." He moved his hands to Todd's chest, fingers dimpling the bare skin around the harness. The noise Todd made when Sir tweaked one of his nipples wasn't something he was proud of, but Sir seemed pleased with it, as he did it again and again. It hurt, but it was a *good* hurt, and Todd felt something hard pressing against his rear. It took him a moment to realize what it was, and when he did, a surge of pride roared through him, clawing at his insides. *He'd* done that to Sir. *He'd* caused that.

Sir's hand rose from his chest and closed around his throat as Sir's lips trailed along his jaw. "Very warm," Sir said. "I can feel your pulse. It's like a little bird."

"Please," Todd whispered, though he didn't know what he was asking for. His brain felt like it was on fire, all coherent thought lost in a sheen of white noise.

Sir chuckled darkly as his nose brushed against the side of Todd's mask. "Oh, am I going to enjoy you." His grip around Todd's throat tightened, not cutting off his air, but then Todd was already having a hard time breathing. "Look at you. Such a good boy. And good boys deserve a reward, don't you think?"

"Yes," Todd said, half out of his mind. "Yes, Sir. Please."

With one hand still on his throat, Sir pressed the other against Todd's chest, running his fingers down to Todd's stomach, fingers flitting against the top of his trousers. Todd thought he was going to dip his hand inside, but instead, Sir went to the front of Todd's trousers, gripping his cock and squeezing. Todd whined lowly, trying to push up against Sir's hand.

"Has anyone every touched you like this?" Sir asked, voice light and almost conversational. It drove Todd up the fucking wall, hearing him like that. As if he wasn't being filthy, as if he had all the time in the world.

"No!"

The grip around his cock tightened. "No *what?*"

"No, Sir!"

Sir laughed again as he let Todd's dick go. Todd thrust his hips in defiance, freezing when Sir growled his name. He deflated, resting back against Sir.

"Good," Sir said, kissing the side of Todd's head. "There you go. That's a very good boy. I'm proud of you. I know what you want. I'll take care of you."

Then his hand returned. Except this time, the deft fingers unfastened Todd's trousers, and Todd cried out when the calloused hand circled his cock, the dry skin rough against his tender flesh. Sir pulled Todd's cock out of his trousers, jerking him once, twice. "You have a pretty cock," Sir said. "Lick." He let Todd's dick go, bringing his hand to Todd's mouth. Todd licked frantically at Sir's palm, tasting skin and a hint of ink from his pen. His tongue went to the webbing between Sir's fingers before Sir pulled his hand away, leaving Todd bereft at the loss.

This time, when Sir gripped him, the wet friction caused Todd to grunt as if punched in the stomach. Sir jacked him slowly, thumb brushing against Todd's slit. "You will not come until I tell you to. Do you understand?"

Todd's mouth fell open, but no sound came out.

Sir's fingers dug into his throat. "Do you understand?"

"Yes!" Todd cried.

"Yes *what*?"

"Yes, Sir! I won't come until you give me permission!"

"Damn right you won't," Sir muttered. He jerked Todd slowly, pinkie finger pressing against Todd's balls. Todd couldn't believe this was happening. He never thought it'd be this good, not even in his wildest dreams. "Good boys listen to those in charge. And I'm certainly in charge of you, aren't I? Look at you. So eager for me. You were waiting for Sir, weren't you? Yes, you were. No one else could have done this for you. They would have tried, but it wouldn't have been anywhere near as good."

"No one," Todd said, wriggling in Sir's lap. "No one else."

"Of course not," Sir snapped. "Because they wouldn't know what to do with a boy like you." He thrust his hips up against Todd's ass. Todd ground down against him before jerking back up against Sir's hand. "It's a good thing I know what boys want. I will ruin you for any other, so much so that you won't even think about anyone else. You're mine, boy, and I will show you why. Come. Now."

Todd let out a strangled yell as he did just that. Spunk shot from his dick, drops hitting his chest, the desk, Sir's hand as he continued to jerk Todd roughly. It became too much, but Sir didn't stop, gripping the head of Todd's cock and *squeezing*. Todd groaned as he arched his back, Sir's hand still around his throat.

"There," Sir whispered. "There, there. You did so well." He let go of Todd's cock, causing it to slap wetly against his stomach. He brought his soiled hand up to Todd's lips. "You've made a mess of me. Clean it up."

Todd didn't hesitate. He licked the spunk from Sir's hand, the taste bitter, but it wasn't like he hadn't tried it before. He was twenty years old, after all, and more than a little kinky. But it tasted different than all the times before, and Todd knew it was because of Sir's skin. He cleaned Sir completely, leaving his hand slick with saliva.

He was boneless when Sir tucked his dick back into his pants, fastening Todd's trousers once more. For a moment, Todd thought Sir would shove him off his lap now that he'd finished. Instead, Sir turned Todd so his legs were hanging off the sides of the chair, his back resting in the crook of Sir's arm. Sir leaned down and kissed Todd's forehead as Todd blinked sleepily up at him. Sir began to rock him gently, feet planted firmly on the floor, the muscles in his legs tensing as he moved them back and forth.

"You did well," Sir said, and Todd warmed at the praise. "Better than I could have hoped for. How was it for you, boy?"

"Blargh," Todd said, his mouth like mush.

Sir grinned down at him, his crow's feet deepening. "That good, eh? I see. And that was only a small part of what I can do for you. *To* you. I can't wait to see what you'll do when I take that arse of yours." He pushed his hips up once more, and Todd trembled, wondering if he was now supposed to reciprocate. But Sir seemed to be able to read his mind as he said, "Ah, don't worry about that. We'll deal with it later. Now is about you, boy." He cupped Todd's head, bringing him against Sir's chest. Todd closed his eyes against the steady beat of Sir's heart, strong and loud.

He drifted, then, drifted on an ocean current, held safe in the arms of a man who whispered soft platitudes, telling Todd he was a good boy, the best boy, and that Sir was so very pleased with him. Todd hummed a little under his breath in acknowledgement, and

Sir rocked them both side to side while Todd floated.

Eventually, awareness seeped back in, and Todd's vision began to clear. He felt loose, relaxed in ways he hadn't been in a long time. And with this thought, reality came crashing in, like a splash of ice-cold water. He stiffened, remembering that this was only temporary.

"What time is it?" he mumbled.

Sir paused his ministrations. "Near eleven. Why?"

If Mama was telling the truth—and he had no reason to think she wasn't—then he still had time. Not much, but this was already more than he'd dared to hope for. He tried to convince himself that it was better to have this for as long as he did rather than to not have it at all, but it was a cold comfort. Soon, the magic would end and he'd have to return to the attic. He didn't know how he'd survive, especially when Sir held him as if he were precious.

"Your ball," Todd whispered. "Don't you need to go back out there?"

"I can do what I want," Sir said, brow furrowing.

"I know, Sir. But you have guests. A host always makes sure their guests are attended to."

"Is that right?"

"Yes," Todd said firmly. "My dad, he…he taught me that. Guests should never want for anything. You need to take care of them."

"Smart man," Sir said. "And I can see you learned well from him. Up."

Todd stood on shaky legs, Sir's hand in his to keep him from falling. Sir rose before him, towering over Todd. For a moment, Todd wished he'd kept his damn mouth shut so they could stay locked away behind closed doors. But before he could voice this— or something equally stupid—Sir said, "We will go out there, then, and see to my guests. You'll stay at my side, do you understand? No distractions." He tugged at one of the D-rings in Todd's harness when Todd didn't answer. "I asked you a question, boy."

"Yes, Sir," Todd said. "I understand."

Sir nodded. "Good." He let the D-ring go, bringing his hand up and scrubbing his face with it. "Then let us head back out there. Might as well get it over with."

"Sir?"

Sir smiled ruefully. "I prefer the quiet. Parties such as this, while enjoyable, cause more stress than I wish. If it wasn't for Gabriel, I'd probably never hold such things." He tilted his head as he looked down at Todd. "Though, for the life of me, I can't blame him this time. It has brought you to me, and for that, he will have my eternal gratitude. Come. Let us see what we see."

Taking Todd's hand in his own, he led them toward the door to the office. He stopped before opening it, looking Todd up and down. He reached up and fixed Todd's crooked mask until it was straight. "I will see this off of you before the night's end," Sir said. "I will see all of you."

To that, Todd could only nod, heart cracking as he knew it would never be. This wasn't a gift from Mama. It was a curse, one that he'd take over again if given the chance. If that made him damned, then so be it.

He thought Sir was going to kiss him right then and there. He did, but his lips pressed against Todd's forehead. He pulled back, but only just, reaching up and tugging on one of Todd's ears. "These, like the rest of you, are wonderful. Every piece, every part. Let's finish this so that we may find out just how far that blush extends down your body." Then he turned and opened the door.

Loud laughter and music bowled over Todd, causing him to shrink back. In here, in the office, it was safe. Out there, the real world lay waiting for them with furious snarls and gnashing teeth. Sir looked back at him, not angry, not upset, merely curious. Todd steeled himself, squaring his shoulders and holding his head high. If Sir could do this, so could Todd. He didn't want to let Sir out of his sight. For all he knew, others lay in waiting, ready to spring a sexy trap and ensnare Sir. Not on Todd's watch, godsdammit.

"Strange little thing," Sir said, sounding absurdly fond. "Soft where it counts, and yet you have fire burning in your eyes. I can't wait to see all that you are."

He allowed Todd to use the restroom, given that his bladder was about to burst. Once finished, Todd splashed water on his face, staring at his reflection in the mirror above the sink. "You can do this," he whispered. "Have faith."

Sir was waiting for him when he opened the door. He took Todd's hand in his, leading him down the hallway toward the sounds of the ball in full swing. When they walked through the double doors, Todd felt all eyes fall on them, and though he wanted to turn and run as fast as he could, Sir held onto him tightly, and Todd took it for what it was: strength and safety. He knew Sir wouldn't let anything happen to him, not under his watch.

Gabriel appeared out of the crowd, a funny little smile on his face, smug and knowing. "Finally," he said. "I was beginning to fear you'd forgotten about us."

Sir scoffed. "I told you I'd be out when I was ready."

Gabriel rolled his eyes. "So you did. But I worried we'd seen the last of you this night. I'm pleased to be proven wrong for the first time."

"Pest," Sir muttered. "That's all you are."

Gabriel ignored him, looking at Todd. His smile softened into something kinder, more welcoming. "And who do we have here?"

Todd didn't feel like speaking, turning his face into Sir's arm, squeezing his hand so tightly, the bones ground together. "This is my friend," Sir said, picking up on Todd's discomfort.

"Your friend," Gabriel said dryly. "And does your friend have a name?"

"He does," Sir said, and nothing more.

Gabriel waited a beat before sighing. "Fine. If that's the way you want to play it, then so—"

"It's Todd," Todd said, glancing at Gabriel out of the corner of his eye. "My name is Todd."

Gabriel blinked. "He speaks! How delightful. Todd, you say? It's a pleasure to meet you, Todd. I do hope you've enjoyed your time here. I can see you've sampled the—"

"Gabriel," Sir said in warning.

Gabriel waved him away, smiling quietly at Todd before looking at Sir. "Come, my lord. There are many people who wish to speak to you. Your absence has caused quite the stir."

"I was busy," Sir said, pulling Todd close as if trying to protect him. "And they are in my home. I don't have to explain myself to anyone. The only reason I'm out here now is because someone reminded me how a good host should act."

Gabriel snorted, looking at Todd with a new appreciation. "Is that right? Well, then. I won't complain. At least you're finally listening to *someone*. Come, come." He bowed low before spinning on his heels and heading off through the crowd, most of whom were whispering as they watched Sir and Todd.

Sir chuckled. "He's got a bee in his trousers. It's best if I do what he asks. Believe me when I say that Gabriel is not a man to be trifled with. Sometimes, we both forget who works for whom."

Todd squirmed, trying to pull away. "I can just…go in a corner or something. Get out of your way."

Sir frowned as he looked down at Todd. "Why would you do that? No, I think it's best you stay at my side. The sharks have smelled blood in the water. I won't leave you alone so that they may feast. You'll stay with me, understood?"

Todd raised his head, looking around at those gathered in the ballroom. Men and women with hungry eyes watched Sir, but quite a few also stared at Todd with the same expression. It unnerved him, those looks, and he almost wished he could go back to how it was before, hidden in shadows as the ball went on around him.

But at least this way, he was with Sir. He knew Sir wouldn't let anything happen to him. "Yes, Sir," he said.

"Good boy," Sir whispered gruffly, and a thrill ran down Todd's spine like lightning. Those two words were enough to make him want to tilt his head back and crow for all to hear.

He went with Sir as he mingled with his guests, Sir making sure to never let Todd go. He didn't ask Todd to speak, nor did Todd offer. He wasn't sure what he could say, and he was relieved when Sir seemed to know this. He was asked after, but he let Sir speak for him. One man tried to get his attention, hand reached out as if to touch Todd, but Sir growled in response, and the hand fell away.

It went on and on, more and more people seeking Sir's attention. Some touched him—a hand on his arm, or a lingering caress against his chest—and Todd had to keep from snarling at them. Sir must have felt his discomfort, because he stepped away from prying hands, the conversation never faltering, even as disappointment tinged with disbelief crossed their faces.

He was about to ask Sir if he could get him something to drink when the crowd parted in front of them. And there, standing in all his resplendent glory, was Gary, Tina and Justin on either side of him. Todd shrank down, blood turning into an icy sludge. He tried to escape Sir's hold, but Sir wouldn't let him go.

"My lord," Gary said as he bowed his head. Justin did the same, one arm across his chest, the other folded behind him. Tina curtsied, her eyes alight with something Todd couldn't quite place. He knew his face was covered, but that didn't mean they wouldn't recognize him. He hoped Sir wouldn't make him talk, or give his name. It would ruin everything, and he couldn't bear the thought of Sir grimacing in distaste if his true identity was revealed. "There you are. We'd wondered where you'd run off too."

Sir frowned briefly before his face smoothed out into a blank mask. "Gary. I do hope you've been enjoying yourself."

Gary raised his head, gaze narrowing at Todd before he smiled. "Oh, I am. These parties are such a treasure in a harsh world. May I present to you my children again? Not that you need the reminder, I'm sure. They're exquisite." He coughed pointedly, and Justin and Tina straightened as if a metal rod had been shoved down their backs. "Justin and Tina, both of age, and very eager to hang on to your every word."

Tina slunk forward, her bosom on full display, her skin lovely and pale. She trailed a long fingernail up Sir's chest as she purred, "Sir. I've heard so many things about you that I feel as if I know you."

Sir snorted as he carefully pulled Tina's hand from his chest, letting it go. It hung awkwardly between them before Tina dropped it back to her side. Undeterred, she continued in a breathy voice. "Tales of your prowess are whispered with such awe, that I almost can't believe them. But seeing you here in all your glory makes me realize that they hold great truth."

"Thank you," Sir said flatly. "Though I assure you rumor is often accepted as fact when it shouldn't be."

Tina faltered for a moment before she laughed daintily. All an act, and one Todd had seen time and time again. She didn't want Sir like Todd did. She wanted him for his money, his title.

The same was true for Justin, who stepped forward, knocking against his sister until she stumbled to the side with a glare. "Lord Tremaine," Justin said, bowing once more, his top pulling tight against the muscles in his arms and chest. He was beautiful; both he and his sister were, and even worse, they *knew* it. They had learned to weaponize their looks, something Todd hadn't, and he grimaced at how ridiculous he must look in comparison. He was too thin, too lanky, and his ears stuck out too far from his head. He wasn't like them, and he worried that Sir would forget him in the face of some new pretty. "I am grateful for your presence. I'd heard you were otherwise…occupied." He glanced at Todd, sneering quickly before smiling at Sir. "I'm glad to see that you've returned to us. If I may be so bold, can I ask you for a dance? I do love this waltz."

"So do I," Sir said, and Todd's heart cracked cleanly in two. "It's why I hired the orchestra. They know how to pluck the strings, don't they? A firm hand is well and good, but sometimes a delicate touch is required for the music to be so sweet."

Justin's lips quirked, his eyes filling with victory. "In that we agree. Shall we, then?" He glanced at Todd dismissively before smiling seductively at Sir. "I'm sure your little…. friend, won't mind, would he? He seems better seen than heard." He laughed, though it didn't reach his eyes.

"*Or*," Tina snarled, stepping up next to her brother as Gary watched them both gleefully. "I could dance with you. I'm light on my feet. *And* off, should the evening require such a thing. Do you like bendy things, Sir? Because I am *very* flexible."

"Not as flexible as I am," Justin said, overriding his sister's outrage. "I can do the splits. Perhaps Sir would like a demonstration?"

Todd waited for Sir to accept either offer. He wouldn't complain if that's what Sir wanted. Perhaps he could go back to his corner, and though it would hurt to see, he knew he'd watch Sir with whomever he chose. He didn't have much time left, and he wanted every memory of this night he could gather to keep him warm when he returned to the cold attic.

"You both seem…eager," Sir said. But he said *eager* the same way others said *obnoxious*, and Todd allowed himself to feel the smallest bit of hope. "And while I appreciate the offer, I already have a partner to dance with." He smiled down at Todd. "Shall we, boy?"

Todd nodded, relief crashing into him.

He ignored the glares Justin and Tina and Gary sent his way as Sir led him to the center of the ballroom, Gary snarling at his children, demanding to know *how* they'd fucked that up so easily. Todd didn't hear Justin or Tina's retorts, his gaze fixed firmly on Sir. The crowd amassed around them, forming a loose circle as Sir took his hand, putting it on his shoulder. Todd gripped Sir's vest as he took Todd's other hand, raising it up in his own.

"Follow my lead," Sir murmured just for Todd. "I will take care of you. I promise."

Todd could only nod.

The strings began to play, the music soft and romantic. Todd sighed as Sir began to move them both. It was clumsy, at first, just a little. Todd's knees knocked against Sir's, and he stepped on Sir's boots a time or two. Sir didn't seem to mind, even as Todd flushed horribly. He didn't want to make a mockery of Sir, not in front of all his guests. He remembered dancing with his mother in their home, standing on her feet, his father watching them with a soft smile as he played the violin, something he didn't do very well, but it was enough for the privacy of their own home. "Listen to the music," his mother whispered. "Feel it in your bones. There you go. Careful, careful. You got this, Todd."

And with this memory, Todd moved with Sir, sinking into the waltz, becoming more confident the further along it went. Sir studied him with a strange expression, and Todd couldn't look away, not even if he wanted to.

He didn't.

Everything else melted away around them: all the people watching with growing fascination, the ballroom, the future that was inevitable. All that remained was the music and Todd and Sir, as if they were the only things in existence. Todd didn't even notice when a clock struck midnight, the twelve chimes melding with the music.

One waltz gave way to another and another and another. Sir swirled Todd around the room, never looking away.

When yet another song came to an end, Sir came to a stop, hands still on Todd. Thinking they were finished, Todd said, "Thank you for—"

Sir kissed him.

Somewhere very, very far away, Todd heard people gasping, but it was nothing in comparison to the kiss Sir had bestowed upon him. Todd groaned into Sir's mouth, which Sir seemed to take as an invitation. His tongue brushed against Todd's, and Todd sagged against him, holding on for dear life. He'd never been kissed before, not like this. He felt clumsy, artless, but Sir didn't seem to mind if the rumbling in his throat was any indication. Sir's grip tightened, holding him close, and Todd wanted Sir to destroy him, wanted Sir to break him apart until he lay in pieces. Only then could he be rebuilt and—

Sir pulled away, but only just, his forehead pressed against Todd's. "You will stay with me, boy," Sir said, his breath warm on Todd's face. "Tonight. Tomorrow. Always. If this is but a taste of what you are, then I can't wait to see the rest. Say yes. Say yes, and I promise you, you'll be taken care of in ways you never dreamed of. You will be my boy, and nothing will take you away from me."

Todd said, "I—"

He never got the chance to finish.

A loud din burst from somewhere in the ballroom, causing Sir to whirl around, shoving Todd behind him. Todd stood on his tiptoes, peering over Sir's shoulder, wondering what had happened. His eyes widened when he saw Sam and Ryan looking around wildly. Ryan saw Todd first, nudging Sam. Sam looked relieved as they both rushed forward.

"Holy shit," Sam breathed when they stopped in front of a frowning Sir. "*You're* Sir? Oh my gods, I totally get it now. Dude, *I* would totally hit that. What the fuck." He brightened. "Wait, that would be your job, wouldn't it? Big ol' daddy hands, giving *such* a spanking."

Ryan glared grumpily at Sir. "You don't get to touch him!"

Sir frowned harder. "I wasn't planning on it. Who the hell are you, and why did you feel the need to interrupt me in my own home? I was speaking with my boy."

"Because it's almost twelve-thirty," Sam hissed, though he said it to Todd. "And boys like our friend here need to get to bed *before it's too late.*"

Todd gasped as he glanced at the clock on the far wall. He only had ten minutes left. No, no, he needed more time, he wasn't ready, he didn't *want to go.*

"Do you know these men?" Sir asked, glancing back at Todd.

Todd nodded, throat closing as the second hand of the clock ticked and ticked and ticked, the sound louder than anything Todd had heard before. "They're my friends," he croaked. "They…"

Sir started to turn when Sam cried, "It's Smashing Time! And fuck *yes*, that was capitalized!"

And then a horse named Tiggy burst into the ballroom, causing the crowd to scream and scatter as he bucked, his hooves clomping against the stone floor, echoing flatly in the room. Sir growled as he started for the horse, shouting for his people to put a stop to this at *once*.

He was distracted, which was all Sam and Ryan needed. They grabbed Todd by the hands, pulling him toward the doors that led to the front of the house. At first, Todd dug his heels in, trying to jerk his arms away from Ryan and Sam. "I know," Sam said over his shoulder, never slowing, never stopping. "But Mama said the magic will end at twelve-thirty. We can't be here when it does. Think, Todd, please."

Todd gave in, knowing Sam was right. This night, no matter how life changing it'd been, was always temporary. Mama had made sure he knew that. And though it hurt more than Todd expected, he'd had his chance. He'd been given a moment where everything felt right, and though it was being cruelly plucked from him, he'd known this was always going to happen.

He didn't try and fight it anymore.

They made it to the doors, and were out in the hall, Tiggy neighing loudly from somewhere behind them. A loud crash occurred followed by shouts, as if Tiggy had knocked over a table or two, followed by the sounds of hooves running after them. Todd glanced back in time to see Tiggy burst from the ballroom, running after them at full speed. He passed them by, mane flying behind his head.

Men and women blocked the exit, but they dove out of the way when Tiggy ran toward them, clearing a path for Sam and Ryan and Todd to follow. They hit the stairs, the carriage awaiting them at the front. Todd crashed into Sam's back as he stopped, ordering Ryan to hook up Tiggy. The mask slid from his face, landing on the last step.

Sam pulled open the door, panicking as he motioned for Todd to climb in. Todd blinked when he saw Sam had whiskers sprouting out from either side of his nose, thin and white. The magic was already failing. They were cutting it too close. Ryan had buck teeth as he hurried to attach Tiggy to the carriage. Tiggy's horse ears grew in length, night black fading to a muddy brown. Todd began to climb into the carriage, and froze when a voice commanded, "*Stop.*"

Sir.

Todd didn't turn around. He couldn't let Sir see his face. He heard others gathering behind him, their voices loud. He thought Gary and Justin and Tina were among them, and though every fiber of his being wanted to obey Sir, he couldn't. Not now, not ever again.

He climbed into the carriage as Sam slammed the door behind him. Face hidden in the darkness of the carriage, Todd looked back at the manor. Sir was rushing down the steps, looking furious. The carriage shook as Sam and Ryan climbed onto the bench. Tiggy made a sound, more mule than horse, and began to pull forward.

Todd turned and watched as the manor fell away behind them. Sir was at the bottom step, shouting after them, words that Todd couldn't hear. Before they went through the front gates and out of sight, Todd saw Gabriel appear next to Sir. He frowned and bent over, picking the mask up off the ground.

And then they were gone.

THEY DIDN'T QUITE MAKE IT BACK home before the magic disappeared. One moment, Tiggy was running as fast as he could, the carriage rattling, and the next, Todd found himself flat on his back, blinking up at the starry sky. A bucket lay on the ground next to him, two rats climbing out of it, a mule snorting and shaking his head.

"Well, fuck," Sam said, a rat once more. He pushed himself off the ground, Ryan leaning heavily against him. "That sucked balls. I mean, I love being a rat, but the human stuff was pretty rad, for the most part."

"You all right?" Ryan asked him, pressing his twitching nose against Sam's fur.

"Yeah," Sam said with a sigh. "You never realize how small you are until a drag queen fairy turns you into a human for a little bit. Also, that's the dumbest sentence I've ever said out loud."

Todd blinked as a mule nibbled on his hair. "Todd hurt?" Tiggy asked.

"No," Todd whispered. "Not…physically."

"Aw," Tiggy said. "It okay, Todd. We get you home and safe. Promise. Up, up, up."

Todd grimaced as Tiggy bit into the front of his tunic, now the same old clothes he always wore. The harness, the trousers, all of it gone. And it hurt more than Todd expected it to. He sniffled, eyes burning. He stood as Sam and Ryan gathered at his feet, looking up at him.

"Hey, dude," Sam said quietly. "I know it seems bad right now, but it'll be okay. You still have us, right?"

"Yeah," Todd mumbled. "I still have you."

"See?" Sam said, putting his little paws on Todd's shin. "That means you're not alone. Yeah, we're probably too small to spank you or whatever you're into, but I can give you an order if it'd make you feel better."

"*Sam*," Ryan spat.

"What?" Sam asked. "I'm trying to help! Our friend's heart is breaking, and we need to take care of him."

Ryan sighed. "Let's just get home, okay? We can figure out everything later. We need to be there before Gary gets back. We don't want him to know Todd hasn't been at home this entire time."

They had a point. Facing Gary's wrath would only make this night worse, and Todd didn't have the strength to deal with that on top of everything else. He bent over, scooping up Sam and Ryan. He held them against his chest and followed Tiggy as the mule led them home.

AN HOUR OR SO LATER, Todd lifted his head from his bed as the front door opened below him. Angry voices filtered up through the floorboards, and Todd rolled out of bed, sinking to the floor and pressing his ear against it. Sam and Ryan were safe in their nest, sound asleep.

"Who was it?" Justin demanded, voice muffled but clear. "Who the hell was that guy? He seduced Sir and then ran away? He ruined everything!"

"He knew *exactly* what he was doing," Tina spat. "Acting all timid and demure and stringing Sir along like that. The audacity is something I can't even begin to contemplate."

"Children," Gary said. "*Children*. That's no way to speak about someone we don't know. Don't be so crass."

Todd frowned. He'd never heard Gary defend anyone. Maybe Gary had decided to turn over a new leaf and—

"After all," Gary continued, "his loss is our gain. Sir will be even more desperate and lonely now, which means he might take a second look at the pair of you. Perhaps this time, though, you can consider *not embarrassing the crap out of me in front of everyone*."

"There it is," Todd muttered.

Tina and Justin began to shout over each other, their outrage a palpable thing. Todd shouldn't have derived as much pleasure from it as he did. He wondered if that made him a bad person.

"Shut up!" Gary growled, his children falling silent. "You've said enough for one night. All I asked was for you to try your best, but apparently, even *that's* too much! I've given you everything you have ever asked for, and this is how you repay me? If you both weren't past your expiration date, I'd consider sending you *back* to the orphanage."

"We didn't do anything!" Justin cried.

"It wasn't our fault!" Tina whined. "We did everything you asked, but Sir wouldn't even give us the time of day."

"That's because you weren't good enough," Gary said. "You're lucky that idiot boy did what he did. It means you both get a second chance." Todd heard Gary's hooves clomping on the floor, as if he were pacing back and forth. "That's exactly how we'll play this. We'll give it a few days, and then we'll call on Sir under the guise of checking in on how he's doing. You'll both need to show him that you're better than any idiot who tries to climb above his station. Sir will be at his lowest, and we'll swoop in and make sure he's taken care of. We'll take it slow at first, but eventually, he'll come to understand he can't live without one of you. I honestly don't care which of you he chooses."

"It'd better be me," Justin said.

Tina scoffed. "Oh please. You've never bottomed in your life. You'll try and top Sir, and he'll throw you out on the streets. No, he needs a gentle hand, someone subservient."

"And that's *you*?" Justin said, aghast. "Give me a break."

"Of course not," Tina said. "But he won't know that. And by the time he figures it out, I'll be so intertwined in his life, he won't be able to get rid of me without paying out his ass. It's the perfect plan. All I'll need to do is act submissive for a couple of months, and then we'll be rich." She began to cackle maniacally. She stopped when no one else joined in. "Isn't this the point where we all laugh evilly?"

"Whatever," Gary said. "I don't have time for you laughing like a weasel getting plowed by a knight. The incompetence of my own children has left me exhausted. I need to sleep. And you *better* not wake me up before at least noon tomorrow. Make sure Todd has my breakfast ready for me when I wake, or there will be hell to pay. For *all* of you."

"At least Todd didn't end up going," Justin said. "Can you imagine if he'd tried to talk to Sir?"

Tina laughed again, less like a weasel getting plowed by a knight, but not by much. "Sir would have kicked him out of the manor before Todd could've started sputtering nonsense." Her voice rose to a higher pitch. "My name is Todd! I think I matter even though I don't!"

"Now, now," Gary said. "Though making fun of Todd brings me joy, we need to focus. I want you both to go to bed and think of ways you will avoid disappointing me in the future. Go, now, before I make you sleep in the barn."

"They really suck ass," a voice whispered near Todd's ear, causing him to yelp as he sat up, looking around wildly. He breathed a sigh of relief when he saw Sam and Ryan leaning out from their nest.

"Don't listen to them," Ryan said as Sam nodded. "You're amazing, Todd. What you and Sir shared isn't something to be dismissed."

"Ryan's right," Sam said, whiskers twitching. "Tina and Justin can die mad about it. It'll all work out. You'll see."

Todd wished he could believe that. He wished that more than

anything. But maybe Tina was right. It wasn't as if Sir knew who he really was. They had shared a moment, yes, but for all Todd knew, Sir did that all the time. Todd might just be another notch on Sir's bedpost, a boy for the night who immediately vacated Sir's thoughts the moment he fled the ball. Out of sight, out of mind. Of course it didn't matter to Sir like it'd mattered to Todd.

"Yeah," he said quietly. "Sure. That must be it."

Ryan and Sam exchanged a glance before looking back at Todd as he lifted himself from the floor and trudged toward his bed. "You can't give up," Sam said. "That's what they want. From what you told us, Sir took care of you when he didn't have to. That has to count for something. Don't sell yourself short, dude. There's a planet of people who'll do that for you. Don't be one of them."

Todd climbed into bed, pulling the comforter up and over his head. Ryan sighed before telling Sam they'd try again in the morning. Sam sounded like he wanted to argue, but ultimately agreed. Soon after, tiny little rat snores came from their nest, and Todd was once again alone.

Cocooned in his bed, he curled in on himself. He grimaced as he rubbed against the ache in his chest. For a moment, he could almost make himself believe it was Sir's hand, rough yet warm. "That's my good boy," Sir whispered, and Todd drifted off to sleep, a smile on his face.

THE NEXT WEEK, Todd was busier than ever. Gary had a chore list a mile long, and every time Todd tried to take a break to breathe, Gary would be there with yet another task for Todd to complete. Clean the baseboards. Wash the walls. Clean the chandelier. Beat the rugs. Go to the market. Make breakfast. Make lunch. Make dinner. Wash all our clothes. Mop the floors, except *I* need the mop for reasons that don't concern you, so, Todd, you'll need to use a sponge.

Todd did all this and more, going to bed every night with an aching back and muddled thoughts. He barely had time to think about Sir at all.

Sam and Ryan tried to convince him to go back to Sir's manor and reveal himself, but Todd told them he didn't have time. For all he knew, Sir had forgotten all about him, and Todd didn't want to incur Gary's wrath, so he kept his head down, doing everything assigned to him without complaint.

He was in the barn, mucking out the stalls when Tiggy said (through a mouthful of grain), "Todd sad?"

"Todd busy," Todd muttered, the handle of the pitchfork scraping against his palms.

"Same difference," Tiggy said as he swallowed. "Give you advice? Tiggy a mule. Mules give best advice."

Todd sighed, wiping the sweat from his brow. "I don't need advice, Tiggy. I need to finish my chores so I can go to bed before one in the morning."

"Tiggy give advice. Ready?"

Todd leaned on the pitchfork, staring at Tiggy.

"Stand tall," Tiggy said. "The more you hunch, the more stuff gets put on back. Todd not pack mule. Tiggy pack mule. Carries stuff because that's what Tiggy does. Makes Tiggy happy. Todd not Tiggy. Todd not carry everything. Not meant to. Tiggy carries because Tiggy a mule. Todd a human. Needs help to carry stuff."

"I can do it on my own," Todd muttered.

"Shouldn't have to," Tiggy said. "We all need someone. Tiggy has you and Ryan and Sam. Todd has us too, but Todd needs more. It's okay to want that. Better than okay."

"It doesn't matter," Todd said dully. "It was always going to be temporary." He looked down at the ground. "The sooner I realize that, the better off I'll be. Sir will find a husband or a wife, and I'll be happy for him."

Tiggy snorted. "Liar. No lie to me. Tiggy your friend. Tiggy don't lie to you."

"It's not a lie," Todd insisted. "I'd be happy for Sir. He deserves to find someone who'll take care of him as much as he takes care of them."

Tiggy looked at him sadly. "Todd better than that. Todd needs Sir. But Sir needs Todd even more because Todd is the best Todd. No other person is you."

"*Todd*!" Gary screamed shrilly from the house. "You better finish out there quickly! I found a cobweb in the curtains, and I'm not happy!"

"No other person is me," Todd agreed. "But this is the hand I've been dealt. I need to make the most of what I have. It's just one more year. One more year, and all of this will go away."

Tiggy shook his head but didn't speak.

EXACTLY A WEEK AFTER THE BALL, someone knocked on the front door.

"Answer that," Gary ordered. "If whoever that is wants a handout, tell them I already gave to charity twelve years ago, and I've regretted it ever since. It's why I joined the organization, embezzled everything I could, and then moved across the city so they couldn't find me."

Gary lay spread out on a velvet chaise lounge, munching on the grapes Todd had been handfeeding him for the last hour. Justin and Tina were on the opposite couch, demanding that Todd peel each grape individually, which was much harder than it sounded.

Todd smiled tightly and went to the door. A page stood on their porch, bright-eyed and grinning. "Hello and good day! I come on behalf of my master, Lord Tremaine the Firm."

Todd's grip on the doorknob tightened. "What?" he whispered. The page seemed to be alone, but had Sir found out who he was? Did he send the page to whisk Todd away? Or worse, tie him up and bring him back so Sir could demand to know what the hell Todd had been thinking, coming to the ball without an invitation?

The page said, "Lord Tremaine is on a mission." He pulled out a scroll from his sleeve, unfurling it and clearing his throat. "I, Lord Tremaine, am requesting a visit to your residence. I will call upon you this Tuesday at promptly three—no, wait." The man squinted down at the scroll before laughing. "My bad. He's going to the house next door at three. Sorry, this is a script that I am supposed to fill in with the little details. Let's say, three-thirty instead."

"Why?" Todd asked.

The page shrugged. "He's looking for something. Don't quite know what, but then I'm not paid enough to know. Can I mark you off my list?"

"What's this?"

Todd whirled around. Gary stood behind him, eyes narrowed, horn as sharp as a butcher's knife. He shoved Todd out of the way, causing the page to take a step back. "Who are you?" Gary asked in a chilly tone. "Why are you talking to my servants? I mean, why are you talking to my dear, sweet stepson who I love as if he were my own, even though he's clearly not?"

The page recovered. "As I was saying, Lord Tremaine will be calling upon you on Tuesday. It won't take long, but Sir is quite adamant that he be allowed to visit every household in the city who have those of age and are single."

"*Really*," Gary purred, and Todd could see the gears turning in his head. "Lord Tremaine, you say? Whatever for?"

The page shrugged. "He's searching for something. Does anyone here fit the criteria?"

"Oh, yes," Gary said. "My children, Justin and Tina fit the criteria perfectly. Both are of age and desperately single."

"Justin and Tina," the page said, marking them down on the scroll with a feather quill. He raised his head, glancing at Todd. "And him?"

Gary laughed. "Oh, no. Ignore him. We do. It's quite easy. No, he's our special little guy. We wouldn't want Lord Tremaine to suffer my stepson's…exuberance. Justin and Tina. That's all you need to consider. I'm sure Lord Tremaine will find them acceptable."

Rage swelled within Todd, harsh and grating. If unicorns weren't protected by laws, Todd would consider ripping off his horn and shoving it down his godsdamn throat. And then he'd go for Justin and Tina and bathe in their blood—

"Uh," the page said. "Is your…servant stepson growling or…?"

"No," Gary said quickly. "That's just the sound he makes when he remembers that every fireplace in the house needs to be cleaned. And he should get right to that *immediately*." He glared until Todd stepped back away from the door. "And you tell Sir that we will wait for his visit with bated breath. My children will do *anything* to make sure Sir's visit is eventful."

"Right," the page said slowly. "I'll just…make sure he knows that. But in the spirit of thoroughness, does he have a name? Just so I can put him on my list."

"Not at all!" Gary said brightly. "He was never given one. Isn't that marvelous? It's a hipster thing, so. Here, dear boy. A coin for your troubles."

"Wow," the page said. "Thanks! See you next Tuesday!" And with that, he waved, jumped off the porch and headed down the sidewalk.

"Farewell!" Gary called after him. "It was so nice to see you! We can't wait for Lord Tremaine's visit! It'll be…annnnd he's gone." Gary slammed the door shut and turned to face Todd. "The fireplaces won't clean themselves. Hop to it." He pushed by Todd, mane trailing after him. "Children! *Children.* I have the best news! You both are getting another chance at Sir, and you *better not fuck this up.* If you do, I'll be forced to commit filicide, and you *know* my skin can't take the dungeons. Mold makes me break out, and I know you wouldn't want your daddy to get pimples on his lovely snout."

Todd stood in the hallway, listening as Gary and Justin and Tina went about making plans to ensure one of them would leave with Sir as their new spouse.

THE NEXT THREE DAYS passed quickly, the house in a tizzy at Sir's impending visit. Gary doubled down on Todd, ordering him to make the house spotless before Sir arrived. "Cleanliness is next to godliness, as I always say."

"You've never said that in your life," Todd muttered without thinking, hands covered in cleaning chemicals.

"What was that?" Gary asked sweetly.

"Nothing," Todd said. "Sorry. Something in my throat."

"Ew," Gary said. "Are you getting sick? You better not infect the rest of us before Sir gets here. I swear to the gods, if you give us the plague or whatever else your shriveled little body is cooking up, I'll sell you to the brothels in Meridian City. Is that understood?"

"Yes," Todd said through gritted teeth. Then, "Will I be in attendance when Lord Tremaine arrives?"

Gary laughed, though he looked startled as he did so. "Why on earth would you need to be there? It's not as if Sir would look at you for any reason. No, I think its best that you stay in the attic while he's here. In fact, I'll insist upon it with a lock on the attic door. I won't have you ruining this moment, not when we're so close to making all of our dreams come true." Then, raising his voice, "Justin! Tina! You better be picking out the best outfits. I won't have either of you looking slovenly in front of Sir!"

The night before Sir arrived, Todd climbed back into the attic, head pounding, hands cracked and stiff from all the cleaning he'd done. He fell onto his bed without changing, not having the strength to do so. Sam and Ryan climbed up onto the bed, settling on the pillow above his head.

"This is your chance," Sam said, petting his hair, the tip of his tail near Todd's ear. "Sir will be here tomorrow. You can't let this moment go to waste."

"There's no point," Todd mumbled. "You heard Gary. I'll be locked away up here. Sir won't even know I exist."

"Unless you make him," Ryan said. "You can't let them take this away from you."

"Seriously, dude," Sam said. "Mama gave you the tools, but you have to learn how to use them yourself. It wasn't magic that made Sir see you. That was all you, man. It didn't matter what you were wearing or who Sir thought you were. He saw you for you."

And oh, did Todd want to believe that, more than anything. He remembered the way Sir had held him, how caring and kind he'd been. By rights, he could have kicked Todd out of the ball the moment he laid eyes upon him, but he didn't. A week removed, it felt like a dream, one that Todd didn't want to wake up from.

"What can I do?" Todd whispered. "Gary won't allow it."

Ryan and Sam didn't speak. Todd lifted his head and discovered rats could look positively mischievous when they wanted to. "What?" he asked.

"We *might* have a plan," Sam said. "Do you trust us?"

"Yes," Todd said immediately. "But—" A tiny paw pressed against his mouth, cutting him off.

"No buts," Ryan said.

"Except for the butt that Sir is gonna play with," Sam said. "We've got you, dude. You're our best friend. We're only rats, sure, but you'll see. We're gonna take care of you. Gary won't even see us coming. The rest will be up to you."

Though Todd wanted to tell them to stop, he didn't. He rolled over onto his back, folding his arms behind his head, staring up at the ceiling. "And if it doesn't work? If Sir doesn't want me?"

"Then fuck him," Sam said fiercely. "He won't deserve you. You need someone special, Todd. And if it's not Sir, it'll be someone else. Only the best for our Todd. Right, Ryan?"

"Right," Ryan said. "Someone out there will want you for all the things you are and none of the things you aren't. But I wouldn't count Sir out just yet."

"I'm probably going to regret much of this, aren't I?"

"Yep," Sam said. "Isn't it exciting?" He and Ryan curled up near Todd's head. "Sleep, dude. You'll need it. We've got a big day tomorrow. Things are gonna change, I just know it."

Todd slept, and for the first time in a long time, he couldn't wait to see what tomorrow would bring.

"THERE," GARY SAID through the closed attic hatch. "Lock is in place, and we're good to go. Todd, I better not hear a single *sound* from you. If I do you'll regret it, I promise you that."

Todd sat on the floor, staring down at the hatch. He waited until Gary left before trying the door, just to make sure. It raised an inch before stopping, barely letting in a sliver of light. He let it fall back down with a thump before he sat back on his legs. He'd seen Justin and Tina before being forced into the attic. They looked beautiful, nary a strand of hair out of place, their clothing accentuating their more considerable assets.

And maybe that would have been enough to force Todd into despair once more. After all, compared to Justin and Tina, Todd thought himself no different than white paint drying on a wall. But Todd was done with accepting the life he'd been living, and though it was easier said than done, he chose to have faith, instead. Faith in himself. Faith in his friends. Faith that Sir would see right through Justin and Tina and Gary to the diseased hearts that beat in their chests. Todd—ever magnanimous—didn't wish them harm. No, he just wished they would go the fuck away. Or—even better!—that *he* would go the fuck away. Preferably with Sir. But even if that didn't work out like he wanted, he was done with this half-life he'd been living since the death of his father.

Anticipation filled Todd, an excitement mixed with an awful curl of dread that he tried to ignore. It was harder than he expected it to be, but Sam and Ryan wouldn't let it overtake him. They sat on the floor near the hatch, waiting until Sir arrived so they could put their plan into action. Todd asked them once more if they were sure; after all, this was dangerous for them as much as it was for himself. However, after the fourth time he'd asked, Sam had told him—in no uncertain terms—to shut the hell up, dude, we're gonna get you your man, so don't even worry about it. We got this. We're godsdamn *rats*. We can do anything.

The tiny clock that sat on the wooden crate next to Todd's bed ticked and ticked and ticked, Todd sure each second passing was actually a year outside of the attic. He paced back and forth before sitting on his bed. And then he was up and pacing again, gnawing on his ragged thumbnail. He'd worn the finest clothes Gary allowed him to own: clean trousers and a tunic that he left untied at the throat. It was nothing like the clothes he'd worn to the ball, nor was it as fine as anything Sir wore in his every day, but Ryan said that clothes didn't make the man. It was what was underneath that mattered most.

By the time the clock struck three in the afternoon, Todd was a sweaty mess, knowing Sir had to be close if his page had the timing correct. He would be in one of the houses in the neighborhood. For the next ten minutes, Sam had to talk Todd down, reminding him that *yes*, Sir was probably talking to eligible citizens of Lockes, but they weren't Todd. Sir wouldn't throw away their night together for some pretty piece of flesh. Todd, as he was wont to do, reminded

Sam that he'd only been in Sir's presence for a couple of hours, and in the grand scheme of things, that was nothing at all. To which Sam replied that Sir had also jacked off Todd while calling him a good boy. Todd spluttered nonsensically for a bit after that, face heated as Sam and Ryan grinned smugly at him.

Todd was so distracted he didn't realize it was three-thirty until a loud knock came from somewhere below them.

With a strangled gasp, Todd rushed toward the sole window in the attic, one that looked out onto the front of the house and the street below. He cursed inwardly as he tried to see who stood on the porch, but the stoop was out of sight, the angle off just enough that Todd couldn't see who was knocking. For all he knew, it was only the page again. Or simply Gabriel. Would Sir really come himself or would he send someone in his stead?

The answer was given a moment later when Todd heard the door open, and Gary exclaimed quite loudly, saying welcome, welcome, come *in*. This was immediately followed by a familiar rumble of thanks, and Todd's brain buzzed as if filled with bees.

Sir was here.

"Operation Land Todd a Man and Ensure He Gets His Butt Reamed is a go," Sam said.

"We really need to talk about the names of your plans," Ryan said fondly.

Sam rolled his eyes. "What? Why? What we're trying to do is *literally* in the name of the op. That's how you know it's a good one."

"Mistake!" Todd whispered fervently. "We're making a *mistake*."

Sam and Ryan ignored him, which was probably for the best. They rose to their feet near the hatch that led into the house. "Todd," Sam said. "It's time. Let's go, let's go, let's *go*." He hopped around, tail slapping against the floor.

Taking a deep breath, Todd knelt near the hatch, pausing with his fingers gripping the metal latch. "Are you sure?"

"Fuck yes, we are," Sam said. "This is going to be fricken *epic*. Bards will sing songs of our triumph, and all the world will know our names as the rats who helped their friend in his quest for true love. I can already hear it." Then, remarkably, Sam began to sing. "Cheesy dicks and candlesticks, and everything you need!" He frowned. "Wait. Why is that song familiar? Man, I hate that. Where the hell did I hear it?"

"Focus," Ryan hissed. "If we're going to do this, we need to do it now."

Sam shook his head. "Right. Todd, lift the hatch as high as you can. We'll handle the rest."

With a nod, Todd did as he was asked, the muscles in his arms straining as he lifted the hatch as hard as he could. The wood groaned, but the lock held. A sliver of light appeared in the small opening Todd had created, and he couldn't quite see how this was going to work.

"How are you going to fit?" he grunted, arms quivering.

Sam snorted. "We're rats. We can fit through anything. Watch."

Todd gaped when Sam went first, stretching out his body until he was longer and thinner than he normally was. With his ears flat against his head, Sam began to squeeze through the opening. Todd was sure Sam would get caught on his back or rear, but Sam popped through with ease, his tail disappearing into the house. A second later, his head popped back up. "See? Ryan, your turn."

Ryan did the same. He was a bit bigger, but it didn't matter. He fit through just as easily. Once Todd was sure Ryan was clear, he let the hatch go, causing it to thump against the floor. Todd turned on his knees, lowering his face toward a crack between the floorboards. Closing one eye, he looked through the crack and saw Sam and Ryan on the floor below. Sam looked up at him, grinned, and then he and Ryan scurried out of sight.

Ten minutes, Todd reminded himself as he sat back up. Sam told him to give them ten minutes, and if they hadn't been murdered, the rest would be up to Todd.

No pressure.

He waited, staring at the clock, willing time to move forward. It did, but at a pace akin to dripping molasses. Todd decided that regardless of what else happened, he was sick and tired of anything having to do with clocks and would destroy every single one he could find. An appropriate reaction in the name of true love.

Or so he told himself.

He heard Gary's tittering laugh, Justin and Tina fawning. Once, he thought he even heard Sir laugh, but he couldn't be sure. He hoped not. Then he felt guilty, because Sir could laugh at whatever he wanted, just so long as that didn't involve sticking his dick in evil.

Exactly ten minutes after Sam and Ryan had gone into the house, Gary shrieked. "Rats! Oh my fucking gods, we have *rats*. Disgusting creatures! Kill them. *Kill them and bring me their heads.*"

A loud crash came from below, followed by the sounds of shouts and cries of revulsion. It was about this time Todd realized that sending rats might not have been the best idea. Thundering footsteps ripped through the house, followed by breaking glass and crunching wood. Justin, for his part, screamed in horror at something Ryan or Sam did, and Tina loudly demanded that the house be burned down *immediately*, and then rebuilt to her specifications.

Todd leapt away from the attic door when he heard shuffling come from the floor beneath him. A moment later, the lock clicked as it was removed, and a furious Gary threw open the hatch, his head rising up, eyes narrowed. "Get down here," he spat. "We have rats. I need you to hunt them down and make them *suffer* for ruining everything!"

"Are you sure?" Todd asked, voice even. "I don't want to interrupt your visit."

"I'm *sure*!" Gary yelled. "Get your ass down here. Don't make me tell you again."

Gary lowered himself to the floor, the hatch open in invitation.

"You got this," Todd whispered to himself. And then he climbed down the rickety ladder.

Gary stood in the hall, snorting sparks of red and violet. "*Rodents*," he snarled. "Of all the—no matter. I'll apologize to Lord Tremaine, and he'll understand. I can still salvage this. Find them, Todd. Find them and make them wish they'd never been born, or you'll find yourself discovering the same. I'll make sure of it."

Todd nodded as Gary whirled around, clomping down the hall. As he reached the top of the stairs, Gary stopped for a moment, shaking his head before fixing a beatific smile on his face. "I *so* apologize for this," he announced grandly as he began to descend the stairs. "We've never had issues like this before, I swear. We keep a clean and tidy home, so I have no idea where this infestation came from. Rest assured, I will have it taken care of."

Todd froze halfway down the hall when Sir said, "No apologies necessary. I grew up on a farm. I've had to deal with a rat or ten in my time."

"You're so *brave*," Tina simpered. "Tell me more about your life of squalor and how you lifted yourself up from poverty into the man you've become today."

"Squalor," Sir repeated, not amused.

"Ignore her, my lord," Justin said airily. "My dear sister means well, but she's a bit addled in the head. Breech birth, or so I'm told."

"We're *twins*," Tina snapped.

"But I was born first," Justin replied. "A go-getter, which is something I apply to my everyday life. Isn't that wonderful, Sir?"

"Lord Tremaine," Sir said. "I'm only Sir to those who kneel for me."

"Of course," Justin said hastily. "And I am the *best* kneeler. Why, I don't even like standing at all! Watch!"

"No!" Tina cried. "Watch *me*. I kneel even better than Justin. Except not on this floor because of the rats. But I promise no one has ever kneeled as much as I do."

"Usually in alleyways," Justin said gleefully. "My sister has a propensity for kneeling in any alley she can find. Why do you think that is, Tina?"

"Only emulating you, big brother," Tina said, voice sticky sweet. "Tell me, Justin. How many men, exactly, have you sucked off this week? Six? Seven?"

"It's not *my* fault I'm good at what I do!"

"Slut!"

"Bitch!"

"*Children*," Gary trilled. "Perhaps we should save this conversation for when our *guests aren't here*. Ignore them, Lord Tremaine. I know it seems as if the rats have also infested their brains, but I assure you that you won't ever find a better pair. And hey! Why choose only one? Have both! Please. I'm begging you. Have them both."

"That's…quite the offer," another voice said. Gabriel. Gabriel was here with Sir, and he didn't sound pleased. "And one I'm sure my lord will take into consideration once we depart. Which we should as soon as possible. It's been a busy day, and we still have more stops to make."

Todd descended the stairs, the hairs on the back of his neck standing on end. The wood creaked under his feet as he stepped off the last stair. He couldn't see into the parlor where the others sat, Gary's considerable rear blocking the view. Gary turned to look over his shoulder, his smile turning into ice. "There's the help," he said. "Finally. You provide a roof over their heads, and yet they still move as if underwater. That should not *be*." Then, dropping his voice. "Find the rats, you little shit, and do it quietly. Don't interrupt us."

Todd nodded, and Gary turned back toward the parlor. "Now, where were we? Ah, yes! Lord Tremaine, you said something about a mask?"

"Yes," Sir said. "A mask was left at the manor. I'm seeking the one who wore it. I have something I need to say to this person."

Holy gods. Todd did *not* need to get an erection at this very moment, but apparently, he was shit out of luck in that regard.

"It was me," Tina said immediately. "I was wearing the mask. Silly thing. I dropped it as I left. Yes, that's exactly what happened. I'm *so* glad you found it. I've been missing it something awful."

"Really," Gabriel said flatly. "You were the boy wearing the mask."

"I was!" Tina said. "Ignore my breasts. Pesky things, those are. I don't even know why I have them."

Justin laughed. "Oh, Tina. This is just *sad*. Obviously, it wasn't you, it couldn't have been because it was me. I was the one who wore it, and I can prove it."

"You can?" Gabriel asked. "Oh, this should be interesting."

Todd crept toward the parlor, back against the wall, trying to keep Gary from seeing him. He heard a small squeak from his other side and turned his head to find Sam and Ryan hiding underneath a small table, peeking out from underneath the tablecloth.

Sam mouthed *go* as Ryan furiously waved his paws toward the parlor. Todd nodded, taking a deep breath and continuing to slide down the wall. Gary didn't hear him coming, stepping further into the parlor as Justin and Tina bickered back and forth.

"Children," Gary snapped. "Would you shut your adorable mouths for one godsdamn second? Lord Tremaine, forgive their temerity. They're in awe of your handsomeness. While I'm sure you're used to it, it's no excuse. Justin, Tina. I raised you better than this. Tina, you silly little twat, try on the mask."

Todd reached the entrance to the parlor. He stuck his neck out, looking around the corner.

Sir sat in a high-backed chair, slumped into it, hand on his chin, the other waving for Tina to get on with it. He looked as wonderful as ever, wearing black trousers that left nothing to the imagination, and a red tunic that Todd hoped to one day see on the floor.

Gabriel stood next to him, looking bored out of his mind.

Todd watched as Tina leapt to her feet, standing before Sir, who nodded at Gabriel. Tina preened as Gabriel sighed, pulling a familiar mask out from the pocket of his thick cloak.

"There it is!" Tina cried. "Just like I remember. Yes, it *is* mine, so I'm glad this charade has come to an end." She snatched the proffered mask from Gabriel's hand. Shooting Justin a dark and malevolent smile, she placed the mask on her face.

Only to have it immediately slide off and fall to the floor.

They all stared down at it.

"Huh," Tina said. "Oops. Just let me…" She bent over and scooped the mask up, giggling nervously. "I don't know how that happened. Stupid mask. I'll have the tailor who made it flogged immediately." She pressed the mask against her face once more. It began to slide off, but she held it up with a single finger. "There! See? It fits!"

"Remove your hand," Sir said.

Tina stiffened, eyes filling with fire. For a moment, Todd thought she'd snarl at Sir that he didn't have the *right* to tell her what to do, but then she smiled weakly, and dropped her hand.

The mask fell again.

"Oh no," Gabriel said flatly. "I was so sure that was going to work."

Tina's face flushed with fury as Justin shoved her to the side. "Poor girl. She tries so hard, doesn't she? Well, as I always say, never send a woman to do a man's job." He picked up the mask and set it on his own face. He hesitated a moment before dropping his hand.

Everyone held their breath.

The mask stayed on Justin's face.

"There," Justin breathed. "See? I *knew* it'd fit!" He whipped his head toward his sister. "And now that I get to leave this fucking hovel, Tina, you are the absolute *worst*. My gods, if you weren't my twin, I would've run you through with my sword ages ago."

The mask clunked to the floor.

"Um," Justin said. "Ha, ha. I was just…kidding?"

"Enough," Sir growled. "I've seen all I need to. You seem to think me a fool. You have done nothing but waste my time, and that is something I cannot forgive."

"Maybe *I* should try it on," Gary said. "For all I know, I was the boy in the mask and—*yes*. That's exactly what it was!" Glittering tears filled his eyes as he took a step toward Sir. "I didn't mean to deceive you, my lord. I was blinded by my love for you. But fear not! I have seen the light, and now we can be together forever!"

"Oh my gods," Gabriel mumbled, turning his face toward the ceiling. "My lord, we are going to have so many words when we return home."

Sir stood abruptly, causing Gary and Tina and Justin to stumble backward. "We're done here," he snapped. "Unless there is anyone else in this house who could be considered, I bid you good day."

Todd whipped his head back around the corner, throat closing. He looked back toward the stairs. He needed to run back to the safety of the attic. He couldn't do this. He couldn't *do*—

"THERE'S ONE MORE!" Sam shouted, voice ringing in the hallway. "HIS NAME IS TODD!"

Silence fell, thick and heavy.

Then: "Todd," said in a strong and growly voice, sending shivers down Todd's spine.

Gary laughed loudly. "Ignore that. We have ghosts who shout random things all the time. Terrible business, that, but then this house used to be a hospital for the delightfully deranged, so it's to be expected. In fact, we have learned to live with it, and sometimes even join in. Isn't that right, children?"

"Oh, yes," Tina said. She began to scream. "MY NAME IS TODD AND I DIED HERE."

"MY NAME IS TODD!" Justin bellowed. "I WAS GROSS AND CRAZY AND DIDN'T KNOW WHEN TO STOP MEDDLING SO I SUFFERED A TERRIBLE DEATH!"

"See?" Gary said, beads of sweat on his snout. "That's all it is."

"For fuck's sakes," Sam muttered. "I hate everything."

"Except for me," Ryan said, bumping his shoulder.

"Except for you," Sam agreed. "Because you're the perfect rat husband, and I cherish everything about you."

"Todd," Sir said. "Is there someone here named Todd?"

Gary bristled. "Well, *yes*, but you don't have to concern yourself with him. He's a servant who has no business getting involved with this discussion. And it's not as if the mask would fit him. He was nowhere near the ball. He was here at home."

"Todd Haversford?" Sir insisted.

Shit. Todd had forgotten he'd given the wrong name to the woman at the door.

"No," Gary said. "That's not his name at all. Pity that. I almost had hopes that he—"

"My name is Todd McAllister."

Silence once more. It took Todd longer than he cared to admit to figure out *he'd* spoken. He slapped a hand over his mouth as Ryan and Sam pumped their tiny paws in the air.

"Todd McAllister," Sir said quietly. "That voice. I...show yourself."

As if his body weren't his own, Todd pushed himself off the wall, following the command. Gary glared murderously at him, Justin drawing a finger across his throat as Tina bared her teeth. But Todd barely paid them any mind, his gaze fixed on Sir.

Gabriel's eyes widened as Todd stepped into the parlor, but everything else melted away as Sir rose from his chair, bending over in one smooth motion and picking the mask up off the floor. Carefully, as if he approached a skittish animal, he walked toward Todd, gaze never leaving his face. Something flitted across his eyes, and Todd thought it was a flash of recognition, though he couldn't quite believe it. He didn't look like he had the night of the ball.

Sir stopped in front of him, inches separating them. Sir studied him, Todd forcing his eyes to remain open, his back straight and proud.

"I know you," Sir said slowly. He reached up and touched the side of Todd's face, a finger trailing down his cheek. Todd leaned into it without thought, sighing at the warmth from Sir's skin.

Sir shook his head as if clearing his mind. Mouth in a thin line, he raised the mask. "May I?"

Todd could only nod, head jerking up and down.

Sir pressed the mask against his face, hands shaking. Todd held his breath as Sir's hands fell away. The mask stayed in place, fitting Todd perfectly.

"It *is* you," Sir whispered. "My gods, I…" And then Todd was being kissed within an inch of his life. He gasped as his knees gave out, sagging against Sir who held him up with strong arms. "My boy," Sir said, kissing Todd again and again. "My good boy. I thought I'd never find you. How did you…?"

"I'm sorry," Todd whispered back, voice cracking. "I wanted to stay, but I—"

"What," Gary said.

"What," Justin said.

"What," Tina said.

Todd glanced at them, a weak retort bubbling in his throat, but Sir grabbed his chin gently, turning his focus back where it belonged. "Eyes on me," Sir said, and the command was clear. "Why were you hidden away from me? I want the truth, boy. Leave nothing out."

"Oh, would you look at the time," Gary said. "I forget that I had an appointment on the other side of Verania in six minutes. I should—"

"Gabriel," Sir said without looking away from Todd. Over Sir's shoulder, Todd saw Gabriel pull a curved sword from his robes, moving swiftly toward the only exit. Gary squawked in outrage as Justin and Tina began to whimper pathetically. "Now, speak, boy. I would hear every word."

Strength, Todd knew, didn't always have to come from within. It could come from another person, one who had searched high and low to find him. With that in mind, Todd spoke, doing exactly as Sir asked. He started with the death of his mother, and the grief he and his father had succumbed to. He told Sir about his father's decision to remarry, bringing Gary and Justin and Tina into their lives. When his voice cracked at his father's end, Sir's expression hardened, but not for Todd, never him. Even as Gary screamed it was lies, all lies, Todd pushed through it all, telling Sir about how he'd been forced into the attic and into servitude, at the beck and call of Gary and his children.

"And how did you come to be at the ball?" Sir asked when Todd trailed off, unsure of how to proceed.

Todd shrugged awkwardly. "Long story, but the gist of it is that my best friends are two talking rats and a smart mule, and then my fairy drag mother appeared and made me clothes out of magic, but it had a deadline, which is why I had to flee the manor even though I wanted nothing more than to stay."

Sir faltered at that. "You…what."

"See!" Gary screeched. "He's fucking *bananas*. No one in their right mind would listen to this tripe. How *dare* you waste Lord Tremaine's time with your silly tales of—"

"Hi!" Sam said, as he and Ryan scurried into the parlor. "We're the talking rats from the story. My name is Sam. This is my boo, Ryan. And if I may be so bold, Todd, Sir is fucking hot. You better get all up on that."

"Hell yeah!" Ryan crowed. "Rats for the win!"

The cacophony that followed was so loud and unruly the constables were called, and by the time they arrived, Sir was sitting in the chair once more, Todd curled up in his lap, head laying against the rise and fall of Sir's chest.

Gabriel had ensured Justin and Tina and Gary couldn't flee, wielding his sword deftly, so much so that Ryan had stars in his eyes, much to Sam's consternation. Gary, of course, shouted maniacally that he was a magical creature, and therefore, knew his rights under the laws of Verania. However, this did not cover the alleged murder of Todd's father, and thusly, Gary's legs were wrapped in manacles. But since he was a unicorn, he only needed to lower his horn to the chains, causing them to fall off. Before anyone could stop him, he crashed through the picture window that lined the front of the house, glass shattering and falling onto the street. Justin and Tina screamed after him, asking why he would leave them behind. The last anyone saw of Gary was him fleeing the City of Lockes, never again to darken the streets. Rumor had it that Gary changed his name to Wanda, and somehow made a living as a courtesan in the distant country of Yennbridge, where there were no extradition laws.

His children weren't as lucky. Both were arrested immediately for their crimes against Todd's indentured servitude. In the ensuing court proceedings, Justin and Tina claimed they were victims of their father, and that any sentence should take that into consideration. When this was dismissed, both decided to plead temporary insanity. However, a jury of their peers saw right through their defense, and Justin and Tina were sentenced to ten years in the dungeon, where they would spend the next decade pooping in buckets.

But that came later.

Now the sounds of a crowd gathering on the street filtered in through the broken window and Justin and Tina swore revenge as they were led away. Todd opened his eyes as Sir rubbed a hand down his back. Sir smiled at him, a small quirk on his lips, and Todd warmed at the pride emanating from Sir.

"Is this real?" Todd whispered.

"It is," Sir said. "As real as it will ever be. The house, the restaurants, all are yours once more as they should have been from the beginning. I'm so proud of you, boy. You were very brave this day." Then he frowned, and Todd swallowed thickly. "However, on the night of the ball, I gave you an order that you disobeyed. Isn't that right?"

"Yes, Sir."

"And what was that order?"

"You told me to stop. But I didn't."

"That's right," Sir said gently. "And there will be punishment for that, mark my words."

"How is it punishment if he likes it?" Sam asked Ryan, causing Sir and Todd to look down at the rats.

"I dunno," Ryan said. "It's a kink thing, I guess." He paused, considering. "Are we kinky?"

"Who the fuck knows, dude. We're talking rats. Let's just deal with that first before we try and figure everything else out. Though, that being said, I have some really freaky ideas for what we can do with that tail of yours. It's so *thick*."

"The thickest," Ryan growled, and Sam began to squeak in ways that would haunt Todd's dreams for years to come.

"I suppose they'll have to come with us," Sir said.

Gabriel sighed. "I was afraid you were going to say that. The mule too?"

"The mule too," Sir agreed. "They're Todd's friends. They will have a home with us just as Todd does."

Todd blinked. "Wait, what?"

"You're going to live with me," Sir said, resuming rubbing Todd's back. "From now on, you'll live in my—*our* house, and—"

"Uh, no?" Todd blurted. Then, "Sir."

Gabriel snorted as the others fell silent. Sir's expression hardened, but Todd wasn't afraid. Not of him. Never him. "What was that?" Sir asked.

Todd paled, but this was important. "You're amazing. Wonderful. The best thing that ever happened to me, but we're still getting to know each other. We need time to figure things out. Like...date. And stuff."

"And stuff," Sir repeated.

"Yes," Todd said. "I mean, honestly, did you really think I'd move in with you right *now*?"

"Yes," Sir said, sounding grumpy. "I thought exactly that." His bottom lip stuck out as if he was pouting, and Todd didn't know what to do that didn't involve demanding Sir deflower him right here and now.

Shaking his head, Todd said, "We have time, now. All the time in the world. I want to do this right, but I also need to learn how to stand on my own."

Sir scowled. "I don't like it. At all. But..."

"But?" Todd asked.

Sir rolled his eyes. "But you have a point. This is as new for you as it is for me. So, yes. You may stay here for as long as you need. But not tonight. And perhaps not tomorrow night either. Or the next night after."

Todd laughed as Ryan and Sam cheered. From somewhere in the back of the house, Todd heard Tiggy yell, "Get yo man!"

Sir tugged on Todd's ear, pulling Todd back against his chest. Todd turned his face into Sir's tunic, breathing him in. "Thank you, Sir."

"My boy," Sir replied. "It is I who should be thanking you."

T RUE TO S IR'S WORD, Todd was punished that night, the skin of his ass reddened from Sir's big hand. After, once Todd had sufficiently recovered, Sir destroyed Todd's virginity quite spectacularly, Todd proving he followed direction quite well. After, mind wonderfully blank, Sir pulled Todd against his chest, holding him close and promising Todd that he would never feel alone again.

It should be said that Todd *did* learn to stand on his own. In fact, he made it an entire three weeks. The managers of his father's restaurants were pleased to see him back in charge. He worked hard during the day, relearning the tools of the trade, and though he always swore he'd sleep in his own bed—the attic still felt like a bit of a haven—he usually found himself in Sir's bed, not quite sure how he ended up there.

At the end of the third week, he looked around his childhood home and realized it was no longer for him. It felt too big, too empty. And it didn't have Sir, which was the most important thing of all. With that in mind, he packed up what he could and loaded it into a rickety cart, Tiggy attached to the front and stomping in excitement. Sam and Ryan climbed up next to Todd on the bench seat, and they left their home behind in search of another.

It did not take long.

Gabriel was waiting for them on the stairs of the manor, eyebrow arched as he smiled. "Finally," he said. "You'd think Lord Tremaine was a child with the way he's been going on and on about you not being here. I really am tired of it. I take your arrival means you've come to your senses?"

Todd jumped down from the cart and flung himself at Gabriel, who laughed as he hugged Todd back. "I have."

"Good," Gabriel said into Todd's hair. "He really is a pain in the ass when he doesn't get what he wants. It's high time he has his equal at his side."

Todd pulled back, mouth agape. "Equal? But I'm…he's…he's *Sir*."

"He is," Gabriel agreed. "But you are Todd, and there is no one on this earth who is better matched with him than you. I expect great things from you, Todd." He lowered his voice barely above a whisper. "And between you and me, he's never been happier. You will be loved beyond measure here as you rightly deserve."

GABRIEL SHOOED HIM into the house, telling Todd he'd see to Sam and Ryan and Tiggy. As it turned out, Sir had constructed a new stable just for Todd's friends, one where they would have all their hearts desired.

Todd walked through the familiar halls of the manor, heading toward the office. He took a deep breath outside the door before knocking.

"Enter," Sir grunted from inside.

Todd pushed open the door. Sir eyed him up and down, eyes alight with joy, fighting a losing battle with a smile. "And what brings you here, boy?" Sir asked, setting down his pen. "I thought you'd be at work."

Todd said, "I took the day off. I had things to do, Sir."

"Really," Sir said, leaning forward, elbows on the desk. "And what did you have to do?"

Todd decided to play it cool. "I heard the lord of this manor was in a foul mood. Seems he's quite the bother when he doesn't get what he wants."

"Is that right," Sir said. "Sounds like a very serious problem. What solution do you propose?"

Todd shrugged, though his body was a bundle of nerves. "That I live here, and keep an eye out on Sir, just to be safe."

Sir barely reacted, though Todd now knew him better than that. Sir was pleased, and it was all Todd could ever ask for. "Sounds reasonable," Sir said. "Get your pillow, boy. I still have work to do before the day ends."

Todd did as he was asked, pulling open the drawer and pulling out the pillow that was now his. He set it down next to Sir's chair and kneeled. A feeling of calm washed over him, and he knew he'd made the right decision.

Especially when the moment his knees hit the pillow, Sir's hand cupped the back of his head, pulling him forward. Todd lay against Sir's thigh, sighing as a hand carded through his hair. It never faltered, not even when Sir picked up his pen with his other hand and got back to work.

Todd drifted as he sometimes did, drowning willingly under Sir's ministrations. He came back into himself briefly when he heard Sir whisper, "Thank you, boy. You've made me very happy this day. I will never forget it. Welcome home."

Todd smiled and closed his eyes.

And wouldn't you know?

They lived kinkily ever after.

DAVID'S Dragon

ONCE UPON A TIME, there was a boy named Sam who looked upon the stars through the tiny window in his room in the slums of the City of Lockes, dreaming for more than what his life had become. Little did he know, the stars were watching him back, waiting for the day his destiny would be revealed. The stars whispered to each other about this boy. Some—the furthest and the oldest of the stars, gods who created the universe simply because they were bored—didn't think he had what it took. How could the fate of the world rest on the shoulders of one so young and foolish?

But there was one who fought for him above all others, one who believed in Sam Haversford with every fiber of its being. And though young itself, this constellation of stars knew about the bonds of loyalty and friendship, of unending love and the power of sacrifice. Paths, this constellation knew, could be set in stone, but stone could just as easily crumble.

This constellation was known as the Star Dragon.

David's Dragon.

The old gods cried, *He's just a child! Even if his magic is extraordinary, how could he possibly hope to conquer what will come?*

To which the Star Dragon replied, *He will, because he won't be alone. He'll have friends by his side, those who will do anything for him.*

The old gods muttered as they twinkled, but eventually, they subsided. *Fine,* they grumbled. *Be it on your head, then. Should the world collapse, we'll start again from the beginning. A new world. We've done it before. We can do it again.*

But the Star Dragon had faith. This world—though messy and chaotic—had moments of beauty so breathtaking it threatened to bring even the strongest to their knees. Even in darkness, hope was a weapon, if only one knew how to wield it.

In the end, the brave boy from the slums accepted his destiny, and though he suffered immeasurable loss, he stood brave and true, surrounded by those who loved him most. He battled the Dark Wizard Myrin…and won.

It was then this powerful wizard made a wish upon the stars, and as the Star Dragon ascended back into the heavens, he came upon a man who hadn't yet passed beyond the veil.

It is done, the Star Dragon said.

To which the man replied, *You were a little rude to him, if I'm being honest.*

The Star Dragon snorted. *Eh. He'll survive.*

He is the better part of all of us.

He is, the Star Dragon said. *And he wishes for you.*

The man smiled, though his eyes were filled with tears. *Truly?*

Yes, the Star Dragon said. *His wish will be granted, a gift for all he's done. It is not your time yet, Morgan of Shadows. Never forget.*

Morgan said, *I won't. I…thank you. For everything.* And then he began to shine as if he were a star himself. But instead of taking his place in the sky, he fell back toward the earth, alive once more.

The Star Dragon climbed higher and higher, searching for the voice that brought peace to his soul. It didn't take long before he heard a whisper. *There you are*, the voice said, glittering brightly. *My friend, my love. Hello, hello. Welcome home.*

The Star Dragon settled in the sky, the tip of his snout back where it belonged, pressing against a bright star that pulsed warmly. The Star Dragon sighed happily, having returned to the one he cherished most.

David, the Star Dragon breathed. *Did I do good?*

You did, David said. *A bit of a dick, but you got your point across. I'm so proud of you.*

With these words, the Star Dragon twinkled brightly. Anyone who chose to look up at the sky would think how strange it was that the constellation seemed brighter than it'd ever been. But then the thought would pass from their head, and the world moved on, as it always did.

But this isn't about what came after.

This story is about what came before.

Before the rise of Myrin.

Before the love between a knight and a wizard.

Before a dragon kidnapped a prince to take him to his tower.

Before Sam ever came to Castle Lockes, before he even knew he had magic.

Before he was born, before the wizards Randall and Morgan made a desperate decision to stop the one who had betrayed them.

Before all of them existed.

One thousand years before Sam stood on the cosmic plane and battled against Myrin, another story took place, one of love and loss, hope and betrayal.

And like most stories passed down through generations, details were changed, fanciful additions and unnecessary subtractions made, though the beating heart remained the same.

But what is to follow here, now, is the truth. The good, the bad, and the ugliness of humanity.

This is the story of a boy and his dragon.

DAVID WAS BORN on the night of a terrible storm that raged above a small village that sat on the outskirts of the Dark Woods. His father—a hardworking man named Jacob who loved with his whole heart—wiped his beloved's brow with a cold cloth, her hand squeezing his own tightly as she gritted her teeth. The midwife, a squat, handsome woman with frizzy hair, whispered soothingly from her spot between the mother's legs. "There," the midwife said. "You're doing so well, miss. I can see the child. Oh, look at all that hair on their head. Yes, it's almost time. One last push. Gather your strength."

The woman—Maureen, she with the golden hair and a

mischievous smile—cried out as thunder rumbled, as lightning flashed.

"I'm here," Jacob said. "I'm so proud of you."

"You can bite my entire *ass*," Maureen growled, causing Jacob to choke on his tongue. "Take your pride and shove it. Next time, you can push out a baby. See how proud you are then."

"I have herbs that can help facilitate that," the midwife said. "Should you decide to go that direction."

Jacob smiled quietly. "Let's get through this first, shall we?"

"Push, miss," the midwife said. "Push with all your might."

Maureen did, and the midwife moved quickly, still speaking encouraging words in low tones as she peered between Maureen's legs. Maureen screamed one last time before sagging back against the pillow, her face pale and slick with sweat.

"There," the midwife said, the sound of scissors snipping through something fibrous and wet. A moment later, she rose from the ground, a tiny child in her arms. At first, the child made no sound, and Jacob felt fear clawing at his chest. And then the midwife suctioned goop out of the child's nose, a sound of life filled the room, small and reedy, but clear.

"A boy," the midwife said, wiping the child down before wrapping him up in a blanket. "Miss, you have a son. Congratulations." She leaned forward, setting the boy on Maureen's chest. "Your work is not yet done. The afterbirth will come soon. Take a moment to breathe. I'll return shortly."

She left the new father and mother to look down in wonder at the tiny bundle against Maureen's chest.

"He's perfect," Maureen whispered, and Jacob fell in love at first sight. The boy—red and wailing—had a head of black hair, his eyes the brightest blue Jacob had ever seen. He had all his fingers. All his toes. A little nose that wriggled, and a gummy mouth that emitted such a strong sound.

"David," Maureen whispered. "His name is David." She looked up at her husband. "After your father."

Jacob smiled widely. "A perfect name. Dad would be honored. I know he's watching us from beyond the veil. A blessing for our first son. What a wonderful day this has been. What a wonderful life we have. Thank you, Maureen. Thank you." He leaned down and kissed his wife on the forehead.

And though they did not know it, another awaited the birth of the boy. Hidden away in the woods, a creature smiled and whispered, *Welcome to the world, little one.*

FOR HIS FIRST SIX YEARS, David grew knowing only love and peace. He was a headstrong boy, talkative and bright, though his head sometimes seemed stuck in the clouds. His mother, Maureen, was the mayor of their village, his father her assistant. Their village—one of hundreds in the kingdom of Verania—had prospered over the years, their crops helping to feed their fellow countrymen and women. The people of the village grew to love David, often finding him seated with his mother at her desk, asking question after question about every single thing she was doing. A lovely family, the village of the people said. Our future.

Every night, David and his parents would sit down for supper, just the three of them, talking about their day. They laughed, they teased, they lived. After all, that was the point of life. To be as good a person as possible, but to also recognize when one made a mistake. "No mistake is too big to apologize for," Jacob told his son, "so long as you mean it. But that doesn't mean you'll earn forgiveness right away. Learn, David. Learn from your mistakes and grow to be the man I know you'll be."

On one such night toward the end of summer, Maureen said, "David. Tomorrow, you'll go to school for the first time as we've discussed. It's going to be a big day. Are you excited?"

David frowned as he chewed on a hunk of meat. He swallowed before speaking, just as his Mom had taught him. "I wanna go to work with you. Do mayor stuff."

Dad laughed. "Already into government work. Maureen, we've failed. We're miserable parents."

"Hush," Mom said, though she was smiling. She looked at her son. "You'll be fine. You'll get to go with the other children. And your teacher is extremely excited to have you in his class. Can you keep a secret?"

David nodded with wide eyes. He loved secrets. "Promise," he said, crossing a finger over his chest.

"There is to be a party," Mom said. "To welcome you. It was supposed to be a surprise, but I think we can still pretend you don't know."

"A party?" David asked in awe. "For *me*?"

"Yes," Mom said. "With songs and little cakes. Streamers and confetti. Can you pretend to be surprised?"

David nodded furiously. "I *swear*. I'll be so surprised."

"Oh boy," Dad said. "This should be hysterical." He grinned when Mom swatted him on the arm. "What? I'm just saying."

That night, Mom and Dad tucked him into bed, and told him a story as he drifted off to sleep, both of them doing the voices David loved so much. As his eyes closed, the blanket up to his chin, he sighed happily. He felt Mom kiss his cheek, Dad running a hand through his hair.

And he dreamed, as he sometimes did. The same dream, one he'd had ever since he could remember. In it, he walked through the forest, but he wasn't scared. If anything, he felt happy, whole, safe. Someone—something?—walked with him, just out of sight. The presence was never threatening, and though David tried to find them, he never could. "I'm here!" he called in his dream. "I'm right here!"

That night, as the stars hung suspended in the heavens, a voice spoke back for the first time, warm and melodic. But instead of being spoken out loud, it sounded as if it were coming from everywhere and nowhere at once. It was in his head, in the sky, in the trees.

It said, *Soon, David. Soon.*

"Surprise!" the teacher and the children cried as Mom and Dad led David into the school. "Surprise, David!"

David said, "Look, Mom! It's the party you said I can't know about! You were *right*."

Dad chuckled as Mom sighed. "David, that's not what we—it doesn't matter. Yes, the party."

The other children—a dozen in all shapes and sizes—swarmed around them. Suddenly shy, David clung to his mother's leg, turning his face into the fabric of her trousers. It was louder than he expected it to be, and he wasn't sure he liked it very much. He calmed some when Mom ran her fingers through his thick hair.

"Hi, David," a boy said, poking him in the arm. "I'm Levi. Can we be friends?"

David peeked out at Levi. He was a bigger boy—perhaps eight or thirty, David couldn't tell—and he was missing his two front teeth, his tongue sticking out in the gap. He had bright red hair and eyes so green, David wondered if they were made of summer grass. "Hi, Levi," he muttered, still shy. "I like your name."

Levi gasped. "You *do*? Oh my gosh, that's awesome. Thank you. I like your name too. We should be friends."

David hesitated, looking up at his mom. She nodded, and he pulled away from her, gaze trained on the floor.

"Levi," Teacher said, a spindly man with a big beard and a twinkle in his eyes. "Why don't you show David where he can put his things? I think there's a cubbyhole next to yours he can use."

Levi grabbed David by the hand, pulling him along, chattering a mile a minute about all the things he and David would do together now that they were friends. Though slightly overwhelmed, David began to relax as Levi showed him where to put his satchel. The teacher was right; the cubbyhole—painted blue with red and yellow butterflies—was right next to Levi's.

"There," Levi said. "It's perfect. Now we get to be by each other every day. Come on! Let's go eat the cake we made for you! It's the sixth one we made, but Teacher said we shouldn't tell you about the other ones, because they turned out gross."

David got so caught up in this strange new world that he didn't notice his parents leaving. In fact, he didn't notice their absence until Dad returned that afternoon. By this time, David had glue in his hair, glitter coating the tips of this fingers, and everything that came out of his mouth began with *Levi said* or *Levi told me* or *Levi thinks*.

"It sounds as if you made a good friend," Dad said, waving to Teacher before leading David from the school.

"*Best* friend," David corrected. "He's so cool. He made me a paper swan!" David pulled it from his pocket, frowning as it looked nothing like the swan it'd been before he'd stored it away. He shrugged before shoving it back in his pocket. "I get to go back tomorrow, right?"

"Right," Dad said as they walked from the village. "And the day after. And the day after that."

"Hurray!" David crowed as people around them smiled and laughed.

They reached the Mayor's office, and right before David walked through the door, something stopped him, a tiny tug in the back of his mind. He turned, face scrunching up. He thought he'd heard someone say his name, but he couldn't see anyone looking at him.

"You all right, kiddo?" Dad asked from the doorway.

"Yeah," David said slowly. "Just…" He shook his head. He was hearing things. That's all it was. He ran past his father into the office, calling out, "Mom! *Mom.* You'll never guess what Levi did! *So many things*, and I'm gonna tell you about *all of them.*"

He forgot about the feeling he'd had. After all, he had more important things to focus on.

A YEAR LATER, when David was seven and sprouting up like a weed, he awoke in the middle of the night, heart thundering in his chest. He'd been in the middle of the same dream, in the forest, the trees towering over him, the presence feeling as if it'd been right on his heels. But when he'd whirled around, all he'd seen were the Dark Woods.

He blinked slowly, falling back against his pillow. "A dream," he mumbled before yawning. "Just a dream." He closed his eyes, hoping he could return to this dream.

David.

He opened his eyes once more. The voice from the trees. The same voice. He sat up in his bed, blankets pooling around his waist. Moonlight poured in through the window, bathing the floors and walls in white. He was scared, but like many boys his age, he was also blessed (cursed?) with curiosity, which outweighed any fear. He looked around his room, trying to see if anything was out of place. Nothing, as far as he could tell.

"Hello?" he said, voice trembling just a little. "Who's there?"

Silence.

"You don't need to be scared," David said. "I promise I'm a good person."

No response.

He frowned before laying back down, half-convinced it was nothing at all. He was about to drop off back to sleep when he thought he saw movement from just outside the window. He rose swiftly, his feet carrying him as he rushed toward the window that looked out onto the village.

He saw the watchmen carrying their lanterns as they patrolled the dirt road. He saw two men, partially hidden in the shadows of an alley across the way. They smiled at each other before one leaned in to kiss the other. He saw a cat, carrying a limp rodent in its mouth as it crept through the cool night air.

But nothing near his window.

"Seeing things," he said. "That's all."

He went back to bed.

He didn't dream of the forest again that night.

"YOU'RE BETTER THAN THIS," Mom said sternly when David was thirteen. "Honestly, David, what were you thinking?"

David rolled his eyes. "We didn't do anything! Levi said that—"

"Levi," Mom said. "It's always Levi with you. Levi, Levi, Levi. If Levi jumped off a cliff, would you follow?"

Yes, he would, because Levi was the best friend he'd ever had, and where Levi went, David was sure to follow. But that wasn't what Mom wanted to hear. "No," he muttered, picking at a loose thread on his trousers even as he thought *yes*.

Mom sighed as she sat back in the chair in her office. He'd been brought to her after he and Levi had been discovered trying to sneak off into the Dark Woods. Levi had dared him to go as far as he could into the woods. David had double dared him back. Then Levi had double *dog* dared him, and David knew there was no bigger dare.

Levi—fourteen and already strong, arms lined with ropey muscle that caused David's stomach to twist slickly for reasons he didn't understand—had taken him by the hand and said, "We'll go together. Not too far, just enough so we can grab something and prove we did."

They'd made it to the tree line, only to be stopped by one of the watchmen, who asked what the hell they were doing. David knew that Levi was probably getting read the riot act just like he was. That didn't make him feel any better.

"You could get lost," Mom said, staring at her only child. "The Dark Woods are vast and deep, filled with dangers and creatures that could hurt you. You need to think, David. If you got lost in the forest, we might not be able to find you."

"I'm not scared," David retorted.

"I know," Mom said. "But you *should* be. Why would you make us worry like that? If you got lost, I would cry for days and days."

David didn't like when his mother cried. It was rare, but when it happened, it made him feel as if his heart was breaking all while making him want to hurt whatever had made her sad. And when he was the cause? Oh, did that make him feel small.

"I'm sorry," he said. "I was just…"

"You were just," Mom said. She folded her hands on her desk. "It happens. I'm asking you to make better choices. I'll keep this between us *this* time, so long as you promise not to do anything like this again."

David sagged gratefully in the chair. "You won't tell Dad?"

"No," Mom said, sounding amused. "I won't. We'll pretend it didn't happen."

"Then I promise so hard."

Her lips quirked. "Good. I'm glad to hear it." Then a funny expression crossed her face. "David, can I…"

He furrowed his brow. "Can you what?"

She looked at him for a long moment. "Do you…care for Levi?"

What a strange question. Levi was his best friend. *Of course* David cared for him. "I love him," David said, without artifice. He knew some boys would make fun of him for saying that, but this was his mother. She'd never make him feel low for speaking his truth.

Mom said, "I know you do. But I meant…you know what? It doesn't matter. I'm glad you have someone like him, even if you don't always make the best decisions when he's around."

"He's good," David said, panicking slightly at the thought of his mother forbidding him from ever seeing Levi again. "He makes me happy. He's my best friend. Please don't take that away from me." By the time he finished, he was panting, eyes bulging from his head.

Mom stood swiftly, hurrying around the table and crouching before her son. She lay her hands on his knees, squeezing gently. "Breathe, kiddo. Just breathe. I promise I'm not going to try and keep you two apart." She smiled ruefully. "I doubt I could even if I wanted to. But there is more to the world than him. You may not be able to see that now, but he's not the be all and end all."

That didn't sit well with David. Levi was everything. Ever since that first day when they'd met, they'd been inseparable, and even when Levi had moved to a different class given his age, he always made time for David. For a while, David had worried Levi would make new friends and forget about him, but Levi hadn't. He was always there, waiting with a sunny smile that caused David's heart to stutter.

"He's my friend," David said, not yet having the tools to articulate beyond that. "He's…"

Mom smiled sadly. "I know. And if…if you ever need to tell me something about him, about *you*, I want you to know that I'm always here to listen and support you no matter what."

David frowned. "What do you mean?"

Mom shook her head as she rose. "You'll figure it out when

you're ready. I've got some work to do before we go home. You can help, seeing as how you don't have anything else to do."

David thought about arguing, but he'd gotten lucky. Better to do what Mom wanted than to have her change her mind about telling Dad.

ON DAVID'S SIXTEENTH BIRTHDAY, Levi kissed him for the first time. It was unexpected, though not, as these things sometimes are. One moment, David was exclaiming over the book Levi had gifted him, and the next, Levi's determined face grew larger and larger until he was all David could see. Levi's breath became David's, and all rational thought left David's head in an explosion of fireworks. His chest hitched as Levi paused, a mere inch separating them, an impossible chasm. Then David was kissed for the first time in his life, the barest press of lips, there for a beat, two, three, and then gone as Levi pulled back, eyebrows near his hairline.

"What was that?" David whispered.

"Something I've wanted to do for a long time," Levi said, face flushed as he scratched the back of his neck. "I…you don't…I just…"

"Do it again," David demanded.

And so Levi did. And again. And again. And again. Until David was dizzy with it, his skin buzzing, his mind hot. He gasped when he felt Levi's tongue brushing against his bottom lip, and he had to keep from launching himself at the older boy.

When Levi pulled away after what felt like thousands of years, David sucked in a sharp breath, chest expanding so wide, he thought he felt his ribs crack.

"You kissed me," David said, touching his bottom lip.

"I did," Levi said, sounding more nervous than David had ever heard him. "Is that okay?"

"Yes," David breathed, and shaky laughter bubbled from his mouth. "Yes. Oh my gods, yes."

Levi smiled, and David was lost.

HE TOOK THE LONG WAY HOME, trying to collect his thoughts. He was sure Mom and Dad would know right away what had happened. Though he knew they wouldn't mind, he wanted to keep this for himself, at least for now. He had much to think on. What it meant. What it *could* mean. What would happen tomorrow, the day after, a year from now. Levi was about to graduate and would join his father as a watchman of the village. He'd already been training for the last year, but now that he was a man, he'd be able to do the job on his own, much to his delight. "And I'll protect your house more than all the others," Levi promised him, turning his head in the grass to look at David, his red hair spilling to the ground like fire. "If anything were to happen, I would protect you."

David believed him, and in the back of his mind, he thought the thoughts of the young in love for the first time: this was the most important thing to have happened to anyone ever, and it would last for an eternity. No one would come between them. It was their destiny to be together forever.

But destiny is a fickle thing, diverting paths seemingly set in stone without rhyme or reason, creating a sticky web, entrapping the unsuspecting.

As David walked along the edge of the village, lost in thoughts filled with Levi, Levi, Levi, another voice broke through the storm in his head, one he hadn't heard in a very long time.

David, it whispered in his head.

He stopped, cocking his head as he looked toward the Dark Woods in the distance.

"I hear you," he said, the sounds of the village fading around him.

David, the voice said again, though louder now, stronger.

He took a step toward the Dark Woods.

It's time, the voice sang. *Come to me. Come, come.*

David hesitated, but only briefly. He looked back over his shoulder at the village, heavy with indecision. But then the voice said, *Please. I have much to show you. We are connected. I have waited for you for so long. I would have you see my face, so that I may gaze upon yours.*

David left the village behind and entered the Dark Woods.

HE WALKED FOR WHAT FELT LIKE AGES, the trees growing thicker, the canopy above blocking out the sky and the sun. Though nervous, he didn't give much thought to turning around and running back home. Foolish maybe, but David had always been brave, much to his parents' chagrin.

He heard movement in the forest around him: birds singing in the trees, animals hidden by shadows as they crept and skulked. Once, he thought he saw a great stag, flowers dangling from its antlers, but it must have been a trick of the shadows, because when he tried to go toward it, all he saw were branches rubbing together in the breeze, the sound like bones rattling.

He didn't know how long he'd walked before he came to a clearing with a large hill at its center, covered in green grass and moss. It could have been an hour. It could have been a year. He wasn't tired, wasn't hungry.

"But I'm lost," he mumbled, looking up at the cerulean blue sky above the clearing. "I don't know how I'll find my way back."

He decided to climb the hill in the clearing, hoping to use the height to find the path home. If anything, he told himself, he'd see the smoke rising from the stacks in the village. He approached the hill, coming to a stop when it rose up and down, as if it were breathing.

He stopped, eyes wide. He'd heard stories of the Dark Woods, of fairies that tricked those lost, of giant trolls that feasted on the bones of their victims, sucking out the marrow as if it were a delicacy. Stories to frighten children, but to a sixteen-year-old boy lost in the woods, they all seemed very real. He liked his marrow where it was, thank you very much.

He kept a distance from the breathing hill, circling around it, trying to see what it was. The grass swayed, the flowers bloomed, the earth rising and falling. Once he was back to where he started, he cocked his head and sat down on the ground, legs crossed, elbows on his knees.

"Are you the one calling to me?" David asked, knowing the shit Levi would give him for talking to a breathing hill. "What are you?"

Your friend, the voice said, as loud as it'd ever been, its rumbling growl deep. *I have been here since you were born. I have watched over you and your village, waiting for the day when it was time to reveal myself to you.*

"You're in my head," David said quietly, plucking at a blade of grass. "How are you doing that?" Then he remembered what the voice had said before he entered the woods. "We're connected."

Yes, the voice said. *Connected in ways unexpected. I do not know what the gods are asking of me, but they have put you in my path, and I would see what that brings. There is a reason for all things, though* this *reason is hidden from me. I am in your head because you are in mine.*

David thought, *Can you hear me?*

He startled when the voice said, *Yes, I can.*

David rose unsteadily to his feet, wringing his hands until his knuckles popped. "I don't know if I like that. My thoughts are my own. What right do you have to listen to them?"

The voice chuckled, low and deep. *Fear not, child. Your secrets are safe. I would never betray you for anything. You are important to me, and I am so very pleased to finally know you.*

"Show yourself," David said, trying to sound as strong as his mother and father. Then, "I mean, unless you're just a hill. If so, that's...uh. Cool? I guess. Who else gets to say they have a talking hill as a friend?"

A wave of amusement washed over him, and David trembled when he realized it wasn't coming from himself. No, it came from the hill. It felt heavy and warm, like a blanket on a cold winter's night. *I am no hill*, the voice said. *I am more.*

And then the hill rose, the earth cracking and breaking apart, dirt sloughing off in large clumps. David stumbled back when he saw the flash of a large amber eye, reptilian and intelligent, trained on him. The eye blinked slowly. David gasped when he saw a *second* eye set back in a massive head covered in green, glittering scales the color of summer grass, the same as Levi's eyes. His stomach sank to his toes as the creature revealed itself, four legs on the ground, black talons digging into the dirt. Massive wings spread, covering the width of the clearing, the membranes a translucent shade of green paler than the rest of its body. The beast shook its head side-to-side, its (his?) spike-covered tail thumping on the ground. Its (his?) head lowered toward David, bigger than anything he'd ever seen before. The creature's black lips pulled back over sharp rows of fangs, and it took David far longer than he cared to admit to realize the thing in front of him wasn't getting ready to attack.

It—*he* was smiling.

"You're a dragon," David breathed, voice cracking. He'd never seen a dragon before. Most people hadn't. It'd been hundreds of years since the last sighting, the beasts hiding away from those who wanted to kill them for their teeth, their scales, their horns. Dragons were supposedly filled with magic, and every piece and part of them was prized. Hushed stories had been told of their existence, stories that spoke of their penchant for death and fire and destruction. Nothing good came from a dragon, David had been told time and time again.

I am, the dragon said, though his lips did not move, still grinning at him. *And you are David. You're taller than I expected. You've grown into yourself.*

"Thank you," David said, remembering his manners. "Also, that's kind of creepy. Are you a stalker, or…?"

The dragon snorted, shaking his head. *Cheeky git*, the dragon said, sounding absurdly fond. *I am not stalking you. Mostly.*

Any fear David had felt dissolved. Excitement roared through him, a billion questions all vying to be the first to escape his mouth. "What kind of dragon are you? Where did you come from? Have you always lived here? Can I touch you? Wait, is that rude to ask a dragon? I don't know! I've never talked to a dragon before. Oh no, please don't take offense! I have no idea what's going on, and I can't seem to close my mouth." Then, "Why can you talk to me? I didn't think anyone could talk to dragons. Oh crap. Is this *my* doing?" He paled. "Okay, so, I didn't mean to smoke that thing Levi wanted me to try with him. He said it'd get us stoned, but was that *all* it did? Gods, I'm going to give him so much crap over this."

The dragon chuckled. *No. It wasn't because you got stoned that one time two years ago. I've heard you long before that, and you me. It has nothing to do with Levi.* This last came out in a strange growl, but before David could ask after it, the dragon continued. *I have never been able to speak to a human before. This is new for me as well.*

"Really?" David asked. "That's weird. Isn't that weird? I think it's weird. Why can't I stop talking? Crap, I don't think I'm breathing." He tried to suck in a breath, but his lungs felt constricted, as if a vise had squeezed them closed. He bent over, hands on his knees as he gagged, his vision graying.

A sharp burst of hot air billowed against his face, jerking him out of his panic attack. He opened his eyes to find the dragon's head near his own. A long, pink tongue slithered out between the lips and flickered. *Calm,* the dragon said. *Calm. You're safe with me. I would never hurt you.*

Oh," David said weakly. "That's…that's good." But he *did* calm, his breaths—though ragged—burning in his chest. His vision cleared, and he marveled at the sight before him. The dragon was as large as the biggest house in the village, and though David had never seen another dragon, he'd always thought they'd be even bigger. Grass and flowers grew along his sides and back over the glittering scales. He had two horns on his head, black and twisting together to a single point. It looked like a crown of sorts. His underbelly was the same pale shade of green as his wings, the colors growing darker along his chest, where they swirled together to make what appeared to be a strange symbol, almost like a keyhole. "Wow," David said as the dragon spun in a slow circle, revealing every part of itself. "You're beautiful."

Thank you, David, the dragon said, and David felt a little flutter of happiness in his head. The dragon was pleased with him. *You're not so bad yourself, for a human.*

"What is your name?" David asked as the dragon faced him once more.

My name is ancient. It cannot be pronounced by the human tongue.

David squinted up at him. "What? That's not cool. You should at least let me try."

So be it. My name is…

What followed was a complicated sound filled with grunts and growls, a symphony of noise that David couldn't follow. It ended with a little trill before the dragon looked at him expectantly.

"Huh," David said. "So it's…" He tried to emulate what he'd just heard but ended up biting his tongue and choking on spit.

Another wave of amusement washed over him. *Something like that. Except you just said something extraordinarily offensive about dragons in my tongue.*

David blanched. "I…I didn't mean to… oh my gods, I'm so sorry."

That was a joke, the dragon said.

Relief, then, though he glared at the dragon. "Well, that's a hard name to say. We'll need to come up with something easier for me. Can't just call you Dragon. That wouldn't be fair since you don't call me Human."

What name would you like for me to have? the dragon asked, cocking his head as he settled down on his belly, legs folded underneath him like the world's biggest cat.

David began to pace, feeling the dragon's eyes on him. "Well, I suppose I should ask what you like. What makes you happy. What brings you joy."

Ah, the dragon said. *I see. So, your name is David because David bring you joy.*

David shook his head. "That's not…my name is David because it's the name my parents chose for me. It was the name of my grandfather. I share his name as a sign of honor."

I did not have parents to choose for me, the dragon said. *I am born of fire and stone and magic. Dragons come into being when they are expected to, and not a moment before.*

"Truly?" David asked, taken aback. "I've heard stories about dragons, but I don't know how much of it is true. I can't imagine not having parents. Doesn't that make you sad?"

You can't be sad for things you never had, the dragon replied. *What would be the point?*

"It happens all the time, unfortunately. At least for some

humans. We covet what we don't have."

Why?

David chuckled. "It's just the way we are. For all the beauty and wonder humans can create, we're still…." He didn't know how to finish.

The dragon did. *You're still young, as a species. You haven't yet learned how to control it. I have met humans in my many years. Some good, some not. Are you a good human?*

David shrugged uneasily. What did it mean to be a good human? Was it doing the best he could with what he had? David wasn't a perfect person, but then he never claimed to be. He could be headstrong to the point of stubbornness, and when things didn't go his way, he could become easily frustrated. "I try to be," he said. "I don't know how often I succeed, but I always apologize if I do something wrong. Mistakes are how we learn to become better people. It shows us right from wrong."

Some humans don't seem to learn that lesson, the dragon said. *They are wrong, and yet they continue down that path without a care for who they step on along the way.*

"True," David said. "But thankfully, I'm not one of them. Tell me, what makes you happy?"

The sun, the dragon said, tilting his head back and closing his eyes. *The way it warms my skin when I lay on rocks. The sky, because my wings need the wind. The feeling of grass underneath my feet, as it reminds me to be grounded when my wings grow weary. The stars at night, because they make me feel small.*

David sat before the dragon, resting back on his hands, ankles crossed. "Do you like feeling small?"

Oh yes. When you're as big as me, feeling small is a lovely thing indeed. No matter how large I grow, there is solace knowing there are still things far larger than I. It serves to show me my place.

"I never thought about it that way," David admitted. "I always feel small."

A guttural, rumbling sound came from the dragon, punctuated by sharp exhales from his nostrils. It took David a moment to realize he was laughing. *You may be small compared to me, but you have a strong heart, David.*

"How do you know?"

You hear my voice. There is no one else who has been able to do the same. I imagine it takes someone with an infallible spirit to converse with me as you have.

"Why is that, do you think?" David asked. "I'm not a wizard or a magician. I have no magic in my blood. I've never heard of anyone being able to talk to dragons, least of all someone like me."

I know not, the dragon said. *But I will not question it. Dragons are solitary creatures. We can spend decades without saying anything at all.*

David winced as he looked down at his hands. "I'm sorry if I'm interrupting your quiet." That wasn't what he meant to do at all. He was about to suggest going home when the dragon's tail appeared, the tip dropping into his lap and twitching. It was heavy, the weight firm against his thighs.

I like your interruption, the dragon said. *Solitude can lead to loneliness. It can be difficult when you only speak to yourself.*

Carefully, giving the dragon time to pull away, he lowered a hand and placed it on the dragon's tail. The scales were much smaller on the end, compact and tight, lined with thick spikes along the top of the tail, the last of which was about the size of David's forearm. He stroked the scales between the spikes and snorted when the dragon's back left leg began to jerk of its own volition.

That's fine, the dragon said with a sigh. *That's just fine.*

David studied the dragon as he stroked his tail, taking in his immense size, the colors, the way his scales caught the light. His gaze rose to the dragon's chest, and that strange keyhole there. It wasn't a perfect keyhole; the edges were jagged, the top of the symbol larger than the bottom as if any key would have to be turned upside down to work. Or a sword, he thought as he swallowed thickly.

Why are you worried? the dragon asked. *You were happy only a moment before.*

David shook his head, shoving down the thought of swords and the anger of men into a box in his mind and locking it tightly. He'd have to be more careful if the dragon was in his head. David didn't want to scare him away. "Sometimes, people can be sad or scared for reasons even they can't explain."

That sounds terrible. I wouldn't like not knowing why I was upset. It'd mean I wouldn't know what to bite to make it stop.

"If only it were that easy," David muttered. Today has been a strange day. He'd never have thought that getting kissed by Levi for the first time wouldn't be the most exciting thing to have happened. "That symbol. On your chest. What is it?"

The dragon turned his head until one eye pointed down toward the ground. *Why? Is it unsightly?*

"No," David said honestly. "There is nothing unsightly about you."

The dragon huffed. *You're good for my ego. I will keep you. I don't know what it is. It's always been part of me. Though I have met other dragons in my life, I've never seen another with the same upon them. What does it look like to you?*

Instead of trying to explain—for fear the meaning might be misunderstood or lost—David formed an image in his mind, of a grand, ornate door with a green lock. A key fit into the keyhole and turned, causing the door to open, white light spilling out.

Ahhh, the dragon said. *I see. I am a lock. You are a key.*

David startled. "That's not…I'm not much of anything."

I don't like it when you speak badly of yourself, the dragon said, the tail twitching in David's lap. *You are a key. You are my key.*

"Keyhole," David muttered, mind racing. "Key. Lock." He brightened. "Lockes! In the Veranian tongue, Lockes means a beacon of hope, a light in all the darkness. What if we called you Lockes?"

Lockes, the dragon said slowly, chewing on the word. *Lockes. A beacon of hope, a light in the darkness. I am the dragon, Lockes. Yes. Yes, David. I will accept the name you have bestowed upon me, and gladly. Thank you. That is much easier to say than what my actual name is. From this day forward, you will be David the Key. And I will be your Lockes.*

David smiled.

He returned to the village as the sun began to set, the sky aflame. He promised Lockes not to reveal the dragon's existence to anyone, and though it hadn't sat well with David, he understood why. Dragons, though not having been seen in decades, were something to be feared. And when people were afraid, they acted unlike themselves, wanting to destroy what they didn't understand. He wouldn't let anything happen to Lockes, even if he wished to shout from the rooftops that he had made friends with a *dragon*.

He'd learned more in a single afternoon than he'd ever had at school. Over the course of his first meeting with Lockes, he began to understand that all the texts about dragons were woefully inadequate, built upon stereotypes and half-truths. Sure, there might be some factual information, but like people, dragons were individuals. The actions of one didn't necessarily apply to them as a whole. He wondered what else that could apply to. Everything, he thought as his house came into view, it could apply to anything and everything.

Mom and Dad looked up from the kitchen table when he walked in through the back door. "There you are," Mom said. "I thought you'd be home before now. What have you been up to?"

David panicked, saying the first thing that came into his mind that wasn't dragon related. "I was with Levi! He…" David blushed, scuffling his boots on the floor.

Mom and Dad exchanged a knowing look. "Levi did what?" Dad asked, sounding like he was trying to keep from laughing.

David rolled his eyes. "He…uh. Kissed me?"

"And how did you feel about that?" Mom asked carefully.

David shrugged. "Good? And weird, all at the same time. I mean, he's *Levi*. He's just…"

"He's just," Dad said, sounding amused. "If you'd like, we can act surprised." His eyes widened as he brought a hand to his mouth. "Levi? You kissed *Levi*. I never would've suspected!"

Mom's hand was at her throat. "This is news to me as well. Even though from the first day you met him, it was *Levi this* and *Levi that*. Oh, how I wish I could have seen what was coming to better prepare myself!"

"Ha ha," David muttered. "I know you both think you're funny, but you're really not."

Mom and Dad broke, laughing as Dad pounded the table with a

meaty fist. "We're just pulling your leg, kiddo," Mom said, wiping her eyes.

Dad rose from his chair and moved toward David, settling his hands on his son's shoulders. "Levi is a good man. Honest and strong. He will make a good husband."

"*Dad!*" David bellowed, cringing as he stepped back, causing Dad's hands to fall from his shoulders.

"Jacob," Mom said.

"What?" Dad said. "He will. And don't tell me you're not thinking it too. A union between our families will benefit us all. What's the problem?"

"I'm *sixteen*," David hissed. "I'm not getting married!"

"Well, not yet," Dad said. He grew stern, pointing a finger at David. "Especially not while you're still in school. While I'm pleased you finally pulled your head out of your ass to see Levi has been pining after you for ages, you need to remember to focus on your studies."

"Mom!"

"He has a point," Mom said, rising from the table and joining her husband in front of David. "Levi is wonderful, but this is your first relationship. Maybe it'll be your only; and will turn into what your father and I have. Or maybe it will be your first, a stepping stone into becoming a man. Regardless, you shouldn't let it consume you. A clear head means a clear heart."

"I know," David said, wishing he'd kept his fool mouth shut. Now, he'd never hear the end of it. He could already see the knowing looks his parents would have whenever they saw Levi. "But it's not...serious. It's not a relationship."

"Uh huh," Dad said dryly. "Keep telling yourself that, kiddo. But I've seen the way you look at him, and how he looks at you. There's something there, and we couldn't be happier for you."

David allowed himself to be gathered up in his father's strong arms, head just underneath Dad's chin. And though Levi was there, smiling handsomely in his head, he dissipated into smoke when a dragon appeared, majestic and glorious.

A secret, and one he'd protect with his life.

DAVID CHEERED FROM HIS SEAT in the audience when Levi was called to the front of the room, Teacher handing him a scroll that signified his schooling had ended. Levi's mother sniffled into a lace cloth, Levi's father wrapping an arm around her shoulders as they watched their son. Levi took the scroll and looked out into the audience, raising a fist above his head. David clapped and laughed, proud of his friend.

Later, once the other graduates had received their scrolls, Levi found David waiting for him at the edge of the small crowd. He looked handsome in his too-small suit, the sleeves ending at the delicate bones of his wrists. David didn't know what Levi had planned; only their parents knew about their new relationship. But the decision was made when Levi cupped his face and kissed him sweetly in front of everyone. Everything else melted away as David grew weightless, feeling as if he would float away into the sky.

"Thank you," Levi said as he pressed his forehead against David's. "I was nervous, but I saw you in the crowd, and you made me feel like I could do anything."

"You can," David said. "I'm so proud of you."

"Because of you," Levi said, nose brushing against David's, causing his heart to flutter. "I wouldn't have made it this far without you."

David shook his head. "You would have done just fine."

"But I won't ever have to know," Levi said. "Because you're here, with me. And I couldn't be happier."

"You big dork," David said fondly. It was only then that he remembered they had an audience, and as soon as he lifted his gaze to the crowd, he saw them all watching. They immediately began speaking loudly, as if they weren't all nosy busybodies. Except, of course, for the two sets of parents watching their sons proudly.

Levi's lips came near David's ear, breath hot. "You should know Grandad told Dad that he needs to offer a goat to your parents in exchange for you as a sort of dowry."

"Oh my gods," David groaned. "Please tell me your father told him to fuck off."

Levi chuckled. "Told him that it'd need to be at least *three* goats."

I like eating goats, a voice whispered in David's head, causing him to freeze.

Levi must have felt the change, because he looked worried as he pulled back. "He was just kidding. You know how Grandad is, stuck in the old ways."

Make it five goats, Lockes said. *Never underestimate your worth. Make it five, and then bring them to me and I will cook them for us.*

I'm not bringing you goats!

Fine, Lockes grumbled. *I can find my own goats. I will bring you twelve, which is more than one or three.*

"David?" Levi asked, pulling him out of his head. "What's wrong?"

David smiled too brightly. "Nothing. Just… thinking. Tell your grandfather that the offer of goats has been rejected."

Levi laughed. "I'll make sure to do that. Come on. Mom and Dad said to invite you and your parents over to celebrate. Dad's been cooking all day, and I'm starving." He took David by the hand, leading them toward their parents. Levi looked back at him, eyebrows waggling. "And then we'll steal away and have our own celebration."

What does that mean? Lockes asked, sounding curious. *Does that mean fornication? Because it sounds like he means fornication. David, are you going to fornicate?*

"Fuck off," David said through gritted teeth.

Levi frowned. "What?"

"Nothing!" David said. "I wasn't talking to—never mind. Yes, let's go eat and then go…do stuff."

"Gee," Levi said. "Stuff. That's romantic."

It's really not, Lockes said. *Romance is spreading the entrails of your latest kill in a pretty display to attract a mate, followed by a dance to show your strength and prowess. David, if he starts to dance on top of intestines, you're being wooed.*

I'm going to straight up murder your face.

Promises, promises, Lockes said.

THAT NIGHT, LEVI TOOK DAVID'S HAND, leading him from his house through the village. He looked nervous, yet determined, as they left the village behind, heading away from the homes and lights. The shadows from the Dark Woods stretched ominously as Levi stopped underneath an ancient oak.

Levi removed the pack he'd brought, opening it and pulling out a blanket. The air was warm and thick, and David was having a hard time catching his breath. He knew what this was leading to, and thought he was more than ready, but this felt big, bigger than he expected. He trusted Levi with his life and his heart, but both were fragile.

Breathe, Lockes whispered in his head. *You are safe. You are loved. I will leave you to your moment, but should you have need of me, all you need to do is call my name.*

Thank you, David thought in reply. *I'm scared but excited. What if I'm not good enough?*

He felt the dragon's annoyance. *That is not the question you should be asking. You should be asking if your Levi is good enough for* you. *You may doubt yourself, David, but I do not. If you are ready to receive what he offers, then take what you're owed. If you are not, then speak up. If he doesn't listen, it will be the last thing he ever does. I will make sure of it.*

The threat from a dragon against his boyfriend should have caused David to bristle. It didn't. In fact, it did the opposite. A wave of calm washed over him, and he smiled as Levi hurried to smooth out the blanket unnecessarily as if even the smallest wrinkle would ruin what he was trying to do. David watched as Levi pulled out a flagon of wine and two wooden cups, along with a container of fruits and cheese. Atop the food sat a golden flower, the same kind surrounding Levi's house, planted by his mother.

"Is this okay?" Levi asked, frowning down at what he'd laid out. "I…I want this to be good for you. No, wait. I want this to be the *best* for you." He looked up at David, brow furrowed as he gnawed on his bottom lip.

Well, Lockes said. *It's not dancing on entrails, but I suppose it'll do. Remember, David: do not force yourself into anything you're not ready for. Also, make sure he stretches your anus before he—*

Bye! David shouted in his head as he ground his teeth together. *We're good! You can go now, oh my gods.*

Lockes chuckled. *Yes, yes. Go, David. I will be here if you have need of me.*

It felt as if a door shut in his mind, and for a moment, David was bereft at the loss. Though he hadn't known Lockes for long, his presence in David's head had become something he'd begun counting on. He was never alone, no matter where he went. And though he sometimes pushed against the boundaries of their connection, Lockes never grew angry with him, always giving him time alone when he requested it. And since David was a teenager, that meant he requested it quite a bit as he often took himself in hand late into the night.

But now?

Now he wished he were with Lockes.

Strange, that.

"David?" Levi asked, sounding worried. "We can go home, if you want. Or we can stay here and just talk. Nothing more."

David shook his head. "No. I...want. To be here. With you." He took in a deep breath, letting it out slow. "With all of you."

Levi smiled so widely David thought his face would split in two.

And later, when Levi loomed above him, David's skin slick with sweat as he cried out in a mix of pleasure and pain, he thought of great wings, and air against his face as he rocked his head back, shouting out to the stars as Levi whispered his name over and over again.

How old are you? David asked, sitting lazily against his dragon's chest, long, scaly legs stretched out on either side of him. The middle of summer had brought a heatwave, and though Lockes could breathe fire, his skin and scales were cool to the touch. David had spent the summer working in his mother's office, but today, he had a rare day off. Levi had asked if he wanted to go somewhere, but David had begged off, saying he wanted to catch up on his sleep. He felt a bit of guilt for the lie, but it faded when he found Lockes waiting for him in the Dark Woods.

He no longer felt the need to converse out loud. Lockes could hear him just as easily in his head, and it seemed pointless to speak his words when he could just think them or send images to explain what he was trying to say. Lockes was pleased with this change in their relationship.

I'm young, Lockes said, pressing his snout against the top of David's head. *Though young to you is different than young to me. Your entire life up to this point is but a blink of an eye to me.*

You didn't answer the question.

The dragon nipped at his head, and David laughed. *I am two hundred and seventy-three years old.*

Whoa. I…huh. I expected something like that, but it's still surprising to hear.

Why?

David shrugged. *Because I'll never know what that feels like, to have that much time pass. In a few months, I turn seventeen. I can't even begin to imagine almost three hundred years on top of that.*

Time moves differently for me than it does for you. He hesitated. *Or, at least it did.*

David tilted his head up to look at the underside of the dragon's jaw. *What do you mean?*

Lockes said, *Your lifetime is marked by events. You're born. You grow. You become a man. You find a love and build a home with them. You age. Eventually, you die. A dragon's life isn't the same. Time is…more fluid for us.*

But?

But, Lockes said, *I have found myself almost stuck in time. With you. I count the hours of every day until I can see you again. It wasn't like that before.*

He couldn't tell if that hurt the dragon or not. The mix of feelings he got from Lockes was too big to parse through with any clarity. *Is that...bad?*

No, Lockes said promptly. *It's not. The opposite, in fact. It has caused me to slow down, to ponder time in ways I hadn't before. Though my life is longer than yours, it is still finite. Nothing lasts forever.*

We will, David said, suddenly sure of himself. *We'll last forever. Whatever life comes after this, we'll still be together. And even though I'll cross the veil first, I'll wait for you, no matter how long it takes.*

Do dragons and humans cross the same veil? I've never spoken with another human about such things before. Isn't it strange that we hold some of the same beliefs?

I don't know, David admitted. *The crossing is supposed to bring peace and everlasting life. Why wouldn't you and I get to have the same thing? I know I won't have peace without you by my side. No matter how long it takes, I'll be with you, in the end.*

Lockes sighed audibly. *I would like that very much. I don't know what the gods have planned, putting you in my path, but I thank them every day for it.*

Me too, David thought, turning his head so his cheek rested against the dragon's chest. He smiled quietly when he felt the consecutive beat of all eight of the dragon's hearts, soft and soothing. *How did you come to be here in the first place? How did you know to find me?*

The tip of the dragon's tail rolled around his body, settling in David's lap. He reached for it without thinking, rubbing the scales between the spikes as Lockes loved.

I was...drifting, Lockes finally said. *I did not know my purpose, why I was born. I had my hoard, but it did not bring me the same joy as it once did. Gold and pretty jewels are wonderful, but they're just trinkets, in the end. Little baubles that mean nothing.*

I know of at least a billion people who'd disagree with you.

Lie, Lockes said. *You do not know a billion people. But I understand your point. A hoard is a dragon's most prized possession, and though it did bring me happiness, it wasn't the same as when I started building it. I felt...unfulfilled. I grew to despair that I wasn't a very good dragon.*

You are, David said. *You're the best dragon.*

I'm the only dragon you know, Lockes said, and David could hear the smile. *Which is fine with me, because I would hate to have to kill one of my own kind in order to keep you.*

But you'd do it, wouldn't you?

Yes, Lockes said. *Because you are precious to me. I awoke one day after a long sleep that had lasted a decade. I had planned to sleep even more, but I felt this…thread of light, extending from my chest and disappearing into the distance. I didn't know what it was, but I knew I had to follow it. And so I did. I flew for days and days, crossing vast mountains and the deepest oceans. I came upon a great wood full of darkness and secrets, and there, I met a god.*

A chill ran down David's spine. *A god. Truly?*

Yes, Lockes said, his voice taking on a dreamy lilt. *An old one, perhaps the oldest of us all. The biggest dragon in existence, the god of all of us, hidden away in what you call the Dark Woods. I stood before him, and he towered over me. He spoke, calling me a child who had been set upon a path. I had much to learn, he said. There would be hardships along the way, but I had a purpose. And that purpose would define who I would become.*

The thread led to a god? David asked in wonder. He couldn't believe such a magnificent creature could live hidden in the forest. David knew the Dark Woods were bigger than anyone knew, but a dragon god? He wondered what other secrets the Dark Woods held within.

No, Lockes said. *The thread was not to him.*

Then who did it lead to?

You, David. The thread led to you. You weren't yet born when I arrived here in this clearing, still growing in your mother's belly. But I felt you, even then. And I knew I only had to bide my time until you were ready to see me for all that I am. I slept a sleep of dreams, and there you were, a light that never extinguished, growing brighter the moment you were born.

"I heard you," David whispered aloud, his skin thrumming. "Ever since I can remember, I *heard* you. Whispers, in the back of my head."

I know, Lockes said. *We're connected, you and I. The old god said that the reasons wouldn't be clear to me, at least at first.*

"Are they now?" David asked.

They are, Lockes said. *But it's nothing as grand as fate or destiny, or facing an encroaching dark as a last stand for the light. The reason you called to me, and the reason I followed you is because I chose to. We are meant to be friends. Brothers. You are my love, and I would do anything for you.*

David's eyes burned as his chest hitched. *Don't you miss your home? Your hoard?*

The dragon rose to his feet. David stood too, turning and looking up at his friend. Lockes lowered his head until he could look directly into David's eyes. Neither of them blinked, watching, waiting. *I do not,* Lockes rumbled. *Because you are my home. You are my hoard, my greatest treasure. You have brought me peace and purpose, and nothing that came before will ever compare. I will be here, always. And when you take your last breath, I will sleep until it is time for me to cross the veil. And if the gods themselves try to keep me from you, I will tear the heavens apart until I am by your side again.*

David flung himself at his dragon, hugging his snout as tightly as he could. Lockes laughed in delight, pulling back. *May I?* he asked, raising one set of talons, and clicking them together in invitation.

Though he didn't know what the dragon was asking for, he agreed readily. He was safe with Lockes.

Lockes closed his claws around David carefully, lifting him up off the ground as he rolled over onto his back. He set David down on his stomach, a sign David took as one of great trust. A dragon's underbelly was their weakness, the softest part of their bodies that could be pierced with a sword or spear. Lockes was showing that he trusted David with his life, and he hoped he could carry that trust for the rest of his life.

For the remainder of the day, they lay there, just the two of them, sometimes speaking, but mostly enjoying the quiet of two beings existing together in this tiny little corner of the world.

"I KNOW YOU'RE LYING TO ME," Levi said through gritted teeth on the eve of David's eighteenth birthday.

David closed his eyes, rubbing the sides of his head, trying to stave off the oncoming headache pulsing against his forehead. "I'm not…" He sighed as he opened his eyes. "I'm not lying to you."

He walked with Levi along the path surrounding the village, wishing he could be anywhere but where he was. He knew this was coming, could see it in the set of Levi's shoulders, the way he watched David with growing hurt in his eyes. It'd been going on for weeks, now, and though David couldn't fault him for that, he didn't know how to fix it without revealing the truth of the matter.

"You go off," Levi snapped. "To only the gods know where. You tell your parents you're with me, but you're not." He looked stricken. "Are you…is there someone else?"

David stopped, staring at Levi. Those words hurt, even if they had a bit of validity to them, though not like Levi thought. "No," he said tiredly. "Levi, I love you and only you. There is no one else I'm interested in. You are my heart."

"Then where do you *go*?" Levi exploded. "People are talking, David. They see you wandering away even though you seem to think they don't. If you're not…if you're not cheating on me, then what the hell is it?"

David's hands curled into fists. "I'm asking you to trust me. I swear to you it's not what you're thinking. There is no one else. There never has been, and there never will be. It's you and me, okay? Nothing else matters." This last felt like a lie, but one buried in truth.

"Then tell me," Levi begged, voice cracking. "Tell me what it is you do. Tell me where you're going. If it's not someone else, why can't you tell me?"

"Do you trust me?" David asked flatly.

"I want to," Levi said, causing David to grunt as if he'd been punched in the gut. "I'm trying to. But I don't understand what's going on with you. I share everything with you, David. Everything.

And I thought you were giving the same in return. But there's always been some part of you that's closed off to me, and I don't get *why*."

A strange anger rose in David's chest, harsh and grating. "Because it's not for you to know," he growled. "It's *mine*."

Levi paled, and David knew he'd gone too far. Lockes was there, in the back of his head, but he didn't speak, didn't do much aside from making his presence known, and for the first time, David wanted the dragon to go away.

I understand, Lockes whispered. *I'll wait until you're ready, no matter how long it takes.* The door shut, and instead of relief, all David felt was guilt.

"Levi," he said, struggling at the loss and trying to find the right words. "That's not…that's not what I meant. It's nothing bad. It's nothing that would hurt you or me. It's time away from everything to clear my head. It's a part of my life that doesn't involve you, just like your watch duties don't involve me. Just because we're together doesn't mean we can't do things on our own."

Levi sagged, head bowed. "I know that. I just…" He grimaced. Then, "I'm not trying to take that away from you, David. I love you too. More than you could possibly know. You're the best thing that's ever happened to me, and it feels like you're pulling away from me. I don't know how to fix it. I can't lose you."

"You won't," David said, moving until he stood in front of Levi, their knees bumping together. He took Levi's hand in his own, raising it until Levi's palm pressed against David's chest, right above his heart. "You're here, with me. Always. And nothing can change that. I'm happy with you. I've never doubted you for a moment." He wished that last hadn't sounded like a dig, but there was nothing he could do about that now.

Levi sighed, fingers curling against David's tunic. "I'll be better. I swear it. I just…you'd tell me if something was wrong, wouldn't you? You'd tell me so I could help you."

David kissed his cheek. "I would. But I promise nothing is wrong. Everything is fine." He wished he could believe his own words, but a curl of doubt blossomed in his heart, the roots digging in deep.

"HAPPY BIRTHDAY!" Mom and Dad said.

"Happy birthday!" his friends cried.

"Happy birthday," Levi whispered.

Happy birthday, Lockes said, tail thumping against David's leg.

I can't stay long, David said, already loathing the idea of leaving his dragon once again. *I'm supposed to be getting ready for my party.*

Will there be cake? Lockes asked. He'd been inordinately fixated on the idea of cake to mark yet another year of David's life. Through their time together, Lockes had shown great interest in human customs, especially those meant to celebrate. He didn't quite understand the importance of an eighteenth birthday, given that dragons didn't mark time in the same way. But he knew it was important to David, so he didn't mock it too much.

Yes, David said. *Would you like me to bring you some?* He lay on the dragon's belly, the sun warming them both in their lethargy.

Lockes lifted his head to look at David. *Does it squeal and scream when you chase it? Does it bleed when you bite down into it?*

Gross. No. It's not alive. It's flour and sugar and eggs.

Then what's the point? Lockes asked, eyes narrowing. *The thrill of the hunt makes food taste better. Why would you eat something that can't run from you?*

David shuddered. *Now I never want to eat meat again. Thanks for that.*

You are growing, Lockes growled, pressing a single talon against David's cheek, the skin dimpling. *You need to take care of yourself. If cake doesn't bleed, it's not enough to keep you healthy.*

What if I was a vegetarian?

Veg-i-tear-ian. What is…that.

It means you don't eat animals, only plants.

Lockes snorted, a tiny lick of fire bursting from his right nostril, disappearing into a wisp of black smoke. *Humans do that?* He sounded horrified.

Some.

Then they are not to be trusted. If they subsist on only plants, their minds have not developed enough to understand their bodies' needs. If you have friends who are vegetarians, you must shun them immediately.

Oh boy. I'll get right on that.

And if you ever *consider following that illogic, seek me out and I will destroy it immediately. Move. I will hunt for you now so I know you're fed. I saw a herd of goats near the edge of the woods. I shall slaughter them all and we will feast like kings.*

David laughed as he thumped his fingers against the dragon's belly. *You can't kill the goats. There will be meat along with the cake. Don't worry about me. I can take care of myself.* His smile faded as another thought struck him. *Please don't approach other humans. They won't understand.*

Lockes cocked his head. *Because of what I am.*

Yes, David said. *They won't see you for who you are. It's not fair, but people fear what they don't know. And when they're scared, they say and do things they might not otherwise.*

This is important to you.

Yes, David said firmly. *I don't want you in harm's way. I can't promise others would see you as I do.*

Of course they wouldn't, Lockes said. *You are David. I am Lockes. We are bound together. I would never have another human like I have you.*

And though it hurt his heart to say so, David knew he couldn't let this moment pass him by. He had never been a selfish boy, and now that he was a man, he needed to remember the lessons he'd learned in his youth. *You...* But instead of finishing in words, he sent images. Of Lockes taking to the sky, flying far, far away. Free to explore the world in ways David could never be. David knew his place. He would remain in the village, working for his mother and father.

Lockes frowned, one of his front fangs hanging out over his bottom lip. *Why would I leave you?*

I don't want you to, David replied. *But are you truly happy here? Staying in one place for so long? Don't you want to see what else is out there?*

Do you?

David sighed. *Sometimes. But then I start to shake with the idea of leaving all I know behind. I don't know if I'm meant to explore.*

Then I will stay here. Where you are, I am. Where you go, I go. I am happy, David. I have food. I have shelter. I have you. What else could I ask for?

The world.

Lockes scoffed. *I have seen much of the world. I've made my choice. I will stay here unless you decide to go elsewhere. Only then will I leave to follow you. Stop thinking such thoughts that suggest otherwise. Do not worry about me.*

Do you worry about me?

Constantly. I don't like it when you're out of my sight.

It's the same for me, David said. *You worry because you care for me. I worry because I care for you. Don't try and minimize that since I wouldn't do that to you, even though you know I can take care of myself.*

Lockes huffed, annoyed. *I know you can. But it's not you I worry about specifically, though I do that too. It's others and what they could do to you. You are a friend of a dragon. That shows your strength of character. But that's enough discussion for now. Today, you're apparently a man even though nothing else has changed. As is custom, I have a gift for you.*

You didn't have to get me anything, David said as he slid off Lockes to the ground before the dragon righted himself, talons digging into the earth.

I am aware, Lockes said, heading toward an ancient tree that grew at the edge of the clearing. *A dragon never does anything they don't want to.*

"That's because you're stubborn," David muttered, chuckling when Lockes's tail thumped his legs in warning.

Lockes lowered his head to a hollow at the base of a tree. His tongue snaked out, pink and forked as it curled into the hollow. When it pulled back, the tip was wrapped around a small bundle of leaves and twigs. He turned and set it on the ground in front of David, looking proud.

What is it? David asked.

Lockes rolled his eyes, something he'd learned from David. *If would not be a surprise if I told you. Open it.*

He sat down on the ground, pulling the bundle into his lap. With great care, he unfurled the leaves and twigs to find a shimmery powder laying at the bottom. He poked his finger against the pile, and his skin tingled warmly.

Thank…you?

Lockes huffed. *You're welcome, even though you have no idea what it is. Take off your shirt.*

David's head jerked up. "Excuse me? I love you, but not like *that.*"

Gods, Lockes mumbled. *Of all the—just take off your shirt!*

David set the bundle carefully on the ground to avoid spilling the powder. He stood, removing his tunic and letting it fall to the ground.

So attractive, Lockes mocked him. *Your pale skin without scales and easily broken ribs. I can't wait to get me a piece of that.*

Shut up, David retorted, but his smile took away the sting of the rebuke.

The powder. Take a handful and rub it against your chest.

David thought about arguing but did as he was asked. Lockes would never do anything to hurt him. The powder was thicker than he expected, and it clung to his bare chest as he rubbed it against his sternum. The tingling sensation grew, but not unpleasantly. It made him squirm as if a thousand tiny fingers were gently poking him.

Do you trust me? Lockes asked as he lowered his head, sniffing the powder on David's chest.

Yes, David said without hesitation. *I trust you in all things.*

I am going to breathe fire on you, Lockes said. *It will not hurt. You will not be burned.*

David's knees grew weak. "Uh, maybe we should talk about this. I'm all for you breathing fire, but not at *me.*"

Hush, Lockes said. *I wish you to carry my mark. It is a source of pride, and it would please me to have it on you.*

David blinked. "What? What mark? What are you…" His gaze drifted to the dragon's chest, to the keyhole, to the lock. *Like yours?*

Like mine, Lockes agreed. *Would you wear it?*

Proudly, David said.

Good. Do not move. My aim is true, but I'd rather keep your eyebrows as they are. Humans look awfully strange without eyebrows.

Alarmed, David said, "*What*? Don't you dare burn off my—"

Lockes inhaled deeply, lips pursing to a tight *O*. He blew out a strong breath, the dark circle of his mouth beginning to glow red and orange. Before David could react, fire shot from the dragon's mouth, the air burning. The stream of fire struck the powder, causing it to sizzle, though David wasn't burned. It was over before he could move, the air thick with smoke.

Brush off the powder, Lockes ordered.

David grimaced as he did. The shimmery powder had blackened, and it fell off in clumps. David's eyes bulged from his head when he saw what lay underneath.

There, about the size of his hand, was a keyhole tattooed on his skin, the exact same shape as the one Lockes had, green in color, the lines wavy. Though Lockes's was bigger, that appeared to be the only difference. It was as if they mirrored each other, and David gaped, unable to speak.

Do you like it? Lockes asked, and for the first time, he almost sounded…nervous.

David touched the symbol as he snapped his mouth shut. The keyhole was slightly raised and bumpy, but other than that, it felt like his own skin. Awed, he whispered, *I love it. Thank you, Lockes. You have made me incredibly happy today.*

Lockes preened. *You are mine, just as I am yours. Wherever you go, wherever your life takes you, I will be part of you.*

Something in Lockes's voice caused David to jerk up his head. *But…you're going to be with me, right? You're not going anywhere?*

Silly man, Lockes said as he nosed against the keyhole. *What did I just say? Where you go, I go.*

It should've made David feel better.

It didn't.

HE WAS ABLE TO KEEP THE SECRET on his chest for only a week. Levi laughed as he shoved David into an empty storage shed, eyes dark, skin flushed. David kissed him again and again, trying to untie Levi's trousers without much success.

"I'm only on break for a little bit," Levi said, grunting as David gripped his length and squeezed. "We have to do this quick."

"So romantic," David teased, laughing as Levi growled and tugged at his tunic. Without thinking, he lifted his arms. Levi pulled his tunic off and let it fall to the floor.

"Romance? I'll show…you…romance. What the hell is that?"

David frowned. "What are you—" He followed Levi's gaze, looking down at his chest. "Oh shit. Uh. Surprise?"

"Did you get a *tattoo*?" Levi demanded, almost sounding scandalized. "When did you do that?"

"Last week," David said, rubbing the back of his neck, trying to ignore Lockes's quiet laughter in his head. "I wanted to do something for me to celebrate becoming a man."

Levi squinted at him before looking down at the symbol once more. "What…is it?"

"A keyhole."

"What does it mean?"

David shrugged awkwardly as he thought quickly. "Keyholes are part of doors. All doors lead to somewhere else. It's to remind me that we're all on the road to somewhere."

Pretty thoughts, Lockes snorted. *How delightful.*

Oh, you're gonna get it, just you watch.

Promises, promises. I'll leave you to it. Do not let him expend on it. That's disgusting.

Lockes!

But Lockes was already gone.

David fidgeted under Levi's examination of the keyhole. "Do you like it?"

"I…guess?" Levi blanched. "I mean, *I* wouldn't get it, but it's your body. You can do what you want, so long as you don't hurt yourself. It…has its charms." He must have realized how that sounded because he hastily added, "It looks good on you."

"Gee, thanks," David said dryly. "That was a ringing endorsement if I ever heard one. Now, if you're done gawking at me, I'd like to suck you off, if it's all the same to you."

Levi's trousers were at his feet even before David finished speaking.

THE ENDING OF ALL David held dear began with something lovely.

On his twentieth birthday, Levi knelt on one knee in front of their friends and family, his jaw tense, his mouth a thin line. He cleared his throat as everyone silenced around them. David couldn't move. He couldn't speak, couldn't breathe.

"David," Levi said, voice cracking. "You have been my best friend for as long as I can remember. In fact, I can't even think of a time when you weren't by my side. I have loved you from the moment I saw you, and that love has only grown. Would you do me the greatest honor and marry me? I swear if you accept, I will make your life one filled with laughter and love. I will fight for you until my last breath. I will—"

"Yes," David blurted. "Yes, oh my gods, yes. I accept. I *accept*."

Everyone cheered as Levi slid a heavy silver ring over David's finger. It fit perfectly. And then he rose swiftly, grabbing David and lifting his feet from the floor, spinning them both around.

I'm happy for you, Lockes whispered. *My love, you deserve this and more.*

I wish you were here with me, David said as Levi kissed him again and again.

I am. I am.

LEVI AND DAVID WERE WED on a warm spring afternoon, the entire village in attendance. They stood before their people and promised loyalty and everlasting love to each other, a gold sash tied around their joined hands.

The Man of the Gods said, "And now you may kiss your—"

David tackled Levi and kissed him for all he was worth.

LEVI AND DAVID HAD A HOUSE built on the outskirts of the village. The construction took three months, and though the time passed quickly, David was relieved when he was finally able to leave the only home he'd ever known. His father cried even though David was only moving five minutes away, and his mother smiled a watery smile as she held her husband.

He looked back at his parents only once as Levi led him to their new home.

You are sad and happy at the same time, Lockes whispered in his head. *How can you be both for the same reason?*

I'm human, David said as he sniffled. *Our feelings don't always make sense.*

Now that I agree with.

I don't know when I'll get to see you again, David said as Levi chattered away about how he thought they should decorate their new house. *It might be a few days before I can get back to you.*

Take your time. You've told me that newlyweds only think with their genitals.

That's not what I said!

But that's what you meant.

I hate you.

No. You love me.

Yes, David thought. And in his secret heart, tucked far away from even a dragon, a tiny voice whispered, *More than anything else.*

THE FOLLOWING YEAR proved hard for the village. The healing rains didn't come, causing a drought that no one could have predicted. The ground dried up, becoming hard and cracked. Crops failed, the plants poking through the ground dying without so much as a gasp. By the end of David's twenty-first year, the people of the village began to suffer.

"What will we do?" someone cried as they gathered before their mayor. David's mother raised her hands to try and quiet the worried crowd. "We have children to feed!"

"We will come through this as we always do," Mom said, looking out at her audience. "Things will be tight for a little while, but the rains will come again. We're not yet to the point where we'll need to ration food, but I ask that each household take stock of what they have." Her gaze grew hard. "No one should be hoarding anything. We must take care of each other. The children and the elderly will be our first priority. Times are lean, but we will pray to the gods and hope for the best. We'll be all right."

Is it bad? Lockes asked. *They sound frightened.*

They're worried, David said, Levi's hand clutched in his own. *Without the rains, the crops can't grow. If they don't grow, we can't sell anything or feed ourselves.*

You will not go hungry, Lockes muttered. *I will provide for you.*

It's not just me, David said. *It's the entire village.*

I care not for your village. Only you.

David sighed. He felt Levi looking at him in confusion, and he shook his head as he smiled weakly. Levi frowned but didn't speak, turning back to listen to David's mother. *I know. But I must think about others too.*

I can help.

David sat straighter in his seat. *No. I told you that you can't show yourself. They would—*

I'm not revealing myself, Lockes said. *I have an idea. It will take me time, but I promise I will return.*

Alarmed, David said, *Return? Where are you going? Are you leaving me?* He began to panic, trying to keep the worst of it from his face.

Calm, Lockes whispered. *Calm. I would never leave you for long. Two weeks, David. If I fly now and go as fast as I can, I will return in two weeks. Do you trust me?*

Yes, David said, the mark on his chest itching. Without thinking, he rubbed his hand against it. *I trust you in all things.*

As you should, my love. I will *come back. I am not done with you yet.*

The door closed in his mind, and David sat in a daze for the rest of the meeting.

TRUE TO HIS WORD, Lockes returned exactly two weeks later. David sat in his mother's office, taking notes as she paced back and forth, her thoughts in a tizzy. The door in his mind flew open, and the pen he held fell to the floor.

You're back!

I am, Lockes said. *I flew as fast as I ever have.*

David's brow furrowed. *You sound exhausted.*

I am, but it's okay. The return trip was harder than I expected, given all that I carried with me. Can you come? I have brought a solution to your problems.

What is it?

Patience, David. Come, and I will show you.

All right. Give me a bit. I'm with my mother. I'll get away as soon as I'm able. His shoulders relaxed, losing the rigidness they'd carried since Lockes had departed. He knew the dragon would return, but hearing his voice again brought a flood of relief.

"—and make sure you include the village council in this missive. We don't want anyone left in the dark when they…David. Are you listening?"

He smiled tightly as he looked at his mother. "I am. Sorry. Got lost in my head a little bit."

She sighed. "This is important, David. I need you here, with me, giving your all. We have to find a way to come through this. I can't have your head in the clouds right now. Focus."

He nodded and slumped in his chair as she continued on.

HE ESCAPED AN HOUR LATER, promising his mother that he and Levi would drop in for dinner the following week. David felt a pang of guilt, knowing the secrets he carried with him, but he knew they wouldn't understand. He had to do what he could to protect his dragon. Levi was asleep at home, resting before another shift as a night watchman. Though David wanted to go to him and curl up in their bed, the thought was fleeting. Lockes was back, and that was all that mattered.

He found Lockes in the clearing, wings spread out on the ground as if he'd collapsed there and hadn't moved. David rushed forward as Lockes opened a single eye, huffing out a warm breath in greeting.

"Are you okay?" David asked, running his hands over the dragon's face, searching for any sign of injury. He found none, but he didn't like how exhausted the dragon seemed.

Fine, my love, Lockes said with a sigh. *It will take time for my strength to return, but I will be well. Look at what I've brought you.*

He raised his head and neck, revealing four bulging sacks as tall as David underneath him. David touched the closest one, frowning at the odd shapes through the burlap. *What is it?*

Open it and find out.

David did, untying the sack. He gasped when he saw what lay inside.

Gold and silver coins in varying shapes and sizes, heavy and thick with faces and strange markings David didn't recognize. And jewels! Jewels of red and blue and yellow and white, some in bulky rocks, others cut into with angular corners and planes. The sack was filled to the brim. As if in a dream, he moved onto the other sacks, opening them all and finding more of the same, along with moonstone dishes inlaid with gold and rubies, ancient chalices that looked religious in nature.

"Where did this all come from?" David whispered, hands shaking.

My hoard, Lockes said proudly. *I flew all the way back to where I came from, gathered what I could and brought it back for you. Will it help?*

Stunned, David choked on a harsh laugh. "Will it *help*? My gods, Lockes. This is enough to support the village for hundreds of years to come!" He blinked against the tears in his eyes. "We...*I* can't accept this. It's yours."

We are one in all things, Lockes murmured, snuffling against David's head. *What is mine is yours. I have no need for it since you are my treasure. I give this willingly.*

David had learned that a dragon's decision—especially one as big as this—was ironclad. To deny the gift could cause great offense. He bowed low in front of Lockes, one arm behind his back, curling his other arm across his chest. *You honor me, Lockes.*

Lockes snorted. *Take your honor and shove it. I did this because I love you. Pretty things are everywhere. You are not.*

Still dazed, David said, "But...what about your home? You... went all the way back and returned? Don't you miss what you left behind?"

Lockes pulled his lips back over his teeth in a smile. *You are my home. I did miss what I left behind, but now I no longer need to, because I have come back to it. To you.*

David threw himself against the dragon's chest, his face against the keyhole. *You're the best thing that's ever happened to me.*

The dragon lifted his wings, encasing them in a cocoon of

darkness as he curled his head down against David's back. *And you to me.*

"A GIFT!" THE PEOPLE CRIED the next morning after a pile of treasure had been found on the doorstep to the mayor's house. "A gift from the gods! We're saved! Oh, bless, bless, bless!"

"Where did it come from?" Levi asked as they watched David's mother and father sort through the treasure.

"The gods," David said. "Who else could it be? They must have heard our pleas and sent this as a thank you for our devotion." It sounded hollow, even to him. It wasn't the gods. It was Lockes, but no one could ever know.

Levi looked away, the skin tight around his eyes.

THE SMITHS MELTED DOWN the larger parts of the treasure, creating bricks of gold and silver that were kept under guard day and night. The coins and jewels were appraised, the jeweler from the next town perplexed at what he found. "Some of this is ancient," he said, face almost inches away from one of the coins. "Thousands of years old with languages I've never seen before." He lifted the coin, putting it between his teeth and biting down. When he pulled it back, little imprints of his teeth remained in the gold. "How in the world did you come by this?"

David's mother said, "It just appeared on our doorstep."

"Then you are very lucky," the jeweler said. "It's real. All of it is real." He looked down at the separate piles he'd created. "There's enough here to feed many mouths, and not just here."

"Everyone will get something," Mom said firmly. "Not just in our village, but all those who have suffered because of the drought. We'll need to be careful to not spread it too thin, but we can't keep this for ourselves. No one should be left wanting."

They needn't have worried about that. This was only a small portion of the treasure, the rest stored away in the hollow of the tree. If the time came when more was needed, all David had to do was return to the forest and gather more. Lockes didn't seem to give one whit either way about the treasure, satisfied that he had David.

"You are gracious," the jeweler said with a bow. "But I would caution you. Greed is a terrible thing, and word is already spreading about what has happened to your village. There will be those who would have this for themselves and would try and take it by any means necessary."

"It will be under constant guard," Levi said. "I have been promoted to Captain of the Watch, and I've already gathered those I trust implicitly to make sure none is taken without agreement by all."

"Agreement," the jeweler said derisively. "Gold drives people mad with desire. I think you'll find not everyone will agree."

"Our village will," Mom said, her tone brooking no argument. "This isn't just for us. It will benefit us all, and though I don't know where it came from, I won't allow us to fall under its spell. We will be smart about this, and if I hear of any dissent, I will deal with it myself."

David shivered at the steel in his mother's voice. There was a reason she'd been reelected time and time again. The people trusted her to do right by them. Her tone and words did not allow for argument to the contrary.

"And what of the King?" the jeweler asked, a shrewd expression on his face that David didn't like. "If he or his court catch word of this, they will send an envoy and demand an investigation. And that doesn't even begin to address how much they'd tax all of it."

"The Port is far from here," Dad said. "Our people understand that we need to keep this quiet. We ask that anyone else who seeks help does the same. We've hidden more from Varden the Cruel."

The jeweler blanched at the nickname given to the bloodthirsty king. David had never laid eyes on him, but he'd heard the stories of the king's terrible might. His castle in the Port was built on the backs of the enslaved, and he had shown he didn't give a single shit about the struggling villages. They'd been on their own for longer than David had been alive, but this was a way to even the playing field.

"On your head, then," the jeweler said, though not so mired in irony that he didn't look as hungry as the rest of them.

SEVEN MONTHS LATER, as the first snows began to fall, David stole away to the forest, his breath streaming from his mouth in a thick fog as his feet crunched on the thin layer of ice. It was early in the season for snow, a portent for the harsh winter ahead. But the people of the village were safe in their homes, fires lit, their bellies full. And so far, news of the treasure hadn't spread beyond the surrounding villages. David was surprised by this fact, but thankful for it. He'd spent restless nights, sure that he'd awaken to the sound of drumbeats and the village alarms, signaling the arrival of the king's knights.

Lockes blinked sleepily, his head dusted with snow as David entered the clearing. *There you are. You're late.*

Sorry. I had to finish up with work before I could get away. Levi was asking questions again.

He always does, Lockes said. *I don't know how you don't tire of them and his incessant prattling. It's obnoxious.*

I ask you questions all the time, David reminded him.

Well, yes. But I love you. You are mine, and if you didn't *ask questions, I'd think you sick. Come. It's too cold for you. I will warm you.* He lifted his wing, allowing David to sit on the hard ground underneath him. He breathed a thin stream of fire above his wings, heating up the air around David. *Is that better?*

Much, thank you. David settled against Lockes, taking in the comfort of familiarity.

You sound tired.

I am," David said, scrubbing a hand over his face. *Levi is…*

He shook his head as he chuckled bitterly. *He's wearing on my last nerve, if I'm being honest. He wants to know where I go. He asked me again if there was someone else.*

Jealousy is useless, Lockes said as he yawned, jaw cracking. *You love him. That should be enough.*

I know, but I am keeping secrets from him. It makes me feel guilty.

Why?

David closed his eyes. *Because you're part of my life in ways he's not. A marriage is meant to be open and honest.*

You are *open and honest.*

Not about you.

Lockes hesitated. *Does that bother you? I've told you that you can bring him if you like. I may not love him as you do, but I can stand him if I must.*

Wow. You're really putting yourself out there.

Oh, hush, Lockes grumbled. *You know what I mean.*

And David did. But he couldn't find a way to articulate how the idea filled him with dread. Lockes was perfectly happy to keep David to himself, and David felt the same. He didn't think anyone else could understand. And if he *did* reveal Lockes to anyone, he would have to answer as to why it'd been years since he'd first met the dragon and hadn't said anything. Lockes was right: jealousy was a useless emotion, but David didn't like the idea of anyone else taking up his dragon's time.

Lockes must have latched onto this thought. *As if anyone would compare to you. Do you think me so fickle that my gaze would wander?*

No. I just...this is our *time. You and me. I need it as much as I need you. I'm not ashamed of you. If I thought I could, I would shout your name from the rooftops. You're my best friend. My love. My everything.* He waited for the guilt to rise again at such thoughts, but it never came.

I am, Lockes said, a rumbling purr coming from his chest, a rare sound that expressed his complete satisfaction. *I wouldn't have it any other way.*

David tilted his head back as he opened his eyes. *Do you...do you ever think about leaving?*

No.

Never?

Never.

What if...

Spill it, David. Your thoughts are jumbled and I can't find what you're trying to say.

"What if I went with you?" David said aloud. "What if we ... left and went somewhere else?"

Lockes didn't speak for a long time. David was about to tell him to forget it when the dragon said, *Where would we go?*

Wherever we wanted to. Away from everyone else. We'd find a place where we didn't have to hide. We could just...be.

Would you like that?

I...

Would you be able to leave your mother and father? Levi? Your friends? The home you have built, the life you've created?

David fisted his hair in frustration. *I don't know. Sometimes, I think I could. I don't know what that says about me.*

It says that you're human. Wonderfully, horribly human. I may not always understand you or your kind, but I know you'd regret it one day.

How do you know?

You need people, Lockes said. *Others like you. What if you began to see me with regret and disdain? My hearts couldn't take it if you blamed me for taking you away.*

I wouldn't!

I know you think so. But it might happen, sooner than you'd expect. Think on it, David. Think on it as hard as you ever have in your life. If that's what you truly want, then yes, I would go with you anywhere you wanted. Back to my keep. Or across the snowy mountains to the land of giants. Beyond even that. Wherever you go, I go. Here, or anywhere else.

I will, David vowed. *I'll think on it. I don't have to make the decision today.*

You don't, Lockes agreed. *Today, let us just enjoy each other's company. Would you tell me a story? I do love the one about the unicorn. I met a pair of unicorns once. Foul creatures, those, always thinking with their genitals. I would hear your terrible story about them again.*

And so David did, the flurries falling around them.

HE LEFT LOCKES BEHIND as the sky began to darken, wanting to get home before nightfall. He promised to return as soon as possible, telling Lockes that the treasure still hidden wasn't needed at the moment. They had more than enough to survive the winter and beyond.

He was halfway home when he looked down at the tracks he'd made on his trip to see Lockes. He frowned, a strange sense of unease sliding in between his ribs when he saw his own footsteps in the snow…next to another set of tracks. Human. Boot prints, set far apart as if whoever had left them was very tall, or had taken exaggerated steps. But to what end? Wracking his brain, he tried to remember if he'd noticed them on his way in. He didn't think he had. There'd been no snow the last time he'd come, and the prints were slightly larger than his own feet, so it couldn't have been him.

David? Lockes whispered. *What's wrong?*

I…nothing, maybe. Have you seen anyone else? Smelled or heard anything?

No. But the winds are blowing away from me, not toward. I wouldn't have caught a scent unless they were close. Is there reason for concern?

I don't know. Be ready, just in case.

In case of what?

To that, David had no answer.

THAT FEELING OF UNEASE only grew as he approached the village. Given the oncoming weather, the village should've been locked up tight, everyone in their homes around the hearth to keep warm. Instead, he saw shadows moving at the center of the village as he crossed beyond the houses on the outskirts, as if a crowd had gathered. No alarms were ringing, but that didn't mean something wasn't wrong. He thought about going directly to his parents, but then he heard his father's voice, loud, angry, the words lost but the intent clear. His father was furious.

David hurried towards the village center, pressing his back against a shop as he sidled down the side to peer around the edge.

What he saw stopped him cold. A crowd of at least thirty people were gathered in the dirt road in front of the Mayor's office. Mom and Dad stood on the porch of the office, wrapped in heavy furs. Dad's face was twisted, his cheeks splotchy as Mom spoke in soothing tones, though she too looked perturbed. The crowd was too thick to see if she spoke to one or all, but torches were lit, and the men had weapons: rusted swords and halberds, taken from the storage shed the watchmen used when they patrolled at night. David couldn't remember a time when the weapons had actually been used, more for show than anything else. He doubted a single person who held a weapon had used it in defense, though they'd all been trained in case the need arose.

And then the crowd shifted, and he saw the one person he didn't expect.

His husband.

Levi looked incensed as he glanced at the gathering behind him before turning back toward David's parents. His voice rose, taking on a cadence David hadn't heard before. "I know what I saw," Levi snapped. "I wouldn't lie, not about this. Not about *him*. This pains me more than you know, but it is *there*. Skulking in the woods, ready to kill us all."

"So you say," Mom retorted. Dad placed a hand on her arm, and she shrugged him off. "I know you love my son, Levi, and you've seen to his happiness. That alone is enough for me to listen to you. But how can you be sure? What were you doing in the woods?"

"I followed him," Levi said, and David's blood turned to an icy sludge. "You know he disappears into the forest. He's done it for years. And none of us has done anything to stop him. I couldn't let it go on any longer. I thought…" He hung his head, his shame evident. "I thought there was someone else. That he…" Levi's hands curled into fists. "But it wasn't. It's worse than that." Levi raised his head, and though David couldn't see his face, the rigid set of his husband's shoulders was enough of an indicator.

"My husband," Levi said, "was with a dragon. A terrible beast with claws and fangs that could tear through any of us in an instant. We are in danger, and David has betrayed us. He was…he was *laying* on the creature. As if he *knew* it."

The crowd murmured, the sound like a harsh wind over old bones.

"That's a serious accusation," Dad snapped. "How dare you. We invited you into our home. Our *lives*. We thought our son was safe with you, but here you are, disparaging his character. David wouldn't betray us, and the fact that you can speak those words so easily makes me regret ever allowing you near him."

"Then where is he?" someone called from the crowd. "If what Levi is saying isn't true, where is David?"

And though David was more frightened than he'd ever been, he wouldn't let them take Lockes from him. He gave brief thought to running back to the clearing, but these were his people. They would listen to him. They had to. He'd make them see.

He stepped out from the shadows, shoulders squared, head held high. He didn't try to hide his approach and a man—*Teacher*, David thought dizzily—turned, eyes wide. "There he is!" he cried. "David is here!"

The crowd turned as one, all eyes on David. He did his best to keep from flinching, not wanting to show any sign of weakness. If they saw it, they'd think he felt guilty. He didn't. He had done nothing wrong, and he'd prove it, no matter what it took.

The people parted as he walked through the middle of the crowd. Levi frowned at him, but David ignored him, heart cracking. He loved Levi, but he couldn't look at him, much less speak for fear he'd say things he couldn't take back. He didn't know what that made him. A coward, most likely.

Dad jumped from the porch, rushing toward his son. He gripped David's arms, fingers digging in hard enough to leave bruises. "Tell them," Dad begged. "Tell them Levi's wrong. That he didn't see what he says he did."

David looked his father in the eyes and said, "I can't."

Silence fell over the village, thick flakes of snow dancing around them.

Dad dropped his hands and took a stuttering step back. "What?"

Run, David thought as hard as he could. *Oh please, run. Fly as fast as you can. Leave. Never look back.*

No, Lockes growled. *I will never leave you.*

Tears prickled his too-hot eyes, though he didn't know who they were for. Himself. His family. His people. Levi. Mom. Dad.

Lockes.

He said, "There is nothing for you to fear. I swear it. I wouldn't bring death and fire upon our village. It's not like that. It never has been."

"David," Mom whispered. "What have you done?"

He hated the pain in her voice, the devastated look on her face, but he couldn't do anything about that now. This was his secret, one he'd carried for years, and now that it was out in the open, he needed to prove to them that Lockes wasn't dangerous. "I made a friend," he said, his voice stronger than he felt. "Someone who protects me. He sees me for who I am. He doesn't expect me to be anything I'm not."

"He!" Levi said. "Are you listening to yourself? *He*. It's not a *he*, David. It's a *thing*. A monster incapable of rational thought."

David glanced back at his husband, stiff neck creaking. Levi looked wounded and furious, an awful combination. "He is *real*," David said. "More than anyone could have known. I talk to him. He talks to *me*."

The crowd's whispers grew louder, no longer a wind but an approaching storm.

"That's not possible," Mom said. "Dragons don't talk like we do. There's a reason they were hunted. They are killing machines, capable of destroying everything they come across."

David shook his head. "You're wrong. I know you've heard the stories, and maybe some of it is true. But this dragon isn't like the others. He's different. He…" Then, "The treasure."

Dad grunted as if struck. "What about the treasure?"

"It was a gift," David said. "I told him of our struggles, how our people were suffering. By rights, he could've done nothing at all.

But our friendship means more to him than anything in the world. He gave me—*us*, his hoard. The reason we survived the droughts was because of his selflessness."

"And what did you offer it in return?" Levi snarled, moving until he stood in front of David, eyes ablaze. "What did you give it to receive such a thing? Have you been telling him about us?" David had never seen him so angry, and he flinched as if Levi was about to strike him. "Did you betray us to the dragon?"

"No," David spat. "I have never betrayed anyone. Lockes wants nothing but my company. That's all he ever wanted. He's my—"

"Lockes!" Levi cried. "You've given it a *name*? It's not a pet. It's *evil*. Gods, David, how could you be this stupid?"

Without thinking, David shoved Levi back. He didn't fall, though it was close. "Fuck you," David growled, sounding more dragon than man. "Don't you dare speak of him or me in such a way. You may be my husband, but I won't allow it. Watch your tongue."

Levi was shocked into silence.

David looked beyond him to his mother. "Lockes has never harmed me, nor has he *ever* harmed a single person, either in this village or elsewhere. He has only ever wanted to help. We wouldn't have survived without him. Do you understand what it takes for a dragon to part with his hoard? It is their *everything*. And yet he didn't hesitate when I told him of our troubles. He offered without reservation."

"Why?" Mom asked faintly. "Why would he give such a thing?"

"Because he loves me," David said. "And I love him. He's not a monster. He's not evil. He is kind and wonderful and—"

"He's been brainwashed," Levi said. "The dragon has addled his mind!"

"He hasn't," David said, trying to keep his voice calm. "I've never thought more clearly than I do at this moment. We owe our lives to Lockes. He has provided for us. And there is more, so much more than what he's already given. Because of him we will never suffer again." He never looked away from his mother. "We have survived because of him. Instead of swords and fire, we should be on our knees thanking him."

"Blasphemy!" someone shouted in the crowd.

"You will stay away from it," Levi growled, gripping David and shaking him so hard, his head snapped back and forth. "You won't go to the woods again. I won't allow it."

David shoved him again. "I can think for myself. You're my husband, but that doesn't give you the right to make decisions for me. Levi, I love you. I do. But you're wrong. All of you are *wrong*."

He looked to his father. Dad stared at the ground, arms across his chest.

He looked to his husband. Levi's face was dark with blood, spittle flecking his lips.

He looked to his mother. Mom had tears in her eyes, her mouth a thin, white line.

And then she shook her head. "I'm sorry, David. I can't take the chance. It's not just about you. It's about all of us. If…if the dragon grew angry, what would stop it from destroying all we hold dear? What if he wants something in return for what he's given us, something that we can't offer? Blood. Our children."

David laughed, bitter and sharp. "Are you listening to yourselves? Are you listening to *me*? I'm telling you he's not a threat! If he wanted to harm us, he would have done it years ago."

"Years," Levi scoffed. "Because that's how long you've known about it, haven't you? You've kept this from us for *years*. How are we supposed to trust you after this? For all we know, you're working with the dragon!" His paused, eyes narrowing as if a thought struck him. "That mark."

"What mark?" Dad asked as David began to sweat.

"David has a symbol on his chest. He said it was a tattoo. But I *asked*. No one in the village has marked David in such a way."

"David?" Mom asked. "Is…is Levi right? Do you have a mark?"

David, Lockes warned. *Leave them. Leave them and return to me. Don't make me ask you twice.*

David ignored him. For the rest of his days, he would remember this moment, when he believed he could get through to his people, that they would hear his truth and know there was nothing to be afraid of. Regardless of what else he was, David was still remarkably, foolishly human. His hope in his people blinded him to the truth, and had he but done as his dragon requested, all that followed might have happened differently.

Yes, this memory would haunt him for years to come: here, in this moment, he still had hope.

"I do," David said. "And I wear it proudly. Because it marks me as a friend of the dragon. *My* dragon. And no one can take that from me."

"Show me," Mom said. "Now."

He did. He unfastened his coat and lifted his tunic, the light from flickering flames dancing along the keyhole carved into his chest.

Dad let out a long, mournful sound. Mom put her face in her hands. The crowd jostled around David as everyone tried to see the mark for themselves, their faces white in terror.

"I told you," Levi said. "Everything I said is true. He wears the mark of a dragon, which means the dragon has poisoned him against us. How could you do this to us. To me? You've broken my heart." He spat at the ground at David's feet.

David bristled. "Because I knew this is how you'd react. You're all so fucking scared, but of *what*? Lockes has done nothing but help us. You fear things you don't understand, and when that fear becomes too great, you fill with bloodlust, wanting to strike down whatever frightens you. If you have ever loved me, if you have ever thought of me as husband or friend or son, then you'll trust me with this. I've earned that much."

Mom lowered her hands, and for a moment, David thought he'd gotten through to her. He thought she'd heard him, really heard him. It shattered like glass when she said, "I'm sorry, David. We can't take the chance." She raised her voice. "We must destroy the dragon before it can attack. Those who can, take up arms. Hide the children in your homes. We will not stop until the dragon is dead."

"*What?*" David cried. "No! You can't—"

"Take him," Dad said. "Lock David up until we can be sure the dragon's magic has been purged from his body. If there's more treasure, then we'll have it for our own." He looked grave when he added, "And a dragon's body is worth its weight in gold. Leave nothing to chance."

Hands descended on David as he struggled, snarling as if feral. He kicked Teacher in the face when the man tried to grab his legs. Other hands grabbed David's arms, pulling them back so hard, he thought they'd pop out of their sockets. Rough rope wrapped around his wrists, binding them behind his back. "No!" he shouted. "You can't hurt him. Oh my gods, please don't hurt him. Mom! Dad! Don't do this. You have to *stop*!"

His mother and father didn't move to stop him from being lifted up in the air, Levi grunting as David's knee connected with his nose. A savage sense of satisfaction rolled through David as his husband's nose gushed blood.

David screamed then, screamed as loud and hard as he could. He put everything into it: his rage, his fear, his anguish. All of it. It echoed in the village and through the woods, causing winter birds to take flight in terror.

And it was met with an answering cry: the roar of an angry dragon.

Everyone stopped.

David, Lockes whispered. *I am coming.*

"No!" David bellowed, back bowing so much that the people almost dropped him. "You *fly*. Across the mountains! Across the sea! Go, and never look back!"

I can't.

David threw his body as hard as he could. The people who held him were caught off guard, hands slipping. He fell to the ground, landing with a bone-jarring crash that knocked the breath from his chest. He pushed through it, gagging as he flipped over, drawing his legs up underneath him and rising. He managed to make five running steps before someone grabbed the rope binding his hands, pulling it taut, causing David to fall on his back in the snow.

A familiar sound rose above the village: great wings slicing through the air. David raised his head in time to see a massive shadow blot out the black clouds above the village. People screamed around him as Lockes reared back, wings spread, eyes bright in the dark.

Lockes folded his wings and hurtled toward the ground. Everyone scrambled out of the way, and the earth rolled as Lockes landed, front legs on either side of David. The dragon's mouth opened, and he *hissed*, an awful sound David had never heard him make before. His tail whipped back and forth, kicking up snow and dirt, hitting the side of a building, which shook and groaned but didn't fall.

Are you all right? Lockes asked as he snapped his fangs at the frightened people gathering in front of the Mayor's office.

You shouldn't have come! I told you to run!

As if I would leave you, Lockes replied angrily. *You needed me. These people aren't to be trusted. I will take you away from here. We will go and never return.* His tail whipped around his body, falling on David and flipping him over. He used the last spike on his tail to slice through the ropes around David's wrists.

David pushed himself up off the ground. Lockes curved his neck around David, shielding him from the crowd. *Are you injured?*

No. They didn't...yes. We will leave. We will leave and never return. Take me away, Lockes. Take me away where we can find everlasting peace.

A loud *thunk* startled David, and he turned in time to see a halberd fall to the ground next to him. Someone had tried to hurt Lockes, but the spear had glanced off his scales.

That wasn't very nice, Lockes said. *I haven't killed a human before. I don't want to start now.*

David pushed his way from underneath the dragon, cold as he watched his people. Their faces were ashen and slack. He couldn't see Levi among them, but it didn't matter. They had both made their choices. "We will go," he said hoarsely. "Away from you. Away from all of this. You'll never have to see me again."

"David," Mom whispered. "No, we don't—"

"Stop," he snapped. "You've proven your point. You won't listen. Yes, I lied to you. I lied to all of you, but that doesn't give you the right to hurt him. You're my mother. You're supposed to listen to me. You're supposed to *protect* me."

"I have to protect everyone," she pleaded. "David, you can't expect us to just—"

"Look!" Teacher cried. "It's there, just as Levi said! The dragon has the same mark as David! It cast his magic on him. The only way to save him is to slay the dragon!"

"Kill it," the crowd whispered. "Slay the dragon. Free David from its spell."

David backed up against Lockes, eyes narrowed, heart thundering. "Stay back. I told you we would leave. You won't have to worry about us again. We'll go far from here, where no one can hurt us."

"David, you're not thinking clearly," Dad pleaded. "It's infected you. Please, son. Stand aside. Let us help you."

You tried, Lockes said. *I am sorry that it's come to this, David. We must go while we still can. Run for the forest. I will follow you. Head for the clearing. I'll meet you there, and I'll take you away from here.*

Yes. Yes. Yes. Away. We'll go away.

He gave one last look at his people, his friends. His parents. Betrayal burned, but they'd made their choice just as he'd made his. Perhaps he would one day regret his actions, but that was not this day. Now, he only cared about saving his friend. Nothing else mattered.

He turned to do as Lockes asked. He only made it a step when a flurry of movement appeared at the corner of his eye.

Levi, sword raised, mouth open in a silent scream of fury, his gaze trained on David.

"No," David whispered, raising his hand.

Lockes moved quicker than David had ever seen him, but not for Levi. He slammed his head against David, knocking him off his feet and out of the way. Before the dragon could recover, Levi stabbed him in the chest, the sword a key piercing the keyhole.

And oh, how David screamed as pain crashed into him as if his own chest had been run through. His mind whited out as Lockes roared, head back, fangs snapping at nothing. The sword jerked from Levi's hand, still lodged in the dragon's chest as Lockes took a staggering step back. Blood, shiny and black in the darkness, gushed forth, splattering the ground. Lockes groaned deep in his throat as he fell to the ground, his right wing crumpled underneath him.

"No," David muttered as he pushed himself up. "No, no, nonono*no*—" He rushed toward his friend, falling to his knees next to the hilt of the sword. He gripped it, meaning to pull it from the dragon's chest, but Lockes whined in pain, eyes squeezed shut, his breaths already labored.

"Stay with me," David begged as he moved to Lockes's head. "Please stay with me."

I am with you, Lockes whispered. *I am always with you.*

David ignored the hushed crowd around him as he held his friend's face in his hands. "I can fix this. Tell me how to fix this."

You can't, David. One of my hearts has been pierced. It's... He groaned again, blood dribbling out of his mouth in a steady stream, coating David's front. *There is nothing you can do.*

David tilted his back toward the sky. "Gods!" he cried. "Save him. If he is one of yours, *save him.*"

But the gods did not answer.

David, Lockes said, and his voice sounded stronger. For a moment, David hoped against hope. But the blood around the sword continued to pour from the mortal wound. *Listen to me.*

David sobbed against the dragon, laying on his snout, head resting on the ridge between his eyes. "You can't leave me. You promised. You *promised me.*"

I did, Lockes said. *And a dragon always keeps his promises. This is not the end. Remember? We will be together again, no matter what it takes. We will cross the same veil and defy the gods and stars should they attempt to keep us apart.*

David screamed and screamed, the people around them shuddering.

My love, Lockes said, voice fading. *My life had no meaning until I met you. You gave me purpose. You gave me a home. Live. Live as long as your life allows and know that I'll be waiting for you when your time comes. We'll find peace. We'll find everlasting life. Together, as we were meant to be.*

"I can't do this without you," David choked out.

You can. And you will. Do you love me?

"With everything I have."

The dragon sighed. *Oh, how that makes me soar. There has never been one such as you. And I love you more than you could ever know. David, I'm...I'm flying. We're flying. Can you feel it? Can you see it?*

David closed his eyes, and there, in his head, was the bright blue sky, the sun beaming down on them. Clouds passed them by as they flew far above the world, together, always together. The image began to dissipate, and no matter how much David tried to hold onto it, it poured through his fingers like sand.

He opened his eyes.

Lockes didn't move. His chest didn't rise.

"Lockes?" he whispered. "*Lockes*. You have to get up. You need—please, get up. Oh my gods, move. *Move*." He slammed his fists against the dragon's face, but the amber eyes he'd known so well had closed for the last time.

David slid from the dragon, falling to his knees. He rocked back on his legs and screamed at the sky. The sound echoed through the village, the forest, and for a long time after, people would speak in hushed whispers about his excruciating wail, the way David's eyes flashed like a dragon's, his teeth bared as if they were fangs.

But that would come later.

Now, they stood as witnesses to the greed and fear of men. They bowed their heads as David's rage washed over them, absolute and never ending.

But David was not a dragon. His human throat eventually closed, his scream cutting off in a wet choke as he fell to the ground next to Lockes, curling around the dragon's mouth. David closed his eyes, and they did not reopen for three days.

THE DRAGON WAS SLAUGHTERED, quartered, blood soaking the earth. Though they did not know it then, nothing would ever grow in or around the village again. It was as if their hubris had poisoned the very earth upon which they lived. Though they would feel regret, most agreed that it was the right thing to do, and the money the dragon meat and skin brought in was more than enough to make up for the loss of crops. And it was made easier when a group of villagers—led by a silent and brooding Levi—came to the clearing and found the rest of the treasure in the hollow of the tree.

A year later, a traveler would come to the village, meaning to trade his wares. He crested the ridge on the road that led to the village, and stopped, his pack mule bleating in fear.

Below them, the burnt remains of the village stood smoldering. Once the traveler returned to the Port, eyes bulging, face as white as snow, he spoke of what he'd seen. A contingent of knights was sent to the remains of the village, and though they went through the blackened wood carefully, they never found a sign of any of the villagers. It was as if they'd all disappeared into thin air.

BUT THAT CAME LATER.

This was now:

David opened his eyes on the third day in the bedroom he'd grown up in. For a moment, he thought he woke from a gentle sleep, but then his sleepy mind reached out for Lockes, only to be met with a gaping chasm where the dragon had once been. In that moment between sleep and wakefulness, he was almost able to convince himself that Lockes was still alive.

Truth seeped in, as it always did.

He wept then; great wracking sobs that made him feel as if he were being torn apart. The storm eventually passed, eyes gritty, throat ragged, heart sore. Cool winter light filtered in through the window.

The door opened, and his mother and father stepped into the room, pausing when they saw he was awake.

"David," Mom breathed. "You…"

He did not speak. He had nothing left to say to them. To any of them.

"David," Dad tried, voice gruff. "I…we know this is hard for you. But we did what we had to in order to keep you safe. You're free now. The dragon's magic no longer has a hold on you. David. Can't you see? You're safe."

Still, David didn't speak. He turned away from them toward the wall.

Eventually, they left him, closing the door.

THAT NIGHT, as the village slept, David rose from his bed. He left his parents' house behind. A year later, it would be the second house crushed under the might of a god.

The first would be where David went after leaving his childhood home. The house he shared with his husband. He kept to the shadows, avoiding the watchmen who patrolled. He didn't look for Lockes. His friend was already gone, and he couldn't bear to see what had been done to his body.

No lights came from the house. He went inside, up to the room he'd shared with a man who he thought he'd be with for the rest of his life. Love, he knew, could also be poison. And how it poisoned every part of his body. He pulled a pack from the closet, packing up everything he thought he'd need. His heart ached, and he rubbed his chest absentmindedly, the symbol on his chest feeling like it burned white hot.

He knew where he had to go.

Only one being could answer his questions.

He shouldered the pack and turned toward the door.

Levi stood there, watching David with haunted eyes.

"You're leaving," he said quietly.

"Yes," David said. "I am. And if you try and stop me, I will tear your head from your shoulders."

Levi flinched, but it brought David no satisfaction. "I believe you."

David sneered at him. "Move. Now."

Levi didn't. He took a step into the room, hands raised in caution. "I…David, I only wanted to help—"

David moved without thought, arm across Levi's throat as he pinned his husband against the wall. "I will never forgive you," he snarled in Levi's face, spittle flying onto Levi's cheeks, his lips, his chin. "You have taken from me. I hate you. Do you hear me? I *hate you.*"

Levi's mouth twisted down, eyes wet. "You're not in your right mind. You—" His words cut off in a choke as David pressed his arm harder into his throat.

"Do not follow me," David whispered. "Do not attempt to find me. If you try, it'll be the last thing you ever do."

He left his husband in their house.

David never returned to the village again.

HE WALKED FOR THREE WEEKS, deep into the Dark Woods, grief heavy on his shoulders. He avoided the clearing on the first day, unable to lay his gaze upon it for fear he'd collapse and never move again. His body would give out, and his skin would bloat and rot until there was nothing left but bone. He'd return to the earth, and as much as it called to him, he wasn't ready. Not yet. Not when he had questions that needed answers.

The days passed in a haze. David rarely spoke aloud, lost in his head, memories of Lockes hanging in tatters. He attempted to gather them together as best he could, but it wasn't the same. He was alone for the first time since he could remember, truly alone.

On a cold night when the snows fell heavily, he camped in a shallow cave. He lit a fire, trying to keep warm. He lay as close to it as he dared, and the fire snapped and popped, embers rising with the smoke. The embers began to dance, pulsing, and for a moment, David thought he was dreaming.

But then one of the embers spoke in a quiet voice. It said, "He waits for you. He knows you're coming, the old god. He hears your sorrow as if it were his own. You will find the answers you seek."

"Who are you?" David whispered.

The embers grew in numbers, alighting around the cave, bright as stars. "We are the Fairies of the Wood," the ember said. "We will guide you to him. You may call me Dimitri. I am the King of the Fairies, and I mourn with you. Your grief is our grief. Your pain our pain."

David drifted after, hovering between sleep and consciousness.

And in this half-life, another voice spoke, old and strong.

Come, David, it said. *It is almost time.*

HE FOLLOWED THE FAIRIES through the woods. He did not speak to them, nor they him. David knew that fairies could be tricksters, but he had no other choice. He had to believe they wouldn't lead him astray.

Toward the end of the third week since he'd left the village behind, the fairies stopped. It was midday, the sun shining weakly, the trees heavy with snow. Before them, a great white mountain rose from the forest, and David worried he'd have to climb it. He didn't think he had the strength left to do so.

The fairies formed a bright buzzing cloud in front of him. One of the lights broke apart from the rest, fluttering in front of his face. "Here," the light said, and David knew it to be Dimitri. "Just up ahead. We'll remain in the trees to allow you an audience with the god. When you are ready to leave, we'll guide you from the forest."

"I'm not going back," David said.

"I know, child," Dimitri said. "Listen to the god. He will show you your path."

The fairies flew past his head, back the way they'd come.

David stared resolutely forward. He didn't know what to expect, but he couldn't back down now. Not when he'd come so far.

He turned his head, looking around. The forest was completely silent. No wind. No birds. Nothing. It was as if the earth itself held its breath.

"Hello?" he said. "I'm…I seek an audience with the dragon god."

Nothing.

David grew angry. "Show yourself!" he shouted, his grief pouring from him. "I *demand it.*"

The mountain shifted. The earth cracked. Snow fell in clumps.

David froze as a massive head rose through the trees, knocking them aside, the roots groaning mightily as they tore from the earth. The sun was blotted out as the beast towered above David.

A dragon. A pure white dragon with eyes of gold, the biggest David had ever seen, but it wasn't fear he felt, then. It wasn't terror.

It was grief, bright and glassy. Grief for all that he'd lost.

David's knees grew week, and he collapsed to the ground, tears streaming from his face.

The dragon's head lowered toward his. David had never felt so small in his entire life. He didn't look away as the dragon studied him, its wings folded at its sides.

"I have traveled far to find you," David choked out. "I need you to tell me why. Why it hurts. Why I can't breathe. Why, oh gods, *why.*"

The dragon did not speak.

David glared up at it, face twisted in a furious snarl. "*Why*, godsdamn you! Why was he taken from me? Why do I have to feel this way? Why do we suffer no matter what we do?"

Why, why, why echoed in the forest around them, mocking him, and his hands balled into fists as he slammed them into the ground, dirt and ice flinging up around him.

Eventually, he tired, slumping in on himself, rocking back and forth. *Please,* he whispered in his head. *Please help me. I don't know how to go on. I don't know how to fill the ragged hole in my chest.*

And the dragon spoke, his voice thundering in David's head. *Child, you ask the same questions that many have pondered before you. In their anger, in their grief, they demand to know the* why *of things, as if they think it can offer an explanation that will satiate the fire burning within. Though I have the answers you seek, I warn you: you are human, and therefore ruled by your emotions. Nothing I can tell you will absolve you of that.*

Tell me, David said. *I don't care about the repercussions. I must know.*

The dragon sighed. *I see that. I won't offer platitudes. You wouldn't take them even if I did. That being so, believe me when I say I share your pain. A dragon's death affects us all. The woods are darker because of the loss, but you must remember that his sacrifice cannot be in vain.*

Did I do this? David asked, stricken. *Should I have sent him away the first day we met?*

He wouldn't have gone had you tried, the dragon said. He shifted above David, raising his wings and cocooning them in darkness. *The one you call Lockes came to me, years ago. He had questions about the thread of light in his chest. He didn't know what it meant, who was waiting for him on the other end. He sought my council, and I showed him the truth of all things, letting him make the decision for himself.*

What truth? Who are you?

The dragon's eyes glittered in the dark. *I am the Great White, the oldest being in creation, born of fire and rock when the world was young. A god, though I have not yet taken my place in the stars. I am balance. I am the crossroads. I am not the judge. I am not the jury. I am not the executioner. I do not take sides.*

Then what's the point of you? David snapped, forgetting momentarily that the dragon could swallow him whole in the blink of an eye.

Instead of anger, the dragon rumbled as if amused. *A question whose answer would require far more time than you have on this earth. Time has no meaning for me, not like it does you. You, as a human, can do only one thing: move ever forward toward your final breath. Even now, you're dying. Not because of the anguish that has consumed you, but because your life is finite. Though you may not believe me, I'm envious of you, knowing that one day, you'll cross beyond the veil. Time slips through your fingers. For me, time isn't a straight line with a dedicated sense of direction. It moves forward and backward. I see all. I know all.*

Did you know? David shouted in his head. *Did you know how this would end?*

Yes, child. I did.

David reared back, furious, teeth bared. *Then why did you— how could you have let him—*

The one you call Lockes knew as well.

David gasped, another piece of his heart cracking and falling away. *What?*

The Great White shifted, lowering his head to the ground, his exhalations heating David's skin, causing sweat to trickle down his face. *He came to me, telling me of the instinct within him, the drive toward a future that was clouded to him. He sought my council, asking why he existed. What his purpose was. I gave him a choice: turn from his path and return to live a full life surrounded by his hoard. Or, continue on as he was, knowing his ending would come no matter what. He chose, child. He chose you.*

David bowed his head, sobs shaking his chest and shoulders. *I don't understand.*

Dragons are solitary creatures, the Great White said. *We can go centuries without ever speaking. And even if we choose to speak, most cannot hear us. You are different, David. You are one who hears the voices of dragons. There have only been a few of you. There will only ever be a few more.*

David was then flooded with images that shot across his mind, almost quicker than he could follow, a storm with fierce winds that threatened to knock him over. He saw dragons of all shapes and sizes, black and red, white with ice feathers that shuddered and shook, a creature like a snake, desert sand kicking up around it as it slithered through a crumbling castle toward a cavernous hole.

And through it all, a boy, standing tall and true, his robes billowing around him, hands raised toward a gathering darkness. For a moment, David stood next to this boy, and then he *was* the boy, his lighting-struck heart fierce and warm. He was frightened, this boy, perhaps more frightened than he'd ever been in his life. But what kept the fear from consuming him was the knowledge he wasn't alone.

The boy faded. The dragons faded. David was left alone, sitting in the snow with the Great White watching him.

What was that? David whispered.

A glimpse, the Great White said. *Of what will come. The path is set in stone, but stone crumbles. He will have a part to play, but he'll only succeed because of you, David. Though it may not seem like it now, the one you loved above all others will only do what he must because of what he learned from you. You gave him purpose. You gave him a home. You loved him without demanding anything in return, and that taught him more than I ever could. He loved you, and that has given him the tools to stand when he must against the face of evil. You were, in a way, his destiny.*

It's not fair! David cried. *I don't care about what happens in the future. I don't* care *about destiny. I want my friend back!*

I cannot, the Great White said, not unkindly. *What's done is done and cannot be undone. Your dragon knew this would happen. And yet he chose you regardless. He saw the time you would have together, and though it amounted to only the blink of an eye in the grand scheme of things, he could not see a life without you by his side. He knew it was better to have you for the time he did than to not have you at all. He was lonely, David, an affliction most dragons never have. But like you, he was different. He didn't want to be alone anymore. And with that quiet wish, he found his way to you, knowing it would mean his death.*

David put his face in his hands as he struggled to breathe.

You suffer, child, because you gave your heart to him, much as he gave all of his to you. Can't you see? Such a love isn't something to be taken lightly. Grieve for him. Grieve for all that you've lost. But then raise your head toward the stars and know that he watches over you still. You will be together again, one day. Your time with the one you call Lockes isn't over. But before you join him in your rightful place by his side, there is something you must do. You have your own destiny, David, and if you're as strong as Lockes believed you to be, you'll see it through.

What is it? David asked as he dropped his hands. *What must I do?*

Another image filled his head, and it knocked the breath from his chest. It went on and on and though he did not know it, days passed, the sun rising and falling, clouds gathering, snows drifting from the sky.

By the time the image faded, David knew what he must do. The how of it was clear, and maybe even the why.

But still…

I'm just one man, he said. *How can I even know where to start?*

As such things always do, the Great White said. *With a cornerstone. All other stones are set in reference to the cornerstone, with the first step. It will hurt, David. It will hurt like nothing else. But this is your destiny. This is the path you must follow, even if the stone crumbles underneath your feet. Take your pain and turn it into something more. Lockes will guide you, and I swear to you that by the time you draw your last breath, you will return to him, and nothing will separate you again.*

David hung his head. *I don't know if I can do this.*

You can, the Great White said. *Because you are a friend to the dragons. We will not let his sacrifice be in vain. Let his fire warm you when you're cold. Let his light chase away the shadows that gather around your heart. You wear his mark upon your chest. A lock, but he is your key, as you were his. Open yourself, David, and you'll do what you must.*

Will I always feel this way?

The Great White lifted his head. *Perhaps. But so long as you remember the time you had together, you will overcome.*

David nodded. *Then I'll do what I must. Not for you. Not for those who come after me. Not even for myself. For him. Lockes. Always Lockes.* He hesitated, chest hitching. *Can I...can I touch you? I...*He blinked rapidly, looking away. *I want to feel dragon scales. To...* He sent an image, one he kept in his secret heart. His hands, cupping Lockes face, the dragon smiling in that quiet way he had.

Yes, the Great White said. *You can.*

David stood slowly, hands shaking as he raised them toward the dragon's face. He closed his eyes as his fingers touched hardened scales. It wasn't the same; he didn't try and convince himself otherwise. But it was still something, and though his sorrow ran deep into his very bones, David took the offered comfort, holding it close.

Look, the Great White said, pulling his head away and spreading his wings. *Look up. Do you see it?*

David tilted his head back, a shout of joy and agony pouring from his mouth.

There, in the night sky, was the constellation of a dragon, one he'd never seen before. The stars were tinged green, the wings wide, the mouth open in a silent roar.

He has earned his place amongst the stars, the Great White whispered. *And you will join him, one day. But until then, know he watches over you, and rejoices in knowing your reunion will come.*

David watched the constellation until the sky began to lighten, the stars fading against a deep blue.

As the sun rose, David looked at the Great White for the last time. *I'll do what you ask. But I'll warn you now. If you or anyone else tries to keep us apart, I will tear the heavens asunder to get to him.*

I believe you, the Great White said. *I promise, child. And a dragon's promise is absolute. Begin, David. Begin so you can end.*

David turned and left the Great White behind.

THE FAIRIES LED HIM from the Dark Woods. They didn't try and speak to him again, for which David was thankful. He was lost in his head, already planning on how he'd achieve what had been tasked to him. The fairies kept a watchful eye, guiding him in the right direction.

When he stepped from the Dark Woods a few weeks later, he was determined. In the distance, he could see the outline of the Port, rising up against the vast sea. The flags of the King's Castle waved in the ocean breeze.

He turned from the Port, pointing his gaze east, toward rolling, empty fields of green. *There,* he thought to himself. *That's where I must begin.*

Yes, a voice whispered in the back of his mind, sounding like a friend lost. *Yes, my love. This is where. I will be with you, every step of the way.*

David smiled, wiping his eyes. "I know you will."

OVER THE COURSE OF TWO MONTHS, he built himself a small, single room dwelling of stone with a thatched roof. It was hard work, and he made mistakes, but he eventually got it right. People were curious about this man, stopping by on their way to or from the Port, asking what he was doing, and if he needed any help. He always invited them in for a meal or a cup of tea, but they left without knowing much more than when they'd arrived.

On a cool Spring morning, David set the first stone. The cornerstone, that which would guide the rest of what he'd create. He cried, then, as he laid the stone, cried great, gasping sobs as he set it in the field where he'd cleared the tallest of the grass.

"I miss you," he said as he touched the stone. "I miss you so godsdamn much."

A dragon's wings fluttered in his head.

"I know," he said. "I know."

With a chisel, he carved words into this first stone, words that came from his secret heart. When he finished, he blew against the words, clearing the dust. He traced his fingers over them, and then he was flying, flying, flying in the clouds upon a dragon's back, and nothing could hurt them. Nothing could take this moment away from them.

VARDEN THE CRUEL, the King of Verania, sent a contingent of knights to find out what David was doing. David ignored them even when they threatened him with their swords, telling him he'd be thrown into the dungeons. He didn't stop, and the knights muttered uneasily about how determined he seemed. They returned to the king, telling him of what they'd witnessed. The king said he'd deal with it himself.

But the next day Varden the Cruel was overthrown, and a new Queen assumed the throne, a woman filled with kindness and grace. Varden lost his head, and everyone cheered as the king's reign finally came to an end.

The queen herself came to David a month later. She wore trousers and a loose-fitting shirt, her brown hair pulled back into a braided ponytail.

David was nervous as she looked at the wall he'd created so far.

It wasn't anything big: ten feet high and twenty feet long, but he worried she would try and stop him.

He bowed before her, trying to wipe his dirty hands on his pants before she could see them.

"What are you making?" the Queen asked as she finished her perusal of the wall.

"A city," David said, wincing at how it sounded.

The Queen nodded slowly. "Why?"

"Because it's what I must do. I made a promise, and I intend to keep it."

He expected her to laugh at him. Or order him to stop. Or to have her knights take him into custody and lock him away in the dungeons.

Instead, she said, "Put me to work. What do you need me to do?"

He blinked, confused. He opened his mouth, but no sound came out. He bowed his head when she gripped his shoulder, squeezing gently. "We aren't in this alone, sir. Though I don't know why you're doing what you are, I see you're a man with a purpose. You remind me of my…" She shook her head, laughing to herself. "Let's just say you remind me of someone I care about greatly. I would help if you'd allow it."

David could only nod.

THE QUEEN CAME BY every now and then to check on the work, but she was still the Queen, which meant her attention was needed elsewhere. But David never worked alone again. She sent her best minds, the people who understood what David was trying to do. She provided the materials, the men and women who didn't mind the back-breaking work, who never questioned David, or complained about the task.

Every night as he fell into bed, exhausted, he'd look out the window and upon the dragon in the stars. *I'm doing it,* he'd think. *I don't know how far I'll get, but I'm doing it.*

The stars watched.

When David turned forty, the queen died. David stopped working for only the second time since he began (the first when he'd come down with pneumonia that knocked him flat on his back for two weeks) to attend her funeral. He ignored the way people whispered at the sight of him when he walked into the Port, his clothes covered in dust from moving stone. He waited in line to view the queen in her eternal sleep. When it was his turn, he pressed a hand against the side of her coffin, and whispered, "Thank you."

He turned to leave but was met with two knights. They took him to the queen's son, the new King of Verania. Though young and having only just lost his mother, the king smiled at him as David entered his office.

David bowed, but the king waved him off. "No need to stand on ceremony," the king said. "My mother loved you, David. She didn't always understand you, but she saw how important your work is to you. Before she passed, she made me promise that I would continue to help you in her stead. Unless you feel otherwise, I intend on honoring that promise."

"Thank you, my king," David said, bowing once more, back protesting. "You humble me."

The king snorted. "I know a man possessed when I see one. You'd continue on by yourself if you had to, wouldn't you?"

"Yes," David said, meeting the king's gaze directly. "I would."

The King nodded slowly. "Then you have my support." He tapped his fingers on his desk. "Though, I must admit, I wish to know why. Why are you doing this? What set you on this path?"

David said, "I loved someone, once. And I love them still. Like you, I made a promise, and I will see it through to the end."

The king studied him for a moment. "Did this...someone love you back?"

David smiled. "He did. He was my friend."

"Was?" the king asked.

David looked away, heart in his throat. Though the grief had lessened over the years, it didn't take much for it to rear its ugly head again. He wished desperately that it were night so he could flee this place and look upon the stars. "He's...gone, now."

"I see. I'm sorry for your loss, David." He swallowed thickly. "I know something of loss."

"Thank you," David whispered. "To you as well."

"You'll have all you need. Anything you require, you have my permission to come to me directly. Can I offer you a house here in the Port? It'd be better than the place you call home."

David shook his head. "I need to stay where I'm at. It's...the Port is too loud for someone like me."

The king considered him for a long moment. Then, "Don't you get lonely?"

"No," David said honestly. "Because I'm not alone."

AND SO HE CONTINUED ON, building up and out. A great wall followed by stone roads that lined the growing city. He became weaker the older he got, and in his seventy-fifth year, suffered a fall that broke his right leg. The healers said that he wasn't as young as he used to be, and that he needed to rest before he was no longer able to walk again. David growled at them until they left. He lay in his bed, mind fuzzy from the liquid the healers had made him drink to chase away the worst of the pain. He pushed himself up from his bed, and hobbled toward the window, hissing at the glassy ache in his leg.

He froze when he saw hundreds of people building in his stead as the first stars came out as the evening wore on. He looked up at the stars, and said, "Soon. I have a little bit more to do, but I'll be there soon."

Soon, the stars whispered back.

THE BOY FROM THE VILLAGE, the friend of a lonely dragon, the man named David, died on the eve of his eighty-second birthday. He knew it was coming, could feel it in the stuttering of his heart, the way he could never quite seem to catch his breath. His hands shook more often than not, and his mind had begun to drift in ways he couldn't control. He forgot names, forgot people's faces, but he never forgot Lockes, not for a moment. The dragon was always there.

On his last night, he wrote a short letter before he left his home, wandering towards the half-completed city. Groundwork had been laid for a castle that would rival any in history. He wished he could be alive to see it, but he knew his people would complete it in his absence. He sat down near the wall, touching the first stone he'd laid decades before. The carving he'd made was still clear, though grass had grown up around it.

He sat down near this stone, and groaned as he lay onto his back, face toward the sky.

"I'm old," he whispered. "And so very tired. But I've done what you've asked. I've played my part. Please. I'm ready to go home."

The constellation of a dragon was as bright as he'd ever seen it. He sucked in a sharp breath when the wings began to move, the dragon's head pulling from the sky and turning down toward the earth.

Are you? all the stars whispered. *Are you ready?*

"Yes," David said, voice rough with age. "I am. I miss my friend. I've lived a long life, but I need to rest with him."

Close your eyes, the stars said. *Close your eyes, David, and see what your love has brought.*

He did.

And there, in the dark, was Lockes.

"Hello," David murmured next to the wall. "Hello, hello, hello."

David, the dragon said. *How I have missed you. How I have waited for you. Come, my love. Come. It's time to come home. And I will be with you each step of the way, for you are mine as much as I am yours.*

David's chest rose and fell, rose and fell, rose and fell…

And then it did not rise again.

He died in the field next to his life's work.

But he did not die alone.

WHEN HE OPENED HIS EYES, all he saw were stars.

Welcome home, Lockes said. *My friend, my love, welcome home.*

And David smiled, his star shining the brightest in all the sky.

THE BUILDERS FOUND HIS BODY, cool to the touch, and covered with morning dew that looked like tears. They knelt before him, head bowed, offering their prayers for a safe journey beyond the veil.

Word spread, and spread quickly, of the death of the man named David. The king, now an old man himself, ordered David buried as if he were royalty, entombed in stone underneath the city he'd dedicated his life to building.

On the eve of his burial, a knight came to the king with a letter.

It read:

To whom it may concern:

My life had purpose. Please do not mourn me. I have returned to where I belong, by his side. Though I may have led a life of solitude, I was never alone. He always watched over me. And that's the point, I think. This life hasn't been easy, but I met each day as if it were the last one.

It is my hope that my work will continue with those who come after me. I only have one request: a name, to show he did not die in vain. If it's not too much trouble, can you please name the city after him? That would make me happy.

The City of Lockes.

I hope it becomes a home for those who want one, and a shelter for those who need it most. A beacon of hope. It's what he would have wanted.

I'm tired, now. More than I've ever been in my life. But it was the life I chose, and I would do it all over again if I had to. For him.

Thank you for all you've done. I couldn't have gotten this far without help. I won't forget it, no matter where I go next.

Sincerely,

David

AND SO IT CAME TO BE. The City of Lockes was named, and two decades later, the last stone was placed into the new castle. The queen—daughter of the prior king—moved into the castle and proclaimed for all to hear that from this day forward, it would forever be known as Castle Lockes as a symbol of a man who loved with his entire heart.

A THOUSAND YEARS LATER, a wizard left the castle behind at dusk. Without thought, he rubbed his hands against the scars that crisscrossed his body, a reminder of how close it'd been. The Dark Wizard had been defeated, and peace was slowly returning to Verania, but it could have just as easily gone a different way.

"Where are we going?" the wizard's husband asked him, taking his hand and squeezing gently.

"Something I need to see," the wizard said.

They made their way through the city in the middle of repairs, and out through the gates. The wizard turned right, leading the knight along the great wall that surrounded the City of Lockes. They walked for a good ten minutes before the wizard stopped, crouching down near a stone at the base of the wall. It was covered in moss and lichen. The wizard brushed it away until he found what he was looking for.

"What is it?" Knight Commander Ryan Foxheart asked.

"A reminder," Sam of Dragons whispered.

"Of what?"

"That stone crumbles," Sam replied hoarsely. Then he smiled as he tilted his face toward the night sky. Above him, a star dragon held watch, the tip of his snout pressed against the brightest star in all the universe. David's Dragon, the constellation was called, and the wizard felt a great and powerful joy in his heart, as if he were flying through the clouds. "Thank you. Even if you were sort of an asshole, thank you."

On the cornerstone, below the symbol of a keyhole, were words carved with a delicate yet steady hand.

In the memory of my dragon, who I loved beyond measure.

Eventually, the wizard and the knight returned to their home and lived, because *that* was the important thing. To live, even when all seemed dark.

UP IN THE SKY, a star whispered, *Did I do good?*

Yes, the dragon replied, voice filled with happiness. *Yes, my love. You did good. I am so very proud of you. Come, come. Let us fly together. We still have so much to see.*

And so they did.

It's said, even now, that if you look upon the stars on a clear night, you will see David and Lockes, wings spread across the heavens.

A boy and his dragon, together for eternity.

TJ KLUNE is a New York Times bestselling author and an ex-claims examiner for an insurance company. His novels include *The House in the Cerulean Sea* and *The Extraordinaries*. Being queer himself, TJ believes it's important—now more than ever—to have accurate, positive, queer representation in stories.

www.tjklunebooks.com

Other Works by TJ Klune

www.ingramcontent.com/pod-product-compliance
Lightning Source LLC
Chambersburg PA
CBHW072347020726
47506CB00004B/1037